Praise for *Plain Murder*

"An excellent addition to the Amish mystery subgenre. Perfect for anyone seeking a gentle read."

—*Library Journal*

"A good mystery that will keep readers guessing."

—*Parkersburg News & Sentinel*

"Delightful characters."

—*RT Book Reviews*

Books by Emma Miller

PLAIN MURDER

PLAIN KILLING

Published by Kensington Publishing Corporation

PLAIN KILLING

EMMA MILLER

KENSINGTON BOOKS
www.kensingtonbooks.com

KENSINGTON BOOKS are published by

Kensington Publishing Corp.
119 West 40th Street
New York, NY 10018

All Kensington titles, imprints, and distributed lines are available at special quantity discounts for bulk purchases for sales promotion, premiums, fund-raising, and educational or institutional use.

Special book excerpts or customized printings can also be created to fit specific needs. For details, write or phone the office of the Kensington Special Sales Manager: Kensington Publishing Corp., 119 West 40th Street, New York, NY 10018. Attn. Special Sales Department. Phone: 1-800-221-2647.

eISBN-13: 978-0-7582-9175-2
eISBN-10: 0-7582-9175-2
First Kensington Electronic Edition: January 2015

ISBN-13: 978-0-7582-9174-5
ISBN-10: 0-7582-9174-4
First Kensington Trade Paperback Printing: January 2015

10 9 8 7 6 5 4 3 2 1

Printed in the United States of America

Plain Killing

Chapter 1

Stone Mill, Pennsylvania

As Rachel Mast turned off the single-lane gravel road and onto the rutted logging tracks, the trees closed in around the minivan like a dark tunnel. It was one of those muggy August days that seemed too hot for central Pennsylvania, an afternoon when not a leaf stirred and even foxes and deer crept into the undergrowth seeking relief from the heat.

Rachel lowered the window and sucked in a deep breath of the still air, savoring the primal scents of old-growth conifers, and the stillness. Her companions, who'd been laughing and chattering in the back of the van, grew quiet and watched out the windows. Sophie, Rachel's white bichon frise, ceased her excited whining to creep into Rachel's lap and thrust a black nose out the open window.

Despite the heat, Rachel suppressed a shiver. *A goose walked over my grave,* she thought, and then chuckled at her own foolishness. She had an MBA from Wharton, and should have left superstition and old wives' tales behind a long time ago, but there was something ominous about the stillness of this remote place today. She'd been feeling it since she turned off the main road onto the gravel road that wound around the mountain. "Almost there," she called with forced gaiety. Glancing down at the console, she flipped the air-conditioning up to max. "That water is going to feel wonderful."

"*Ya,*" her sister agreed. Sixteen-year-old Lettie was riding shotgun and had had to contend with Sophie's nonsense for most of the ride.

"This was one of your better ideas," their cousin Mary Aaron said from the bench seat in the middle of the van. "Good day for playing hooky."

Rachel agreed. It had been a crazy week at her B&B. Three couples had reserved rooms for a long weekend and then canceled on Friday afternoon; then two decided to come anyway, a day later. Her computer had crashed, and she'd had to have the plumber out when one of her guests' children flushed three washcloths and a bar of soap down the toilet. The clothes dryer wasn't working right. . . . The list seemed endless. She couldn't think of a better escape than to go to the quarry for a swim and a picnic with her friends.

And she hadn't fled duty and responsibility by herself—Rachel and Mary Aaron had collected a gaggle of young Amish women, most of them relatives, for a few hours' respite from their summer chores. Rachel was the only Englisher, the only nonmember of the Amish faith, among them, which meant she was the only one with a vehicle and a driver's license, both considered by some in the Old Order Amish to be evils. Rachel, her license, and her vehicle were all guilty of abetting hardworking females who wanted to slip away from summer gardening and canning chores for an afternoon of illicit, if innocent, fun.

They made up a party of seven, eight if Sophie was counted. Too many bodies to cram into Rachel's four-wheel-drive Jeep. Instead, she'd borrowed her next-door neighbor's van, which provided room aplenty for passengers, towels, and coolers of food. An ice chest full of ripe peaches, local pears, and a huge watermelon made perfect picnic fare. It would all be washed down with lemonade Rachel's housekeeper had made fresh in the kitchen of Stone Mill House that morning.

At last they made the final downhill curve and reached the mossy clearing beside the aggregate quarry that had filled with water years before. Rachel coasted to a stop near an ancient oak tree and shifted into park. "We're here!"

Mary Aaron and Lettie slid out, and the rest followed. No one but Rachel had worn shoes, and soon modest dresses and prayer *kapps* were cast off, leaving the lot of them scandalously clad in cotton shifts and undergarments.

"Remember that it's deep," Rachel cautioned as they approached the steep edge. Crystal blue-green water glistened at her feet.

"Really deep," Mary Aaron added, looking down. "More than a hundred feet. *Dat* says they mine until they can't keep pumping water out, and then they just move on to dig another quarry."

Lettie's eyes widened as she peered over the edge. She was the youngest of the group, and this was her first time at the quarry. Her *mam* had let her go on the picnic only after delivering the severest of warnings to behave herself, to listen to Rachel, and not to go into the water. Her *mam* had also wagged a finger in her face and admonished her to not allow Rachel to drive the automobile at a reckless speed, which meant anything faster than a horse could trot.

As children, none of them had ever dared to swim here; parents were adamantly opposed, besides, more compelling to youthful imaginations, the quarry was rumored to be haunted. But most had ventured to this glen on summer afternoons every August since age fifteen, when Amish girls traditionally became considered young women.

The quarry was a secluded retreat where they could relax and set aside the strict rules of Old Order Amish dress and behavior for a few hours. Here, amid a tangle of old-growth hardwood, rhododendron thickets, and intertwined pine, spruce, and hemlock, the temperature—due to the flooded quarry—was at least ten degrees cooler than the rest of the valley.

Giggling, Lettie joined the other women as they carried blankets and coolers out of the van, all the while sharing family and valley news and bits of harmless gossip. Rachel helped spread the blankets on the thick moss and unpack the lunch baskets while Sophie ran in circles, chasing butterflies.

"Last one in is a rotten egg!" Mary Aaron dared and made a dash for the edge of the quarry.

Rachel, clad only in a T-shirt and panties, darted after her and dove deep into the shimmering depths. The icy water came as a shock, but she quickly adjusted, then reveled in the silky sensation of the blue-green water against her skin. Mary Aaron, always a strong swimmer, crossed in front of her before lazily rising to the surface. When Rachel came up for air, her cousin was floating on her back, her long sandy-blond hair drifting loose around her head and shoulders. Rachel dove under again and came up beneath her, flipping her over. Mary Aaron shrieked as she righted herself and returned the favor by splashing water in Rachel's face. From the sheer-cut rim, Elsie, Mary Aaron's nineteen-year-old sister, shrieked with laughter and plunged in to join them.

Soon everyone, including Lettie, was in the water. They remained there for a good half an hour before the water temperature began to temper their high spirits. Lettie was the first to admit that she was cold. "I'm freezing," she said. "Can we eat?"

"*Ya,*" someone agreed. "I skipped lunch and I'm starved."

"Me, too," Mary Aaron said. Elsie nodded in agreement, and one by one, they climbed out, threw towels around their shoulders, and made their way to the blankets. Lettie passed around wedges of watermelon that her mother had contributed, and Rachel bit into a slice. It was so sweet and delicious that she closed her eyes and groaned with pleasure.

"It is *goot,* isn't it?" Elsie agreed as she wiped at the juice running down her chin. "This was a great idea, Rachel." She spoke in Deitsch, the old German dialect that the Amish used among themselves.

"*Ya,*" Lettie said, eager to add to the conversation. "*Mam* grows the biggest watermelons in the valley. She promised to tell me her secret when I get married."

"Rachel must know," Elsie teased.

"*Ne.*" Rachel shrugged. "*Mam* never did tell me, and now . . ." She spread her hands in a gesture of hopelessness. Gardening and cooking secrets or everyday greetings, it was always the same. Her mother never spoke directly to her. Her mother hadn't spoken a word to her since, as a teenager, she'd abandoned her Amish upbringing, left home, and joined the Englisher world. Anything her mother had to say to Rachel was always passed to her through someone else. Rachel recognized it as the ultimate act of love. As awkward as it was, she knew her mother desperately wanted her to return to the safety of church and family.

"Lemonade?" Rachel poured an ice-filled paper cup nearly to the brim and offered it. "Ada made it this morning. Tart and cold."

Sophie, who'd been on the blanket begging watermelon only a minute or two before, let out a piercing bark from a distance. Rachel glanced around. "Sophie! Where are you?" She couldn't see the dog, but from the sound, she wasn't on the path that led to the quarry from the clearing but in the underbrush. "Sophie, come here!" she repeated, knowing full well that the stubborn little dog would probably ignore her.

A miniature white poodle-looking dog of about fourteen pounds would not have been the dog of Rachel's choice. Basically, she'd inherited Sophia Loren when a dear friend had gone to prison a few months earlier.

Sophie's barking became a low growl.

"That dog." Rachel rolled her eyes. "Only for George would I do this." She stood and slipped her feet into zebra-striped flip-flops. Still clutching the towel around her, she plunged into the underbrush, pushing through the thick rhododendron. "Sophie! Come, girl! Come!"

"Don't go in there!" Lettie called. "It might be a bear."

"Not likely," Rachel answered over her shoulder. "Not with all the noise we've been making." Branches scratched her bare legs and arms and twined around her ankles. "With my luck, you're trapped in a thicket of poison ivy," she grumbled at the dog. She couldn't imagine what had Sophie in such a fuss. Maybe a snake.

Sophie loved chasing snakes, although what she'd do if she ever caught one, Rachel had no idea. The thought that the bichon might have startled a rattler gave Rachel pause. "Sophie, come here!" As much of a pest as the dog could be, she had become a bit of a companion, and Rachel didn't want anything bad to happen to her. "Sophie!"

The growls grew fiercer.

"Rae-Rae," Mary Aaron called after Rachel. "Wait, I'm coming with you."

"Me, too," Lettie called. "I don't want a bear to eat you."

Rachel, now unable to see the girls in the clearing, forged ahead. Another ten feet and she pushed aside a thick evergreen bough to catch a glimpse of the white, fluffy bundle bounding up and down. Sophie's plumed tail was at full sail. Her protests rose to a fevered pitch as she fiercely held some perceived enemy at bay with every ounce of will.

"Sophie! What have you—"

Rachel froze. Sophie had taken her stand only a few inches from the edge of the water. Rachel stared through the braches of a massive hemlock, a tree that had grown out over the water. Beneath the intertwined roof of foliage, nearly hidden from view, forty feet from where Rachel and the others had been swimming, a body floated.

Rachel's mouth went dry. She blinked, hoping that what she'd glimpsed was only a figment of an overactive imagination. But when she dared to look again, the awful sight was all too real . . . and all too still.

Suspended facedown on the surface of the water was the body of a woman in full Amish dress, a white prayer *kapp* still on her head.

"Mary Aaron!" Rachel screamed as she took the few steps to the edge, threw off the towel, and plunged into the water. She had no idea who it was. None of those with her had been dressed in Sunday clothes.

Adrenaline pumped through her veins as she reached out. Grabbing a hold of the woman's arm, Rachel seized a low-hanging hemlock bough and, vaguely aware of the crashing sounds of brush as help came, rolled the woman onto her back.

Her eyes were china blue. Not the blue of human eyes, but glass blue. Hard, cold, and lifeless.

Chapter 2

For just an instant, in shock, Rachel released her grip on the body. The girl was dead. Her blue eyes were empty of life and beyond any earthly help. There was no question in Rachel's mind. She looked up to see Mary Aaron, her mouth agape, staring down at her.

Mary Aaron's face was nearly as white as the girl's, and her pupils were dilated in fear. "Is she . . ." She didn't say the word *dead,* maybe because speaking the worst out loud would make it real.

"My phone's in the van," Rachel managed, grabbing the girl's sleeve. The girl's prayer *kapp* began to sink and Rachel grabbed it, wrapping her fingers around the ties. "Call 9-1-1. Now. Run!"

Mary Aaron turned and pushed back into the underbrush as Lettie halted at the edge of the quarry. She took one look at the floating body and screamed, a high-pitched shriek of utter terror.

"Lettie!" Rachel called sharply. "Listen to me." She got her arm under the woman's armpit and looked up at her sister. The other girls were right behind Lettie now. They were crying, one nearly hysterical, but Rachel barely noticed them. Rachel kept her gaze focused on her sister, her voice steady. "Lettie, you'll have to help me lift her over the edge. I can't do it alone."

Rachel was afraid to let go of the girl. The bottom was so far below. She could imagine the cold body slipping through her grasp, sinking down and down to rest on the bedrock of the quarry. This young woman, whoever she was, was someone's daughter, possibly someone's wife. No matter what her story was, she didn't deserve this. No one did.

Then, it occurred to her the body wouldn't sink. Not if she'd found it floating. But she still couldn't let go. Wouldn't.

"I can't . . ." Shaking her head, Lettie backed away from the edge.

"You can do this," Rachel insisted. "Mary Aaron has gone for help. I need you, Lettie. She can't hurt you," she added softly.

"She looks *dead,*" Lettie wailed. "Her skin is blue."

She was right; the young woman's skin was cyanotic. What was it her biology professor had said about drowning? Cold water made the skin of a victim dusky blue.

"It's not for us to decide," Rachel said calmly. It was what one did in emergencies. She knew the girl was dead, long dead, but it wasn't up to her to determine that. What was up to her, at that moment, was to get this poor soul out of the water. "We can't leave her here," she reasoned aloud, to give herself courage as much as Lettie.

"*Ya.*" Features stark, lips drawn tight, Lettie hesitated, then dropped to her knees. She followed Rachel's instructions without faltering: lift here, pull there. Lettie helped to get the woman onto solid ground, gave Rachel a hand up out of the water, then turned away into the bushes and vomited.

Rachel's teeth began to chatter with cold, and one of the other girls dropped a towel around her shoulders. "She's dead, isn't she?" Elsie murmured, staring at the body gazing sightless at the sky.

"Yes," Rachel answered. Gently, she pulled down the young woman's tangled shift and skirt to cover her naked legs, and placed the sodden prayer *kapp* over the fair hair.

Lettie was weeping now. Softly. She joined the other girls, who stood in a semicircle.

They all stared at the dead girl at their feet.

Rachel supposed that she should have been horrified, even disgusted by the body, but all she felt was grief and compassion. She removed the towel from around her own shoulders, thinking that she would cover the victim's face. It wasn't until she knelt that she realized the dead girl looked familiar. At first, the young woman's face had seemed more like a doll's than a human's, but now—"Elsie . . . is this one of the Glick girls?"

Her cousin gasped. "*Ya.* It looks like . . . it's Beth."

Lettie returned to Rachel's side. "It is," she whispered. "I know her. She came to our class at school and taught us how to crochet when I was in eighth grade."

"Beth is the one who left almost two years ago," Elsie added. "The Glick girl who was . . ."

"*Die meinding,*" Lettie whispered. "Shunned." And then she gagged again.

Silence settled around them. Rachel pressed her lips together. Being shunned was the worst fate that could happen to a member of the Old Order Amish, a punishment reserved for extreme cases of misconduct. The thought was even more frightening than finding a dead body.

"Go back to the van," she instructed quietly, running her hand down her sister's arm. "All of you, go and dress. English men will be coming soon."

"Oh." Elsie covered her mouth with her hand. "Come, Lettie. Hurry."

"Take Sophie, Lettie," Rachel told her.

Lettie scooped up the little dog in her arms, then glanced back. She was eager to get away but obviously didn't want to desert her sister. "You'll be all right? Alone here?" she asked, hugging the dog to her.

"I'll be fine," Rachel assured her. "Someone should stay with her."

Elsie, Lettie, and the others made themselves scarce, and oddly enough, once she was alone with Beth Glick, Rachel felt a calmness settle over her. She had covered the girl's still face and staring eyes, but she couldn't leave her side. "You're not alone, Beth," she murmured. Taking a slim, cold hand in hers, Rachel silently prayed for the soul of this unfortunate young woman.

Twigs snapped, and Rachel opened her eyes to see Mary Aaron hurrying toward her from the direction of the van. "They're coming!" she called. "I called 9-1-1. They're sending the paramedics."

Rachel remained where she was, still holding Beth's hand.

"Do you think you should touch her?" Mary Aaron asked as she came to stand beside her. "Will you be in trouble?"

"It's Beth Glick." Rachel pulled the towel away so that Mary Aaron could see the dead girl's face.

"It is," her cousin breathed.

Rachel placed Beth's hand on the dead girl's abdomen and arranged the other hand carefully so that one lay over the other. She wasn't a large girl, and her pale hands were small and slender. "Elsie said Beth was shunned when she left the church."

"Ya," Mary Aaron agreed. "She had been baptized, so they had no choice." She nibbled at her lower lip. "Her family never speaks of her." Mary Aaron held out Rachel's clothes. "Best you make yourself decent before the Englishers get here."

Rachel nodded, surprised by how calm she was. Calm, except for her trembling hands. She went back to the edge of the quarry and rinsed her hands in the water. Then she began to dress.

"What was Beth doing here? Did she come to drown herself?" Mary Aaron had taken the time to put on her own dress and apron. Now she hastily twisted and pinned up her hair. She put on her white prayer *kapp*. "Was it a suicide?"

Rachel turned back to her cousin as she pulled her shorts over her wet panties. Her gaze dropped to the still form on the ground. She shook her head. "I don't know. Why would she? If she'd come home—if she repented of her sins before the church elders—she'd have been forgiven and welcomed back into her family."

"*Ya,* so what was she doing here?" Mary Aaron glanced around her nervously. "No one comes here alone. How would she even get here without a car or a buggy?"

"I don't know." Rachel pulled off her wet T-shirt and pulled a dry one on over her wet bra. "Did you bring my cell with you?"

Mary Aaron fished in her pocket and produced the phone. "Who are you calling?"

"Evan." Rachel hit the numeral *1* on her speed dial. "I don't want Lettie and the others to be here any longer than they have to."

Evan and Rachel had had supper together and watched a movie at his house the previous night. He was on day shift this week. "I think he's working traffic," she said, more to herself than to Mary Aaron. His phone was ringing. He kept his personal cell with him. If he wasn't busy, he'd pick up. *Please pick up, Evan,* she willed.

She felt responsible for bringing the girls today, and it would be her fault if they got into trouble. While spending time with her in frivolous pursuits wasn't forbidden by most of the families, it certainly wasn't encouraged. The Amish way was to remain apart from the world, and being in the middle of the discovery of a drowning victim, especially a shunned runaway, wasn't where parents and church members wanted their young people.

The phone clicked in her ear.

"Rachel?"

She let out a sigh of relief. "Evan. I need you to come. Right away."

"What's wrong? Are you all right?"

"*Ya.* It isn't me." She quickly explained what had happened and where they were. "I need you to call Coyote

Finch. I don't think I can talk to her, or anyone just yet." She took a breath. "I'll forward you her cell number. Ask her if she can come right away. She can drive the Amish girls home. Maybe she can get here before things get crazy."

"Not much chance of that. Not if you've already called it in."

"Please, just call Coyote. Ask her to take Black Bear gravel road to the old lumber mill. It's not far from here. I'll send them through the woods. The girls can meet her there."

"I don't know, Rachel. If they're witnesses, the investigating officer will want to question them."

She turned away from Mary Aaron, who was looking anxious. "It will be all right. Mary Aaron is here with me. She'll stay. Why would they need to talk to more than two of us? Evan, I—" She stopped and started again. "I think she's been dead for a while. . . ." She trailed off.

"Hang in there. I'm coming." He was calm, professional, caring. She knew she could count on him. "But if I can't get hold of Coyote, you're on your own with the girls."

"She'll pick up. Afternoons, her husband puts the baby down for a nap. She'll be at her pottery wheel."

"Be there as quick as I can," he promised.

Rachel ended the call, forwarded the number to him, and glanced at Mary Aaron. "Is that all right? Will you stay?"

She offered a wan smile. "What are best friends for?"

Uncle Aaron would not be pleased, and neither would Rachel's aunt, but they were used to Mary Aaron's objectionable dealings with Rachel. Mary Aaron hadn't been baptized yet, so she was still permitted some leeway in her behavior. When Evan was there, the two of them could at least shield Mary Aaron from the Englishers who would arrive in their emergency vehicles. And they could make certain no one photographed her, if the press showed up.

"It was the only thing I could think of," Rachel said. "Asking Coyote to come for the girls."

"*Ya*, it's best." Mary Aaron motioned toward the picnic site. "Elsie used to go with our brother when he bow-hunted up here. She can show them the way to the abandoned lumber mill."

The wail of a siren came from the mountain road. "Hurry," Rachel urged. "Tell Lettie to take Sophie for me. Get the girls into the woods before they get here. I'll walk to the road so I can show the paramedics where Beth is."

"It seems a shame, indecent almost—strange men taking her away."

Rachel sighed. "I know, but it's the way the authorities work."

"Foolishness. Better to call the bishop and Beth's family to carry her home. She needs prayers, not doctors."

Rachel agreed with her, but knew she would be wasting her breath trying to justify Englisher regulations. Mary Aaron knew more than most about how the English world worked, or at least how it worked in the valley. Her family and their Amish community, however, may as well have been living in the nineteenth century. They were practical people of faith, and much of what the English did was beyond their ability to comprehend.

With a last look at Beth, Rachel followed her cousin back to where the other girls waited. As she expected, they were all eager to be away from that place. Elsie was sensible. Rachel could count on her to guide Lettie and the other three to the pickup spot. And Rachel knew that Coyote would be there to get them and see them home safely. She was a new friend, but the kind Rachel could count on.

Evan was only five minutes behind the first paramedics from Stone Mill's volunteer fire company. Rachel watched gratefully as he pulled his patrol car into the glade and got out of the vehicle. As always, he looked bigger to her in his state police trooper's uniform than he did as a civilian.

"You came."

He put out his arms and she went into them. She closed her eyes as he hugged her and brushed a kiss on the crown of her head.

"Did you think I wouldn't?" He gave her a final hug and they stepped apart. "I'm really sorry that you had to be the one to find her." He brushed dust off the fabric of his pants. "Road construction," he explained. "I've been eating dirt all afternoon."

"Trooper!" One of the volunteers stepped out of the trees. He was a stocky redhead, a few years younger than Evan. Rachel thought she'd seen him shopping in Wagler's Grocery. "I think you'd better see this," he said.

"What is it?" Evan asked, suddenly all policeman.

"The 9-1-1 call was for a drowning," the redhead said. He looked down at the ground, then up at Evan. "But it looks like a possible homicide to me."

Rachel looked at the paramedic. "Homicide? Beth Glick was murdered?" Rachel felt light-headed. "That couldn't— Are you sure?"

"No," the man said. "But this isn't my first drowning." He returned his attention to Evan. "Something doesn't look right. Some kind of marks on her neck." He drew his finger across his own neck at one shoulder. "Like she's been choked."

"Stay here," Evan told Rachel. "And don't repeat that to anyone. Cause of death is up to the investigating team and the medical examiner."

"I want to come with you." Rachel looked up at him. "I'm the one who found Beth's body."

Evan frowned and shook his head. "Wait in the van. And ask Mary Aaron to stay there with you. You'll both need to give a statement to a detective when he arrives."

"But—" she began.

"Please, Rachel." Evan strode past the man, back straight as a soldier's on parade, muscles tensed. The paramedic quickened his step to keep up. He was still talking, but Rachel couldn't make out what he was saying to Evan.

She motioned to Mary Aaron, who'd been stowing a cooler in the back of the van. Rachel's cousin came around the vehicle and slid into the front seat. Rachel got in by the driver's door. She wondered if she looked as bad as Mary Aaron. Mary Aaron's normally rosy complexion was blotchy, the muscles around her mouth drawn. Dark shadows smudged the hollows beneath the wide, intelligent eyes that now glistened with moisture.

"You heard?" Rachel asked, her voice barely a whisper.

Mary Aaron nodded. "Who would want to kill Beth? She never did an unkind thing to anyone in her life."

Rachel gripped her cousin's hand, acutely aware of having made the same gesture earlier. Mary Aaron's grip was strong, her flesh warm in contrast to poor Beth's stiff, chill flesh. "We can't jump to conclusions. The paramedic could be wrong. We don't know that someone murdered her. It could have been an accident."

"*Ya*, an accident," Mary Aaron said. "That would be better, I think. Better than if she'd done something terrible to herself. Or that someone deliberately harmed her."

"He said she had marks on her neck, but she must have been in the water for several days." Rachel squeezed Mary Aaron's fingers harder. "She could have hit her neck on a rock when she fell, or maybe from lying on the quarry floor."

"Under the water," her cousin finished. "*Ach.*" She shivered. "All that cold, dark water. So deep to sink and then come . . . rise up again."

"But a blessing that we found her," Rachel said. "At least she's not alone anymore."

Mary Aaron's throat flexed as she swallowed. "Your friend will come for the girls, won't she? She won't leave them there, waiting at the mill?"

"No," Rachel answered firmly. "Coyote won't let us down. She's a good friend."

Coyote, her husband, and their children had moved to Stone Mill only a year and a half earlier, but they had knit seamlessly into the tight community. She was definitely a free spirit—a runaway California hippie, she had told Rachel.

Coyote Finch was a talented artist, an excellent mother, and a positive force in the town. She wouldn't ask questions. She'd drop what she was doing and pick up Elsie, Lettie, and the others. And because she was a woman, the Amish girls wouldn't feel uncomfortable riding with her, not something they would have felt right doing with an Englisher male.

"I don't want to go . . . to leave Beth," Mary Aaron said. "But *Dat* won't like it if I'm late getting home for evening chores."

Rachel nodded. "I know, but . . ." She shrugged. "He'll understand when we tell him what happened. It's not as though we can just drive away without waiting for the police investigators."

"Here comes Evan." Mary Aaron pointed.

He approached the van, cell phone in hand. "There's been a change of plans," he said, coming to Rachel's open window. "The detective has been delayed. Another case. Sergeant Haley says that you can go home. He'll contact you this evening or first thing in the morning."

"So we should go?" Rachel asked hesitantly. A part of her wanted to get as far from the quarry as possible, but a part of her didn't want to abandon Beth while she was still lying there in the grass.

He nodded. "But you're not to discuss what happened with anyone. Go home, write down everything you can remember, and wait for the detective to call."

Rachel glanced at Mary Aaron and back at Evan. "They can't call Mary Aaron." Everyone knew the Amish didn't have phones.

"I told him that," Evan said. "You can give him directions to the Hostetler farm."

"Or I can go with him," Rachel said. "You know how my aunt and uncle can be with Englishers."

Evan grimaced. "That's probably best. I'm sorry you had to be involved in this, any of you, but we have to follow procedures. I don't know how long I'll be. Hours, I suspect. There's only one medical examiner available today, and she's on the scene of another accident."

"What will they do with . . . with Beth?"

"Once they take photos of the scene—" He glanced at Mary Aaron. "I'm sorry. I know how you feel about photos, but it's a part of the investigation. No one will see them who doesn't need to." He paused. "Once we're done here, she'll be transported to the hospital for a cause of death . . . exam."

Mary Aaron nodded and folded her hands in her lap.

He returned his attention to Rachel. "Go home and try to get some rest. And don't dwell on the worst-case scenario. This could very well have been an accident; the paramedic was speculating. She could have been swimming alone and simply drowned."

Rachel frowned. "In her dress and stockings and bonnet?"

Mary Aaron said something in Deitsch too low for them to hear.

"I've got to get back to the scene." He tapped the windowsill. "Go straight home. I mean it. And talk to no one about this until you speak with the detective."

"Be careful," Rachel said, touching his sleeve lightly. "Call me when you get off."

"It might be late."

"Call me anyway."

She started the van, backed into the area where they'd spread their picnic earlier, and turned the vehicle around. Neither she nor Mary Aaron spoke until they reached the gravel road.

"What do you think?" Rachel asked. "Should we go to Beth's parents and tell them that's she's dead?"

"Evan said not to talk to anyone."

Rachel thought for a moment. It wasn't as if she were a rebel or anything. She'd been Amish once upon a time, for heaven's sake. But she tried to follow her instincts and her heart, and her heart told her she couldn't just go home and wait for the police.

Among the Amish, death was accepted as a natural part of life. Dying young was a tragedy, but this life was not as important as the next one. For Beth Glick's family, their daughter's fate was one much worse than death.

The penalty for dying outside the mercy of the faith hovered in the humid air between Rachel and Mary Aaron. Beth's family and religious community would believe her a lost soul, lost not to this life but to the eternal one, which was what mattered.

"Beth's family shouldn't hear this from the police," Rachel said.

"*Ne,*" Mary Aaron agreed. "Better from one of their own. But she wasn't from our church district. I don't know her mother and father so well." She looked at Rachel. "Maybe we should take this to our bishop first. See what he thinks is best."

"*Ya,* that's a good idea." She kept both hands on the wheel as the van bumped over the rough road. "He'll know what to do. It'll be a shock to the Glicks, and they'll need the support of their church leaders."

"And if the Englisher policemen are angry that we do this?"

"We have to do what's right for our people," Rachel said. "That comes first."

Chapter 3

A few minutes later, Rachel turned off the gravel road into a small clearing in the forest where there was a natural spring. "I better change now," she told Mary Aaron. If she was going to see the bishop, shorts and a T-shirt wouldn't do.

Campers, hikers, and hunters often stopped at the spring to drink and to fill their jugs with clean water. Years previously, someone had inserted a copper pipe into a crevice in the rocky outcrop, and an unending stream of sweet, clean water gushed out into the natural rock hollow before trickling away downhill.

According to Native American lore, the spring held healing properties and the spot was sacred. The thought that Beth Glick probably passed this way surfaced in Rachel's mind as she parked the van.

The sheer horror of the young woman's death, either by mischance or violence, was hard to grasp. It seemed too absurd to be real. If someone had killed her, why? Who would do such a thing?

It was hard for Rachel to wrap her mind around the fact that they'd all been having such a good time swimming in the quarry while poor Beth's body had been floating nearby. She shuddered, wondering if she was in shock. She exhaled slowly, willing herself to calm down, as she stared out the van window, hands on the steering wheel. What mattered right now was doing what she could for Beth's family, and she'd be useless to the Glicks if she were a basket case.

"A pretty place," Mary Aaron murmured.

"It is," Rachel agreed. The clearing was a showcase of wildflowers, all thrusting up through the peaty mat of leaves toward the light: purple violets, Virginia bluebells, forget-me-nots, lady slippers, and stark white Indian pipes.

Rachel climbed out of the van. From the back, she removed a midcalf-length denim skirt and a shapeless blouse with a modest neckline and three-quarter sleeves. She walked around to the passenger's side. Without being asked, Mary Aaron held a half dozen bobby pins and a blue head scarf out the window. Rachel quickly braided and pinned up her hair, then tied the scarf over it. Her cousin made no comment, but nodded her approval.

The Amish communities around Stone Mill were extremely conservative. Unlike Beth, Rachel had left the faith before being baptized, so she wasn't in danger of being shunned. She hadn't broken a covenant with the church. Rachel was free to come and go, to visit friends and relatives, and to take part in Amish family life when invited. She had learned since returning to Stone Mill that being both Amish and English enabled her to move between the two communities as an outsider couldn't. She had a knack for facilitating solutions to difficulties that arose from cultural differences. Since she had returned, she'd been assisting her Amish family and friends with modern advances: running computer websites, dealing with government regulations, and getting the best medical care.

Everyone was used to seeing her now. But when she interacted with members of the church, Rachel always took care to dress in a manner that wouldn't offend them. Otherwise, she would find herself politely, but firmly, dismissed, as most Englishers were. She might buy eggs or a loaf of bread at a roadside stand, as any tourist could, but few Amish would speak to her on a personal level if she wasn't decently clad, with her head covered. It was a compromise that Rachel understood. Most English, including Evan, didn't.

"It makes no sense," he'd said a dozen times. "They know you aren't Amish anymore."

Usually, she'd shrug and try to find the humor in the situation. "Of course they do. But if I dress modestly, then I'm not as threatening. I'm not throwing it in their faces that I walked away from the life they believe in."

It was a small price to pay, especially this afternoon when she and Mary Aaron had such grim news to carry to an unsuspecting family. Evan would be annoyed that she hadn't followed his instructions, but how could she just go home and wait? The Glick family needed to be told of their daughter's death, and not by Englishers. But not by near strangers, either. This was too delicate a situation for her to barge in with; she hardly knew the Glicks. Bishop Abner Chupp—the religious leader of the church group that Rachel's and Mary Aaron's families belonged to—would know the best way to proceed.

Rachel pulled the skirt on over her shorts, then stepped out of her shorts. She buttoned the blouse over her T-shirt. She got back into the van and drove out onto the main road that led around the mountain, toward home. The bishop's farm wasn't far from her Uncle Aaron's, and the sooner they got to his home, the better. Neither she nor Mary Aaron spoke as they wound down the steep and twisting route. She'd made the last sharp grade when her cousin reached for the cell phone. "We'd best see if your friend got the girls."

Rachel nodded.

Mary Aaron found the number and made the call. Coyote picked up on the third ring, and Mary Aaron put it on speaker so Rachel could hear. "Hey," Rachel said. "Did you find them?" She slowed down and steered around a pothole, a result of the previous winter. The road was in bad shape, and she didn't want to risk blowing a tire.

"Are you okay? I just dropped your sister off," Coyote

said, concern in her voice. "She was the last one." Coyote didn't ask why she'd been asked to play taxi driver, and Rachel was certain that none of the girls would have told her about Beth's death.

"I'm fine. I'll fill you in later. Thank you for picking up the girls." Rachel tapped the brakes as a doe and her fawn darted across the road ahead of them. Mary Aaron tensed and grabbed the dashboard. Rachel shook her head. "Not even close."

"What?" Coyote asked.

"A jaywalking deer."

"They're bad this year. Blade nearly clipped one Sunday night." Blade was Coyote's pierced, tattooed, and scary-looking husband. A nicer man you would rarely meet, but he was somewhat of a shock on first acquaintance.

A truck passed them, going uphill. The driver waved, and Rachel waved back. "Just wanted to say thanks," she said to Coyote.

"No problem. It gave me an excuse to get out of the house, and your mother gave me a pear pie. The kids will be ecstatic."

Rachel said good-bye, and Mary Aaron set the phone on the console.

"It doesn't sound like the girls told Coyote about Beth. You think they told anyone else?" Mary Aaron said.

"I'm sure my *mam* knows by now. Lettie would tell her."

Mary Aaron gazed out. "And you think Elsie won't tell our mother?"

Rachel grimaced. "We'll have to hurry if we're going to get the word to Beth's family before the Amish telegraph does."

It was an undisputed certainty of life in Stone Mill. None of the Plain people had house phones, and few owned cells, which were used strictly for making business calls and were kept in the barns. But news of any kind that affected them spread fast. By nightfall, Amish living as far away as the west end of the valley would know that Beth's body had been discovered.

* * *

The Chupp home was a white, nineteenth-century frame farmhouse dwarfed by the huge stone barn across the single-lane gravel road and framed by a garden and an orchard on either side of the dwelling. A stone supporting wall ran along the front yard, which was higher than the roadway by at least six feet. Pots of black-eyed Susans and daylilies spilled a riot of color over the wall from the lawn, and neat flower beds and grapevines added to the charm of the small house. Stone steps led up from the mailbox, and at the base of the steps stood a deep concrete water trough. Spring water ran from a pipe in the wall, and a ledge above the trough gave locals a place to set and fill their jugs. The water ran into the trough, which overflowed into a narrow stream below.

As Rachel pulled the van into the parking area, a pickup truck with West Virginia plates was just pulling out. The woman sitting beside the driver waved, and Rachel waved back. "Tourists," Rachel said. "Let's hope they stop in Stone Mill and buy something."

Rachel and Mary Aaron got out, climbed the steps and approached the front door. Rachel was about to knock when Naamah Chupp came around the corner of the house with a basket of fresh-cut flowers.

"Rachel! Mary Aaron!" White teeth flashed as Naamah's round face creased into a merry smile. "So good to see you!" she cried, her double chin bobbing.

The bishop's wife was a good fifteen years younger than he was, but topped him in both height and weight. She wore a russet-brown dress with elbow-length sleeves, a full black apron, and a slightly askew white *kapp*. Naamah's hair was walnut brown with a sprinkling of gray. She spoke to them in the Deitsch dialect. "You must come in. I made a fresh pot of coffee not an hour ago, and *streuselkuchen*." She beamed. "So good of you to stop by."

Mary Aaron took a deep breath and dropped her gaze to the ground. "We need to see Bishop Abner," she said. "Something . . ."

"Bad," Rachel supplied. "Bad news."

"Not your mother, Mary Aaron? That sugar of hers. I told her. Listen to the Englisher doctor. Vitamins are good, but you must watch your diet and take the pills."

"Ne," Mary Aaron said, shaking her head. "*Mam* is fine. It's someone else. A sudden death in the community."

"In another church district," Rachel said. "But we need to consult Bishop Abner."

Naamah clapped a hand over her mouth. "God have mercy. Not a child, I hope."

Rachel shook her head. "A young woman. Beth Glick."

"Beth, you say? The Beth who ran away? The girl they put the ban on? *Ach.*" Naamah's dark-brown eyes widened and then grew moist. "So dangerous, the English world. Not for us. Poor girl. And her poor mother. To lose a child is terrible."

Rachel nodded. It was no secret that the bishop and his wife longed for a baby. This was his second marriage; his first wife had passed away, but they'd not been blessed either. Now, after ten years of marriage, Naamah would soon be past the age of giving birth. For Amish women, whose lives centered on family, being childless was a great heartbreak. Naamah, however, always cheerful, seemed to have filled her life with flowers and other people's children.

"Abner is in his workshop," she said, pointing to the barn. "Sharpening saws, I think he said. You must go to him." She made shooing motions with her hands. "And then come back to the house for coffee and something in your stomach. Even in a time of trouble, you must eat to keep up your strength."

"Thank you, but not today," Rachel said. "I have to get Mary Aaron home, unless we go on to tell Beth's parents."

"Such a pity," Naamah said. "I'll make my *grossmutter*'s pound cake to take to the Glicks. And a pot of soup, bean or German vegetable. What do you think? Either make *goot* for feeding a crowd." She shook her head, looking at the flowers in her hand. "*Ach,* poor woman, the mother, first to lose her daughter to the Englishers and then to death. Breaks my heart to think of it." She glanced at Rachel and Mary. "Best you go. He will know what is best to do." Again, she pointed to the barn.

Rachel followed the sound of metal screeching against a sharpening stone, toward the barn across the road; Mary Aaron walked at her side. They found Bishop Abner where his wife had said he would be, wearing safety glasses and grinding the edge of a scythe. He was seated on what appeared to be a bicycle frame and pushing foot pedals to rotate the stone by means of a series of straps and pulleys. The rasping noise was so loud that Rachel clapped her hands over her ears.

"Bishop Abner?" Mary Aaron moved forward to tap his shoulder.

Surprised, he started, then stopped what he was doing, pushed back the glasses, and smiled at them. He rose from the bicycle contraption. He was a small man with very little hair on top of his head and a long, scraggly reddish-gray beard that he'd tucked into the top of his overalls. He carefully laid down the scythe and scooped up a brimless straw hat. He put it on. "Forgive me. It's warm in here," he said by way of excuse for being hatless.

Rachel glanced around the workshop. The work area was clean enough to be her kitchen after her cook had finished tidying up at the end of the day. The cement floor had been swept; the tools were hung on wall pegs or stacked on shelves, and nothing was out of place. She smiled back at the bishop. As the religious leader of their church community, he was a devout, hardworking, and selfless shepherd to his flock. She liked him, despite the fact that he never missed an opportunity to try and lure her back into the fold.

"Rachel, you've come to talk with me?" he asked as he picked up the scythe and carried it to a wall of farm tools. He hung it beside a sickle and the wrought-iron head of a pitchfork. "Your mother was just saying to me last Sabbath that she thought you might be ready to—"

"*Ne,* Bishop Abner," Mary Aaron interrupted. "This isn't about Rachel. We've come on a sad matter. We hope you know the right way to do what must be done."

He stroked his beard. "*Ach.* Come outside. We'll sit under the maple tree in the shade. There's always a breeze coming up the valley."

Behind the barn, beneath the tree were several benches and a rocking chair. Bishop Abner waved them to a seat just as Naamah appeared with a jug of cider and three mugs full of ice. "Thought you might be parched," she said. "Not staying. I never interfere with my Abner's church business, but I don't like anyone to go away from our home thirsty." She poured the cider, handed the mugs around, patted Mary Aaron's shoulder, and left them alone.

The bishop took a sip and then nodded to Rachel. "What is it? What sad news have you come to share?"

"We went up to the quarry, a group of us," Rachel began. Mary Aaron supplied the names of each of the young women. All but Rachel were members of his church. He had known most all of their lives.

"We went for a picnic," Rachel explained. "And then . . ." She went on to tell him the rest of the grisly story.

Bishop Abner listened intently, his faded blue eyes filled with concern. He didn't speak until Rachel finished. He waited a moment, letting them all settle on what had been said. "And you believe that Beth's mother and father will be told this awful thing by the police? Tonight?"

Rachel nodded. "Soon, I imagine. The authorities will want one of the family to make a positive identification of the body."

His brow furrowed, and he tugged absently at his beard. "But why would they do such a thing when you all told the policeman who she was?"

"Regulations," Mary Aaron said, leaning forward. She'd set her mug on the ground without tasting the cider. Her face was pale, and she still looked as if she might burst into tears.

"The English have lots of regulations. We thought that we should ask you what to do. Rachel will drive me to the Glicks' if you think—"

"*Ne, ne,* no need for that," he answered gently. "You girls were right to come to me. I will go to their bishop. This is for him to do, or maybe the two of us together. Such news should not come from strangers."

"Will that be okay?" Mary Aaron asked. "You know she left us. She'd been shunned." She hesitated. "Will they still give her a burial?"

Bishop Abner pulled a spotless handkerchief from his pocket and wiped his nose. He didn't reply for long seconds. "I can't say what the elders of their district will decide. Know this, my daughters. If the bishop of the Glicks' church will not give this child Christian burial, I will." He shook his head. "We don't know the state of her mind, do we? There may have been circumstances we don't understand that led her to drift away from the true path."

Rachel tugged at a loose thread on her denim skirt. "But people say that Beth's family considered her already dead to them."

He removed his hat and rubbed at his bald head thoughtfully. Lines creased around his eyes. "I have heard the same rumors that you have, but I cannot believe that they will not feel differently now. Ours is a stern God, but a forgiving one. And who among us is not guilty of sin? I do not presume to know what He will do with such a wayward one. But I will do what I can to save her, even now." He smiled sadly at them. "Go home. You both have kind hearts, but you have done all you can."

"Can I drive you there in the van?" Rachel offered.

He shook his head. "*Ne.* I'll hitch up my roan mule. That way I won't be at Bishop Johan's home before I have time to ask God to give me the right words to say. That is one of the good things about depending on a four-legged creature for transportation. Your world is too fast, Rachel. Not enough time for silence. Not only do driving horses and mules give us years of faithful service, as well as good fertilizer for our gardens and fields, but they give us time to think."

He got to his feet, which Rachel took as the signal that the discussion was over. They thanked him and went back to the van.

Naamah stood waiting beside the vehicle with two jars of pickled green tomatoes. "Take these to your mothers," she said, handing one jar to each of them. "My pickled tomatoes turned out especially good this summer. Give them my best and tell them that they remain in my prayers. And remind your mothers of the quilting bee here on Saturday afternoon. We're sewing a layette for Verna Herschberger. The midwife says she's expecting twins."

As they pulled away from the bishop's home, Rachel's cell rang. The ringtone told her it was Evan.

When she didn't reach to answer it, Mary Aaron glanced at her. "You're not going to see what he wants?"

"Battery's almost dead. I better not."

Mary Aaron picked up the phone and checked it as the ringtone ended. "You really should replace the battery. You said it's using its charge too fast."

"Just have to find time to go to the cell phone store in State College." Rachel concentrated on safely passing a wagon full of milk cans. Both she and Mary Aaron waved at the young man driving.

The ringtone on the phone started again.

"Maybe he knows something," Mary Aaron suggested as she carefully set the phone on the console between them. "Maybe he's calling to say that the paramedic was mistaken. That she just drowned."

Rachel hoped so, but she doubted it. There was no way the medical examiner could have determined the cause of death yet.

She glanced at the phone. If she answered it, Evan would

want to know where she was. And then, she'd have to admit that she and Mary Aaron had not gone home but had instead taken the news to Bishop Abner. Evan would not be happy. "I don't want to use up any more of the battery. I don't like to let it go dead; you never know when there might be an emergency. I'll call him after I get back to Stone Mill House."

"You should hurry. You can drop me off at the crossroad."

"And leave you to face your parents alone? I don't think so." Rachel wasn't looking forward to telling her aunt and uncle that she'd involved Mary Aaron in *another* death. The family was still reeling from when Mary's father, Rachel's Uncle Aaron, was accused of Willy O'Day's murder. Aunt Hannah was a resourceful and self-reliant mother of twelve children, but the world outside of her Amish community frightened her. She was especially vulnerable where her daughters were concerned. Rachel knew that her aunt was worried that Mary Aaron might follow her out of the faith. It was important to reassure her that Mary Aaron was in no danger. Otherwise, her aunt and uncle might severely limit Mary Aaron's contact with her, with the B&B, and with those outside the church.

Mary Aaron, younger than Rachel, was her best friend, more like a sister than a cousin. Since Rachel's return to Stone Mill three years ago, they'd become closer than ever. Rachel didn't know what she'd do if Aunt Hannah and Uncle Aaron decided that she was a bad influence on their daughter. Uncle Aaron, especially, disapproved of Rachel leaving the valley and her family for an education and the English world. They were on better terms since she'd helped him navigate the legal system, but it wouldn't take much to have him return to his former opinion of her. The path she walked between Amish daughter and owner-manager of a nearly successful B&B that welcomed Englisher guests was a narrow and precarious tightrope, one she sometimes thought impossible.

"Do you think Beth was murdered?" Mary Aaron whispered.

The van crossed a narrow stone-and-concrete bridge. It wasn't far now to her uncle's farm, and she thought back to what Bishop Abner had said. A horse-drawn vehicle gave you time to think. She wasn't sure what would be the best way to break the news to her aunt and uncle and to her own parents. Maybe she should get rid of her Jeep and get her own driving mule.

But as they drove up the long Hostetler lane and pulled into the farmyard, she quickly realized that she needn't have wasted time trying to figure out how to tell her aunt and uncle what had happened. Although it was the supper hour and all should have been quiet on the farm, children spilled off the porch and from around the house. Rachel's niece, Susan—her brother Paul's daughter—came running toward the van. Rachel's nine-year-old sister, Sally, was right behind her.

"They must know," Mary Aaron said.

"I think you're right."

Aunt Hannah and Uncle Aaron came out of the house. They weren't alone. Her own parents were with them. Uncle Aaron, arms folded and features grim, stopped on the porch. Her father, mother, and Aunt Hannah hurried toward them.

Mary Aaron got out of the van and went to hug her mother.

"*Vas is?*" Rachel's mother asked. She directed her question to Mary Aaron.

Rachel's father came to stand in front of her. "You are not hurt?"

"We're fine," Rachel assured him. "We went straight to Bishop Abner. We thought it best if he carried the news to Beth's church leaders."

Her father nodded. "That was wise. Elsie and Lettie, they told us what happened. That you had the English potter woman drive them home so they would not have to talk to the police. Was *goot*." Unlike most of the Amish in the valley, her father usually spoke English to his children. "Your mother was worried, so we came here."

Uncle Aaron and her mother were brother and sister. Sometimes Rachel wondered if her father felt that her mother valued Uncle Aaron's advice more than his. But she'd been born a Hostetler, a family not known for change. And if she was often rigid in her ways, Rachel's father made up for it with his easy temperament and jovial nature.

"I knew that quarry was no place for you girls," her mother fussed to Mary Aaron. Rachel knew the message was for her.

"Poor girl, poor, poor girl," Aunt Hannah murmured, clinging to Mary Aaron. Then she noticed the children around her, released Mary Aaron, and clapped her hands. "Away, all of you. I'll call you when supper is on the table." And then she said, "Rachel, come in. Tell us how you found the . . ."

"Body," Rachel's *mam* supplied. "Whatever was Beth Glick doing up there alone?"

"Maybe she wasn't alone," Uncle Aaron called from the porch. "She has been gone for years. Strange that she should come home only to drown in that quarry. Not natural."

For once, Rachel agreed with him. It wasn't natural, not natural at all. And if she'd been murdered, then nothing would ever be the same in the valley. Women felt safe to walk or drive here at any time of the day or night. English or Amish, people rarely locked their doors. The thought that all of that could change was chilling.

Her cell rang faintly from inside the van—Evan's ringtone. Everyone turned to stare at the vehicle.

Rachel hurried back to the van, grabbed the phone, and silenced it. She would call Evan the minute she got back to the B&B. Hopefully, he would have good news for her. Hopefully.

Chapter 4

Rachel pulled the van into her driveway as dusk was falling. She had intended to return the vehicle to her next-door neighbor that day, but decided that the following morning would be soon enough. Hulda Schenfeld was a lovely woman and a good friend, but Rachel simply didn't have the energy to deal with the nonagenarian that night.

To Rachel's relief, the public parking area for the B&B was empty except for a single car: a lime-green VW with *Coexist* and *Save the Redwoods* stickers displayed on the rear bumper. That meant she wouldn't have to go inside and chat with guests.

The vehicle belonged to a college professor from California who was writing a screenplay featuring a talking cat. She was here for an extended stay. The screenwriter, Professor Li, was an ideal guest. She had reserved a room for six weeks and paid in advance. She just wanted to be left alone to write. Her only requests had been that the housekeeping staff leave clean sheets and towels outside the door rather than disturb her, and that she have use of the kitchen twice a day to make her own juice. Apparently, Professor Li lived entirely on raw vegetables and fresh fruits, which she processed in her own juicer. She was smartly dressed and pleasant enough if Rachel passed her on the stairs or in the hall, but for all the interaction she had with her hostess or the staff, she might as well have been a ghost. That was a blessing now because Rachel was in no condition to be a good hostess, or any hostess at all, for that matter.

She was exhausted. Had it only been hours since they'd discovered Beth Glick's body in the quarry? It seemed as though it had happened days ago.

She eyed her cell phone, still lying on the console, as the van crawled down the driveway. She'd been avoiding Evan, but she knew that she had to call him back eventually.

Rachel didn't regret going to the bishop. It had been the right thing to do. As close as she and Evan were, there were things he didn't understand about her position in the Amish community. He didn't want her to do anything to impede the authorities' investigation of Beth's death, but news of a child's death couldn't come to an Amish household from an outsider. Especially under these circumstances. It just couldn't.

As Rachel drove around the fieldstone farmhouse, she considered the idea of just jumping into the shower and going straight to bed. She could deal with Evan after a night's sleep. In the end, they'd work it out. No matter what they quarreled about, and it was rare that they ever did, he never held a grudge. Evan was the nicest guy she'd ever met.

She swung the van around the house and jammed on her brakes. Evan's police cruiser was parked in her spot.

"Oh, good," she muttered under her breath. She put the van in reverse and considered making a run for it, but good sense prevailed. How foolish would that look? Evan would probably follow her; he might even turn on his lights and siren. He'd been known to do it before when she tried to avoid him.

Slowly, she got out of the vehicle, taking her cell phone with her. Her goats bleated from the stone barn. It was past their evening feeding. "Coming," she promised.

"Rachel," Evan called. He was sitting in the backyard on the glider in the grapevine arbor. It was one of her favorite spots at Stone Mill House and one her guests loved. She had built the arbor with her own hands, using lumber from a collapsed barn that she'd had torn down. It was now covered with grapevines and surrounded with bee balm and butterfly bushes.

Her feet felt as if they were weighed down. "Hey," she said as she approached him. Butterflies, absent this evening from the arbor, fluttered in her stomach. "Still need to get a new battery for my phone." She held up the phone, then slid it into her skirt pocket.

"Sit." Evan's expression was serious, but he didn't seem angry with her. More resigned, she guessed. His eyes were gray, almost pewter in color, interesting eyes with thick lashes that she would have given a pinky finger to own. "You didn't come straight home." He didn't wait for her to reply. "Where did you go? Please tell me you haven't been to the Glicks' farm."

She shook her head. "No, Mary Aaron and I went to Bishop Abner. After we talked to him, he went to meet with the Glicks' bishop. I imagine Bishop Schroder went right to Beth's family with the bad news."

"Rachel. It's not your place or the bishops' to—"

"I'm sorry, but I couldn't let strangers tell them, Evan." She stood at the edge of the arbor. "I just couldn't," she repeated.

"We have a protocol. Troopers should have been the first to tell them."

She didn't say anything.

She could see that he was trying hard to contain his annoyance with her. "Rachel, you understand that you can't get involved with this case. Right?"

She settled onto the glider, conscious of the goats still pitifully bleating. It wasn't as if they were truly starving; she'd fed them that morning.

The glider was oversized, painted blue, with a high back, and wide enough for three people to sit side by side. She'd left a gap between them. "I'm already involved, Evan. I found her."

"This is a matter for the authorities. It's police business. You're a civilian. Anything you do could interfere with the investigation." He was still wearing his uniform, which meant he'd come straight from work. Now, he removed his campaign-style trooper hat and placed it on a wooden table. He ran a hand through his short, dark hair. "Sergeant Haley asked me to assist on the investigation, because I grew up here."

"You may live in Stone Mill," she agreed, "but the Amish still consider you an outsider." She kicked off her flip-flops and tucked one leg up under her skirt.

He studied her bare foot for a moment. "Amish wearing sandals, now?"

"When I left the house at noon, I was just going swimming. We didn't expect to get caught up in . . . in this."

He didn't comment on her skirt or hideous, oversized shirt, for which she was grateful. She rubbed her temples. "Is the detective still coming to talk with me tonight, or are you supposed to question me?"

"He'll be here in the morning."

"Good. That's better than tonight." She glanced toward the barn, now in full shadow, then back at him. "I'm sorry if I caused you a problem, going to the bishop, but Beth is a touchy subject in the Amish community. This had to be handled carefully."

He brushed dried dirt off the hem of his trousers without speaking. The crease was sharp.

She thought back to when she and Mary Aaron were in the van, getting ready to leave the quarry. "Was he right?" she asked. "The paramedic at the scene. Did someone murder her?"

"I'm not qualified to say. The medical examiner . . ." He sighed and lowered his head, staring at his polished boots. "I wanted you to know I didn't leave her alone, Rachel. I waited, and I followed the ambulance to the hospital."

She raised her chin and gazed into his eyes. "That was a kind thing to do."

He flushed. It was one of the qualities she found endearing about Evan. Tough cop or not, he could never hide his humanity. "She wasn't a member of your family's church? Is that why you had to have one bishop talk to the other?"

"Yes. Beth's family belongs to another church district," she explained. "They're the ones who drive the black buggies with the gray tops. They're very conservative."

"Two-tone buggies make them *more* conservative?"

She shook her head, raising a hand to him. "Don't even get me started on the color of buggies, what wheels can be made of, or what shade of blue is the most appropriate."

He gave her a half-smile. They'd talked about the intricacies of various Amish sects many times, and he knew the subject made her crazy. "So Beth's church is more conservative than your family's?"

"Yes. Small differences to you and me, maybe, but not to them. Straight pins on the women's dresses, even the little girls'. No buttons. And the men's hat brims are wider. And they have more fasting days than we do." She corrected herself. "Than my *parents'* church does. Most of their young people accept baptism right out of school, when they're sixteen."

"That's young, isn't it?" he asked.

The hunger cries grew more incessant. Goats could be drama queens.

Rachel glanced in the direction of the stone barn, distracted. "Not for—" She looked back at Evan. "I'm sorry. I've got to feed up. Otherwise they'll never shut up." She rose and walked out from under the arbor. The backyard was illuminated by two security lights mounted on poles that came on automatically at sunset.

Evan followed her.

She opened the side door to the barn, which held a spacious pen for three long-eared goats. A door on the far side of the indoor enclosure led to the pasture, but it was closed. Ada, Rachel's cook, must have closed it when she left; it wasn't safe for goats to be out at night. Too many predators. "It's coming," she soothed.

The goats danced and leaped in the air, tails up, ears twitching in anticipation. Rachel circumnavigated two stacks of bushel baskets she'd borrowed from her father, slid the lid off a feed barrel, and scooped out a generous amount of goat chow. Ada said she was overfeeding them. That they were going to get fat.

"Could you turn on the water at the wall?" she asked Evan. When he'd done it, she lifted the handle of the faucet and water poured into the stainless steel trough. She pulled off a chunk of timothy and dropped it into the hayrack. Tails twitched as the goats dove into their supper.

Evan leaned against the stall, a lean hand gripping the top rail. "So, you were saying that Beth Glick had been baptized?"

"Probably at sixteen." Rachel dusted the loose hayseeds off her hands.

"I understand she's been gone almost two years." He straightened. "Did she go to another Amish community?"

"No one knows, but that's doubtful. Her parents woke up one morning to find her *kapp* on her bed and her suitcase and purse missing." Rachel pulled a bobby pin from her hair that was poking her and stuck it back in somewhere else. "When you leave your *kapp* behind, you leave that life," she said softly.

The natural progression of thoughts normally would have taken her back to the day she left *her* parents' home. And her *kapp*. But she refused to go there tonight. She just didn't have the emotional energy.

Evan was probably thinking something along the same

lines. But if he was, he didn't say anything about it. Instead, he asked, "How old was she when she left? She barely looked more than sixteen."

Rachel exhaled, trying to think. "She left when she was about eighteen, so she would be—would *have been*—twenty."

They were both quiet for a moment, lost in their own thoughts. Then she looked up at him. He'd had an awful day, too, and she doubted that he'd eaten anything. "Come inside," she said. "We'll see what Ada left in the refrigerator."

"I didn't come to eat." It was a weak protest.

"Well, I'm hungry." Which wasn't really true, but she knew that if she didn't eat, he wouldn't. She shut off the barn light and the water, and they went outside.

"You think she ran away?" Evan walked toward the house with her.

"I assume. She left with seventy-five dollars of her mother's chicken-and-egg money. It was taken from a sugar bowl in a cupboard, according to my Aunt Hannah. She makes it a point to keep up on local gossip."

"So Beth stole from her parents and took off. And no one has heard from her all this time? There must have been some contact. Letters, a phone call to a friend." He grimaced and shrugged. "Okay, no phone calls. But someone must know something about where she was all that time."

Rachel opened the screen door, and Sophie launched herself through the air, barking excitedly. She jumped up and down at Rachel's feet as though she'd been left alone for days rather than just a few hours. "Outside, girl. Do your business."

Sophie stopped spinning and yipping long enough to race out into the grass and disappear into the darkness. A minute later, she shot back through the door that Rachel was still holding open.

The kitchen was dark. Rachel hit the switch. The counters and floor were spotless, thanks to Ada and her cleaning crew. Turning back to Evan, who'd followed her in, she said, "As far as I know, no one heard from Beth after she left. Not a word."

"Strange," he commented.

"Not really." Rachel washed her hands at the big soapstone sink, dried them on a tea towel, and scooped out dog food from a cookie jar for Sophie. She poured it into a small blue crockery dish on the floor, and the dog stopped hopping long enough to stare suspiciously at the dry nuggets. Rachel groaned. "She's spoiled rotten. She wants people food, but the vet says that this is what she should be eating."

Evan regarded Sophie without comment. He liked her, and he was always slipping her bits of food under the table. Rachel guessed that if it were up to him, the dog would have whatever they were eating.

She opened the refrigerator door and peered in. Ada had left potato salad, a plate of sliced tomatoes and onions, fresh from the garden, and a roasted chicken covered with plastic wrap. "I think we hit the jackpot." She began to pull out the dishes and hand them to him.

"So no one, to your knowledge, heard from Beth? No word in two years?" He carried the chicken and potato salad to the table for two, by the window.

Rachel set out plates, silverware, and cloth napkins. "Iced tea?" He nodded, and she went on. "Beth's bishop doesn't approve of phones, not even for businesses in the community. In an emergency, members of his congregation reach out to Amish from another district who might keep a cell phone for emergencies. Or even Englishers. They'll flag down a passing car, but they won't use a phone. Beth couldn't have called them if she wanted to."

Bishop, her big, seal point Siamese, appeared in the doorway and meowed. She glanced at his dish on the windowsill, high out of Sophie's reach. "You still have food," she said to the cat. "No begging." She poured two glasses of tea.

"But they get mail. She could have mailed them a letter or something."

"I don't think she ever did," Rachel said grimly.

He was quiet for a minute, then asked, "If Beth left after her baptism, that's serious, isn't it?"

She indicated he should sit. They took their seats, and he waited as she bowed her head for just a moment of silent grace. It was a habit that even fifteen years away from Stone Mill hadn't ended.

"Serious enough that her family declared her dead to them." Rachel picked up her fork. "Before you're baptized, sins are far more easily forgiven. The assumption is made that a person doesn't know better. It's more complicated than that"—she gestured with her fork—"but you get what I mean."

"Right." He took a bite of potato salad. "Maybe she was hiding with some other Amish group. This is good."

Rachel shrugged. "What does Ada make that isn't good?" Bishop strolled under the table and rubbed against her bare ankle. She toyed with her fork. As much as she liked potato salad and roasted chicken, she wasn't sure she could eat even a forkful. She had the feeling that if she closed her eyes, she'd see Beth's white face. "I suppose anything is possible, but Beth left her *kapp*." She shook her head. "Chances are, she didn't go to another Amish community. She became English."

They ate in silence for a couple of minutes. She knew what he was wondering: If Beth had left the Amish, why was she in Amish clothes when she died? Rachel was wondering the same thing, of course. She pushed a piece of roasted chicken around her plate.

"How long will the autopsy take?" she asked. "By custom, family and friends sit with the body after death. I don't know if that will happen or not, since she had been shunned. But the funeral is usually twenty-four to forty-eight hours after death. They don't believe in keeping the dead above ground any longer than possible."

"No embalming?"

"No. We don't embalm." She wondered if the Glicks would

agree to bury Beth at all or if they'd refuse the body. "Off the record," she said, looking at him across the table from her, "do *you* think someone killed her?"

He didn't answer.

She went on. "You must have seen what the paramedic was talking about: the marks on her neck."

"We'll wait and see what the medical examiner's report says," he hedged.

She watched him. He kept his gaze fixed on his plate. "But you'll tell me when you find out?" she asked.

"I shouldn't." He hesitated. "But it's possible that I'm going to need your help when I go to talk to Beth's parents. Sergeant Haley told me he hasn't, personally, had much luck talking with the Amish on some other cases. I think he's hoping that since I'm from here, they'll be more willing to talk with me."

She didn't know that they'd be any more willing to talk to Evan than to Sergeant Haley, but she didn't say so. She suspected Evan already knew that. "If you're going to try to talk to the Glicks, you need to wait until after the funeral," she warned. "That time should be private."

"It's not my decision, Rachel. Sergeant Haley wants me to interview them first thing tomorrow. My lieutenant wants me to do whatever the detective needs."

"If you push them, they'll refuse to talk to you."

He considered that for a moment. "Will you come with me?"

"Not unless you wait until after the funeral. It wouldn't be right to intrude on their grief."

"Even if it helps us find out what happened to her?"

She laid her fork down. "That's not the way they'd see it, Evan. They're not going to care all that much about what happened. Don't you understand?" she asked, trying not to be frustrated with him. "What matters is that she's dead and was unrepentant. To the Glicks, to any Old Order Amish person, what happens in this world, or has happened, isn't important. It's what happens in the hereafter."

"That may be their belief," he said quietly, "but if she was killed, the sooner we find out the truth of where she's been all this time, the quicker we'll bring her murderer to justice. And maybe save the life of another young person who's left the Amish."

"You think this has something to do with Beth leaving?"

He dropped his gaze to his plate. "I don't know. But I plan to find out."

The next morning, Rachel was up before the sun. She'd slept poorly, repeatedly waking in the darkness, heart pounding. Beth Glick's body kept floating past her or slipping out of her grasp and sinking into a bottomless, still well of blue-green water. At five, she gave up trying to sleep, jumped in the shower, and pulled on a pair of capris and a T-shirt.

Letting her damp hair hang loose over her shoulders, she unplugged her cell phone from the wall and took it with her. She made her way quietly down the front stairs from the third story, with Sophie running ahead of her and Bishop ambling one step behind. She let the dog out the back door and left her to play in the grass for a few minutes; she wouldn't wander far.

The Siamese watched as Rachel filled the kettle and set it on the commercial-sized gas range. A dull ache settled behind Rachel's eyes as she measured loose Assam into a porcelain teapot. She could enjoy coffee at a social event, but real tea, hot or cold, was her staunch ally. When the water was almost boiling, she poured it over the tea leaves and counted off the minutes until it was ready. She added a liberal amount of apple blossom honey and then padded, barefoot, out onto the back porch.

Questions about the dead girl surfaced as Rachel sat on an Amish-made chair, but she pushed them away. She had things to do this morning. Business matters. She needed to check her email for reservations and new orders for her shop. She had to make certain the changes she'd made to the website were up and running. She couldn't keep going over and over the previous day's tragedy when there were practical things she had to attend to. And nothing could get done until she'd had at least two cups of tea and cleared her brain of cobwebs.

She sighed and stared out into the first purple streaks of the coming dawn, her mind a tangle of pressing problems. When she'd quit her six-figure job in a rising company to return to her hometown, she had been determined to make a difference here. Stone Mill, like so many other small rural towns, had been dying. The lack of employment for young people was the biggest culprit. Traditional livelihoods, such as farming, coal mining, and manufacturing, had all but vanished.

The Amish community remained entrenched in their land, but like their Englisher neighbors, they suffered from the economic changes and the lack of available farmland. Large, growing families and the price of land suitable for growing crops meant that only a handful of Amish boys could hope to make a living as their fathers and grandfathers had. In some ways, the isolation of the valley, hemmed in by mountains, was a blessing because it insulated the communities and protected traditional ways of life. But isolation also had its drawbacks. The Amish might not want to be part of the modern world, but without cars to drive the distance to State College or Huntingdon, they needed local grocery stores, English doctors, feed mills, and places to sell what they produced. It was clear to Rachel that if the town ceased to exist, her Amish relatives and their neighbors would have a difficult time remaining.

Rachel sipped her tea. Sophie came up onto the porch and dropped to a sit.

When Rachel first left the valley, she hadn't expected to ever return for more than a visit. She found the challenge of surviving in the English world exhilarating, first in college and then in corporate America. But as the years passed, she'd discovered something lacking in her success. She'd been homesick for family, for the slower pace of her girlhood, and for the joys of small-town values. When she'd returned to Stone Mill, she'd had a plan. Restoring Stone Mill House and opening the B&B was just the beginning. Without a thriving town, no one would come to stay in her charming rooms. Her problem hadn't simply been how she would survive but also how she could help Stone Mill, both English and Amish, to prosper.

Extensive research had convinced her that it was possible for Stone Mill to survive the economic downturn. The valley and surrounding mountains had natural beauty, clean water and air, a rich history, and virtually no crime. What had been needed were jobs, up-to-date medical care, and good schools. She'd hit upon the idea of making Stone Mill a quaint tourist attraction. Luring visitors to the area would bring money, and higher incomes would provide stability.

Lancaster had become a national destination for tourists wanting the Amish experience. What she had dreamed of was for Stone Mill to provide a genuine window into Amish culture, without twenty-foot-high plastic whirligigs and souvenirs made in China. She hadn't thought that it would be easy, and it hadn't been. But in the three years since she'd returned, she could count a dozen new businesses in town, and her Amish crafts website was slowly gaining momentum. Artisans using centuries-old skills fashioned quilts, baskets, furniture, and kiln-fired pottery that were in high demand in New York, Houston, and Los Angeles, and sold over the Internet. And young people who might have left family and friends to work in a big-box store in the next county, or moved West to live with family, stayed in Stone Mill and apprenticed to experienced elders.

Her most pressing problem right now was that, so far, no one else had come forward with the Internet and marketing skills needed to ensure continued success. Mary Aaron showed an aptitude for business in general, but religious restrictions limited her to dealing with the craftsmen and filling orders once they'd been received. It was up to Rachel to manage the website, travel to meet with prospective resellers, and handle contact with Englishers. All these tasks had been added to running her B&B. It was a juggling act, and sometimes she wondered if she'd taken on more than she could handle.

She drained the last drops of tea from her mug and started to rise. A gray mist seeped in from the fields, seeming to distort the morning sounds of roosters crowing and an owl hooting from the loft of the old stone barn. Abruptly, a shape materialized out of the shadows.

Sophie rose and barked.

"It's only me. I didn't mean to scare you." Hulda took hold of one of the porch uprights and eased herself up onto the open porch. "Saw your light on," the small woman said. "Came to the front door, but it was locked. Gracious, Rachel, when did you start locking your doors?"

Last night, Rachel thought as the adrenaline drained out of her muscles, making her sink back into the chair. Apparently, Hulda hadn't heard about Beth.

"You startled me," Rachel admitted, trying to make light of her overreaction. Hulda was often up early, and it wasn't unusual for her to wander over for a cup of tea and a sweet. "Sorry I didn't bring your van back last night, but—"

"I know. That nice young man of yours was here. I saw his police car come in not long before you got back." Hulda tilted her head. "I'd come out to water my geraniums, the ones in the big pot on the front step, and there he came, still in his uniform. I think it's nice that you find time for friends your own age."

"I was just going back in for another cup," Rachel said, holding up her mug. She wanted to tell Hulda about Beth, but she wasn't comfortable being the source of the information. Not yet, at least. Not until she confirmed that Beth's parents had been told. "Would you like one? I don't know what Ada left in the sweets cabinet, but I'm certain there must be apple muffins or something."

"I don't want to put you out, but a cup of tea would go well," Hulda agreed.

Rachel stood back as the white-haired woman strode past her and entered the kitchen. As usual, Hulda was dressed in a pantsuit and sensible black shoes, her hair and makeup done. Rachel hoped she had half of Hulda's energy when she reached her nineties.

"Expecting more guests this weekend?" Hulda asked. "I'm surprised you haven't been busier. Last month you were turning people away."

"I know," Rachel said, eager to move past the subject of why she'd locked her doors last night. There would be time enough to talk about it later, when they had more concrete information. She was just taking Hulda's favorite mug out of the cupboard when her cell phone on the counter rang. Rachel stared at it. What time was it? *Too early for anyone to call with good news.*

"Are you going to answer that?" Hulda asked. "Who could it be at this hour?" She looked at the vintage timepiece she wore on a gold chain around her neck. "Six oh-three."

Rachel picked up her phone. "Hello?"

"Rachel. It's Evan. I'm sorry it's so early."

She had a bad feeling about this.

"I've been to the hospital and spoken to the medical examiner. The paramedic was right. Beth Glick was murdered."

Chapter 5

Rachel drove past all-black buggies, gray-topped buggies, and open buggies that lined the narrow road that led to a stone-walled lane and the Glick farmstead. She parked in the field near the end of the dirt driveway, got out, and threaded her way between rows of horse-drawn vehicles and pickup trucks to walk to the two-story frame house. Dressed modestly in a navy calf-length riding skirt and two-button jacket, she was obviously an Englisher, but no one, not even her mother, would find fault with her clothing.

Before leaving Stone Mill House, Rachel had twisted her hair into a chignon and covered it with a dark-blue Italian scarf, similar in appearance to the ones Mary Aaron wore to work in the garden. Tonight, it felt, if not comfortable, then at least appropriate. Wasn't there a saying about not being able to take the Amish out of the girl?

Rachel didn't know how much discussion, or argument, there had been within the Glick household, and within their church, concerning whether or not the Glicks would accept their lost child's body for burial. In other places, in similar circumstances, families had refused to accept the bodies of shunned family members, and the state had been forced to bury them. Thankfully, the innate good in those involved had prevailed, and Beth's body had been brought home so that family and loved ones could pay their respects before burial. Where she would be buried had not yet been determined.

Families, friends, and neighbors, both Amish and English, stood in the yard, on the wide porch, and inside the front hall. In the heat, all the doors and windows to the home were propped open. It seemed like everyone in the valley was there. Tragedy brought the people of the valley together, and differences in race, religion, and age didn't seem to matter when one of their own was grieving. It was what made Stone Mill a special place, and what Rachel had missed most in her time away. Wherever she fit, and she still wasn't certain where, this was and always would be her home. Even in such a time of sorrow, there was a feeling of comfort knowing that your neighbors were there to catch you and support you if you stumbled.

It was nearly eight o'clock in the evening when Rachel approached the Glick farmhouse. The sun had already settled behind the mountains, and twilight would soon turn to darkness. Evening chores complete, Amish neighbors and church members would come and go late into the night. Others would come and stay, joining Beth's brothers, sisters, and parents in keeping vigil over the deceased.

Rachel entered the front hall of the house, nodding to one person after another. Conversations and voices were muted, but she felt welcome, and knew almost everyone there. She hadn't seen her parents or brothers and sisters yet, but she had no doubt that they'd already stopped by or would arrive soon. Even though they were not close friends of the Glicks, they wouldn't fail to pay their respects.

Rachel steeled herself to view the body. She didn't fear the dead; since she was a young child, she'd attended wakes and funerals. But neither was she eager to again see the tragic face of a girl who'd been wrenched from this world far too soon. She paused and whispered a silent prayer for Beth's soul.

"She's in the parlor. There to the right," a rasping voice

said. A tall woman in a black bonnet motioned toward an open doorway. Rachel knew that by *she,* the woman meant Beth. By tradition, the name of the newly dead was rarely spoken, even at her own wake.

Rachel moved to the doorway.

According to custom, and despite her separation from the Amish church, Beth had been laid out in the kerosene-lamp-lit parlor off the main hallway. Garbed all in white, she rested in a wooden coffin held up by two sawhorses draped with blue quilts. Straight-backed chairs lined the walls, but only a few were occupied, and those few by elders. Most of the furniture had been removed to make room for the coffin and the mourners.

Several middle-aged Amish women stood together near the cast-iron woodstove, cold now in deference to the August heat. From the open windows, a slight breeze fluttered the plain white curtains. The room smelled of floor wax, cinnamon, and too many people. There were no flowers.

Rachel held her breath as she entered the room. Her mouth felt dry and her palms damp as she forced herself to approach the coffin.

Beth Glick looked smaller than Rachel remembered. Thankfully, someone had covered the young woman's face and throat with a man's white linen handkerchief. Beth was clothed in a white dress and white stockings; only her bare hands were visible, fingers folded stiffly around a worn German Bible. Rachel exhaled softly. Such small hands . . . wrinkled from their immersion in water. Her eyes stung as she stared at Beth's swollen and discolored flesh, two fingernails broken off raggedly at the quick.

Rachel swallowed once and then again, determined not to break down and cry. *Whatever happened to Beth, she's no longer suffering,* Rachel told herself as Evan's report echoed in her mind: "According to the medical examiner she was strangled unconscious before she met death by drowning." Evan had gone on to say that the water in Beth's lungs was identical to that of samples taken from the quarry, proving that death had occurred there. "No evidence of sexual assault," he had added hastily.

Sounds of subdued weeping pierced her musing. Figures in Plain clothing moved around the coffin, and Rachel caught the scent of sour sweat.

"Good of you to come, Rachel."

Rachel turned toward the familiar voice. "Bishop Abner?" She took another breath, grounding herself. It wasn't *his* body odor that had offended her. His was a clean wholesomeness: green apple soap, licorice chewing gum.

Rachel glanced back at Beth's pale form. "Thank you for this," she whispered to the bishop. "I'd worried that the family would . . ." She trailed off, not wanting to speak of what she'd originally feared, which was that the Glicks would refuse to accept their runaway daughter's body. She had been afraid that no one would give her the last rites of her faith.

"It was the least I could do. Who is more in need of our prayers?" Bishop Abner laid a lean hand gently on the edge of the pine box.

"Bishop." A stern face beneath a white *kapp* appeared on the other side of the coffin, and the breeze from the open window carried the odor of unwashed underarms and clothing in need of airing. Rachel steeled herself so as not to flinch. It was something she'd had to get used to again after fifteen years away from the valley, and she'd discovered that she found it far more distasteful than she had as a girl. Her family had always used deodorant, but some Amish considered it forbidden as too worldly.

"Her poor mother," the woman intoned. "To lose a child with no hope of salvation."

"Yet," Rachel murmured, her gaze downcast, "the Bible tells us that He is a merciful God." She had plenty of opinions on the subject, but this was neither the time nor the place to discuss theology.

The woman stiffened and stared at her for a moment before her lips thinned and hardened. "For one who has broken her promise to the Almighty, there is no hope of salvation."

"We are all sinners, and we can always hope," Bishop Abner said. He glanced meaningfully at Rachel and then toward the door. Rachel nodded and followed him quietly out of the parlor. "Beth's mother asked to speak with you," he murmured.

"Me?" She wondered if she'd offended the Glicks with her presence. But there were many Englishers from the town, so she didn't think so. A wake was a public event.

The main hall was crowded with Amish. She and the bishop worked their way past a cluster of elderly women in black prayer *kapps,* and several men who were members of her parents' church community. Three little boys dressed in black trousers, black suspenders, and white shirts sat solemnly on the stairs that led to the second floor, straw hats in hand, feet decently covered in black stockings and high-top leather brogans. The bishop led the way toward the back of the house.

"Bishop Abner?" Eli Rust, her Uncle Aaron's next-door neighbor, tugged at the bishop's sleeve. "A moment of your time?" Rachel noticed that Eli's brother was with him. Both men were members of Abner's church community.

Joab Rust nodded in her direction. She nodded back.

Abner raised one finger in a gesture that she assumed meant she was to wait. "How can I help you?" he asked the men.

Rachel half turned to give them some privacy in the crowded space and stepped back against the wall to allow Polly and Ed Wagler by. Ed's eyes were swollen, as if he'd been crying. "Polly. Ed." The Waglers ran the town grocery, and Rachel had known them since she was small.

"Terrible business, this," Ed said. "I can't . . ." He choked up, pulled a red handkerchief from his pocket, and blew his nose loudly.

"To think that something like this would happen here, of

all places." Polly embraced her, enveloping her in a cloud of gardenia cologne. "And you had to be the one to find her."

"Terrible," Ed repeated. "Words can't express . . ." Again, he seemed unable to go on.

Well-meaning Polly had no such obstacle. "Such a young girl, with so much life ahead of her, a lovely Christian girl, always so pleasant when she came into the store." Ed blew his nose a second time, almost drowning out his wife, but she went on. "We brought a lunchmeat-and-cheese platter, the large one."

Ed's Adam's apple bobbed in his thin neck. "No need to mention it, Polly. Least we could do."

"Ed said he'd do the same again in a few weeks," Polly said. "When our Calvin passed, Ed was fine during the funeral, but later, he just fell apart. Just sat and stared at the pond. Couldn't seem to eat a bite or take pleasure in anything."

"So much to do right afterwards, a body doesn't have time to think. But later, later it all sinks in. Good thing the Glicks have their faith to sustain them," Ed added. "It's something you admire about the Amish. They accept death as part of life." He took his wife's arm. "Best we go in and pay our respects," he said.

"Have you been in to see . . ." Polly glanced down the hall. "They say she looks peaceful, just like she's asleep."

Rachel said nothing. She'd never felt the dead looked like they were sleeping. They looked dead.

"Let's do it, Mother," Ed said.

The kitchen door at the end of the hall slid open, and a stout Amish woman carrying a wailing baby pushed through. "We're holding up the show," Ed said. "See you in church, Rachel."

"Talk to you later," Polly said, and they moved toward the parlor.

A minute later, Bishop Abner returned. "Shall we find the parents?" he suggested.

Rachel nodded and followed him toward the back of the house. She could smell the food before they passed through the pocket door at the end of the passageway.

The huge kitchen and attached dining room were women's domain, and the amount of food and drink amassed there could have easily fed half the valley. Every flat surface of table and counter space was laden with bowls, platters, and plates of food. Pies, cakes, gingerbread, and sweet rolls stood cheek by jowl with trays of roast beef, fried chicken, and smoked hams. The sea of aproned women with rolled-up sleeves and sweaty foreheads parted. Nursing mothers whisked blankets over exposed breasts and babes, and toddlers were shushed from begging for bites of this and that.

Everyone stared at Rachel and the bishop.

"Bishop." A plump-cheeked woman closed an oven door and stepped back to give them room.

"Bishop Abner."

Rachel didn't recognize the teenage girl who spoke, but her red and swollen eyes and the haunted expression on her face hinted at someone near and dear to the deceased.

"*Mam,*" the girl said, "Bishop Abner's here."

A tall, thin woman with sad eyes rose from the table. "Bishop, it's good of you to come." A young mother with a newborn wrapped in a shawl got up as well, and Rachel noted a strong resemblance to the dead girl. *A sister?* Under the table, Rachel caught sight of a toddler sucking a thumb. The child wore a close-fitting white baby cap and a shapeless white dress. Rachel couldn't tell if it was a boy or girl. Wisps of brown hair curled around the baby's rosy cheeks.

"I am so sorry for your loss," Bishop Abner said. He turned to Rachel. "Do you know Mabel Glick?"

"You are the one who found our Beth?" the woman asked. She sounded as if she'd been crying for a long time, and her cheeks appeared sunken. "Thank you."

Rachel added her condolences to those of the bishop. She recognized Mabel as someone she'd seen at the grocery and at the farmer's market, but she couldn't remember if she had ever spoken more than a few words to her. Mabel's eyes were blue, her hair streaked with gray.

Did she know that her daughter had been murdered?

The young woman with the baby slipped an arm around Mabel but said nothing. The infant squirmed in the blanket and began to whimper. Rachel tried to think of something appropriate to say, but nothing seemed adequate. The kitchen was stifling, and she needed fresh air. She backed away from the table. "If there's anything I can do to help, please just let me know."

The thought of retracing her steps back through the kitchen and central hall was daunting, so Rachel edged toward the back door. As she opened it, she heard a man's strident voice. The angry words were in Deitsch, telling Rachel that the speaker was Amish. She couldn't quite hear what he was saying, though.

She glanced back at Bishop Abner, who had obviously heard the man as well. One rarely heard a raised voice among the Amish, and it was certainly even more unusual considering the circumstances of the gathering. As she stepped out onto the back porch, she immediately spotted the cause of the uproar.

A Pennsylvania State Police car was parked in the yard. Standing beside it, she saw Evan in full uniform and a small, red-faced Amish man. The bearded man was obviously angry, because he was shaking a fist at Evan and delivering a verbal tirade in Deitsch. And from what Rachel could now hear, she was thankful that Evan's grasp of the language wasn't good. Shocked by the violent gesture she rarely witnessed among her people, Rachel descended the back steps and crossed the yard toward them. Abner followed her, but she didn't wait for him.

"I only came to pay my respects," Evan said. "I know that today is—"

"Not for outsiders, with your guns of the hand and your shiny buttons!" the little man exclaimed, switching back to

English. "This is my land, my home. Tonight we sit with the body of our daughter, who is lost to salvation because of you Englishers."

Evan caught sight of Rachel and flushed an even deeper red than his accuser.

Bishop Abner spoke up quietly. "Mose, I'm sure that this officer of the police meant to give no offense. He is a good man, trying to do the proper thing."

Mose. Aunt Hannah had told her that Beth's father was Mose. "This is the trooper who was with Beth," Rachel explained in Deitsch. "At the quarry. He stayed with her until the ambulance took her to the hospital. Bishop Abner is right. This Englisher is a good man. He was a good friend to my Uncle Aaron when he had his trouble over Willy O'Day."

Mose glanced at her, unclenched his hand, and dropped his arm to his side. "Not today is he welcome here," he said firmly in English. "Not with my Beth lying cold in there." His eyes, nearly hidden behind round, black-rimmed glasses, were full of pain.

Rachel looked back at Evan. "Maybe it would be better if you came another day," she said, "unless Mose is required, by law, to speak to you now—"

"No. No." Evan shook his head. "I only wanted to let the family know how sorry I was, to show my respects for their loss." He seemed to recover a little of his composure. "I didn't want to cause you further upset, Mr. Glick." He offered his hand, but Mose stepped back, ignoring it.

"I want no gun of the hand here for my children to see. Such a gun is not for hunting. Only for shedding the blood of other men."

"I'm sorry," Evan said. "I should have thought . . ." He grimaced. "I was on my way to fill in for another . . ." He shook his head. "I'll leave you, Mr. Glick. I just wanted you to know how badly I feel about what happened to Beth."

Mose's beard bobbed as he swallowed. He stepped back and pointed. "Leave now."

Evan gave Rachel a stricken look and got back into the police car. Mose folded his arms and stood stiffly as Evan backed up the vehicle and drove back around the house.

"I think that he meant well," Bishop Abner told Beth's father. "Did he come to ask you more questions?"

Mose shook his head. "*Ne*. He did not. Early this morning, another two Englishers with guns came. They had many questions, but what could I say? She has been lost to us for a long time. We do not know where she goes or what she does. What evil people she might have . . ." He trailed off.

"This is a terrible time for you and for Mabel and for your other children," Rachel said. The bishops had broken the news of Beth's death to the family, but it was the police who had come to them this morning to tell them that she had been murdered. "But Evan Parks is a good man. He will help find the person who did this awful thing. They will be brought to justice."

"You believe this?" Mose regarded her intently. "You think that finding the murderer and putting him behind bars will right the wrong?" He shook his head. "It will not. 'Vengeance is mine, saith the Lord.' It is for God to make justice on the sinners, not man." He made a choking sound and turned away. "I will not allow hatred for a bad man to make my heart as black as his. I will find a way to pray for his soul, that he may yet be saved."

Rachel was at a loss for words. The Amish way was to forgive the sin and forgive the sinner. Revenge wasn't a concept they accepted.

"When the police find the killer and bring him to trial, he will be put away for the rest of his life," she said. "To make certain he will never do to another human what he did to your daughter."

Mose walked away without answering. A group of middle-aged Amish men standing beside the barn parted to let him into their midst, but he walked through the space between them without speaking. He didn't pause when a tall man in a black coat and hat uttered his name.

"That is Mose's bishop, Bishop Johan Schroder," Bishop Abner explained. "And those are the elders of his church." He raised his gaze to meet hers. "This isn't easy for any of them. Deciding what should be done with Beth. With her body. Where she should be buried. They don't know what is right."

"You know what's right," Rachel said, fixing her gaze on her family's bishop. "You took pity on Beth. You did what you could for her, despite her having left the faith."

"Some think I interfered where I should not have. Even some of my own church feel that I am not firm enough in condemning her."

"I'm glad you didn't," Rachel said. "I'm glad we came to you first."

He sighed. "I wish I could be glad. And I wish I could be certain that my detractors are not right. Maybe I am too lenient in my decisions."

"Or maybe you are a wise leader," Rachel said. "One who knows the true meaning of love."

Rachel sat in Evan's driveway outside his house the next morning at eight ten; it was his day off. He was a creature of habit, so she knew he'd be back from the gym any moment.

The evening before, she'd left the Glick house soon after Mose had ordered Evan to leave. After another fitful night's sleep, she'd risen early and worked in her office. Then she'd scooped up some of Ada's sticky buns and brought them to Evan's.

When she saw him pull in, she got out of the Jeep.

"Still mad at me?" he asked as he joined her in the driveway. He was dressed in athletic shorts and a T-shirt. He drank water from a green Nalgene bottle she'd given him for his birthday. "I pretty much made a fool of myself last night at the Glicks', didn't I?"

She rose on her toes and kissed his cheek. "I know you meant well."

"I didn't go there to interrogate her parents. I just wanted to express my condolences."

"I know that." She held up the plate of sticky buns she'd covered in plastic wrap. "I thought I'd make breakfast for us. You jump in the shower, and I'll whip up a cheese omelet."

He groaned. "No cheese. I ate the last of it on a slice of stale bread last night."

She chuckled. "I thought there might not be." Evan was notorious for having an empty refrigerator. The ingredients for his pasta sauce, yes. Other staples, not so much. "I came prepared." She went to the back of the Jeep and retrieved a bag with a dozen eggs, a green pepper, mushrooms, and cheese. "Do you have milk?"

"I think so." He took the bag.

"Good, then we're making progress." She walked up the sidewalk, waited while he unlocked the back door, and followed him inside the small, neat rancher.

"It's pretty early in the morning," he said. "Are we going to ruin your reputation if anyone sees your Jeep in my drive?"

She smiled up at him. "I'll just tell them that I'm *rumspringa*."

He grinned back at her. "Thanks for coming. I still feel bad about what happened last night. You warned me to stay away, but I thought that since I hadn't come on official business . . ." He stopped and started again. "Guess it was dumb to come in the car and the uniform, but with the overtime hours . . ." He exhaled and downed the rest of the water in the bottle.

"Don't worry about it." She walked past him, into his kitchen. "What's important is that you find out who did that to Beth. Quickly."

"I fully intend to."

"That's what I told Beth's father."

"But *you* aren't," he warned, pointing at her. "You know

what happened when you got involved with Willy O'Day's murder. You took chances you shouldn't have. You're not to try and play detective with this case. It's not safe."

She held his gaze steadily, the bag of groceries between them. "That thought never occurred to me."

"Right." He frowned. "Well, good, so we agree on this. I'm the cop. You—"

"I'm the proprietor of a B&B." She set the plate of sticky buns on the kitchen counter and went back to him for the bag of groceries.

"You're more than that to me, Rachel." His voice grew husky. "I care about you."

"I know. Why do you think I'm here? I thought you needed a friend this morning."

"I won't let you put your life in danger again."

She nodded, taking the grocery bag from him. "I hear what you're saying, but—"

"But nothing. It's not up for discussion. I shouldn't have called you yesterday with the medical examiner's report. It won't happen again. No more privileged information. It just encourages you."

"Fine," she said, offering him a smile. "Now let me start this omelet before we ruin a pleasant morning by quarreling."

"I'm sorry you ever went to that quarry." He touched her cheek. "Sorry you had to see something like that."

"Me, too," she agreed, taking the bag to the counter. "But not nearly as sorry as I am that Beth Glick had to die like that."

Chapter 6

Rachel suppressed a shudder as the massive steel door slid shut behind her. Gooseflesh rose on her arms, and she thought of a hundred places she'd rather be on a Saturday afternoon than in prison. She had been here several times already, but the atmosphere creeped her out now as much as it had the first time. At least now, even as she felt that the walls were closing in around her, she knew what to expect. She would pass through several sets of doors, each guarded, then enter the reasonably cheerful lounge where prisoners received their guests.

Hopefully, George had received the box she'd mailed to him a week ago: books and educational material he'd requested. The items would have all been inspected and approved before they were delivered to him. The rules of what was and wasn't permitted and how it had to be sent were numerous and unyielding. As much as she would have liked to bring George some of Ada's homemade treats, baked goods that were not commercially packaged were on the forbidden list, even on his level of relatively low supervision. Maybe lots of convicts had Amish women baking tiny files into their blueberry muffins.

Rachel had been afraid that the unframed photograph of Sophie she clutched in one hand would be confiscated, but the burly, shaven-headed guard at the next set of doors examined the picture closely, remarked on how cute the little "poodle" was, and then handed the snapshot back. She was tempted to explain that Sophie was a bichon frise, not a poodle, but she held her tongue. People mistook her for a miniature poodle all the time.

"Enjoy your day, miss," he said, with a wide smile that revealed dazzling-white veneers. Despite his imposing appearance and his jailhouse pallor—the man was as gray as tallow—he was both soft-spoken and cheerful.

"You, too," Rachel replied, forcing a smile. How could anyone have a pleasant day in prison? She couldn't imagine coming to work here every day, let alone being locked up for years as poor George would probably be. She hadn't really felt like coming today; Beth's death and the funeral the day before were all too fresh in her mind. If there had been any way to wimp out without disappointing George, she would have. But she knew how much he was looking forward to her visit, and she hated to break her promise to a friend.

Another set of barred doors loomed ahead. The escort guard was replaced by a tiny, gray-haired female officer with the demeanor of a Buddhist nun and arms like a Ukrainian wrestler. "Right this way," she said kindly.

Rachel gave her name to the uniformed officer behind a bulletproof glass window the guard led her to. The man checked her name off a master list, and once all the visitors were cleared, she and about two dozen others were ushered down a long hall to a set of glass double doors marked *Reception Area*. The wrestler/nun grandmother punched in the code in the keypad, opened the door, and waved the visitors inside. The high-ceilinged room was painted pale blue and furnished with round white plastic tables and red chairs, many already occupied by eagerly waiting inmates.

"Rachel!" George's hearty welcome greeted her as she stepped into the room. She saw him at once as he hurried toward her. "First in line," he said, beaming. The gray jumpsuit he wore was overlarge and sagged around his middle; his full head of white hair was close cropped in a short military cut. Stenciled letters identified him as a prisoner. To her surprise, George threw his arms around her, hugged her, and kissed her cheek.

Rachel stiffened and glanced around, half expecting a guard to tase them. They hadn't hugged during her previous visits. "I didn't think we were allowed to touch," she whispered.

George chuckled. "You've been watching too much TV, honey. Everybody gets one hug, coming and going." He gestured to the other prisoners and their visitors exchanging hugs and kisses. "This isn't Alcatraz," he continued. "For criminals, we're a pretty civilized lot." He caught her hand and tugged her to a table in the corner of the room. "Sit, sit," he urged. "Would you like something to drink? A soda? Water? Chips?" He waved toward the row of snack and soda machines along the far wall. "My treat."

She sat in a red molded plastic chair. "No, thank you. I'm good." She held out the snapshot of Sophie. "I took a video of her chasing a ball last weekend, but it's on my iPhone and I couldn't bring it in."

"That's right. No electronics." George took the chair beside her and studied the photo with obvious affection. "That's my Sophie," he pronounced. He looked at Rachel. "She looks a little thinner. Is my girl eating well?"

"Sophie is fine," she assured him. "The vet said that she could even stand to lose a pound or two." She patted George's arm. "She misses you, but I'm taking good care of her."

George's sparkling blue eyes began to water, and he removed his glasses and mopped at the tears. "Dry air in here," he muttered. "Poor duct work." He forced a wan smile. "I knew she'd be happy with you." He glanced at the photo again. "I'm going to put this on the wall right next to my bed so I can see her last thing before the lights go out." He clasped his forearms and leaned forward, elbows on the table. "I had a letter from Ell. She has exciting plans for expanding the bookstore."

"It is exciting, isn't it? And the package I sent. It arrived?"

His kindly face creased into a grin. "It did. I can't tell you how much we appreciate it. Our classroom is sadly lacking in up-to-date textbooks and notebooks. Mine is the most popular GED course offered. We had to turn people away, if you can believe that. Twelve is the limit, but I've applied for another time slot. I can easily fill another class. You know, I've always taught teenagers, but most of these men are at or below sixteen-year-olds emotionally. And only a few of them can read on a seventh-grade level. Educate them, and you'll cut the rate of recidivism dramatically. But . . ." He paused for effect and then went on in a rush. "I'm going to have to brush up on my Spanish. One of my students doesn't speak a word of English."

Rachel listened as George rattled on about his class. He was in better spirits than when he first arrived. He seemed to be adjusting well, and it was clear to her that he was thrilled to feel needed.

"I'm sorry," he said after a few minutes. "I'm not letting you get a word in edgewise." He sat back in his chair. "Tell me what's going on in Stone Mill."

She hesitated and glanced away. When she looked back at George, tears stung the back of her eyelids.

"What is it?" He took her hand. "Rachel, what's wrong?"

She had seriously considered not telling George about Beth's murder, but she knew that he received the Stone Mill newspaper by mail. She'd seen that morning's edition. The same edition that George would receive in a couple of days. Owner and editor Bill Billingsly, who was always looking for a way to increase his readership, had plastered the details of Beth's murder across the front page. He had included photos of the Glick farmhouse and of the buggies lined up at the cemetery. The funeral had just been the previous afternoon; she couldn't imagine how he'd gotten the edition out so quickly.

"It's just awful, George."

He rubbed her hand between his dry, wrinkled ones, and she told him everything there was to tell. She told him about finding Beth in the quarry, about the bishops, the medical examiner's report, and the wake. George was a good listener who didn't interrupt but knew when to speak an encouraging word to help her relay the story.

When she was done, she sat back in her chair, hands in her lap, feeling spent.

"What a terrible tragedy," he said softly. "I'm so sorry you were there. That you had to find her. Are you all right?"

She nodded.

He was quiet for minute. "If I may ask . . . where did the Glicks bury their daughter? I know that someone shunned cannot be buried in their cemetery."

"Outside the fence, on unconsecrated ground," she said. "I know that some in their church, in the whole Amish community, weren't happy about it, but I think it was a good compromise." She looked up at him, her sadness almost overwhelming. "I went to the funeral. A nice funeral. As funerals go," she added.

"Are you sure you wouldn't like something to drink? You're looking pretty peaked."

She sighed. "No, thank you. I just feel so awful for her . . . for everyone. I can't imagine who would do such a thing."

George glanced around the visiting room, and his expression hardened. "There are a lot of heartless people out there in the world, Rachel. Some are not in their right minds, and others are . . . just evil. Most humans are innately good, thank the Lord, but those who aren't can be terrible. It troubles me that good folks have to live in fear of them."

"And that people like Evan have to risk their lives chasing them," she added.

He rubbed his palms together in a way she'd seen him do many times, usually when he was upset. "We get complacent. We think that bad things won't happen to innocents in a place like Stone Mill, but evil creeps in when we're least expecting it." He looked down at the photo of his dog on the table, then back at her. "I suppose the police have no leads."

She shook her head. "They're not having much luck getting Beth's family to answer questions. I may go and try to talk to them myself. In a few days."

He regarded her for a minute. "I know I don't have to tell you to be careful, Rachel."

She met his gaze, but didn't respond.

"I wouldn't want anything to happen to you," he said.

"I can take care of myself." At least, she thought she could. And if she'd had a sheltered childhood, the years between leaving home and being admitted to Wharton had been tough. She'd lived and worked in some pretty unsavory neighborhoods, and more than once, she'd had to use her wits to get out of a dangerous situation.

They talked about other things, safer things, for the better part of an hour. Then an unseen buzzer went off notifying the visitors that there were only fifteen minutes remaining. "Send me a list of what else you need for your classes," Rachel said. "Between Ell and me, we should be able to find the material—"

"No need," he answered. "I've made arrangements. I've spoken with my attorney, and he's going to contact my accountant. Ell can make a donation toward our education fund from one of my personal accounts. Then I can order what I need in the way of books, supplies, and media directly. Anything I want."

Rachel's face must have shown her disbelief because George laughed. "Educational materials only. It's not as if I can place an order for dynamite or plane tickets. I'm thinking of starting a book club and maybe a creative writing class. We'll need recording devices for that. None of my students have the basics for writing in the traditional manner, but we'll get there. Baby steps. But some of these men have led amazing lives. Telling their stories may go a long way toward giving them goals and a sense of self-worth."

"*You* be careful," she warned. "If anyone is too trusting, it's you, George. You always think the best of everyone."

"No, that's not me," he said with a grin. "That's my little Sophie. Bring more pictures next time you come. You will come back, won't you?" His eyes narrowed anxiously. "I know it's a lot to ask, but I have only you, Ell, and Sophie left."

"I'll be back soon, probably in two weeks," she promised. Others visitors were getting up and saying their good-byes. "And I'll bring more photos of Sophie." She got up from her chair.

"Bless you, Rachel. I knew I could count on you." He rose and put his arm around her shoulder. "Hopefully, by then all this trouble will be over, and you can get back to making Stone Mill House the best B&B in the state."

"Hopefully," she said, but secretly, she was afraid that Beth's death wouldn't be that easy to put behind them. Even if the police caught the killer, losing one of their own would cast a pall over the valley for a long time . . . maybe forever.

Monday morning, Rachel decided she needed some fresh air and took a walk downtown to The George to pick up a book she'd ordered. Her guest, Professor Li, had apparently written several mystery books featuring a talking cat detective. That character was to be the basis for the screenplay she was writing. Rachel didn't know how she felt about talking detective cats, but she thought it might be fun to read the book.

The bookstore sat on the corner of Main and Poplar and had originally been constructed as an opera house in 1904. In the '30s, it became a movie theater but fell into disrepair in the '70s and was closed. It was her friend George who, after retiring from teaching, had repurposed it as a bookstore and opened the doors again three years ago.

Rachel walked into the front room, with its curved barrel

ceiling, that had once been the lobby. "Good morning," she called. "Are you open? Door was open."

"If the door's open, The George is open," sang a familiar voice. George's niece, Ell, who was now, in her uncle's absence, the proprietor of the bookstore, popped up from behind the counter that had once displayed candies and popcorn.

"First customer of the day, I guess," Rachel said, walking across the old brocade carpet.

Ell, just twenty-two, had a long, thin face, dark eyes, and a pale complexion marred by acne scars. Her round Irish nose was adorned with a shiny piece of hardware vying with the multiple piercings in her eyebrows, lower lip, and ears. She had inky-black, spiky hair and was dressed head to toe in black, but the moment she spoke, she lit up the room.

"I . . . I wasn't expecting you this morning."

"Came to pick up that book I ordered," Rachel said.

"Ah." Ell began to move stacks of books around on the counter. "I could have brought it by. After work."

"It's okay. I needed to get out of the house. Ada is in one of her moods. Apparently, there was a mouse in the kitchen last night. Bishop is in big trouble."

"I bet he is." Ell laughed and slid a stack of newspapers away from the edge of the counter just as Rachel walked up.

Rachel caught a glimpse of the front page as Ell, not so slyly, set a cookbook down on top of the pile. There was something familiar about the photograph.

"Is that the *Harrisburg Patriot-News*?" Rachel asked, turning her head to get a better look.

Ell looked up at her, obviously trying to hide them from her. "I'm sorry?"

Rachel reached across the counter and slid one of the newspapers out from under the cookbook.

"I was thinking about just recycling them all," Ell told her, tucking her arms behind her back.

Rachel stared at the four-by-six photo of a line of Amish buggies at the Stone Mill Amish cemetery. Stone Mill had made the bottom-left corner of the *Harrisburg Patriot*. Two columns. “Every paper in town?” she asked Ell with a frown.

“Bill Billingsly,” Ell scoffed. “He’d put his mother in her nightie on the front page if he thought it would sell papers.”

Rachel studied the article’s headline: *Amish Girl Plain Killed,* it read, with Bill Billingsly’s byline. She skimmed the first column. It was the same article he had published in the local paper on Saturday. The article was continued on page five.

“Don’t do it,” Ell warned as Rachel licked her finger and turned the pages.

There were more photographs, photographs not included in the local paper. One was of a group of Amish men and women in their Sunday clothes, walking down a dirt road. It had to be a photo he had taken previously and was just waiting for the opportunity to use it. They were wearing winter coats and cloaks. And photos of the Amish of the community gathered in the cemetery, heads bowed. There was also a small photo of a woman in a black skirt and jacket, her hair covered, walking away from the camera. “That’s a picture of *me!*” Rachel spun the paper around for Ell to see.

“He mentions you, too.” She chewed on a stubby fingernail. “And Willy’s murder and how you were instrumental in finding the killer.”

Rachel groaned.

“Says we’re all waiting for you to step in and solve the case.”

“Unbelievable,” Rachel breathed.

Ell worked on another fingernail. “Think you should sue him or something?”

“It would only encourage him. I don’t sue people. I wasn’t brought up that way.” She looked at the photo again. “How did he get this in the Harrisburg paper?”

“I guess the Associated Press thought it was newsworthy. Can’t be many Old Order Amish girls who are—”

Rachel folded the paper and slapped it on the desk, cutting Ell off. "Unbelievable."

Ell reached for her coffee cup, which was in the shape of a tabby cat. "Bill never misses an opportunity to exploit the Amish." She took a sip. "They won't care much for the publicity, will they? The Amish?"

Rachel sighed. "No. Absolutely not. It's bad enough for the Glicks, for the whole Amish community to have something like this happen, but then to see it in newspapers? Photographs," she muttered.

Ell stood there, mug between her hands. She was wearing a Batman T-shirt over a long black tulle skirt. "I'm really sorry about this, Rachel."

Rachel pushed the paper back toward her. There was no way she would buy a paper. She already had tossed her Saturday *Stone Mill Gazette* right into the recycling bin. "It's not your fault." She offered a quick smile. "You said my book was in?"

"Oh, right. Sure. I've got it right here."

A few minutes later, Rachel walked out of the bookstore. Evan was waiting for her, parked in his police cruiser out front. He put down his window when he saw her.

"I tried calling you," he said.

She walked slowly over to his car, tucked her book under her arm, and leaned in. "Not sure where my cell is."

"I set up that app on your laptop after the last time you lost it, remember?" he asked.

"It's probably in the house somewhere, unless I dropped it at my parents' last night, in which case the battery's dead." She rolled her eyes.

"At least you'll know the last location, if you run the app." He met her gaze. "Got a minute? I need some advice."

"Really?"

"Really."

From the tone of his voice, Rachel suspected that he wasn't having a good morning. The expression on his face confirmed her suspicions. "You want to stop by after work to talk?" She didn't want to get into his car. It just didn't seem like a good idea, mixing work with their personal lives.

"Nah. Get in." He lifted his chin.

"You sure?"

"Yeah. I've already been out to the Glicks'. Them being early risers and all." He unlocked the doors.

She slid into the cruiser, and he put her window up. The air conditioner was blasting. She glanced at the computer screen between the two of them. There were names on it. He hit a button that cleared the screen.

"So it didn't go so well?" she asked.

"Not only won't they talk to me, they won't answer any of Sergeant Haley's questions about their daughter. He met me there this morning. And neither will any of their neighbors or relatives. It's as though they've suddenly lost the ability to understand English. They just stared at us. And any attempts to explain the importance of tracking the perp down . . ." He sighed with exasperation. "We've got nothing. Nowhere even to start. Almost two years ago, Beth Glick vanished, and the first time anyone sees her again, she's dead, floating in that quarry."

Rachel waited, not speaking, simply listening. She knew how badly Evan wanted to catch this guy, and she knew that the girl's death was causing him sleepless nights. She could see it in the shadows under his eyes and the grim creases on either side of his mouth.

"I keep going over and over it in my head," Evan said, staring out at the street.

A white station wagon went by, hitting its brakes when it spotted the police cruiser.

"Where was she?" Evan mused. "How could she show up back here, dead? Where has she been? And what could she have possibly done in that time that would cause someone to want to kill her?"

"The detective doesn't have any hunches?" She'd talked to

Sergeant Haley the previous week. His questions had been brief, and the interview had taken less than half an hour. She hadn't really formed an opinion of the middle-aged detective. She hadn't liked or disliked him. He'd just come off as a bit of a nonentity.

"No. I got the impression he was disappointed that I wasn't more help."

She rested her hands on *The Kitty Catastrophe* in her lap. "You know I'll help in any way I can," she said. "I would anyway. I want to catch whoever's responsible as much as anyone. It will be a long time before I can forget seeing her in that quarry." She felt a shiver run up her spine. "You can't let what Mose Glick said get to you—that it was partly your fault that Beth died. He was just hurt and . . ." She didn't finish her sentence.

"I know. He was talking about society in general. Which is why I wanted to be a state trooper to begin with. To keep this place safe for the Glicks, for you, for everybody. And I'm not naïve enough to think that we can chase bad guys without wearing a weapon. I didn't join the force to hurt people."

"I know you didn't." She closed her hand over his forearm. "You're kind and thoughtful, Evan. The nicest guy I know."

He didn't say anything. The dispatcher came on the radio, and he turned it down.

"What about the families of the other runaways?" Rachel said, thinking out loud. "I think everyone knows about Rupert, Eli Rust's son. He left and joined the military. He's fine. I talked to him a few months ago. Then there was a boy from the same church as Beth who left about a year before Beth did. Did you try—"

"Enosh Kline. His father shut the door in my face. Another man turned his back on the detective and walked off into a cow pasture." He looked into her eyes. "Don't they care about their children?"

"They care as much as any other parent." She leaned back

on the seat. "Their leaving complicates things. And talking to the police after Bill Billingsly has—" She didn't finish her sentence. She wouldn't dignify Billingsly with such attention.

They were both quiet for a few long moments. "I don't know what I should do next, Rachel. I don't know how to do my job."

"I guess . . . we need to think through this logically," she said.

"Like, how did Beth get back here?" he agreed. "Why was she in Stone Mill?" He tapped the steering wheel rhythmically. "The simplest scenario is that she was coming home. She'd dressed in her traditional clothes to make her return to her family and church easier."

"So our best chance is to find out where she's been, who she was with, and start untangling the threads there."

"Not *our* best chance." He looked at her. "You aren't the investigator. All I need you for is to facilitate communication between the Amish and me. Nothing more. And the first thing I need you to do is to try and convince the Glicks to talk to me. I need to try to find out why she ran away. Where she might have gone. They must have some idea."

"Some do. Most families have a child or a nephew or niece who couldn't remain in the church." She smoothed the cover of the paperback novel on her lap. "I don't know how much they know, honestly. It's usually young men who choose to leave because they can at least find a job in construction. Most of the girls who leave come back in a matter of weeks. Four girls from this community gone and never seen again in the last two years is a lot. I know my parents have discussed it. They worry about my younger sisters."

"But none of these worried families have filed missing persons reports."

"They wouldn't do that," Rachel said. "Their kids left because they wanted to escape the life; their parents are ashamed. They would never go to the police."

"So, I'll try to find out where those missing girls are. But you leave the detective work to me. I know you, Rachel. I know how you can be. This could be dangerous." He slid his hand across the car seat and took hers. "I don't know what I'd do if something bad happened to you."

"You're the second person to say that to me."

Evan arched a dark eyebrow. "George?"

"*Ya,* George."

"How is he?"

"Coping. He misses Sophie. And he's really invested in teaching his GED course. I'm glad. Despite everything, he's doing something positive to help others. He says the supplies I sent will really make a difference."

"You've got a big heart, donating to prisoners," Evan said. "It's what I love most about you. You care more about others than yourself."

She felt her cheeks grown warm, and she pulled her hand from his. "Enough, already. I'll ask around. Beth has sisters. They may be willing to talk to me, if not to you. Usually, friends, siblings or . . . a favorite aunt. When young people walk away, they don't vanish into thin air. Someone probably knows more than they're saying. Running from an Amish life into the English world, you can't imagine how difficult it can be. I took my birth certificate when I left, but most of these young people go off with nothing, not even proof that they exist. An eighth-grade education leaves you so unprepared to survive out there."

"But you made it."

"I did," she answered. *But clearly not everyone does.*

Chapter 7

"I better get going," Evan said from behind the wheel of his police cruiser.

"Right." She reached for the door handle.

"You come on your golf cart?" he asked.

He always seemed amused by her campaign to persuade the locals to use electric golf carts instead of cars on their errands around town. The carts were environmentally smart: they used less energy, put out no gas fumes, and were quiet. Best of all, they traveled at about the same speed as an Amish buggy and didn't spook the horses. In her opinion, using golf carts when possible added to the small-town ambiance of Stone Mill.

"It's not that hot yet. I walked."

"You want a ride home?"

"No, thanks. I can use the exercise." They agreed to have supper together Thursday evening, and Evan drove away.

Heading for home, Rachel started down the sidewalk. She waved to one of Hulda's grandsons, Saul, who was walking into the bank next to the bookstore. Rachel wondered if he was making the previous day's deposit, which she knew was a no-no in Hulda's book. He waved back and hurried inside, the telltale fabric bag under his arm. Deposits from Russell's Hardware and Emporium were always dropped off in the night box after closing, never held overnight in the store safe.

Hulda wouldn't be pleased that Saul hadn't followed her instructions yet again, and she would find out. For a woman in her nineties, she was difficult to get anything past, and she controlled her family business with an iron hand.

Rachel yawned. She hadn't slept well. In fact, she'd hardly slept at all since she'd discovered Beth's body. This morning, instead of getting right up, she'd laid in bed for a while, thinking about Beth and the possible scenarios that could have brought the poor girl to the quarry.

Eventually, Rachel had risen and gotten on with her day. When she'd checked her email, she'd been pleased to see that more people wanted to come to Stone Mill House the following weekend than she had room for. She was glad for the business, but now, she couldn't help wondering if the national coverage of Beth's murder had something to do with the sudden popularity of Stone Mill and her B&B. She hoped not, but a woman who had called that morning to make reservations had specifically inquired if the B&B was located in the same town where the *Aim*-ish girl had been found dead. It seemed ghoulish that visitors would want to come because of Beth's murder. Maybe the woman had been asking simply to make conversation while Rachel waited for her reservation calendar to load. Rachel couldn't fall into the trap of trying to read her guests' minds and attributing the worst to them. It might simply be the end of summer and more travelers wanting to squeeze in a last vacation.

Ada had showed up promptly at her normal hour, but when Rachel had left Stone Mill House, the girls who usually came in to help with housekeeping hadn't yet arrived. When Rachel had asked Ada why they hadn't come to work, she'd shrugged and mumbled something suggesting that she didn't intend to discuss it.

If Ada's helpers still hadn't arrived by the time Rachel got home, Rachel knew that she'd have to fill in. Besides the vacuuming and dusting of the rooms that weekend guests had checked out of, there were linens to wash and woodwork to polish. Stone Mill House required a lot of elbow grease to keep it shining. Cobwebs and dusty furniture wouldn't do for guests, not if she wanted the B&B to be a success. Plus, Ada had been complaining that the dryer wasn't drying properly, so that needed to be looked at. Any repairs Rachel could do herself, rather than calling a repairman, was money in her pocket that she didn't have to waste.

"Please be there, Minnie," she murmured. Hoping for the sight of the girl's plain, freckled face peering over a heaping basket of laundry, Rachel quickened her step. Minnie, who was a favorite relative of Ada's and, therefore, impossible to dismiss, worked exceedingly slow and had to be reminded of how to use the appliances. But she was usually dependable. Without her, Rachel would be lucky if she got everything done today.

At three, Rachel was on her knees in the stone-floored laundry room when Mary Aaron walked in. She'd heaved the dryer away from the wall and collected a pile of lint from the vent hose that she intended to scatter in the garden. Birds and squirrels would collect it for nesting materials.

"Here you are," Mary Aaron said cheerily. "I saw Ada hanging sheets in the backyard. She said you might still be in here." She studied Rachel, behind the dryer. "What are you doing?"

"The vent hose was clogged. I think that's why it was taking so long to dry stuff." Rachel made a final sweep with the brush she had been using, laid it on the floor, and began clamping the hose back on to the dryer. Her cousin leaned on the dryer and watched as Rachel tightened the screw on the clamp. Then Rachel reconnected the other end of the hose to the wall. "There. Now, if you'll help me push the dryer back."

Together they slid the heavy appliance into position.

"I don't know how you do all these things," Mary Aaron remarked. "With the tools. You know, if you had a husband, he could do it for you."

Rachel ignored her cousin. Next, Mary Aaron would be

telling her how handy Evan was and how any woman would be lucky to have him. In her midthirties, Rachel was all too aware that, by Amish standards, she was an old maid. It was rare for an Amish woman not to marry, and her family reminded her of that often. "I don't mind these kinds of chores. In fact, I kind of like them," she said, gathering her tools.

Mary Aaron looked unconvinced. "*Dat* does all that at our house," she replied, slipping into Deitsch. "Or one of the boys. *Mam* wouldn't know what to do with a screwdriver. It's man's work, she says."

Rachel shrugged. "It's easier than scrubbing floors."

"But washing and scrubbing, hanging clothes, and cooking, those are women's jobs. Chores of the house. Husbands and sons should do the heavy moving and fixing. I'm glad I was not born English. Worldly women are not so fortunate, I think, to have to do women's work and men's work as well."

"Male or female, cleaning out the vent hose is one of those things you have to do when you have a dryer, especially one used as much as this one." She used the English word for dryer. Translating *clothes dryer* into Pennsylvania Deitsch was a mouthful. "Besides taking longer to dry the laundry, if the hose is clogged, a buildup of lint could cause a fire."

"I don't understand why you need one of these things. You've got the expense of buying the contraption, and then you have to pay for the electricity to run it. Better you hang the clothes outside for the sun and wind to dry them, *ya?*"

"I've hung my share of clothes outside when it's so cold they freeze like boards, and I've helped *Mam* try and dry laundry for a big family in the cellar when it's raining outside. I like my electric dryer, thank you very much."

Mary Aaron regarded the appliance suspiciously. "Don't you worry in the night that it will burst into flames, maybe burn the house down around you?"

"No more than I worry about lightning strikes." Rachel returned the tools to her red toolbox. "They cause fires, too."

"*Ya,* they can do that. The Peacheys' barn burned last summer. Remember? They barely got their horses out."

"I remember."

The entire valley had gathered to build a new barn for the family. It was one of the things Rachel treasured about her Plain heritage. Amish might not believe in insurance, but they all came together to help one another in times of emergencies. And the Peacheys had made out well. Their old barn had been dilapidated, and their neighbors had replaced it with a larger one, built with solid timber that would last for generations—if lightning didn't strike twice in the same place.

"Do you have time for a glass of iced tea?" Rachel asked, changing the subject. "I could use a break, and I think Ada baked cookies."

Mary Aaron was wearing a faded green dress, no shoes, and a navy scarf rather than a white *kapp,* which meant she hadn't come by to pack orders and take them to the post office. She always wore her *kapp* when she went downtown, and none of the Amish would be seen barefooted on the street, for fear of Englishers staring. Mary Aaron often helped out at Stone Mill House, but she wasn't an employee. Like most things in Rachel's life, her relationship with her best friend and cousin was complicated. Mary Aaron wouldn't tell her why she'd stopped by this afternoon until she was ready, and rushing her would be rude.

"*Ya,*" Mary Aaron said. "Iced tea would be good."

Fifteen minutes later, the two sat in chairs under the shade of a spreading beech tree, each with a cold glass of tea in her hands. Rachel's tasted so good that she let her eyes drift closed and sighed with content.

"It is *goot,*" Mary Aaron agreed.

Rachel opened her eyes in time to see her cousin staring at her intently.

"Rae-Rae, are you having nightmares?" Mary Aaron asked.

She twisted one bare foot into the thick grass and quickly dropped her gaze to her own foot. "About . . . about seeing Beth like that?"

Rachel nodded. "I am. I think because I'm so worried. The police need to find out who did it." When Mary Aaron didn't respond, she went on. "Evan's helping with the investigation, but the Glicks won't talk to the police. Mose told Evan to get off his farm. He said other things, worse things, and Evan feels bad about it."

"You know how our people are about talking to an Englisher, especially police. I don't think Mose blames Evan. He might have said it, but only because he was upset. Mose is a good man."

"*Ya,* he is."

"I bet he blames himself," Mary Aaron continued. "Maybe he thinks that if he'd been a better father, Beth wouldn't have left and she'd still be alive. He can't admit that, so he takes it out on your Evan." She looked up. "You're going to help find her killer, *ya?*"

Rachel nodded again. A mockingbird lit on a branch and scolded them. "I think I have to."

"Maybe *we* have to. I was there, too. I saw." Mary Aaron sighed. "Maybe if we found the evil man who did this thing, we could both sleep again."

They sat there for a few minutes more, neither saying anything, until Mary Aaron added, "Hannah Verkler went away a year ago. Do you remember? She was a nice girl, a good friend. I knew that she had trouble accepting rules, but she was a good girl. She had good parents, not so strict as the Glicks." She hesitated. "Last night I dreamed I was at the quarry again. And this time, the girl in the water wasn't Beth. It was Hannah."

Rachel reached for Mary Aaron's hand and gripped it. "We could try together to reason with the Glicks. Maybe not the parents. Another family member, maybe? I saw a young woman in their kitchen who looked like Beth. A sister, maybe?"

"Beth has sisters, but I don't know that they'll talk to you." Her cousin nibbled at a lower lip. "I had an idea. Timothy wants me to meet him at a singing Thursday night. I think you should go with me."

"To the singing?"

"*Ya*. Some of Timothy's buddies will be there, and they used to belong to the Cut-Ups. You know, one of the young people gangs. The Cut-Ups aren't really wild; they don't get drunk or cause much trouble, but . . ." Mary Aaron shrugged. "Some of them probably have cell phones or radios, and I know some sneak off to movies in State College. They might know something about Beth . . . or Hannah."

Rachel suspected that Mary Aaron had ventured to a few of those movies herself, with Timothy, but she didn't say so. Precourting among the Old Order Amish youth was usually a private matter, and since neither of the two had been baptized yet, rules were somewhat flexible. It wasn't until there was an official courtship that a young man and woman were considered a couple. "Timothy won't mind if I show up with you?"

"He likes me. He wants us to start walking out together. He might mind, but he won't say so." She smiled. "Besides, it's a long way to take the horse and buggy, especially coming home at night. *Mam* would be worried to let me go alone with a killer loose out there. If we take your Jeep, we'll be safe."

"And you think Timothy's friends might know where Beth was all this time?"

"If anyone knows about young people who have left our community for the English, the Cut-Ups will."

Thursday evening, instead of having dinner with Evan, Rachel found herself driving Mary Aaron to the youth singing at the Beiler farm. John Hannah and Alan, two of Mary Aaron's single brothers, sent by their mother, were squeezed into the backseat. Apparently Rachel's aunt wasn't confident that the

Jeep would allow the women to escape a crazed killer. Either that, or the boys wanted to appear cool, arriving not by buggy but in a candy-apple-red Jeep.

Out of consideration for her hosts, Rachel parked the vehicle in the pasture, out of sight of the house. The Amish kids knew that Rachel and her cousin hadn't come in the usual fashion, and the hosting parents suspected, but no one said anything. There were already dozens of young people assembled in the yard and long, open picnic area. The Beilers of courting age, a girl and a boy, were the babies of the family. The father made his living by cutting timber, and he'd done well. The house, barn, and outbuildings were large, sturdy, and spotless. And after raising fifteen children and marrying off thirteen, the senior Beilers were accustomed to hosting singings.

The gathering brought back a wave of warm memories of Rachel's own teenage years in the community. A farm wagon with straw bales for seating stood beside a dozen topless buggies. Boys in short-sleeved white shirts led sleek horses to an open shed beside the stable, while girls removed cakes, pies, and baskets of cookies from the backs of carriages amid a friendly chorus of teasing and greetings. Everyone loved a singing, where young people could meet up with others of their own age and enjoy an evening of fun and innocent romance. The laughter and soft Deitsch greetings were so familiar that Rachel closed her eyes and, for a few seconds, remembered the excitement and hopes such evenings had raised in her when she was young.

She recognized a few of the youths, but most were from church districts other than her family's. Everyone was dressed in his or her best clothing: the girls in blue, green, or lavender dresses, white *kapps,* black stockings and shoes. The boys sported black vests over their white shirts and black pants. Some of the black felt hats boasted brims wider than customary, a few rebelliously narrow. But there wasn't a single ball cap, cowboy hat, or bareheaded male in sight. Tables laden with snacks, sodas, and sandwich makings attracted knots of young men, while the giggling girls tended to gather at the far end of one of two long tables set up for the singing.

"Mary Aaron!" Timothy waved and hurried toward them. He was a tall, Nordic-looking fellow with long legs, a wide chest, and a cheerful, freckled face. Timothy stood to inherit a substantial dairy farm from an aging grandfather with whom he lived. According to Mary Aaron, he attended church regularly, was obedient and respectful to his elders. He promised to be an excellent candidate for marriage, if and when she decided to allow herself to be courted. What Timothy didn't appear to be was someone who would associate with members of the outer fringes of Amish youth society, a gang such as the Cut-Ups. Which proved, as Rachel knew, that you couldn't tell a book by its cover.

"Timothy." Rachel smiled. He nodded politely, but his attention was all on Mary Aaron. Her brothers had already scattered. Alan was talking animatedly to a red-cheeked girl in a maroon dress and seemed oblivious to his friends' exhortations to join them at the food table. John Hannah had loped off to join a circle of young men near the barn.

Mary Aaron exchanged a few words with Timothy, and then the two of them strolled toward the coolers of sodas.

Rachel introduced herself to the elder Beilers. The mother, Roberta, she knew from the farmer's market held on Saturdays in Stone Mill. Both Beilers were pleasant and welcoming, and neither mentioned the obvious, that she was the only non-Amish at the singing.

Rachel had taken special care to dress modestly this evening, but she'd refused Mary Aaron's offer to borrow one of her dresses. Rachel hadn't wanted anyone to think she was posing as Amish. She'd stitched up a russet, midcalf A-line skirt, a matching shirtwaist blouse with hidden buttons, and a triangular-shaped scarf of the same material. Her mother had been complaining about the state of her navy-blue denim skirt and shapeless top that she usually wore when visiting the Old Order Amish. Sewing was something she'd learned as a girl from her mother, and even if she did resort to a late-model Singer, Rachel was pleased that she could still turn a seam and sew a pleat with confidence.

"Now they are beginning, I think." The jolly hostess waved toward the long tables where boys and girls were taking seats on opposite sides. Rachel didn't join them but found a place on the grass nearby. She'd always loved the singings, but she would have felt awkward sitting between young women seeking beaus and husbands.

Among the Old Order Amish, there was no dating as the English world understood. While marriages were by choice, not by arrangement, it was understood that the sacrament was intended to increase and support family. Family and community unity were more important than individual happiness. What was important was that Amish couples wed in the sight of God and raise children who would honor the faith, so few brides or grooms chose spouses whom their parents or church community found unacceptable. And no one was less acceptable than a person considered morally weak or lacking in faith. Thus, young couples in Stone Mill were strictly chaperoned and bound by tradition to remain pure until their wedding night. It didn't follow the social mores of wider American society, but it had worked well for the Plain folk for centuries and produced, on the whole, strong families.

One of the older girls stood and announced a fast hymn. There was no accompanying music and no songbooks, but everyone knew the hymns by heart. The song leader suggested three more before yielding her place to a boy with a deep and melodious baritone voice. His first selection was "Michael, Row the Boat Ashore," and the group joined in enthusiastically, clapping to the beat and swaying back and forth. Rachel had never seen anyone moving to the music at a singing before. She glanced at Roberta Beiler in astonishment, but the older woman merely shrugged, while her husband shook his head and went into the house. Rachel chuckled. Change came slowly to Stone Mill, but apparently, it *did* come. And when the leader's next song was the spiritual "Wade in the Water," Rachel couldn't help but sing along.

After an hour, the first song leader called for a break, and everyone quickly assembled around the food. Mary Aaron motioned to Timothy, and the two of them joined Rachel at the edge of the yard. Her cousin glanced around to see that no one else was within hearing range and then said quietly, "I told him"—she indicated Timothy—"that we were trying to get some information about the girls who left Stone Mill." She nudged him. "Tell her what you told me."

Timothy glanced at his feet. Rachel noticed that he smelled of Old Spice. He shuffled his feet. "I don't know about the girls," he said. "But a boy, Enosh, who left was one of my pals."

"Enosh left before Hannah and Beth," Mary Aaron elaborated. "Do you remember him? He left around the time you moved back, but after, I think."

Rachel knew the name but didn't think she had met him.

"He's living in Harrisburg," Mary Aaron explained. "He's got a job as a roofer."

"So he's safe?" Rachel asked. "Nothing bad has happened to him?"

Timothy glanced around nervously. "Nothing more than going without a few meals and being homesick."

"Didn't Lucy Zug leave around the same time?" Rachel asked Mary Aaron as she tried to recall.

"*Ya,* a little after, I think."

"You don't know anything about Lucy?" Rachel asked Timothy.

He shook his head. "Know who she was, is all. Her being older than me."

Rachel nodded. "Is there a way for you to get in touch with Enosh? I'd like to ask if he knows anything about Beth or the others."

"I don't think he'd talk to you," Timothy said slowly. "He doesn't want anyone to know where he is. He's afraid his family will find out and make him come home."

"It happens," Mary Aaron said. "Last year, Lemuel Yoder's *dat* tracked him down near Belleville and talked him into coming back."

"I don't want to get Enosh into any trouble," Rachel assured Timothy. "He's an adult. I won't go to his parents," she promised. She lowered her voice. "This is really important, Timothy. Mary explained to you, didn't she? Other girls, maybe boys, might be in danger, too." She let that settle for a minute before she asked, "Do you have Enosh's address?"

"*Ne*. I did have his phone number, but . . ." Timothy shook his head. "My grandfather found my cell and smashed it on the chopping block. Had minutes left on it, too."

"Could you give me the number?" Rachel asked the young man. "It would help a lot."

Timothy looked sheepish. "It was in the phone. I didn't write it down anywhere." He shrugged. "Sorry, I don't remember it."

"But someone else must have his number, right?" Rachel asked.

"I . . . I don't know," Timothy said.

A young man approached, and Timothy took a step back from Rachel and Mary Aaron.

"Come and eat," the other boy encouraged.

"You know Harvey Beiler," Timothy said. "His parents own this farm." He introduced Rachel.

"Glad to have you." Harvey waved toward the sandwich table. "My mother will be upset if we don't eat the spread she put out for us. Every bite of it."

Mary Aaron flashed her a look, and Rachel followed the other three to the refreshments. She helped herself to a plate and a glass of cider, then found an unoccupied bench to sit and watch the others. Groups of boys and girls broke into couples to eat together. A young man sitting next to a cute, plump girl named Vi waved a flashlight. The others laughed.

Rachel understood the joke. The boy would be driving his girlfriend home, and they'd creep into her parents' house in the dark. With no light but that provided by the batteries, they'd sit in the living room and talk and hold hands until after midnight. It was daring but acceptable behavior, and propriety was maintained by the knowledge that parents and extended family might wander through the downstairs at a moment's notice.

Someone called for the singing to resume, and the boys and girls noisily assembled on either side of the tables again. A different song leader began with "What a Friend We Have in Jesus." Rachel, noticing Roberta Beiler and another middle-aged woman begin to refill the food trays and snack baskets, went to help them. They seemed pleased, and Rachel spent the next half hour assisting them.

There was more eating and more songs, but according to custom, the singing officially ended at ten o'clock sharp after several slower and more traditional hymns. Almost immediately, a few buggies arrived to pick up younger teenagers, while the older guests gathered for a few moments of friendly exchanges and more food before heading out.

Seeing nothing more that needed doing, Rachel retreated to a seating area near the back door of the farmhouse. She didn't know if Mary Aaron intended to ride home with her or if she had accepted Timothy's offer, but she hoped to speak with Timothy again before leaving. He was clearly reluctant to help them, but surely he would realize how important it was that Evan talk to Enosh. When she saw someone coming toward her in the darkness, she thought it might be Timothy, but it was her cousin John Hannah.

"Mary Aaron says she'll meet you at the Jeep," John Hannah said. "Alan's going with Andy Peachey and the Gingrich sisters." He came to stand close beside her. "You find out anything that might help you?"

"I don't know. Maybe." She wondered how much Mary

Aaron had told John Hannah. "Wasn't there a girl you wanted to take home tonight?"

"She turned me down," he admitted. "She's riding with someone else. An older fellow." He offered Rachel a root beer, which she accepted. "Good singing, though," John Hannah said. "Mostly fast hymns. Not worship hymns."

Rachel nodded. She was trying not to feel disappointed that they were leaving without any more information than they came with.

The crowd got thinner. Young men hitched horses and helped girls into the open buggies. Four or five young women climbed onto the wagon Rachel had seen earlier and found seats on the bales of straw. Three boys, obviously unsuccessful in finding dates, drove off together. Rachel and John Hannah finished their sodas and walked back down the lane to the Jeep. Mary Aaron was already there, sitting in the front seat. There was no sign of Timothy.

Rachel got in and started the engine. "Timothy already say good-bye?" she asked Mary Aaron.

"*Ya.*" Her cousin shook her head and sighed. "He wasn't too happy that I wouldn't let him drive me home."

Rachel waited as two buggies rolled down the lane past her before carefully pulling out onto the road and turning in the direction of Stone Mill. "I thought you liked him."

"I do," Mary Aaron said. "I'm just not ready to get serious yet."

"He's a good guy," John Hannah said.

"I know he is," Mary Aaron agreed. "But . . ."

Rachel knew that baptism would have to come before a wedding, and she wondered which one Mary Aaron was more reluctant to commit to. "Don't let anyone rush you," she advised.

"That's what *Dat* says." John Hannah fastened his seat belt in the back. "He and *Mam* walked out for two years before they tied the knot."

They rode in silence for a few minutes before John Hannah spoke again. "Doesn't anyone want to know what I found out?"

"About what?" Mary Aaron asked.

"About Hannah and them other girls that left."

"You found out something?" Rachel asked, pulling the Jeep off the road and braking to a stop.

John Hannah laughed. "*Ya.* Well, maybe. Timothy told me you were asking about Enosh. He felt bad that he didn't have any way to contact him. I told him he should ask his friends, but I think he was worried about getting somebody in trouble." He shrugged. "So I did some of my own asking. Talked to one of them Cut-Ups. Found out who Enosh works for. It's a small Englisher company called J. M. S. Roofing. They've got some other ex-Amish kids working for them."

"Do you have an address or a phone number?" Rachel asked.

"Nope. But Pete said anybody can find them. They're in the Harrisburg yellow pages."

Chapter 8

Midafternoon the following day, Evan, Rachel, and Timothy turned into a housing development in a small town west of Harrisburg. It had taken a little persuasion to convince Timothy to agree to go with them to find Enosh. Especially when he realized Mary Aaron wouldn't be going because she had committed to an outing with her mother. But in the end, Timothy genuinely wanted to help the police find out who had murdered Beth, so he agreed to go with them as long as no one would know he had gone and he'd be home by milking time.

A call to J. M. S.'s office by Evan had produced the address of the current job site. Roofing was underway on three spec homes. There were several trucks with the J. M. S. Roofing logo painted on the sides, and a crew at work on each house.

Rachel was at the wheel of her Jeep. "He may be working under the table," she explained to Evan. "A lot of these runaway Amish kids don't have the paperwork to prove their ages, and they certainly don't have social security cards. Obtaining them takes time."

"I think that might be him on that ladder," Timothy said, pointing as Rachel parked. "Let me go and talk to him. I'll see if he's willing to talk to you."

Rachel watched Timothy walk down the sidewalk and approach the ladder. He called out to a young man wearing jeans and a hard hat. No shirt. Knowing Amish standards of modesty, Rachel could appreciate how much of a stretch that might be for Enosh. Some Old Order Amish kids went crazy when they left the strict communities. They started drinking alcohol and engaging in risky behavior. Those individuals rarely made it on the outside. The leap from Stone Mill to the English world was a big one, and only the steadiest and more resilient could succeed. For Enosh's sake, she hoped he was one of the few who would.

The boy came down the ladder, and he and Timothy exchanged greetings. Rachel couldn't hear what they were saying, even with the window down, but Timothy and Enosh soon drew the attention of an older, bearded man. The man walked over to join them, followed by two of the roofers and one of the truck drivers. Enosh kept glancing in the direction of the Jeep, then at the men, then back at the Jeep again.

Evan put his hand on the door handle. "I think we'd better join them," he said. "Our boy looks as though he might be getting ready to pull a vanishing act."

As she and Evan got out of the car, the bearded man broke off from the group and strode toward them. "Jake Sweitzer. I understand you want to talk to Enosh. Is there some problem?" He thrust out a hand to Evan, but the expression in his eyes was wary. He was a big man, stern but not morose, with the look of someone who'd spent a lifetime working outside.

Evan returned the handshake and introduced Rachel and then himself. "Enosh isn't in any trouble. We're hoping he can give us some information on a young Amish woman who left her community about the same time he did. You may have seen something on the news. Beth Glick?"

Jake nodded. "The girl who was murdered. *Ya,* I saw that in the paper." He glanced back toward Enosh and Timothy. Several of the crew stood protectively on either side of them. "Is this an official visit, Officer?"

"No, not at all. We're tracking down all leads, no matter

how small. Frankly, the investigation has hit a stone wall. Beth Glick vanished from her home and community and showed up two years later, dead. If we had any idea what happened to her in the time she was gone, we might have a place to start."

Jake frowned. "Enosh is a good kid. He works hard, pulls his fair share, and the guys like him. He's not someone the police would be questioning in a murder."

"We're not looking at him on this," Evan explained. "I was just hoping that because he left the same Amish community, he might know something about how Beth Glick was able to leave. Who might have helped her in Stone Mill and on the outside."

Jake glanced at the knot of men. "He says he knew Beth, but not anything about her leaving. He doesn't know where she went or how she left. He left Stone Mill three years ago."

Evan nodded. "You said Enosh is a good worker. You know how he spends his time when he's not at work?"

"I'm telling you, Officer, he's a nice young man. Has a girlfriend, taking GED classes two nights a week. He keeps his nose clean. Always the first in on Saturday nights."

Rachel met the man's gaze. "The first in? Meaning . . . he's staying with you?" She knew it was done. Good souls, often ex-Amish themselves, opened their homes to young people to help them get on their feet while they found work.

"*Ya,*" Jake agreed reluctantly. "Sleeps over our garage."

Rachel watched him closely. "I'd guess he's not the only house guest you have."

He gave her a steady look. "Mast, you said? You wouldn't happen to be the woman I read about in the paper a few months ago—opened the bed-and-breakfast in the old mill house?"

She answered his question with one of her own. "Is Enosh the only ex-Amish you have working for you, Mr. Sweitzer?"

"Why do you ask?" His eyes narrowed, and she was afraid she might have stepped over the line.

Rachel was relieved that Evan knew to just keep quiet at this point and let her steer the conversation. He stood next to her, listening.

"You own a construction company," she said. "Amish boys are good carpenters. It's one skill that translates to the Englisher world. By your name, I'd suspect that you are first or second generation away from a horse and buggy yourself." She shrugged. "I can spot them. I bet you can, too." She offered a quiet smile. "I left when I was eighteen."

He grimaced. "Sure *you* aren't the cop? You hit the nail on the head. I left at sixteen, twenty-six years ago. For the first two years, I nearly starved to death, and the next, it's a wonder I didn't end up in prison."

"So you help where you can," she said, with understanding in her tone.

Jake shrugged again. "Amish kids find their way to my door. I feed them, give them a bed and the chance to earn an honest dollar. If that's against the law, put the cuffs on me." He offered callused hands, and Rachel saw that half of his left index finger was missing. Jake flashed a crooked grin. "Skil saw. First week on the job."

Rachel winced. She could see it all in her mind's eye: a skinny, scared kid with a bad haircut. One mistake, and a lifetime of paying for it. She held up her right thumb revealing the shiny scar of an old burn. "Electric stove top."

"I win," Jake said. "No contest."

"*Ya,*" she agreed. "You win." She sensed that a connection had been made between them. For a few steps, she and Jake Sweitzer had walked the same path. "Do you ever think of going back?" she asked him.

His mouth firmed. "Do you?"

Emotion made her voice thick. "More often than I like to admit."

Jake nodded. "I know the feeling. Three kids, an English wife that I'm crazy about, and two mortgages. Still . . . the old life, it calls to me. You know what I mean?"

"I do," she admitted. She looked up at Evan, saw the puzzlement in his eyes, and offered him a rueful smile. "But I'm not giving in to it."

Jake nodded toward the men on the nearest roof. "I've helped twelve, fourteen Amish kids over the years. Maybe half went back home and joined the church. Of the others, I only lost one to the pleasures of the world. But Enosh is the best of the lot. I'll not see him hurt. He's come a long way, but he's still fragile."

She gazed at Timothy and Enosh and the other men who had joined them. "Did you have any girls pass through?"

Jake shook his head. "*Ne*. Girls are a lot trickier. Most don't stay away from the old life for long. And any who have shown up on my doorstep, I've passed them on to other people. My wife, Jen, and I have three boys. I wouldn't know the first thing about girls. It could be that Enosh knows something about one or more of them. But, like I said before, not Beth Glick. We talked about it, Enosh and me. He went to school with her. He was shocked as h—" Jake caught himself. "Shocked as the rest of us when he heard about her murder. Was she trying to go back to her family?"

"We don't know," Rachel answered. "That's what we're trying to find out."

"We'd still like to talk to Enosh," Evan said quietly. "With no details, we have no motive. If we don't catch whoever killed her, he might kill again. If Enosh could do anything to prevent that . . ." He left the rest unspoken.

Jake considered and then nodded. "My crew's a little spooked. I've got three others here who left the Amish." He thought for a minute, then spoke again. "There's a diner about a mile from here. We usually stop there for coffee after work. Enosh likes the apple pie. He says it reminds him of his *grossmama*'s. Take him over there. He'll talk to you if I ask him. Just don't put any pressure on him to go back home." He smiled. "Enosh isn't much for coffee, but he likes the hot chocolate with whipped cream just fine."

Ten minutes later, Rachel and Evan sat in a booth at the diner across from Timothy and Enosh. Enosh was blond, short, wiry, and clearly nervous. "Like I told Jake," he said in Deitsch, "I know nothing about Beth. Haven't seen her since I left Stone Mill."

Evan frowned. "English, please," he said.

"*Ya,* sure thing." Enosh plucked a napkin from the stainless steel holder on the table. "But I can't tell you nothing." He glanced at Timothy. "Don't know why you told 'em I was here."

"He didn't," Rachel said. "One of the Cut-Ups told where you were working, not to me but to one of my cousins." That was safe enough, she thought. She had so many cousins, Enosh would never know where to put the blame.

The young man sat back in the booth, looking very much like a defiant Englisher kid.

"Have you been in touch with any of the girls who left the valley?" Rachel asked.

The waitress came to the table with their orders, a hamburger and fries for Timothy, coffee for Evan, and pie with ice cream for her and Enosh, plus his hot chocolate with whipped cream. When the waitress walked away, Rachel named the other missing girls: Hannah Verkler, Lucy Zug, and Lorraine Yoder.

As she named each one, Enosh shook his head. "*Ne,* none of them," he said. But he twitched and his ears reddened when she mentioned Lucy Zug.

Evan stirred his coffee. The white mug was oversized and bore the image of a silver guitar on the outside. "I hear you have a girlfriend."

"She's English," Timothy put in.

"My cousin Mary Aaron Hostetler is good friends with Hannah Verkler," Rachel said. "She's really worried about her. Are you sure you don't know Hannah? She left after Beth."

Enosh sighed. "I *knew* Hannah, but I haven't seen her. I

told you, I don't know nothing about any of them girls. Not since I left Stone Mill." He dug his fork into the apple pie and took a large bite.

"Except Lucy," Rachel said, taking a forkful of apple pie.

Enosh chewed, keeping his gaze fixed on his plate.

"You won't get into any trouble, Enosh," Evan told him. "We need your help."

When he didn't respond, Rachel said, "How would you feel if what happened to Beth happened to Lucy?"

Enosh swallowed. "Nothing's going to happen to Lucy. She's fine."

Timothy elbowed his buddy. "You might as well tell them what you know about Lucy. I know Rachel, and she won't leave you in peace until you do."

Enosh ran a hand through his close-cropped, white-blond hair. He didn't look twenty-two; he could have passed for sixteen. Only his eyes appeared old and world-weary. "She's fine," he insisted. "I talked to her last week."

"Where is she?" Evan asked, abandoning his coffee.

"State College. She's got a job taking care of a baby for some teacher at Penn State."

"She works as a babysitter?" Rachel asked.

"Nanny." Enosh used the Deitsch term, which translated as "nurse for a baby." "She lives with the family. They treat her good. They even bought her a car."

"So how is it that you know where Lucy is but none of the others?" Evan asked, taking out his iPhone. "Can you give us an address? Her phone number?"

"She's got a good job," Enosh said. "Lucy likes it there. Don't make trouble for her."

"We're not making trouble for anyone." Rachel pointed at him with her fork. "We're trying to prevent trouble and to find whoever murdered Beth Glick. If you care about Lucy, you'll tell us how to contact her."

"Don't worry. We can trust Rachel and him. They won't

make her go home," Timothy said. "And they won't tell her father where she is."

"Lucy was pals with my sisters," Enosh said slowly. "They told me to look out for her when we . . ." He filled his mouth with pie.

"And you are looking out for her," Rachel assured him when he didn't finish. "More than you know."

Beads of sweat broke out on the boy's forehead, and he wiped them off with the back of his hand. Rachel folded her arms and gazed at him. "You want to do the right thing, Enosh. I know you do."

He squirmed in his seat and absently mopped up a drip of melted ice cream on the table with a napkin. "Okay," he said reluctantly. "I don't know the house address, but I can give you her phone number. If she won't talk to you, it's not my fault."

Twenty minutes later, Rachel, Evan, and Timothy left the diner. Enosh remained where he was, working on his second piece of pie and second cup of hot chocolate while he waited for a ride.

None of the three spoke until they got back into the Jeep.

"A network," Evan said, as she backed out of the parking place. "Jake Sweitzer as good as admitted that there's a network of people helping these kids once they run away. They're finding them places to stay, jobs. I had no idea."

"*Ya,*" Timothy agreed. "Englishers." He shook his head in amazement. "I never heard about that." And then he asked, "Will I be home in time for night milking?"

"You will," Rachel promised. "We'll drop you off on the way."

"On the way to where?" Evan asked.

"State College."

The house was large, a block from a park, and situated on a wide, tree-lined street in an upscale part of town. It was seven forty-five, and lights were beginning to come on in the neighboring homes. Deep shadows fell across the lawns and sidewalks.

"Nice place," Evan said as Rachel pulled to the curb a few properties down from the house they'd been looking for. "Nice to know someone in the state has money."

"Hiring a live-in nanny isn't cheap," Rachel said. "Not that I'd know personally, but I've known business associates who had them."

Contacting Lucy Zug had been almost too easy. And the young woman had agreed to speak with them if they could get there before nine p.m.

Rachel reached across to take Evan's hand and give it a squeeze. It had taken all her negotiating skills to convince him that they should try to speak with Lucy before bringing in the detective. Evan was hesitant, but it made perfect sense to her. What if Lucy knew nothing about the other girls? Her safety might lie in the fact that no one knew where she was. Once the officials got into it, word might leak to the press, and she could find her picture in the morning paper. Whatever life Lucy had made for herself in the two and a half years or so since she'd left Stone Mill could be jeopardized needlessly. It was a leap to suppose that if her whereabouts became public knowledge, she might become a target for the killer, but who knew? Anything was possible. And if Lucy was keeping her new life a secret, what right did she and Evan have to risk her privacy?

"You know that if she gives us any leads," Evan warned Rachel, "I have to take them to the sergeant."

Rachel nodded. "I know. And I agree. But there's no sense in us giving him false trails to follow. If Lucy has nothing to add to the investigation, then we don't need to mention her name."

They got out of the car and followed the sidewalk to the driveway of the house where Lucy had said she was staying.

She'd asked them to come to the side door. Trees, shrubs, and flowers made the velvety lawn a showplace, and looking at it gave Rachel a few ideas for giving Stone Mill House a bit more year-round color.

A path led to a stone patio and an oversized blue door with an elegant bronze knocker. A basket of fresh flowers hung from a small, glazed, multipaned window. Evan rang the doorbell. He waited, then rang it again. Rachel waited, trying not to show how nervous she felt. What if Lucy had changed her mind and decided not to talk to them at all? A minute passed and then two more. There was no answer. Evan glanced back at her. "Did we blow it?" he asked.

Just then, the door swung open.

"Lucy?" Rachel asked the young woman standing there. She looked vaguely familiar. Maybe. Things had been crazy when Rachel first moved back to Stone Mill; she couldn't honestly remember if she'd ever met Lucy or not.

"Yes, I'm Lucy Zug." She was a plain girl with full, ruddy cheeks, brown hair pulled back severely into a knot at the nape of her neck, and large hazel eyes. She was dressed in a navy shirtwaist dress and white canvas boat shoes. She hugged herself protectively, thin elbows pressed tightly against her flat chest, fingers locked into fists.

Evan introduced himself and then Rachel.

Lucy's voice was high and reedy. "Can we talk outside, Officer? If any of the neighbors saw you, I wouldn't want Professor or Mr. Thornford to think I had people in when they weren't at home." She stepped out, leaving the door open behind her. "Baby Evelyn is sleeping," she explained. "I'll hear her if she wakes up." Lucy's English was precise, but she still retained her Pennsylvania Dutch accent, and that endeared her to Rachel.

"I call myself Lucy Baker here, but that's not against the law, is it?"

"We aren't here to cause any problem for you." Rachel

knew the girl had to be scared. It had taken Rachel years to become comfortable in her new skin after she left the Amish. "We're simply trying to—"

"I know why you're here. Enosh called me this afternoon, just before you did. He said you wouldn't tell my family where I am."

"We won't," Rachel assured her.

"Professor Thornford and Mr. Thornford know my real name. They're very understanding, but I don't think they'd like it if they knew police were here questioning me. At their house, I mean. They're very protective of Baby Evelyn." She smiled nervously. "First child. Lucky for me that I'm used to babies."

"You have lots of brothers and sisters?" Rachel asked.

"Oldest of nine." She waved stiffly toward a table and chairs. "Would you like to sit down, sir?" She balanced lightly on the balls of her feet, almost as if it took all her effort to keep from floating off the ground. "I don't know what I can tell you. About Beth." Distress showed on Lucy's face. "Who would do such a thing to her? She was such a good girl. Everyone knew how kind and hardworking she was. Pretty, too."

"We won't sit," Evan said. "We just have a few questions and then we'll be on our way. We're trying to find out where Beth was in the time she was gone from Stone Mill. Did you see her? Hear from her or anyone who might have come in contact with her?"

Lucy shook her head and glanced behind her to the open door. "I never saw her or heard anything about her. I told Enosh that. Beth and I were never friends or anything. Different church districts."

Evan looked frustrated. "Do you know any of the other girls who left the Amish community recently?" He read the names from a little notebook he carried in his pocket.

"*Ne.* I mean, *ya*—yes, I knew who they were. But I didn't even know they had left." Lucy's thin voice trembled.

"You can't help us at all?" Rachel asked. The girl was clearly shaken by their coming, but whether she honestly didn't know anything or was reluctant to talk to them, Rachel couldn't tell. It made her feel bad that they'd upset Lucy so. She looked as if she was about to burst into tears at any moment.

A loud wail rose from inside the house. "Baby Evelyn!" Lucy exclaimed. "I have to pick her up. Professor Thornford doesn't like her to cry. She says it's emotionally damaging for an infant when their needs are left unfulfilled." She threw Rachel a desperate look. "Please, is there anything else? I'm sorry that happened to Beth, but I really don't know anything about any of the others."

The baby's howl rose to a full cry. Lucy backed toward the door. "You won't say anything to the Thornfords, will you? I don't want to lose this job."

"I see no reason to." Rachel reached into the bag on her shoulder. "I'm going to leave you my phone number. If you think of anything, no matter how small, that you think might help us, please don't hesitate to call." She handed the girl a business card with the B&B's number on it. "One more thing. When you left home, did you have help? Finding a place to stay? Assisting you to find work?"

"*Ne*. I left on my own. Nobody helped me." Lucy accepted the card but held it as if it were hot enough to cause blisters on her fingertips. "I really have to go, Officer."

Evan thanked her, but the door was already closing.

Together, Rachel and Evan walked back down the sidewalk.

"So, where does that leave us?" Rachel asked as they walked back to the Jeep through the gathering twilight. A scent of roses wafted on the breeze—heavy, almost cloying.

Evan sighed, obviously frustrated. "Nowhere, other than to cross Enosh and Lucy off the list."

"But we haven't found Hannah or Lorraine."

"They could be anywhere. Even working in a house across

the street." He held out his hand for her keys. "Want me to drive home?"

She handed him the keys and slid into the passenger's seat. As cooperative as Lucy had seemed, Rachel had sensed she wasn't quite telling everything she knew. There was something about the pitch of her voice, particularly when she told Evan she had left the Amish on her own, without any help. And neither Lucy nor Enosh had explained how they had known where the other was. It was an unanswered question that worried her like a loose thread on her new jeans.

Chapter 9

After church on Sunday, Rachel repeated the entire conversation she and Evan had had with Lucy to Mary Aaron. Rachel had attended early service at the Methodist church in Stone Mill, but for her cousin and the family, this had been a visiting Sunday, a day set aside for relaxing with friends and family. Among most Old Order Amish, formal worship services were held only every other Sabbath. Each household within a community church district took turns hosting the services in their homes, a holdover from the perilous times before coming to America, when the Amish, Mennonites, and other Plain folk who practiced adult baptism risked their lives to worship in secret.

Rachel had been pleased to find her cousin waiting for her on the back porch when she'd gotten home from church. Although she was close to her own brothers and sisters, Mary Aaron preferred spending visiting Sundays with Rachel, when she could steal away. Laughing and feeling like kids who'd played hooky from school, the two grabbed snacks and hastily retreated to their spot in the attic, the one place in Stone Mill House where no one could disturb them.

It wasn't that Rachel didn't like her guests. Normally, she adored welcoming visitors to Stone Mill House and helping them enjoy their stay in the valley to the utmost, but sometimes she grew weary of always being on call and needed to get away for an hour. With a house full of visitors Friday and Saturday night, Rachel was ready for a break. Even if it was just to escape having to smile so much and answer the same questions over and over again.

It was the perfect day to find refuge in the attic, where no one would think to look for them. Intermittent rain fell in sheets and drummed against the attic windows, shutting out the world. When Rachel was a child, her mother's attic had been a retreat, and she'd been drawn to this spot from the first day she'd purchased the house.

This attic was large, divided into multiple rooms, and was a treasure trove of old furniture and cobwebs. Rachel and Mary Aaron had laid claim to one wainscoted chamber that embraced the double chimney on the west side of the original stone house. They'd spent long afternoons cleaning the grunge of years from the golden pine paneling and polishing the wavy-glass window panes until they caught the sunlight and sparkled. They'd scrubbed the floor, spread quilts over an old church bench and a pair of painted Windsor chairs, and laid an antique hooked rug on the floor.

On clear days, one of them would push open the window and they would lie on an old bedstead on their stomachs, propped up on elbows, to gaze out over the lush valley. In the winter, when the weather was inclement, the hideaway, made cozy by the warmth from the stone chimneys, was a delight. Rachel sometimes came up here alone to read or pray, but she was happiest when she could share it with Mary Aaron. Despite the difference in their ages, it seemed to Rachel as if Mary Aaron understood her better than anyone.

"So you think Lucy knows more than she's telling," her cousin suggested. Mary Aaron was seated cross-legged on the rug, a bowl of baby carrots and cherry tomatoes in her lap. Mary Aaron loved carrots, and she was fascinated by the petite, precut and peeled carrots Ada used for her vegetable plates when she was short on time.

Rachel nodded. "I am, and I can't help thinking she was

holding back because Evan was there. He tried to win her confidence, but . . ."

"He's an Englisher."

"Exactly. And a man. And a cop. Lucy was clearly afraid that her employers would come home and find a police officer there. I kept thinking that if I'd gone alone, she would have told me more."

Mary Aaron held up a baby carrot. "If they make these by whittling down normal-sized carrots, what do they do with the rest? At the carrot factory. Feed them to the chickens?"

It was all Rachel could do not to chuckle. "No chickens. I'm not sure what they do with the scraps. Throw them away probably."

" 'Waste not, want not,' *Mam* says," Mary Aaron said. "Sometimes the English are difficult to understand."

"*Ya,*" Rachel agreed, and quoted one of her father's favorite sayings, " 'Use it up, wear it out. Make it do, or do without.' "

"*Dat* said you changed out there among the Englishers. But not too much, I think." She finished off the last carrot from the bowl. "And these are *gut* even if they are English."

Rachel laughed. "They are, aren't they?" Funny the little things that could make a person happy. Sometimes she longed for the times before she'd gone out among the English: simpler times, simpler pleasures. But her Amish world had always felt too small, and when she had become a teenager, she'd realized that the Plain life was not for her. At least, most of the time she felt that way. Only now and then, the old ways tugged at her heart . . . sweet memories.

Rachel swallowed, tracing the outline of the stylized flower that added rich color to the old rug. Had Beth been like her? Had Beth longed for a larger world with more freedom to spread her wings? And, if so, who had put an end to her dreams so violently? "I think I should go back and try again . . . with Lucy," Rachel said. "Alone."

Mary Aaron tossed a round red tomato at her. Rachel

caught it and popped it in her mouth. "You can't just leave it to the police?" her cousin asked.

"Lucy wouldn't talk to Evan. I suspect she's not going to talk to any other authorities."

Mary Aaron regarded her solemnly. "You want I should come with you?"

Rachel considered the offer. Maybe Mary Aaron's presence, in the clothing Lucy once had worn, the clothing Beth was wearing when she died, might encourage her to say whatever it was she had been holding back. "Would you?"

"I could probably get away tomorrow afternoon. We're doing Monday washing in the morning, and then I promised to help *Mam* can tomatoes. If I pick the ripe ones before breakfast, Elsie and Magdalena can take my place canning in the afternoon. They'll do it if you'll help me run the dresses they cut out on Saturday. You know how Elsie hates to put in a hem, and Magdalena keeps running the needle into her fingers and getting blood on the material."

"I can do better than that," Rachel promised. "If you'll come and help me interview Lucy, I'll finish the dresses myself. It won't take any time on my sewing machine."

Mary Aaron looked wistful. "It does make a nice even seam." Neither of them mentioned that the Singer in question was powered by electricity, or that Mary Aaron's father had forbidden her to touch it. Why the bishop had declared Rachel's sewing machine to be prohibited and the vacuum cleaner not, neither Rachel nor Mary Aaron had been able to figure out. But since the ban didn't extend to clothing that Rachel sewed on her electric machine, the logic wasn't worth contesting.

"Meet me at one o'clock at the end of your lane?" Rachel asked. She drew her knees up and hugged them tightly. Her mind was already racing, going over what she could say to Lucy to convince her that they needed her help.

"Better make it one thirty," Mary Aaron replied. "That

will give me time to clean up the dinner dishes." She smiled. "I think I like this detectiving. It's a little scary but fun. You said Lucy lives in State College?"

Rachel nodded.

"And I know a place in State College that has real tasty Italian ice."

"Near the Grand?" The Grand was a restored movie theater that showed mostly G-rated films, a spot Rachel had heard was favored by the Amish youth daring enough to sneak away for a motion picture.

Mary Aaron nodded. "*Ya,* Giavanni's."

"And how would you know about *Giavanni's?*" Rachel teased. "Is that where Timothy takes you on Saturday nights?"

Mary Aaron giggled. "Do I look like a girl who would go to a picture show with a boy? And if I did, would I be wooden-headed enough to admit it?"

The following afternoon, the two sat in Hulda Schenfeld's van across the street from the Thornford residence. Rachel had borrowed the van again because her red Jeep was too conspicuous. She didn't want any of the neighbors to notice the vehicle and remember it as the same one that had been there a few nights earlier. She tried to tell herself that she wasn't adopting the methods of a TV detective, but there was no sense in being too obvious and alienating Lucy by causing trouble for her.

"How does this work?" Mary Aaron asked. "Do we go up and knock on the door?"

It was exactly what Rachel had been wondering, but she didn't want Mary Aaron to know that she didn't really have a plan, other than getting here and having Lucy give them information she hadn't wanted to share earlier. Information she wasn't certain even existed. "I don't know. We'll just wait here a bit and watch the house," she said. She'd recently started reading amateur sleuth novels and found that she couldn't get enough of them. She just wished she had more time to read. "See if an opportunity presents itself."

Mary Aaron nodded sagely. The street was quiet. A mail-woman strode past, carrying letters and packages to each door. The only sound through the open van windows was birdsong. The mail carrier rang the bell at the professor's house, and when the door opened, Mary Aaron whispered, "There she is." She had known Lucy, though not well, back in Stone Mill.

Lucy accepted the package, chatted with the postal worker for a moment, then closed the door again.

"Okay, so we know she's home," Mary Aaron said.

"She goes by Lucy Baker here," Rachel explained. "I think she's afraid that her family will find out where she's at."

"And try and make her come home." Mary Aaron tugged on one of her *kapp* strings. "They do that. If me or one of my sisters ever left, *Dat* would track us down all the way to Canada. You can be sure of it."

Rachel rested her hands on the steering wheel, thinking back to when she had left Stone Mill. She wondered if her father had searched for her. It was something she had worried about, back then. She considered asking Mary Aaron but decided against it. Some rocks were better left unturned.

The mailwoman moved from house to house, going down the block. Rachel was just about to suggest that they go to the door when Lucy came around the house, pushing a stroller. "She must be taking the baby for a walk."

They watched as Lucy continued on to the sidewalk and turned right. "I saw a park down the street," Rachel said. "That's probably where she's going."

"So we follow her, *ya?*"

Rachel nodded. Having Lucy take the baby out was better than trying to get her to open the door to them because if she was reluctant, there would be nothing they could do. With

Lucy out in the open, however, it would be harder for her to get away from them. "Let's give her a minute."

Mary Aaron nodded, watching Lucy. "What did Evan say when you told him we were coming back today?"

Rachel turned the ignition and pulled away from the curb. "I thought it would be best to wait until we'd talked to Lucy. No sense in involving him if we don't find out anything."

Her cousin rolled her eyes and chuckled. "That's what I thought. As *Mam* says about *Dat,* what a man doesn't know won't hurt him."

They approached Lucy in a small fenced-in area of the park reserved for children three and under. It was perfect, since she and Mary Aaron were between Lucy and the gate. What she hadn't expected was for Lucy to take one look at them and burst into tears.

"*Ne, ne,* don't cry," Mary Aaron said, rushing forward and putting her arms around Lucy. "It's so good to see you, Lucy. To see you doing so well."

Lucy only sobbed louder and clung to Mary Aaron. She was saying something in Deitsch, but she was crying so hard that Rachel couldn't understand a word. The baby, still in the stroller, startled by the newcomers and Lucy's outburst, began to wail as well.

Rachel had to pick up the child, who was somewhere around eighteen months old, to comfort her.

"You must think me a woodenhead," Lucy said after all the tears had been dried and the three were sitting on a bench under the trees while Evelyn dug in a sandbox with a red shovel Lucy had brought with her. "I was startled, that's all. To see you, Mary Aaron. As crazy as it sounds, I miss everyone at home."

"We understand," Rachel soothed. "And we don't think you're foolish. It's hard, what you've done, to come away alone and start over in the English world."

A tear glistened in the inner corner of Lucy's eye. "*Ya,* hard," she agreed. "But you did it."

"Not completely alone," Rachel confided. "A Mennonite widow who used to buy eggs from us helped me for the first few weeks. She was my first connection to the English world." She hesitated. "Someone did help you, didn't they, Lucy?"

"I didn't want to say anything to the policeman," she explained, looking down at her hands, folded in her lap. "I wouldn't want to get anybody in trouble. And . . . I was a little scared."

Mary Aaron took Lucy's hand. "You don't have to be scared. Not of us. We only came to you because you're the only one who might be able to help us. But we would never tell anyone that you're here. I give my word."

Lucy looked from Mary Aaron to Rachel. "I don't understand how I can be any help. I don't know anything about Beth. I didn't even know her."

"Just tell us how you came to leave Stone Mill." Rachel met her teary gaze. "And the truth, this time."

Lucy watched her charge for a moment. "It was Enosh. He sent me a bus ticket, and he told me the address of people who would let me stay with them until we got work. We lived there, me and Enosh, for a few months. Not—" She blushed. "Not *together,* but in the same house."

"In Harrisburg?" Rachel asked. "Did you stay with the man Enosh works for?"

Lucy shook her head. "No, we were in Huntingdon. Enosh got the job later." She pursed her lips. "Mary and Emmett DeStephano. On Oak Street, near the Baptist church. They were good people. Really nice. Emmett was in a wheelchair, and the house was big. Mary needed help, and we were glad to do what we could." She straightened her shoulders, removed a tissue from her dress pocket, and blew her nose. "But I didn't leave home to clean somebody else's house and have them take care of me. I wanted a job. Mary's granddaughter went to school at Penn State, and she knew that

Professor Thornford needed a nanny. Mary arranged for them to meet me, and they hired me." Lucy looked up at Rachel. "I didn't want Enosh to get in any trouble, you know? That was the only reason I didn't tell when you and the policeman came."

"Don't worry," Rachel assured her. "We won't tell."

"You and Enosh, you like each other?" Mary Aaron asked.

"*Ya,* but not as boyfriend and girlfriend. Enosh is my friend, like a big brother." She got up to brush sand out of Evelyn's hands. "No, Baby, don't put it in your mouth. Dirty." She returned to the bench.

"Do you think the DeStephanos might have taken Beth or Hannah in, after you left? There was also a girl named Lorraine Yoder."

Lucy shook her head. "Emmett passed right after I left. Mary went into one of those retirement places near her daughter."

Rachel tried not to become frustrated. "And the family Enosh is staying with now, they didn't help Beth?"

"No. I'm sure of it. And none of the other families we know of helped her," Lucy insisted. She seemed more comfortable, now. "I'm sure of it. It's a small community—people who help Amish kids leave their life. I'd have heard of any other girls from Stone Mill."

Rachel looked at her, trying to assess if she was telling the truth.

"If I knew anything that would help, I'd tell you," Lucy said. "It's terrible that somebody did that to Beth, but maybe she met a bad person and it just happened. It would be scary if you didn't have a safe place to sleep or to work."

"And the other girls, Hannah and Lorraine?"

Lucy shook her head. "Just me and Enosh, we're the only ones from Stone Mill I know."

"Your mother must be bad worried about you," Mary Aaron said. "Especially since Beth's murder."

Lucy lowered her lashes. "She doesn't know where I am, but she knows I'm all right. I send her a letter every two weeks. Sometimes, I send a money order for the children. Maybe one of them needs new shoes or medicine. I help when I can." She hesitated. "I think one of my sisters wants to come out when she gets to be eighteen. Then I'll find her a job, and we can get an apartment together. But not yet."

"Your mother knows you are in State College?" Rachel asked.

"*Ne.* She didn't want to know where I was. That way, if *Dat* or the preacher asks, she can say she doesn't know. She has a post office box. I send the letters there. And I have a post office box, too, but in a different town." She offered a wan smile. "I'd rather not say where. She writes me back, sometimes."

"So it's a secret from your father?" Mary Aaron asked. She squeezed Lucy's hand. "Is he strict?"

"I know he worries about my soul," Lucy admitted. "Someday, I'll go home so they can see how well I am, but probably not for a long time. I'm going to get my high school diploma. Then I can go to college and get a certification in child care. I want to teach nursery school. I think maybe I can do that."

Rachel smiled back at her. "I think you can, too. I think you can do anything you want to do. Do you like working for Evelyn's family?"

"I do. They're good to me. They bought me a car and helped me study for my driver's license. I wouldn't want to leave Evelyn yet. She needs me. But when she's old enough to go to preschool, I have to get a better education. I miss home, but I'm never going back. Not to stay. It's good for a lot of people, but it isn't the life for me."

Rachel glanced at Mary Aaron. It was time to go. She was disappointed that Lucy hadn't been able to give them any information on where Beth had been in the time between when she had left Stone Mill and been murdered there, but she was glad to hear how well Lucy was making the adjustment from Amish girl to English. She was glad for Lucy; glad, too, that

Lucy was using an assumed name. If someone was stalking Amish girls, she would be safe. Who would know?

After they said their good-byes and promised to keep in touch, Rachel and Mary Aaron started to walk away.

"Wait," Lucy called after them.

They turned back.

"There's something," she said hesitantly. "It might be nothing, but . . ."

"But what?" Rachel asked.

"I heard a rumor once." Lucy met Rachel's gaze. "It was at a singing. A boy from another district—I don't know his name. We were talking about leaving, you know, just about what if we did, and . . . he said that he'd heard that somebody in Stone Mill would help kids."

"Did he say who?" Rachel walked back to Lucy.

Lucy shrugged. "If he did, I didn't hear. At the time, I hadn't cared because I hadn't thought about leaving. I don't know if there was any truth to it."

"So you don't know if it was a man or a woman?"

She shook her heard. "An Englisher, I guess, but he didn't give a name."

Rachel glanced at Mary Aaron, then back at Lucy. "If anything else comes to you, or you hear something, promise you'll call me."

"I promise." She patted the pocket of her dress. "I have the card you gave me with the B&B phone number."

Rachel hesitated. "Lucy . . . if we hadn't come back today, would you have ever called me?"

But Lucy only smiled and walked over to scoop Evelyn out of the sandbox. "Come back to visit," she said. "You, too, Mary Aaron. I have Wednesday and Sunday off. You can tell me all the news from Stone Mill."

It was Saturday evening before Rachel saw Evan again. He picked her up at the B&B at seven thirty sharp.

"Anything new on the case?" she asked him as he held the car door for her.

"Nothing. And I'm starting the three-to-eleven shift on Tuesday. Back on the road." He closed her door, went around the car, and climbed in behind the wheel. "I have a feeling my investigation days are over."

She sat back in her seat and gazed out the window as they pulled out of her drive and onto Main Street. She'd called Evan Monday evening to tell him about the rumor that someone in Stone Mill was helping Amish young people to leave the valley and enter mainstream culture, but he hadn't been impressed. He'd said he would pass on the information but that some Amish kid trying to impress a girl at a teenage gathering didn't hold much credibility.

They were on their way to Huntingdon to Evan's favorite restaurant, an authentic but modestly priced Italian place. It had been a busy week, and Rachel would have been satisfied to go to his house for their usual spaghetti and meatballs, but Evan had his heart set on taking her out for a *real date*. So she'd worn an azure-blue dress with a modest V-neck and lacy cap sleeves. She was glad she had because he'd shown up at her house in a dress shirt and tie.

"The truth is, we don't have much evidence in the Glick case," he told her. "A few partial boot prints that might not even have been from the day Beth was murdered. Men's work boot, size 10. Could be anyone's. The case is pretty much cold. You don't get anything in the first forty-eight hours"—he shook his head—"the chance of ever solving the case goes down significantly."

"And now it's been almost three weeks," she mused.

He turned to look at her and smiled. "Let's talk about something else. Want to listen to the radio?"

"Sure."

So they drove through the warm twilight with the air-conditioning on high and the radio playing pop songs from the '90s.

A few miles from Stone Mill, he turned off the steep road that climbed out of the valley and drove a short distance down a gravel lane that led to a picnic area beside a waterfall. Dusk had already fallen as he parked the SUV.

"What's up?" she asked.

"Thought maybe you'd like to see the waterfall at night. Reservations aren't until eight thirty."

He got out of the car and came around to her door. He took her hand, and they walked across the open area to a table and benches. Rachel was a little apprehensive; she'd heard that teenagers sometimes came here to make out. Surely Evan didn't have any ideas in his head. He knew her better than that, didn't he?

But Evan was a perfect gentleman. He spread his sports jacket on the wooden bench for her to sit on and sat beside her. It was peaceful, with the rush of water and the cool mist in the air. Around them, small animals rustled in the forest and frogs chirped and croaked. "Thank you for bringing me," she murmured. "It's so beautiful here."

He cleared his throat and took her hand. "Rachel, how long have we been friends?"

She felt a warm rush of emotion. "Three years, I suppose. Since I came home to Stone Mill."

"And neither of us is getting any younger."

"What?" She looked at him.

He exhaled, and she realized he was nervous. Now she was curious. What on earth was going on?

"I . . . need to tell you something, and you need to listen and not interrupt. If you interrupt, I'll lose my nerve and look even stupider."

She looked at him, now a little wary. "Evan—"

"Rachel, I'm just going to say it," he cut in, taking her hand. "I'm just going to . . . come out and say it." He took a breath. "Will you let me court you?"

"What?" She turned on the bench so that she was facing

him more directly. She didn't know what she'd expected him to say, but that wasn't it.

"I love you, Rachel. I think you know that. I haven't pushed you because I know how you are. But I know you care for me. And I've been thinking that we should do this the Amish way. So you're comfortable. I want you to walk out with me." He was gaining momentum. "And if we find that . . . we're . . . happy together, I want us to move forward. With marriage," he added quickly.

Among the Plain people, young people courted for months, sometimes years. While they did, they went out exclusively with each other. It was a trial engagement, and either the man or the woman could break off the relationship at any time without losing face.

"Evan, that's very sweet, but . . ." She looked away. She'd thought they were just going for a nice dinner. She hadn't expected any sort of serious conversation. She wasn't really prepared for it.

"This can't come as a surprise to you. Did you think we could go on for years just being friends?" He was very close, not threatening, just Evan, big and solid and comfortable. "I know you want children, a family of your own. And I don't see you—"

"Evan, please." She put two fingers of her free hand over his lips. "I do care for you, but things are so crazy now." She looked away, and then made herself look at him again. "I don't think I can do this right now."

"What do you mean?"

She exhaled, trying to find the right words. She didn't want to hurt Evan's feelings. She didn't even know that she wanted to turn down his offer . . . She just . . . She closed her eyes, then opened them again. "I mean that, right now . . . today, I can't think about this. I can't get Beth and what happened to her out of my mind. I think about her day and night. I can't think about my personal life right now, and I need to be absolutely sure because . . . for me, marriage is forever." She looked down and then up at him again. "I guess what I'm saying is that I need more time."

He pulled his hand away from hers. "And people say it's always the guy who's afraid of commitment."

Chapter 10

The next night, it was eleven thirty when Rachel climbed the stairs to her third-floor bedroom. Most of her weekend guests had checked out, but two couples remained. The Barbours, Les and Bonnie, had just returned to the United States from Australia. He was an engineer who specialized in designing dams, and he and his wife had spent many years living abroad. They were friendly and interesting, so much so that she'd invited them to share a late supper with her. She and the second couple, Jenny and Charles Abernathy from Vermont, had spent an evening in lively conversation with the Barbours, sharing their experiences in Europe, South Africa, and Queensland.

The Abernathys were return guests, so Rachel felt like they were old friends. This was their third visit to Stone Mill, and Rachel enjoyed their company more each time they came. Having visitors like the Barbours and the Abernathys was a delight, but she'd found most of her guests to be pleasant. Days like this were why she'd decided to open the B&B.

Sophie shot up the stairs ahead of her. Bishop followed, tail swishing back and forth.

Evan had accompanied her to church services that morning, but his manner had been reserved, and after worship he'd said something about visiting his mother and made a quick good-bye. Rachel thought it just as well. She didn't want to rehash the previous evening's discussion about the two of them courting. She'd been honest with him; she *wasn't* sure how she felt about him. Certainly she cared deeply about him; maybe she even loved him. But agreeing to spend the rest of her life as his wife was a big commitment. She couldn't make such a life-changing decision right now. Maybe after Beth's killer was found . . . after Lorraine and Hannah were found, maybe then she would feel differently.

Upstairs, Rachel undressed, grabbed a fresh terry cloth robe, and stepped into the hot spray of her shower. The water was amazing. Her bathroom, with its heated tile floor and rain showerhead, was her one luxury in her private living quarters. And the girl who'd grown up using an outhouse reveled in it. Whatever challenges tomorrow would bring, she'd be better prepared after a relaxing shower, organic melon shampoo, and a good night's sleep. She had just stepped out onto the rug and was wrapping her hair in a thick towel when the phone on her desk rang. It wasn't her cell, which might have been Evan, but the landline. The B&B number.

"Who in the world would be calling me at this hour?" she grumbled to Bishop. Clutching a thick terry cloth towel around herself, she made a dash for the phone.

"Hello?" The line hummed, but no one spoke. *A wrong number?* "Hello?" she repeated. "Stone Mill House." Still nothing. She considered hanging up; it was probably a wrong number, or maybe a prank call. "Stone Mill B&B," she repeated. This time she couldn't keep the faint annoyance out of her tone. "Is someone there?"

Rachel heard a girl's voice, a low whisper. "Rachel? Rachel Mast?"

Rachel couldn't make out what she said next, but whatever it was, the woman was speaking Deitsch. "Who is this?"

". . . Hannah. Hannah Verkler."

Rachel clutched the receiver tighter, feeling almost as if she were speaking to a ghost. "Hannah? Oh my goodness. I . . .

it's so good to hear from you. Mary Aaron's been so worried about you."

"I need help."

The hair prickled on the nape of Rachel's neck. "Okay. Tell me—"

"I don't know what to do," she went on, almost as if she was talking to herself. "There's nobody else to ask."

"Hannah, are you in danger? If you are, call 9-1-1. The police will—"

"No!" she said. "No police, no police," she repeated. "Promise me you won't involve the police."

"Okay," Rachel said.

"I need you . . . someone to come and get me. Please?" Hannah's voice broke on the last word.

There was a burst of loud music and then a staccato rapping that could have been a fist against a closed door.

"I have to go," Hannah said quickly. She sounded terrified. "He's coming."

"*Who's* coming?"

"I have to hang up. I'll try to call back," she said shrilly.

"You have to tell me where you are. I can't just—"

The banging started again.

"I'm serious about the police," Hannah whispered into the phone. "If you call them, you'll never hear from me again. No one will."

"Don't hang up," Rachel said quickly. "I'll come. You have to tell me where you are."

"New Orleans. Above the—"

Rachel heard a loud bang, then a gruff male voice, and abruptly the line went dead. "Hannah? Hannah?" she called into the phone.

Seconds passed, and then she heard the familiar computer-generated recording: "If you'd like to make a call, please hang up and try again." It was followed by a loud, pulsing tone.

Rachel hung up and went into the bathroom to retrieve

her robe. Pulling it over her still-damp body, she went back into the bedroom. She stared at the phone, willing it to ring again. It didn't. She picked it up and clicked the receiver to see if she still had a dial tone. She hung it up again.

She didn't know what to do. Had the call been real? Was that Mary Aaron's friend Hannah, or was it someone's idea of a bad joke?

The call couldn't have been a joke. The woman on the other end had seemed so desperate. No one was that good an actor, were they?

"Call me back," Rachel murmured. "Hannah, call me back."

But what if she didn't?

Rachel started to pace. Her pets—Bishop on the bed, Sophie on a throw rug—watched her.

Hannah had said she was in *New Orleans*. What would Hannah Verkler be doing in Louisiana?

For a few seconds, Rachel closed her eyes and uttered a silent prayer for Hannah's safety: *You've kept her safe this long. Could you do it a little longer?*

When she opened her eyes, she knew she had to go to New Orleans.

Of course she couldn't go to New Orleans.

Common sense warred with impulsiveness. She had guests. She had a business to run. She just couldn't take off on a wild-goose chase, could she? She'd never been to New Orleans, but she knew it was a large city. She'd never find Hannah. The phrase *finding a needle in a haystack* came to mind.

Rachel unwrapped her hair from her towel and went to the bathroom for a wide-toothed comb.

It was the middle of the night. Tomorrow would be soon enough to sort this out . . . to decide what was best to do.

But waiting until morning was easier to say than to do. In front of the bathroom mirror, she blow-dried her hair.

Evan should be off work by now. It would be easy to reach

him, but she'd given her word to Hannah. No police. Evan was her friend and she trusted him, but he was also a cop. If she went to him for advice, would he feel compelled to report the call to Sergeant Haley as a possible lead in the Glick case? Hannah had said that no one would ever hear from her again if Rachel contacted the police. Did she mean *she* wouldn't contact anyone again, or had she meant something more sinister? If the police became involved, would Hannah's life be in danger?

If she didn't go to Evan, there was only one person she could confide in. Mary Aaron. But lights-out was at ten o'clock at Uncle Aaron's. Mary Aaron had no cell phone, and short of going to her house in the middle of the night and throwing stones at her bedroom window, there'd be no reaching her until morning.

Another half hour of waiting for the phone to ring put Rachel past the point of caution. She reached for her cell and punched in the single digit for Evan. "Hey," she said when he picked up. She could hear voices, the wail of a country western singer, and the rattle of glasses in the background. "You at a bar?"

He chuckled. "When have you ever known me to go into a bar except to break up a fight? I stopped at the diner for a bite with Pete after our shift."

Pete was one of the veteran corporals at the troop, an older guy who'd taken Evan under his wing since he'd been assigned there. "How was your shift?"

"Five hours of nothing and then a pileup about a mile from the troop. Failure to yield the right-of-way. Three cars, one of them a trooper's personal vehicle, but she's fine, and it could have been a lot worse." He said something she couldn't hear, probably to Pete, then back into the phone, "What's up? I know you didn't call me at this hour to chat."

"Will you be leaving soon?" she asked. "I wondered if you could stop by for a few minutes. I'll put the teakettle on. Unless you'd rather I make coffee."

"You want me to come over, now? Tonight?"

"It's important, Evan. Otherwise, I wouldn't ask you—"

"I'll be there in half an hour."

"I don't know. It sounds suspicious. It could be a hoax," Evan said when she'd finished telling him about the mysterious phone call—after he'd agreed that their conversation was strictly off the record.

They were sitting at the little table in the kitchen. He stirred honey into his mug of Earl Grey, tasted it, and then added more.

"She sounded sincere." Rachel cupped her mug between her palms, waiting for her tea to cool. "I don't know, I think it might have been her." She thought for a minute. "No, the more I think about it, the more I'm *sure* it was Hannah."

"Think about it. If it was really Hannah, if she had access to a phone and could call you, she could have called 9-1-1," Evan reasoned. "Does it make sense that someone in danger would call a stranger halfway across the country?"

What he was saying made sense. Perfect, logical sense. But Englisher sense, not Amish sense. "Would it be possible to trace the call? To find out if it *did* originate in New Orleans?" She looked up at him across the table. She was in her bathrobe over PJs, him still in his uniform. "That would prove it was genuine, wouldn't it?"

His eyes narrowed. "I could get in a lot of trouble for trying to trace a call, Rachel, for nonpolice business."

She gave him what she hoped was her most appealing look. "You know somebody who could do it, though, unofficially, don't you?"

He frowned. "Your caller was probably some Amish teenager, maybe even Lucy."

"I don't think so. Lucy's not a teenager anymore, and she's not the type of person to want to cause harm. Even as a joke."

"You're quick to judge someone you've just met."

She considered his statement before shaking her head. "If I make an error in judgment, I'd rather it be that I'm too trusting rather than being too cynical. Isn't that what you always tell me about upholding the law? Treat everyone as you'd want them to treat you?"

"I do try to do that, but I don't look at the world through rose-colored glasses. In some ways, Rachel, you're still naïve. The Amish I meet are no better and no worse than anyone else."

Bishop jumped up into her lap, and she gave her attention to the big Siamese, petting him and scratching under his chin as a way to keep from answering immediately. Finally, she said, "Lucy didn't call me pretending to be Hannah. We just talked to her. I would have recognized her voice." This would have been the time to confess to Evan that she and Mary Aaron had gone back to talk to Lucy a second time, but she was afraid that confession would lead the conversation away from the problem at hand.

"Okay, so if not Lucy, then someone else who knows we've been asking around about the missing girls." He toyed with his spoon before looking up. "I was trying to give you a little space, but . . . have you given any thought to what we were talking about last night? About us?"

It wasn't something she wanted to revisit tonight, but she nodded. "I have, I've thought about it all day, but I stand by what I said last night. I'm too distracted, Evan. I can't get Beth's death off my mind. Once this is behind us . . ." She trailed off and smiled at him. "Please, Evan. This call may be the first break we've gotten. I need to know if the call came from New Orleans."

"Highly unlikely."

"But if it did?"

"It would prove that your call originated in Louisiana. And what then? Are you going to run down there and start knocking on doors?"

She shrugged. She wasn't sure what she was going to do,

but one thing she *did* know: If Hannah Verkler had reached out to her for help, she couldn't turn her back on her without even trying.

Rachel caught a few winks of sleep between four and six, but then gave up trying and got up for the day. She desperately wanted to talk to Mary Aaron, but she kept hoping that Hannah would ring her back or that Evan would come through with information on exactly where the call had come from. He hadn't said he would look into it. In fact, when he left her house, he had said he wouldn't have the call traced, but she just kept hoping he'd have a change of heart. She understood that it was breaking the rules and that Evan was all about rules, but who would it hurt?

Rather than just sitting around all day, waiting, Rachel threw herself into the list of to-dos around the house. She packed a picnic lunch for the Barbours, called back prospective visitors, and cleaned the gift shop—dusting, scrubbing, and rearranging with a passion. She checked the Abernathys out, and before leaving, Jenny ordered a baby quilt and a handcrafted maple cradle. They were expecting a first and long-awaited grandchild, and it seemed that they loved the cradles Rachel's brother Paul made.

Twice the phone rang and Rachel dropped everything, literally, to run for it, hoping that it would be Evan or Hannah. Neither were the calls she was hoping for, although one was a three-day reservation for two couples traveling together. By one o'clock, Ada had housekeeping well in hand and was baking an apple strudel. Hulda had walked over from next door and volunteered to watch the office for the afternoon. Rachel couldn't wait any longer. She had to talk to Mary Aaron to see what she'd make of the previous night's mysterious phone call.

Since she was going to her aunt and uncle's home in search of Mary Aaron, Rachel took pains to make herself presentable. She changed into the long skirt, modest blouse, and head scarf that she wore when visiting any of the Old Order Amish, left Hulda in charge of the phone, and hurried out to the Jeep.

She was just pulling out of the driveway when her cell rang. She braked and answered it.

"Rachel?"

"Evan?" She sat up straighter in her seat.

"I'm sorry I couldn't help you. What we talked about last night. You know I'd do anything for you, but . . . I just don't want there to be any hard feelings."

"I understand." She sighed, trying not to be disappointed. She knew Evan. She knew he didn't break rules, and she knew she couldn't pick and choose a friend's traits. The fact that he didn't break rules was something she loved about him. Most of the time. "I shouldn't have asked. It's fine."

"You're mad at me."

"No, of course not."

"Well, you sound unhappy. You're not good at hiding your feelings."

She closed her eyes for a second. "I'm not mad. Just . . . preoccupied. I was just pulling out of my driveway. On my way to Uncle Aaron's to see Mary Aaron. Hannah was her friend. I have to tell her about the call."

He gave an exasperated sigh. "Did you hear anything I said last night?"

"Every word. I just want to see what Mary Aaron thinks. Talk about our options."

Evan's voice grew terse. "No options, Rachel. We're . . . *You're* doing nothing."

Her own voice grew terse now. "I don't work for you, Evan."

"Please don't do anything stupid."

"Somebody called me in the middle of the night and asked for help. How can I turn my back on that?"

"Look, I know the call spooked you, but that doesn't

mean you have to do anything crazy. You aren't Pennsylvania's answer to Sherlock Holmes."

"I never thought I was."

"Good. Just let the whole thing drop. We'll find the guy who killed Beth. Your part will be to testify if called to. Nothing more."

"Right."

"Right," he repeated. "I'm about to head in for my shift. Breakfast in the morning? Ten thirty? My place? Bacon and eggs?"

"Sure. Probably. Call me. Be careful out there." It was what she always said to him before a shift.

"Back at you."

Rachel eased to the end of the driveway and waited for two cars to crawl past. As she waited, she glanced over to see Hulda standing on the front steps of the B&B with her grandson Saul. Hulda's arms were folded over her chest, and she looked like nothing so much as a small, angry bluebird, feathers ruffled, eyes fixed on the object of her disapproval. Rachel heard her voice but not what she was saying. Saul's face was red, and he took several steps back. Clearly, Saul was in trouble again, and Rachel had little sympathy for him. Saul was forty, give or take a year, and he'd proved himself again and again to be undependable. How such a shrewd businesswoman as Hulda Schenfeld had produced such shallow sons and grandsons, Rachel couldn't imagine. Fortunately, the girls in her family were made of stronger stuff.

Hulda glanced her way. Rachel offered an embarrassed smile and drove on down the street. She couldn't help but wonder what Saul had done now that had infuriated his grandmother. She supposed that even considering the possibilities made her a nosy neighbor, but she was all too human when it came to being curious about the affairs of her friends and neighbors. She genuinely cared about Hulda and hated to see her taken advantage of by Saul and his cousins. At ninety-something, she didn't need the worry. But Hulda carried on, seemingly indestructible, a blessing for Russell's Hardware and Emporium and those who loved her.

Rachel had gone hardly a mile out of town when she saw two people in Amish garb walking along the edge of the road. One was a child, a small girl, and the other had a familiar tilt to her head. Rachel slowed the Jeep and pulled up alongside. "Mary Aaron! Hi! I was just on my way to your house, looking for you."

"*Goot,*" her cousin replied with a grin. "Now you can give us a ride home." She caught the child by the hand. "This is Joab Rust's granddaughter Aggie."

Rachel tried to place the child. She knew Joab and his family pretty well, but she couldn't remember Aggie. Joab was a skilled mason whom she'd hired to rebuild a crumbling stone wall in the old gristmill on her property. She'd had an idea that it might make a charming vacation rental, but like all her other schemes it was taking longer and costing more than she'd expected. She smiled at the little girl. "I'm pleased to meet you," she said.

"Aggie and her mother are visiting from Lancaster," Mary Aaron explained. "She's Joab's oldest stepdaughter's child. She walked over to Bishop Abner's with me." Mary Aaron helped Aggie up into the backseat. "It's all right," she said to the child. "Your *grossmama* won't mind if you ride with me and Rachel."

"Seat belt," Rachel reminded. There were no seat belts in buggies, and even with Mary Aaron, she had to be vigilant to make certain that she buckled up when she rode with her. Regardless of the laws, most Amish put their trust in the Lord rather than safety apparatuses.

Mary Aaron chuckled. "Seat belt. *Ya.*" She snapped Aggie in and climbed into the front passenger seat. "We can drop her off at Joab's, if you don't mind. *Mam*'s waiting dinner for me. We picked our first limas this morning."

"Mmm," Rachel said. "Lima beans and dumplings?" Her aunt made the best slippery dumplings.

"And fried chicken. She'll be hurt if you don't sit down to table with us."

"Wouldn't miss it," Rachel replied. She wasn't really all that hungry, but she couldn't hurt her aunt's feelings by saying so. If she wanted to discuss the phone call with Mary Aaron, she would have to wait until after the midday meal.

"*Mam* had some itch cream she wanted me to take to Naamah," Mary Aaron explained. "Bishop Abner got into some poison ivy. You know how allergic he is. Anyway, that cream she sends away for really dries up the rash." She sat back in the seat and wiped the sweat off her face. "It's warm out there for walking."

"You couldn't take the buggy?" Rachel asked.

Mary Aaron chuckled again. "You know *Dat*. When it's this hot, he doesn't like us to use the horses if we don't have to. And it wasn't all that far, was it, Aggie?"

"Ne," came the small voice from the backseat. Aggie was an adorable little girl. Dark curly hair, bright blue eyes, and red cheeks. Today, someone had dressed her carefully in a blue dress the exact color of her eyes, a black apron, and a starched white *kapp*. Over her *kapp,* she wore a tiny black bonnet. She looked like one of the angelic paintings of Amish children that adorned every gift shop in Lancaster, down to the dusty bare feet.

Five minutes later, Rachel pulled into the Rust farmyard and delivered Aggie to her adoring grandmother. Joab, barefooted and drinking water from a Mason jar at the hand pump, nodded in their direction. He was a big man, square and stocky, with large hands. He didn't talk much, unlike his brother Eli, but Rachel was pleased with the stonework he was doing for her. "Joab," she said. He grunted in reply.

"Grosspapa," Aggie shouted. "I rode in the red car. Did you see me? We went fast."

"Too fast, I think," Joab replied. And then to Rachel he said, "I should be back at your place next week. As soon as I finish up at the Peacheys'."

"Whatever suits you," Rachel said. In any case, the mill house was a long way from being ready for use. Joab had warned her that it would probably need an entire new roof, which had not been in her budget when she'd started making plans for the restoration. As her father always said, "You can have a job done fast or you can have it done right, but not both." In any case, it was too late to change her mind about the restoration project. She certainly didn't have enough nerve to tell the dour Joab that his services were no longer needed.

Mary Aaron waved at Aggie and her grandmother. Rachel turned the Jeep around, being careful not to run over any of the geese or the cats in the yard, and pulled out of the Rusts' driveway. A few hundred yards from the mailbox, she turned onto the old dirt logging lane that ran across the fields to her aunt and uncle's place. The distance from one house to the other was barely half a mile, and Rachel had time only to give Mary Aaron the briefest rundown of the previous night's phone call.

"Hannah *called* you?" Mary Aaron stared straight ahead, in obvious shock. "It was her for sure?"

"I don't know for sure. Evan thinks it was a prank."

"Who would make such a joke, to ask for your help and tell you not to call the police?" Mary Aaron looked at Rachel. "What would Hannah be doing there? And who is she afraid of? Maybe the man who killed Beth? What are you going to do?" she added quickly.

"I don't know." Rachel pulled the Jeep up to her uncle's barn and put it in park. "That's why I needed to talk to you."

"What's there to talk about? If Hannah is in danger, you have to help her."

"I know."

"So, my Englisher cousin. How do we go about it?"

Chapter 11

"We?" Rachel said. "*We* aren't doing anything. You—" She broke off abruptly as she saw her aunt come out onto the back step. "Don't say anything to your mother about Hannah's call."

Mary Aaron nodded. "*Ya,* it would not go so well with her, I think. Hannah being in such a place as New Orleans. She will think Hannah has truly been lost to us."

Hannah Hostetler's thoughts and opinions were very important to Mary Aaron. While she might strain at the restrictions a young woman in an Amish household was expected to live by, she would never go against the wishes of her parents or the elders of her church. Until she married, she was expected to be guided by them. Bonds of love and tradition surrounded them. For Rachel, the constraints had been too great, and the call to independence impossible to resist, but sometimes she wondered what her life would have been had she stayed, given her vows to the faith, and married a Plain man.

She swallowed against the constriction in her throat. For better or worse, she'd chosen her path, and she must take each day as it came. And today, what was important was deciding what to do about Hannah's plea for help.

Her aunt waved. "Rachel! Come in! We're just sitting down to dinner. Hurry, hurry, girls. The children grow hungry."

Rachel glanced at Mary Aaron, who shrugged. Neither

had to say that it was probably Uncle Aaron who was put out that his midday meal had been delayed. Like most farmers, he rose early, worked hard, and was ready for his dinner once the sun was high. And he wasn't alone. Rachel's own *dat* grew grumpy when his stomach was empty. Both Mary Aaron and Rachel got out of the Jeep and walked quickly to the house.

"Is wonderful to have you here," her aunt said as she held open the kitchen door for them. "Wash up. We're just sitting down to table." Mary Aaron's mother was easygoing and usually smiling, though she was shy around Englishers. She was a perfect foil for Uncle Aaron, who had a short temper and took a more dour view of the world.

"Magdalena, set a place for Rachel. She'll be joining us for dinner," Aunt Hannah said. "Look, Aaron." She beamed. "Our Rachel is here to break bread with us."

Uncle Aaron folded his copy of *The Budget,* a publication that catered to Plain folk around the country, and nodded to her. His grunt and half-smile were as warm a welcome as she was likely to get. Still, Rachel thought, he'd come a long way since his avowed disapproval of her when she first returned to Stone Mill. Uncle Aaron was her mother's brother. No one could deny that the two were faithful members of the Amish church, unselfish parents, and hard workers, but they were true Hostetlers, a family known to be both serious-natured and stubborn. Honest to a fault, none of them could be said to accept change easily, but if a neighbor was in trouble, you could count on a Hostetler to be the first to offer a helping hand. Uncle Aaron was not well liked in the community, but he was respected.

"I expected you to be back sooner from your errand," Uncle Aaron grumbled to Mary Aaron.

Fortunate I came along when I did, Rachel thought, because if Mary Aaron and Aggie had walked the whole way, dinner would have been at least twenty minutes later. Mary Aaron made no comment. Respect for parents and elders had been instilled in them all since early childhood, and Mary Aaron's being in her twenties was no excuse for sassiness to her father. Instead, she washed her hands, exchanged her visiting apron for a faded and patched work apron, and joined her sisters in carrying hot food to the table.

"Call the children," Aunt Hannah waved to John Hannah. He did as he was asked, but it wasn't really necessary. His brother Alan and his twin sister, Elsie, were already in the kitchen. The remaining Hostetler siblings had seen the arrival of the Jeep and—faces scrubbed and hands washed—came pouring in the doors and took their assigned seats at the long kitchen table, with a minimum of fuss. There were twelve in all, ranging from Mary Aaron, who was the eldest, down to bubbly seven-year-old Gracie, a strawberry blonde with innocent blue-green eyes and freckles.

Rachel had found another apron hanging near the stove, tied it around her, and used the hem to protect her hand as she pulled a pan of yeast rolls from the oven. "Another minute and these would have burned, Aunt Hannah," she observed. She slid the rolls into a cloth-lined wicker basket and carried them to the table before taking a seat on the bench beside Mary Aaron.

"Mother?" Uncle Aaron said, looking at Aunt Hannah.

"*Ya,* Aaron, we are ready." She took the chair at the opposite end of the table from her husband, and together everyone bowed their heads for a moment of silent grace.

Long seconds passed without a sound except for the ticking of a large schoolhouse clock until Uncle Aaron signaled an end to the prayer by intoning, "And thank your mother and older sisters for this good food that their hands have prepared."

As one, the younger Hostetlers murmured, "*Danke, Mam,*" before placing their cloth napkins in their laps and beginning to pass around dishes and bowls of all manner of delicious food: fried chicken, chicken and dumplings, the famous lima beans and slippery dumplings, creamed celery, pickled beets, mashed potatoes, and sliced tomatoes fresh from the garden. There was little conversation. Dinner was for feeding the body as the unspoken grace had fed the soul, but the atmosphere was loving and genial. As much as she loved her own parents and brothers and sisters, Rachel sometimes enjoyed eating at her aunt's table more, because Aunt Hannah, at least, had accepted her as she was. Rachel might not be Amish anymore, but her aunt considered her a respected part of the family. And she knew that although he might not show it, her uncle was pleased to have her here as well.

Rachel would have enjoyed the wonderful meal even more had she been hungry, but her mind was still on Hannah's phone call. Was she going to act on Hannah's plea for help? Should she go to New Orleans and search for her? If she did, how would she go about it? She couldn't help thinking that her task would have been a little easier if she had a photograph of Hannah Verkler to show, but naturally, as Hannah had been raised Amish, there were no photographs.

Maybe Evan was right. The idea that she could just go and find Hannah was unrealistic.

"Rachel, you're not eating," her aunt admonished. "Aaron, pass Rachel the lima beans and dumplings. You're too thin, *madel*. You need to eat more so that your cheeks are fat. How else will you get a husband?"

Two of Mary Aaron's sisters exchanged glances and giggled.

"Listen to your aunt," Uncle Aaron said. "Good advice, she gives. What man wants a beanpole of a wife? Better a sturdy helpmate, someone who will work beside him and fill his house with children."

Mary Aaron pinched Rachel's leg under the table, and it was all Rachel could do to keep a straight face. This was familiar territory. Amish couples welcomed as many children to their families as God would send. The notion that she might give birth to nine children, as her mother had, or equal Aunt Hannah's twelve, was daunting to Rachel. She hoped to marry someday and have a baby or two, but she was not the stuff of her mother or her aunt. Out of respect for her uncle, she only nodded, wisely keeping her radical Englisher opinions on family size to herself. Instead of arguing, she busied herself by buttering a yeast roll so light that it was all she could do to keep it from floating out of her hand up to the ceiling, and making a show of devouring it.

Dinner at the Hostetlers' was a leisurely meal, and if conversation was sparse through the main portion, it picked up as the girls cleared away the meat, potatoes, and vegetables, and carried gingerbread, rhubarb-pear pie, bowls of sugared, sliced peaches, and lemon pound cake to the table for dessert. Mary Aaron went to the propane-powered refrigerator for another pitcher of honey-water, which she poured into waiting glasses, and her uncle called upon the children, one by one, to tell what they had accomplished in the morning.

"I put a halter on Dick today," Jesse volunteered.

"Jesse did good with the colt," one of his older brothers said. "Jesse's got a gentle touch with horses. I wouldn't be surprised if he didn't have it in him to make a blacksmith."

Uncle Aaron nodded. "*Ya,* I saw you working that foal. By the time you have him broke to drive, we'll have to look for a two-wheeled cart for you. Soon enough, you'll be leaving school and need a way to get to work."

School for Old Order Amish children ended with eighth grade. Then, the girls stayed home to learn sewing, cooking, and managing a house from their mothers, aunts, and grandmothers, while the boys either apprenticed in their father's trade or went out to work for someone else. As Jesse was the youngest son, he might remain at home to care for his parents in their old age and inherit the farm someday. Or he might choose to be placed with a blacksmith until he reached twenty-one. In any case, he would have to decide his future far sooner than any English youth. For that, Rachel was sorry, because if she knew her uncle, it would be more of Jesse's father's decision than his own.

As eager as she was to get Mary Aaron alone, there was no hurrying dinner. This was family time, and each member of the household looked forward to being together, sharing successes and failures, and being encouraged by parents and siblings. Unlike the English, Amish families ate breakfast, dinner, and supper together. It was a major part of the fabric of Plain life. Rachel knew that she might as well curb her impatience, relax, and try to enjoy the companionship, the friendly teasing, and the genuine affection.

As she had feared, nearly two hours passed before she and Mary Aaron were able to retreat to the stone-walled cellar and talk in private. The farmhouse was built into the side of a hill, and the lower level remained cool, even in August heat. It was a favorite spot to hide out when they wanted to get away. Here, seated on the stone steps, Rachel was able to tell Mary Aaron everything about the phone call and her conversations with Evan.

"Lucy wouldn't do that. It had to be Hannah," Mary Aaron declared. "And she must be in great trouble to call you." She thought for a minute. "I wonder what made her think to call you?"

"I have no idea. She left around the time I bought Stone Mill House, right? Maybe she just remembered that your Englisher cousin was moving to town."

Mary Aaron looked to Rachel. "I guess why she called you doesn't really matter, does it? There's no question what we have to do. Hannah is one of our people. You and I have to go and bring her home."

"You want to go to *Louisiana* with me?" Rachel was a little surprised, but she probably shouldn't have been. "You know we'd have to fly there. Driving would take too long."

"So?" Her cousin shrugged. "I'll fly."

"I don't know," Rachel hedged. "Me going is one thing, but I doubt your family would agree to let you accompany me. It's probably going to be a wild-goose chase. And it might be dangerous. I don't know what we'll discover down there."

"You think I am too backward to deal with them English?"

"Of course not," Rachel replied. "But you've never been on a plane. You have no idea what a city is like."

"Doesn't matter," Mary Aaron folded her arms, and for an instant, Rachel saw the steel of Hostetler stubbornness staring back at her out of her cousin's eyes. "How are you going to find Hannah on your own? You don't know what she looks like. You could pass her on the street and not recognize her." She grimaced. "Unless she is still wearing her *kapp*. An Amish girl wearing a *kapp* in the French Quarter, now that—"

A sound behind Mary Aaron made Rachel turn. Standing at the top of the stairs was her aunt. Frantically, she patted Mary Aaron on her knee, trying to get her to stop talking, but it was already too late.

"*Vas is?*" Aunt Hannah demanded. "You have talked to Hannah Verkler and said nothing to us? And her mother worried half to death that she is floating in a pond somewhere?"

Rachel flushed and looked up. "How much did you hear?"

"Enough to know that the two of you plan to go to hunt for her. Would you tell us that you leave? Or just I should wake up and find my daughter and niece gone, like all the others?"

"*Mam.*" Mary Aaron rose and started up the steps toward her. "We were just talking, just trying to think what we should do. Hannah called Rachel and asked her—"

"I heard." Aunt Hannah's normally jovial voice was stern. "I was not snooping on you. I just came down to bring these jars of peaches." She held up two Mason jars. "And is best I did overhear. We must tell your father. He is the head of the house. It will be for him to decide."

"I think we know what Uncle Aaron will say," Rachel interjected. She could imagine her uncle's outburst. They'd be lucky if he didn't call for her mother and father to try and talk sense into her. At the least, he'd probably order her out of his house and forbid Mary Aaron to see her again.

"*Mam* is right," her cousin said. "We should ask *Dat*. It was wrong of me not to."

And so it was with a sinking heart that minutes later Rachel sat dejectedly in her aunt's parlor as Mary Aaron repeated the story to her father. She told it simply, neither adding nor taking away from all that Rachel had told her.

"So you see, Uncle Aaron—" Rachel began.

"Hist." Her uncle held up a broad hand. "I have questions."

She swallowed, waiting for the explosion, wishing she were anywhere else.

"You believe this to be true, what Mary Aaron says?"

"I do," Rachel answered.

Uncle Aaron glanced at his wife. Aunt Hannah's face was pale, her hands clenched in her lap. "You have prayed on this, Rachel?" he asked.

She nodded. "I have."

"And you think this is what God wants you to do? To go to this New Orleans and find Hannah Verkler? To bring her home?"

"Yes, I do."

He frowned. "But your friend Evan Parks, the policeman, thinks that you should do nothing?"

Rachel sighed. "That's true."

Uncle Aaron's features hardened. "Then it is plain to me that there is only one thing you must do."

Rachel held her breath. Now that the decision was about to be made, she realized that she wanted Mary Aaron to go with her. She didn't want to do this alone.

"You must do what you know to be right," Uncle Aaron said. "You must go to this city and look for her."

For an instant, Rachel was speechless with surprise. "I . . . I'm not even sure it isn't a waste of time. I don't know how we'll find her. New Orleans is a big city. I have no idea—"

"God will lead you," Uncle Aaron interrupted firmly.

Rachel wasn't sure she believed that, but she knew better than to speak her misgivings.

"I agree," Mary Aaron said. "And I have to go with her because Hannah is my friend. Rachel doesn't even know what she looks like."

Uncle Aaron looked at Aunt Hannah. "Do you agree, Mother?"

Tears ran down her aunt's cheeks, and she pulled a handkerchief from her apron pocket. "I will not sleep for worry for you both, to go so far among them Englishers," she pronounced. "But Rachel must not go alone. Better they go together to watch over each other."

Her uncle cleared his throat and got to his feet. "*Ya.* Both must go. You will need money for the ticket of the airplane. Tell me how much is the expense, and I will give you what you need."

"We will call on the bishop," Aunt Hannah said, "so that he can ask everyone to pray for your safe return."

"After they are on the plane," Uncle Aaron added. "If Bishop Abner is unhappy that I let you go, he can be unhappy with me, but he cannot stop you."

"I . . . I have money," Rachel said, still almost tongue-tied by their reaction. Never in her wildest dreams had she imagined that Uncle Aaron would urge her to go off to New Orleans on a wild-goose chase, nor insist that Mary Aaron accompany her. "You don't have to give me—"

"Thank you, *Dat,*" Mary Aaron said, cutting her off. "But I have savings from the sale of my quilts."

"Do you insult me?" he asked gruffly. "That I cannot assist my daughter and my sister's child to accomplish this brave, good thing? I will buy your tickets, and there will be no more discussion about it. And you will go tonight."

"You can use my new suitcase," Aunt Hannah said to Mary Aaron, between audible sobs. "The little . . . little black one that I bought to go to Ohio. It's on . . ." She wiped her tears. "On the attic stairs." Her mouth quivered. "And you must take care that you are not robbed in the airport. I hear about thieves of the pocket. They rob travelers. You must trust no strangers and stay only in decent lodgings. Maybe there is a Mennonite church. They would help you."

"I doubt that they will find Mennonites in such a city," Uncle Aaron said. He looked from his daughter to Rachel. "You must be wise and trust in the Lord to protect you. Stay away from places where strong drink is sold, and take your Bible, daughter, so that you can read from the good book at night."

"Well, what are you sitting here for?" her aunt said, making shooing motions. "Go. Pack your suitcase and go and get Hannah. I will wrap some sandwiches. Lord knows what you will find to eat in the airport."

Still in a state of shock by the turn of events, Rachel followed Mary Aaron up the stairs to retrieve the black suitcase and then to the bedroom Mary Aaron shared with two of her sisters. She watched in silence as Mary Aaron placed the suitcase on the white iron bed, opened it, and began to remove clothing from an old oak dresser.

"You might want to wear some of my things," Rachel suggested. "So that you won't . . . won't stand out on the plane or in New Orleans . . . To keep people from staring at you."

"Your things?" Mary Aaron gave her a puzzled look. "You mean I should wear English clothes like you?"

"It might be easier. Better."

"*Ne.* Best you should go back to the Jeep, get your cell phone, and call the airline for reservations. I will wear my own clothes, cousin. I may be going among the heathen, but I'm not yet one of them." Calmly, Mary Aaron began to pack the small black suitcase. "I will pack clothes for Hannah, and I will wear my good leather shoes," Mary Aaron said, "because I don't know how far we will have to walk to find Hannah." She gave a wry grin. "I will ride on this airplane, and I will ride in a taxi cab, but I will not go in a subway under the ground like a mole." She shook her head. "No way will I do that."

"I think we're safe on that account," Rachel answered with a chuckle. "New Orleans has horse-drawn carriages, taxis, buses, and trolleys, but so far as I know, no subway."

Mary Aaron closed the suitcase and snapped the lock shut. "I'm ready, cousin. What are you waiting for?"

Rachel moved away from Mary Aaron and the waiting passengers to an area by the window as she waited for Evan to pick up. It was late, nearly two in the morning here in the airport, and she'd been trying to reach him since before she'd left home. They'd been lucky to find two open seats to New Orleans on this flight out of Harrisburg.

"Come on, pick up, Evan," she said.

Reluctantly, she'd accepted a stack of cash from Uncle Aaron to pay for the tickets to New Orleans. Sort of. She didn't have the heart to tell him what last-minute tickets would cost or that they had to go on her credit card so she could purchase them over the phone.

She'd been worried that Mary Aaron wouldn't have an acceptable ID to be allowed to board at all, but her cousin had surprised her by producing a two-year-old Pennsylvania driver's license. How or why Mary Aaron had a driver's license was a mystery, and when she'd asked, she'd received only a shrug and a smile for an answer. "It's real," Mary Aaron had assured her.

Mary Aaron was still seated, engrossed in an amateur sleuth novel she'd found under the front seat in the Jeep. An elderly woman stopped and stared, but whether it was because of the book cover or Mary Aaron's Plain garb, Rachel couldn't tell. Because it was Harrisburg and Amish were a fairly common sight in the area, they hadn't attracted as much attention as Rachel had thought they might. She supposed that this woman must be from out of town, but as usual, Mary Aaron paid no attention. She may as well get used to it, Rachel supposed, because her attire would definitely not be run-of-the-mill in the French Quarter.

A clipped voice came through the speakers. "Now boarding at Gate 14, US Airways Flight 132 for New Orleans."

Mary Aaron caught Rachel's eye and pointed toward the boarding gate. An attendant began taking boarding passes and allowing passengers to move through the open doorway.

The phone clicked. "Rachel?"

"Evan? I've been trying to get you."

"It didn't occur to you that I might be asleep at this hour?" He sounded grumpy, and she guessed that she'd woken him. Of course she had. He'd gotten off at eleven. "What's up?"

"Uhh, just wanted to check in and let you know that I'm at the airport. I'm going to New Orleans."

His reply was definitely not G-rated.

Rachel lowered her voice. "You don't have to worry about me. Mary Aaron's with me," she continued in a rush.

Mary Aaron stood and picked up both of their carry-ons. For the first time, she was beginning to look anxious as she gestured toward the boarding gate.

"I'm coming," Rachel said. "Just a sec."

"Mary Aaron? Mary Aaron is going with you?" Evan's volume rose. "Did you get another phone call?"

"No, just the one. Listen, I've only got a moment. They're boarding. I just didn't want to leave without telling you I was going. We're not going to do anything crazy. Have you got a pen? So you can write down where we're staying?" She gave him the name of a hotel on Canal, near the French Quarter. She'd found it on the Internet when she'd gone back to her place to get her bag.

"Rachel, this is crazy. No way you can find this woman down there. You're wasting your time, and it could be dangerous."

"Evan, it's not like I haven't traveled before. For work. Remember? I've even been to Florence, Munich, Prague. All by myself. Was pickpocketed in Prague, as a matter of fact."

"You should have stayed home," he argued. "If that *was* Hannah Verkler, she might call again."

She started walking toward the dwindling boarding line. Mary Aaron was ahead of her. "I had all the B&B calls forwarded to Hulda's cell, and I asked her to call me immediately if there was anything else from Hannah. Or anything suspicious. Hulda's going to mind Stone Mill House for me while I'm away."

"Is there anything I can say to keep you from getting on that plane?" he asked.

"No," she said truthfully. "Don't worry, tourists survive Bourbon Street all the time."

"If you run into any trouble, call NOLA PD. Do you want me to give them a heads-up?"

"And tell them what? That your girlfriend is visiting their town and needs protection? No, don't call them. Hannah made it clear she didn't want the police involved, and I promised her."

"Final call for boarding, US Airways Flight 132 to New Orleans," came an announcement.

"Got to go," Rachel said.

"Rae-Rae!" Mary Aaron called from the doorway. "Come on."

"Call me," Evan said.

"Will do," Rachel told him. "And don't worry."

He was still talking when she powered down her phone and hurried to hand over her boarding pass.

Chapter 12

"The coffee shop should be on the next block, across the street," Rachel told Mary Aaron. "The bellhop said it's called PJ's. She said you can't miss it."

Canal Street was crowded, but not as much as she'd expected. The afternoon heat was probably keeping people indoors. By the time they'd picked up the rental car and driven in from the airport early that morning, it was daylight. Hotel parking was dear, but in an unfamiliar city, Rachel was glad that she'd reserved a room for the evening before and took advantage of the valet parking. She and Mary Aaron had showered and fallen into bed for a few hours of much-needed sleep, and now were hungry for breakfast, despite the hour.

"I don't know why people go on about the heat here. It's no hotter than home," Mary Aaron said, striding along the main thoroughfare with a self-assured gait in her sturdy black leather high-tops. She seemed unperturbed by the gawking passersby, the polyglot assortment of tourists, the tattooed and spike-haired natives in scant attire, or the multitude of in-your-face massage parlors that lined the street. The only things that did seem to draw Mary Aaron's wide-eyed attention were the red-and-yellow streetcars that rattled past.

"But you have to admit, it's more humid here." Rachel wiped her damp forehead.

She'd donned modest walking shorts, a short-sleeved flowered T-shirt, and a favorite pair of slip-on Toms while her cousin was in full Amish dress, including apron and *kapp*. Yet despite the ninety-degree heat, the high humidity, and the dust and noise of the traffic, Mary Aaron's white prayer cap was crisp and spotless. She had not a hair out of place, and her fair and rosy-cheeked German complexion revealed not a drop of perspiration. Over one shoulder she carried a black nylon purse shaped like a horse's feed sack and every bit as voluminous. In it, Rachel had seen her tuck all manner of articles, including the mystery novel she'd been reading in the airport.

"You can leave it here in the hotel room," Rachel had advised. "The maid won't move it." But Mary Aaron had paid no attention, as if fearful that a cat burglar would break in and snatch up *Chocolate Chip Demise* before she could finish it and learn who'd killed the bakery chef.

"I've read it," Rachel had said. "If it does get lost, I can always tell you how it ends."

"Don't you dare," Mary Aaron had hissed in Deitsch. "You'll ruin the story for me. The most fun is trying to guess who to trust and who is the villain." So the book had accompanied them on their quest for breakfast, although Rachel couldn't imagine when Mary Aaron would find time for reading.

They halted at a side street, and Rachel pushed the WALK button. Again, Mary Aaron watched but made no comment. When the pedestrian light flashed, the two dodged potholes and delivery trucks, reaching the safety of the far sidewalk just before a tour bus wheeled past, expelling a haze of diesel fumes. Dozens of pairs of Asian eyes peered curiously from the windows. Mary Aaron smiled and waved, and one teenage Japanese girl waved back excitedly. "Tourists," Mary Aaron observed. "They must feel a long way from home."

And you don't? Rachel thought as she glanced at her cousin with admiration. So far as she knew, Mary Aaron had never in her life ventured to a city larger than Lancaster. She had an eighth-grade education, and she'd never been to a train station or taken a commercial flight before yesterday. If anyone had the right to feel out of her depth, Mary Aaron did. Yet, as always, she seemed completely at ease. Rachel didn't doubt that—armed with a street map, her ready cash, and her common sense—Mary Aaron was equal to any challenge New Orleans could offer.

"There!" Mary Aaron grinned and pointed. "PJ's." Triumphantly, she pushed open a heavy glass door, and the two were hit with a welcome blast of air-conditioning. She threaded her way through a throng of customers, leading the way to an area crowded with small round tables and chairs. Nearly every table was occupied, including two that teetered on a raised platform that must have once served as a clothing store's display case. A couple with a baby was just getting up, and Mary Aaron maneuvered around a table of senior citizens to secure the two chairs. "A latte for me and whatever else looks good," she said, motioning toward the line at the register. "I'm starving."

Rachel nodded. It was her turn to pay because Mary Aaron had bought them each a sandwich and iced tea at the airport. When Rachel got to the counter, she snagged two yogurt parfaits and an assortment of Danish pastries to go with the coffee. The young man at the register stared past Rachel at Mary Aaron. "First time here?" he asked. "Been to the Quarter yet?"

"Yes and no," Rachel replied. She didn't usually answer questions from strangers, but he seemed harmless and friendly enough.

"Are you Quakers?" he asked as he took Rachel's twenty.

"Amish."

"Enjoy your visit," he said, handing her the change, two paper cups, and a bag with the pastries, yogurts, and plastic spoons. "You should take a carriage ride from Jackson Square. But wait until later in the day, when it's cooler. Better yet, take the night tour of the cemetery. Spooky!"

She smiled politely, not wanting to explain that they hadn't come to New Orleans on vacation, or that a carriage ride, while pleasant, really wasn't anything special to either of them.

A second employee, a ponytailed young woman wearing a tee that read *PJ'S CANAL ST* across the front, came out of the back carrying a fresh tray of baked goods. She caught sight of Mary Aaron and did a double take. "Look!" she said in a stage whisper to the boy. "Isn't she that girl from *Breaking Amish*? You know, the show on TV?"

Rachel pretended she hadn't heard her as she dropped the change into the tips can. She then carried the coffee and bag to the table where Mary Aaron was waiting.

"What did he say to you?" Mary Aaron asked.

Rachel shrugged. "He wanted to know—"

"Behind you. She's coming over." Mary Aaron reached to take a cup of coffee and gestured.

The employee with the ponytail approached the table. She was wearing denim Daisy Dukes shorts. "Are you that TV star? What's her name? I'm a big fan. *Breaking Amish*?" She whipped a phone out of her pocket. "Do you mind?"

Mary Aaron didn't miss a beat. She smiled at the girl, raised her apron over her face, and replied with a flood of Deitsch.

"No photos, please," Rachel said. "It's a religious thing."

"Oh, yeah, sorry." The enthusiastic fan lowered her phone. "You mean, she's the real deal?"

"She's Amish," the boy at the register explained. "Her friend told me."

Ponytail stood there, blue eyes wide and eager. "Right. Sorry. No offense. But . . ." She snatched a brochure advertising a plantation house tour from a display in the window. "Could I have an autograph? It's not for me. It's for my boyfriend. He thinks you're hot."

Rachel glanced around the room at the interested spectators, then spoke quietly to Mary Aaron in Deitsch. "I don't know which would be easier, to sign or not sign, to get rid of her."

"I don't look anything like those girls," Mary Aaron said, still hidden by her apron. "But I'll give you my autograph if you'll promise not to take our picture."

"Sure." The woman glanced around at the other customers. "She needs her privacy. No pics." She waved the brochure. "Could you make it for Gia?"

"I thought it was for your boyfriend," Rachel said, reading the woman's nametag: *Gia.*

Gia giggled.

Mary Aaron lowered her apron, dug a ballpoint with the name of the hotel on it out of her bag, and signed the brochure with a flourish:

For Gia, from your good friend, Mary Hostetler

Two older women at a table near the entrance clapped. Ponytail gushed her thanks, and Rachel hurried Mary Aaron out of the coffee shop, grabbing some napkins as they went out the door.

"Why did we have to leave?" Mary Aaron asked. "It was nice and cool in there."

"Why are you giving autographs? Have you forgotten why we're here?"

"I signed my own name. What was wrong with that?" Mary Aaron took the paper bag. "What did you get?"

"Muffins and scones. We'll have to find a place to sit to eat. A bench, maybe."

Rachel sighed. She'd hoped that she and Mary Aaron would be able to sit, have their breakfast, and brainstorm. Now that she was here, she had no idea how she was going to find Hannah. She kept thinking that Hannah would call again, or something would come to them, but so far, neither had happened. The suspicion that Evan was right and this was a wild-goose chase went through her mind.

Holding her coffee in one hand, she fished her cell phone out of her bag; she'd made sure it was fully charged before they left, but she would have to keep an eye on the battery level. Having her cell phone die here would be a disaster. "I'm going to check in with Hulda to see if Hannah called again." She didn't have much hope of that being true. Hulda had her cell number, and she would have contacted her if she had. But at least it was taking action rather than standing here in the middle of Canal Street without a clue.

"We could go back to the hotel and eat there," Mary Aaron suggested. "They had that garden with the fountain and the flowers. I think I saw some benches."

Hulda picked up. They exchanged pleasantries. Hulda assured her that everything was fine at Stone Mill House, and there'd been only two calls, both prospective guests. It was raining there, and the main traffic light in town was out. She wanted to know if they'd been to Bourbon Street yet.

Hulda was still talking a blue streak when Rachel saw that another call was coming in. "Sorry, got to go. I'll call you back later today," she said and hit the button to switch calls. "Hey," she said to Evan.

"You're all right? I was worried when you didn't call this morning."

"We slept in."

He didn't sound worried. He sounded upset, annoyed, on the verge of angry. "Do you want me to take off and fly down there? Better yet, maybe you two should get on a plane and come home. You have no chance of finding—"

"Evan. Peace." She exhaled and then spoke calmly. "Look, if there's no way we can find Hannah, then we're just going to wander around, see the sights, and come up empty-handed. And if we're really wasting our time down here, then there's no reason to worry. Right?"

"Seriously, I can take vacation days."

"That's sweet of you, but we're fine. Right now we're taking coffee and Danish back to our hotel. If we don't step out in front of a streetcar, I think our chances of getting back to the hotel are pretty good."

He was quiet on the other end of the phone for a moment. "Do you still have the number from the caller you think was Hannah?"

"I do." She'd put it into her notes on her phone. Not that she'd needed it. She'd memorized the number, a weird thing of hers. She remembered numbers. She gave it to him. If he was asking for the number, obviously he was having second thoughts about trying to help her. "That's a New Orleans number—I checked the area code."

"I'll call this guy I know, Larry," he said.

She waited.

"He owes me a favor. But it'll take time, maybe a day or so. Go back to your hotel and stay there. I'll get back to you as soon as I find out anything. It's probably a cell, but he might be able to get a location at the time the call was placed."

"That would be wonderful, Evan," she said excitedly, making eye contact with Mary Aaron. "Just having an idea of where to start. Maybe she was calling from her apartment or something."

"Go back to the hotel. Understand? No running up and down back alleys and playing Sherlock Holmes."

He hung up. He was obviously pretty angry with her.

"He wants us to go back to the hotel and stay there," Rachel told Mary Aaron. "But he's going to try and find out where Hannah's call originated."

Mary Aaron munched her Danish and arched one brow.

Rachel grimaced. "Sitting in the room doesn't sound very productive, does it?"

"I don't think Hannah is staying in our hotel, do you?" Mary Aaron offered the remaining Danish to Rachel.

"You're right," Rachel said. "It would make a lot more

sense if we took advantage of the city. What harm could it do for us to do a little sightseeing?"

By evening, Evan hadn't called back, and they still hadn't returned to the hotel. Instead, they'd spent the afternoon wandering through the French Quarter, peering into quaint shops, admiring the ornate ironwork balconies, the varied architecture, and the narrow cobblestone streets. They'd stopped for coffee and sugary square doughnuts called beignets and stood in line for forty minutes outside a tiny restaurant on a side street to share a supper of crawfish and shrimp po'boys. They strolled down Decatur and Royal, stopped to listen to live jazz played by musicians in porkpie hats and striped vests, and walked up to watch boats passing on the Mississippi. Afterward, they returned to Jackson Square to admire the displays of artwork and the line of carriages and mules waiting to take tourists around the French Quarter.

Sometime after seven, Mary Aaron convinced Rachel that they should take a carriage ride, if only to rest their feet and to get a better knowledge of the history of the old section of New Orleans. When their guide stopped outside the walls of one of the oldest of the city's cemeteries, Mary Aaron refused to budge off her seat. "You go, if you want." She shook her head. "Not me."

"I'll stay here with you," Rachel said.

The four other passengers who had shared their carriage climbed down and followed the driver into the cemetery. Only then did Mary Aaron move from her place. She got out of the vehicle, walked to the front, and offered half of a crumbly beignet to the gray mule. Rachel climbed down, too.

"This is a good animal," Mary Aaron said in Deitsch, holding the doughnut in the flat of her hand and letting the mule eat it. "Strong and smart. *Dat* would like him." The mule finished the last morsels of the treat, and she rubbed his soft nose and stroked the broad face before turning back. "Do you still think Hannah is here in this city?" she asked.

They'd spoken very little about Hannah all day, but Rachel guessed that the missing girl had been on her cousin's mind as much as she'd been on hers. "I think she might be," Rachel answered. "*Ya,* I believe she is. Somewhere."

Mary Aaron patted the mule's neck. The animal was gray, with long ears, a cropped mane, and massive hindquarters. "Most people don't realize the worth of mules," she said. "They can be stubborn, but if you treat them well, they'll work willingly all day."

"If Hannah's here, she must be in real trouble," Rachel said, knowing Mary Aaron all too well, knowing that she was using the mule to find her balance in the midst of all this strange English world. "Or she wouldn't have called me for help."

"The same trouble that Beth found? Is it possible?"

"It might be."

Mary Aaron walked to the curb and scrambled up to the board seat. "They didn't leave the valley together, but both went and no one heard from either of them until we found Beth's body in the quarry." She reached for Rachel's hand. "Lucy ran away, but people knew where she was. *Somebody* always knows, like with Enosh. It's a secret, but not really."

"And nothing from Lorraine. Not a word, unless whoever knows isn't talking."

Mary Aaron squeezed Rachel's fingers. "The English world is a bigger place than I thought. Maybe Hannah found that out, too."

"Are you sorry you came?" Rachel asked her.

"*Ne,* I'm glad. If you'd told me about New Orleans, I'd never have seen it as it is: the smells, the feel of the old streets, the strange way people dress and talk."

"You were right this morning," Rachel said. "Jackson Square is a long way from Stone Mill."

"But if you think back to the first Amish who came to this country, the ones who fled persecution in Switzerland and Deutschland, it makes me proud to think how brave they were. The bishops tell us that pride is a sin, but how can you not admire their courage? If they hadn't crossed the ocean to a new land, our faith would have burned to ashes in the fires of those who hunted us. I think maybe you have some of that courage, Rachel, to leave your mother's house and go out among the English. Maybe Beth and Hannah, Lucy and Lorraine, carry that same bravery in their hearts."

"Coming to New Orleans isn't quite the same as coming to the American wilderness."

"I think maybe it is," Mary Aaron insisted. "I can see that this could be a good home for some people. New ways and old . . . they fit together like the pieces of cloth that go into my quilts." Mary Aaron smiled wistfully. "It's not a Plain city, but it's not English either. It's different, but not as evil as my father believes. I think I'll remember it always."

"But you couldn't live here."

"*Ne,* I couldn't. And I don't think Hannah could either. We have to find her, Rae-Rae."

"We will, if she's here."

"Promise me? We won't leave her?"

The murmur of voices drew their attention. Rachel glanced toward the gate and saw their driver coming out of the cemetery. The two couples hurried close behind him. They were talking excitedly, and one of the women was laughing. The driver opened a cooler in the front of the carriage and passed frosty bottles of water all around. Rachel unscrewed the cap and took a long drink. She was glad that she'd passed on the graveyard tour and stayed with Mary Aaron. She'd been doubting her decision to come here, but Mary Aaron's determination gave her more confidence.

The driver flicked the lines over the mule's back, and the animal began the trek back to Jackson Square. Neither Rachel nor Mary Aaron spoke on the ride to where the tour had originated. There, they thanked their driver, tipped him, and got out of the carriage. There seemed to be more visitors than before, now that it was dark, in the street and park area.

Rachel supposed that they should be heading back to the hotel before it got too late, but by mutual agreement, they found themselves sitting on a wall and watching the tide of locals and tourists thronging the sidewalks and park area. There were so many people all around, all enjoying themselves immensely and all in good humor, that Rachel wondered how Evan could have supposed that she and Mary Aaron would be in any danger.

A crowd gathered around a makeshift stage across from the line of carriages, where an older African-American gentleman began to play a banjo. Mary Aaron seemed captivated by his performance. Old Order Amish forbade their members to play or listen to any type of musical instrument. Even the hymns at worship service and at youth singings were always sung without accompaniment. Yet everywhere they had walked throughout the French Quarter today, they'd encountered musicians, and Mary Aaron hadn't found fault with them. Instead, she'd seemed to take great pleasure from the novel experience. Strictly speaking, since she hadn't been baptized, she was permitted a certain amount of leeway in her behavior, but Rachel knew that her aunt and uncle would disapprove of the worldly music. And she couldn't help feeling somewhat guilty that she was the one who'd exposed Mary Aaron to the outside influences. Certainly, Uncle Aaron hadn't been thinking of street jazz when he'd insisted that his daughter accompany her on this rescue mission.

They sat on a bench near Café Du Monde for more than an hour before Rachel found herself yawning. She checked her phone to make certain that she hadn't missed any calls before suggesting that it was time to call it a night. Her thoughts drifted back to Hannah. If she was here in New Orleans, how had she gotten here and what was she doing? Had the music and ambiance of the Big Easy drawn her? And why did she believe her life was in danger? She didn't want to imagine the calamities that a young innocent woman without an education or knowledge of the twenty-first century might fall prey to. *Hannah, where are you? Are you safe, or are we already too late?*

Rachel and Mary Aaron finally got to their feet. They followed St. Peter to Royal, and then took that in the direction of Canal Street and their hotel, but when they came to Toulouse, the haunting strains of a violin drew them toward it. Halfway down the shadowy street, a ragged figure stood, head bent over his instrument. Mary Aaron stopped in her tracks, eyes wide and mouth open in wonder.

"I don't know if we should . . ." Rachel began but then turned and followed her cousin, who had begun to walk toward the musician. He seemed alone on the street, his only audience a large yellow mongrel lying at his feet.

It was impossible to tell the man's age or race; dreadlocks fell from under a stained ball cap; his dirty feet, bare, showed twisted, horny toenails. The ragged garment that covered his gray body was a pair of faded jeans held up by a length of rope passed over one bony shoulder. As Rachel neared the man, she caught a sour whiff of unwashed body that nearly made her gag. She reached out and grabbed Mary Aaron's hand to pull her back, but her cousin seemed not to notice the smell or the wild look on the violinist's face. "Mary Aaron . . . it may not be safe."

"Shhh," Mary Aaron whispered. "Listen." The music poured forth from the violin, each note blending perfectly into the next.

Rachel knew the piece from a music appreciation class she'd taken in college. Stravinsky. This homeless vagrant was playing a melody from Stravinsky's *Firebird* with a passion and clarity that Rachel had never heard, and in his hands he cradled a satin-finished violin that must have cost more than her Jeep, new. She suspected that the man might be mentally ill, might suddenly behave irrationally, yet she found herself caught up in the same trance as Mary Aaron. The sad-sweet melody flowed over her like warm honey, sending chills down her spine and bringing tears to her eyes. Together, they stood mesmerized as he played, unable to stir until the final note died in the warm, moist night air.

"Danke," Mary Aaron whispered. And before Rachel could speak, Mary Aaron pulled two ten-dollar bills out of her bag and dropped them into the plastic dog bowl on the ground in front of the musician.

"Bless you," the musician said as he gave her a courtly bow. "Igor?" The dog barked once, which seemed to please the man for he gathered up the bowl and violin case and made his exit down a narrow, unlit alley. The dog trotted after him.

"What was that?" Mary Aaron asked.

"Stravinsky."

She nodded as if confirming the composer. "He was nice." She stared into the darkness. "I think that this is the music the angels must play in heaven . . . God's music."

For the first time, Rachel became aware of the lights and noise coming from the cross street ahead of them. It ran the same way as Royal. She wasn't sure, but she thought that it might be Bourbon. "Mary Aaron, I'm not sure that we want to go this way."

"We can't stay here. Come on. I'm sure I know the way to the hotel. If we go left, it should take us to Canal, where our hotel is."

And so, reluctantly, again she followed her Amish cousin through the night into the madness of nighttime NOLA. She'd never been on Bourbon Street, but as crazy as it might be, she wasn't certain if the tourists would be prepared for Mary Aaron Hostetler in her traditional Plain dress and prayer *kapp*.

Chapter 13

Rachel had heard about Bourbon Street, and she'd read about it, even seen glimpses of the crowds at Mardi Gras on the evening news, but nothing had prepared her for the sheer excess. The thoroughfare had been blocked off to vehicles, and groups of laughing, singing people walked, staggered, danced, and wheeled themselves down the street, a few on bicycles, two in wheelchairs, another on a skateboard, followed by a pair of bike-powered rickshaws carrying inebriated college students. Most of the scantily dressed revelers brandished oversized drink containers and were taking photos of themselves and each other with cell phones. To post on social media websites, no doubt.

The noise level was deafening. Groups of street musicians vied with individuals, all playing different styles, ranging from blues to hard rock, competing in turn with the music from bars, clubs, restaurants, and shops selling tacky souvenirs.

Mary Aaron clamped an arm over her handbag, straightened to her full height, and moved to the center of the street, eyes gazing straight ahead, features set. She avoided a woman in a Hawaiian hula skirt and sequined bikini top leading a white duck on a leash, stepped aside to avoid a gentleman in a speeding wheelchair, and dodged a puddle of something nasty on the street. Rachel hurried to catch up with her, trying not to gawk at the pole dancer in a yellow nightie gyrating to a rock beat in a storefront window or at the red-nosed clown in a striped topcoat and top hat who seemed to be sleeping in the midst of the chaos.

No one seemed to notice her or Mary Aaron. Apparently, her cousin's Plain attire was far too mundane to merit photographing, especially when there was a redhead in a T-shirt leaning over a wrought-iron, second-floor balcony railing, promising strings of plastic beads to everyone willing to expose themselves. Mary Aaron's snowy-white prayer *kapp* may have seemed tame compared to the performer in a flesh-colored body suit and gold crown weaving through the tourists while playing a harmonica strapped to his mouth and walking on his hands.

To her credit, Mary Aaron maintained her composure and kept walking. She seemed not to see the drunks, the panhandlers, the gaping tourists in their silly hats, or the two girls dressed as professional wrestlers, attempting to lure customers into a dark doorway wreathed in artificial smoke and flashing the word *Hades*.

"It's not far to Canal," Rachel said, raising her voice to be heard above the shrieks of laughter from a group of young women. "We'll just—" Her cell rang. When she pulled it out and saw Evan's picture, she seized Mary Aaron's hand and tugged her toward the corner of Conti and Bourbon. The cell kept ringing, but Rachel didn't pick up until they'd turned onto Conti and left the frenzy of Bourbon behind them. The phone had gone to voicemail, but she returned the call.

"Were you asleep?" Evan asked when he answered.

"No," she replied. "Not in bed yet." She couldn't make out Mary Aaron's face in the semidarkness, but she imagined that she saw her smirk with amusement.

"Where are you? What's that noise? Are you in your hotel?"

"Not yet."

"Exactly where are you, Rachel?"

"Conti Street. It's quiet, well lit, mostly small hotels. Quite respectable." She motioned to Mary Aaron and moved under the lighted marquee of a small hotel. This street was much quieter, with only a few people.

"It's after dark."

"We're fine. We just walked down to Jackson Square." Not a lie. They had just walked down nine or ten hours earlier. "You're worried for nothing. There are people everywhere. It's perfectly safe."

"So you're out sightseeing? At this time of night?"

"It's New Orleans, Evan. It would be foolish to come here and not see anything. Have you found out where Hannah's call came from?"

"Not yet. My guy said he could do it, but it would take time. I was just checking in with you."

"That's sweet of you," she said. "You really don't have to worry about us. I'm not going anywhere I feel uncomfortable or unsafe." *And I'm not going back to Bourbon Street,* she promised herself. She wouldn't have believed the party atmosphere if she hadn't seen it with her own eyes, but as shocked as she'd been, she really hadn't felt that they were in danger. It wasn't her type of fun, but the crowds had seemed good-natured. "It's really a beautiful city, so much history."

He didn't say anything.

"Okay, well . . . call us as soon as you hear from your friend, no matter what time it is."

"And then what? You're going to start wandering around New Orleans in the middle of the night?"

"Let's not argue, Evan."

"Are we arguing?"

"No, we're not. You're a peach to help me out." She paused. "I know you didn't want me to come, but I had to. I couldn't live with myself if I didn't and something bad happened to Hannah."

"I couldn't live with myself if something bad happened to you or to Mary Aaron."

"It won't. I promise you."

"And if I'm right? If New Orleans is a strikeout?"

"Then we'll get back on a plane and come home, none the worse for wear."

"Okay. Just remember how you got into this. Something bad happened to Beth Glick."

"How could I forget?"

Evan's voice grew husky. "I'll call as soon as I know anything. Take care."

"You, too."

Evan hung up, and she glanced at Mary Aaron. "I wasn't dishonest, was I? About where we were?" She felt guilty, but not guilty enough to tell Evan that they'd been in the midst of Bourbon Street. He'd never let her live it down, and if Mary Aaron's folks found out . . . She swallowed. If her father had any idea that she had been in such an area, it wouldn't be pretty. But they had, and they'd come out with no harm done . . . yet.

"Who am I to judge you?" Mary Aaron shrugged. "We don't always tell everything. Not even *Mam* tells *Dat* everything. Men would like to control us all the time, but we can't allow that. Maybe we shouldn't have gone onto Bourbon Street, but once we did, what good would it have done to tell Evan and frighten him?"

Rachel chuckled as she felt a rush of affection for her cousin. Every time she thought she knew everything about Mary Aaron, the young woman surprised her. "Are you sorry we did?"

"*Ne.*" Mary Aaron sighed. "More foolish than evil, I think. We should pray for them, but Bourbon Street is not a good place for either of us."

"You're right. It isn't." They followed Conti to the next corner and then turned onto Canal. It had been a long day, and Rachel would be glad to climb into bed and get some sleep. They stopped in a small shop for frozen yogurt, ate it there, and then walked on to their hotel. The room was quiet, the beds made, and everything in order.

"Dibs on the shower," Mary Aaron said. Rachel pulled a face. Mary Aaron threw a pillow at her, and they both laughed.

"I'm so glad you came with me," Rachel admitted. "You're good for me. You keep me grounded."

Mary Aaron paused and glanced back. "And you showed me what it was like to fly."

Their mood was suddenly serious. "I don't want to lead you astray," Rachel said. "The path I've chosen . . . it's hard. Most of the time, I don't know where I belong."

Her cousin smiled. "Don't worry about me, Rae-Rae. I know what I want."

"I wish I did."

They had slept maybe an hour when Rachel's cell vibrated. She reached for it, knocked it off the nightstand, and groggily fumbled for it on the floor.

"Rachel?"

Her heart skipped a beat. It was the same voice. "Hannah?" She sat straight up in the bed. "Hannah, is that you?"

Mary Aaron sat up in the other double bed and turned on the light. "It's Hannah?"

"I talked to the woman who answered your phone. Hulda." The young woman slipped into Deitsch. "She said you were here and gave me your cell phone number. I can't believe you came for me."

"Where are you?" Rachel demanded.

"Can you come? Now?"

Rachel blinked, trying to clear the cobwebs of sleep from her head. She thought she could hear music, a clatter that might have been the sound of breaking billiards, and mingled voices in the background. Was this real or a dream? "Tell me where to come for you."

"Where are you?" the girl asked.

Rachel named the hotel.

"On Canal?" Hannah asked. "I know where that is. I'm only eight, maybe ten blocks from you."

"Can you tell me where you are?"

"Doesn't matter. I'm walking out now. Come and get me. You have to come now."

Mary Aaron was up, throwing off her nightgown and pulling on her clothes. "It's her? Tell her I'm with you."

Rachel got out of bed. "Mary Aaron is here." She started gathering her clothes. "Hannah?" She didn't answer, but Rachel could still hear the background noise: a saxophone, a clink of glasses. "Are you there? Don't hang up! Tell me where to meet you. We're coming!"

Hannah's voice was breathy. "Do you have a car? Tell me you have a car."

"Yes, a rental."

"Good. I'm so scared. If they find out that I'm . . ."

"Hannah?" There was only silence. Rachel dropped down onto the bed to pull on her shorts. "Don't be gone," she murmured.

Now there were street sounds, and the cell reception wasn't as good. "I'm outside, now," Hannah said. "Get your car."

A horn blared. Someone shouted, "Watch where you're walking!"

"Hannah?" Rachel said.

"I'm all right. I was crossing the street and . . . It doesn't matter. Call me at this number if you don't see me when you get there."

"Where are you?" Rachel asked, frantically searching for her shoes under the bed.

"I think I can make it to Conti and Bourbon. Hurry!"

The connection broke.

"She wants us to come and get her now." Rachel stared down at her cell. "She said to bring the car."

Mary Aaron tied a blue scarf over her head and put her

Bible back into her bag. Rachel hadn't known she'd brought the scarf with her.

"Are we coming back to the hotel?" Mary Aaron asked.

"I don't know. Take your things in case we aren't." Rachel finished dressing. She threw her pajamas into her suitcase. "She sounded desperate, said she was walking out now."

"Walking out of where?"

Rachel shook her head. "I don't know. I only know we have to get to her before she vanishes again."

The elevator was empty; the single clerk at the front desk glanced curiously at them as they hurried by but didn't question why they were headed out of the hotel at this hour with their suitcases. Rachel didn't stop to give an excuse. They had her credit card number, and she'd already called ahead for valet service to bring her car.

"I don't know if we can take the car on Bourbon," Rachel told Mary Aaron. "Some of the streets were blocked off. I noticed when we were walking. I'll get as close as I can, and then we can—"

"You stay with the rental. I'll find her and bring her back."

"You'd go alone?"

Mary Aaron laughed nervously. "Unless you want *me* to drive the getaway car." She offered a rueful look. "Just because I have a driver's license doesn't mean I can actually drive."

Finding their way the few blocks to where Hannah had promised to meet them seemed to take forever. A mist had rolled in, cloaking the streets, alleys, and buildings with a thick, hazy fog. There were still people on the streets, but all the figures were swathed in shadows so that one couldn't tell if they were male or female, young or old. The air was thick and moist, still warm enough to bring beads of sweat to one's forehead.

This was exactly what Evan had warned her against—

doing something crazy. She was going out in the middle of the night to a seedy area to meet who-knew-who. What if this was some kind of setup and Hannah had someone else with her? What if it was Beth's killer? And it wasn't just her own safety; she might be putting Mary Aaron in danger. Rachel's heart was in her throat, her pulse racing.

A bulky silhouette loomed out of the darkness and thumped the right fender of her car, making her catch her breath and Mary Aaron squeak in surprise. Laughing, the intoxicated man stumbled away. Rachel edged the vehicle ahead slowly. She couldn't see more than a car-length ahead. "I'm not going to be able to get onto Bourbon. I'm not sure which way to go now."

"Pull over," Mary Aaron ordered. "Conti and Bourbon, it's only a block that way." She pointed. "I'll go find Hannah and bring her to the car. You just have to wait for us."

"You're sure you want to do this?"

"*Ne,* but I'm doing it just the same. Hannah is my friend. If it was me, she wouldn't let me down."

Rachel signaled and pulled into an empty parking space along the street. "All right. But be careful." She murmured a prayer under her breath as Mary Aaron dug in her bag and came up with her hairbrush. "What are you doing with that?"

"If a bad person comes after me, I'll whack them over the head."

"You're going to fight off a mugger with a hairbrush?"

"*Ya.* It's a heavy brush. I'm Amish, not stupid. Would I stand still and let a pig bite me? I would whack him with a shovel. I have no shovel, so the brush will have to do. You stay here, Rae-Rae. Lock the door. I'll be back with Hannah in the flick of a lamb's tail."

"God willing," Rachel murmured.

Mary Aaron got out of the car and in a few steps was gone. A minute passed and then another. Why had she let her cousin go alone? If anything happened to her, she would never forgive herself. She shivered as she watched the digital clock on the dash; she'd left the engine running. "I'm being silly. She'll be back any—"

A shapeless form emerged from the gray haze, then divided into two. A few steps behind, another shape emerged. Then the shapes were running toward her. Rachel gasped, momentarily frozen. Then she flipped on the headlights.

Mary Aaron flew by the car and threw open the back door. "Get in!" she screamed.

Rachel twisted around to see Hannah, in a school uniform, scrambling into the backseat.

"Go! Go, now!" Mary Aaron shouted, leaping into the car.

As Rachel shifted into gear, the third figure materialized in front of the car. A man in a skullcap.

"You better get out of that car!" he bellowed, passing the driver's side door, slamming his hand on the window.

As Rachel hit the gas, she glanced up in the rearview mirror to see Mary Aaron struggling to close the back door. "No, you don't!" she hollered.

"Don't let him in! Don't let him get me!" Hannah screamed.

As Rachel pulled away from the curb, she heard the man cry out, then the slam of the back door. "Lock the doors!" Mary Aaron ordered.

Rachel hit the lock button on the door, screeching tires as she pulled away down the dark street.

"Faster!" Hannah insisted.

Rachel speeded up, glancing in the rearview mirror. The man had started to run after them down the middle of the street, but now he was slowing down. Giving up. "Where are we going?" She gripped the wheel. "Back to the hotel?"

"Not until we're sure we've lost him," Hannah said. Her voice was tremulous, her breath coming in quick gasps.

Rachel flew through an intersection, not entirely sure where she was, although she knew that Canal Street and their hotel were still on the right. "Should I call 9-1-1? Find a policeman?"

"Ne!"

"Best not," Mary Aaron said grimly. "She wants to go home."

Rachel clutched the wheel as she peered through the murk. Here and there, faintly, ghostly illumination from closed business windows and streetlights shone feebly through the fog but did little to help her see where she was going. Cars and trucks, construction cones, and trash cans parked willy-nilly on either side of the street didn't help. From the back-seat came the sounds of Mary Aaron whispering and Hannah softly weeping.

"Do you want me to drive to the airport?" Rachel asked.

"We can't go on the airplane," Mary Aaron said. "She doesn't have identification. She doesn't have anything."

At a traffic light, Rachel turned right and then right again, onto the brighter, broader Canal Street. She glanced in the rearview mirror again. "He's gone."

Twenty minutes later, they were safely back in their hotel room.

Hannah—petite, sandy-haired, gray-eyed—was still pretty and plump. In the uniform she barely looked sixteen. Except, maybe, for the bright lipstick.

It was hard to believe this young woman who'd run away from her traditional upbringing and found her way south to New Orleans had gotten herself admitted to a private girl's school. She'd spoken barely a word since they'd left the car, not to explain who she believed was chasing her or where she'd been all this time.

Mary Aaron followed her into the bathroom, and Rachel heard the shower running. When the two emerged a half hour later, Hannah's hair was pinned up and she was wearing one of the two nightgowns Mary Aaron had brought. The school uniform had vanished; Rachel suspected it had gone into the dry-cleaning bag that her cousin stuffed into the trash can.

"Will someone tell me what's going on?" Rachel asked.

She was so tired that she could barely keep her eyes open. She couldn't remember when she'd last had a decent night's sleep. But she was overjoyed that her wild-goose chase had paid off. They'd found Hannah, and from all appearances, she was eager to go home with them to Stone Mill.

Hannah crawled into one of the beds and buried her head under the pillow.

"She doesn't want to talk about it," Mary Aaron said. "Tomorrow, we will decide what to do. For now, we rest."

Rachel had volunteered to take the pullout couch in the sitting room, and she was too weary to pursue answers tonight. They'd sleep, and then they'd eat breakfast, and then maybe she'd get some of the answers she wanted. She had assumed that falling asleep would be the least of her worries, but sleep didn't come easily. She kept remembering the man chasing Mary Aaron and Hannah and couldn't stop her mind from going places she didn't want to go. What if Mary Aaron hadn't slammed the door on him? What if he'd gotten into the car? And Beth Glick was never far from her thoughts.

Yet they'd done what they set out to do. In a few hours, she'd start to put everything into perspective. She'd insist that Hannah tell her why she'd needed them to come for her, and she'd ask if she knew anything about Beth's whereabouts for the past two years. And she'd call Evan to tell him that they'd found Hannah and were bringing her home, if not by plane, then, she supposed, by car. She could just keep the rental and drive home.

Not what she'd planned, but then, when did her life ever go as she'd planned?

Chapter 14

Neither Hannah nor Mary Aaron stirred until after nine the next morning. Rachel left them drinking coffee from a courtesy pot in the room and went downstairs to request that the rental car be brought to the front door. She'd valet-parked.

"Give me fifteen minutes," she told them as she left the room, "and then meet me in the lobby." She was eager to call Evan to tell him that they'd found Hannah and she was safe, but she didn't want to talk to him in front of Mary Aaron and Hannah.

She found a bellhop to call for her car, checked out, and then found a secluded nook in the lobby from which to ring Evan. "You're not going to believe this," she said when he answered. "We found Hannah. She's with us."

"You found Hannah?" he repeated, obviously dumbfounded. "How . . . Rachel, I . . ."

"I know. Divine intervention? Anyway, I can't talk now. Hannah and Mary Aaron will be down in a minute. We're getting ready to leave the hotel. I just wanted to let you know that we're driving back to Pennsylvania."

"Driving? Why aren't you flying?"

"Hannah has no ID, so we have to drive."

"I can't believe you found her." He still sounded stunned. "She okay? How the hell did you find her? I haven't heard back from Larry on the trace."

Rachel pressed her hand to her forehead, honestly not sure how to answer the question of whether or not Hannah was okay. "She's not hurt. The short version is that Hannah called the B&B again last night and Hulda gave her my cell number. We picked her up in the French Quarter. Wherever she was, she just walked away. Or ran."

Rachel glanced toward the elevator. Someone was coming down. "I need to go. Hannah seems unhurt, but she's scared to death. She insists we get out of New Orleans as soon as possible. I think she believes that someone may come after her."

"Does she know anything about Beth or Lorraine?"

"I don't know anything yet. She hardly said two words last night. She didn't have anything with her, not even a purse, and she was wearing a schoolgirl uniform: knee socks, Mary Janes, and way too much red lipstick."

"A *school uniform?*"

Rachel lowered her voice, even though there was no one nearby. "Like what a grade school girl would wear: white blouse, plaid skirt, navy tie. Evan, it was . . . very odd."

The elevator opened, and Mary Aaron and Hannah stepped out into the lobby. Both were dressed in Amish clothing, Hannah's hair tucked beneath Mary Aaron's *kapp* and her cousin's head covered with the blue scarf.

"I have to go," Rachel said into the phone.

"Rachel, I don't like the idea of—"

"I have to go, Evan. I'll try to call you later." She hung up and turned to greet them with a smile.

Fifty miles northeast of New Orleans, Rachel pulled off I-59 and into Timmons' Family Restaurant. Hannah hadn't said a word since they left the hotel that morning, and she remained quiet through breakfast. After they finished a meal of eggs, bacon, and pancakes, she excused herself to go to the ladies' room. Rachel watched her walk away and then murmured to Mary Aaron, "Do you think she'll come back? Maybe you should go with her."

Mary Aaron shook her head. "She's not going to run away. She wants to go home," she said, switching to Deitsch.

Rachel thought for a moment. "Why now? Why not six months ago? Why not a year ago, when she first left?"

"I think she was being held against her will. I get the idea that it's only been over time that someone, whoever was holding her, loosened the reins." Mary Aaron set her utensils around the rim of her plate, one at a time. "None of it matters now. She's safe. Her family will take her back if she makes confession before the church."

Rachel wanted to think Mary Aaron was referring to the more minor sins an Amish woman in the English world must have committed. But she knew that wasn't what they were talking about. "What does she have to confess?"

Her cousin gave her a look that said nothing and everything, a gaze so innocent and yet wise in the ways of the world that Rachel stared at her in surprise. "She didn't say, exactly, but I think bad people kidnapped her." She glanced in the direction of the ladies' room. The hallway remained empty other than a stout woman dragging a reluctant and whining three-year-old toward them. "They made her do things . . ."

"With men?" Rachel crumbled her napkin as her eyes clouded with tears. "You mean—"

Mary Aaron gently raised a palm to silence her question. "I told you that she didn't say. Best not to dwell on evil. It is the good thing about our faith—a woman or a man can turn his or her back on sin and be welcomed into the bosom of the church. Whatever happened to her or didn't happen, the water of baptism will wash away the sorrow and guilt."

Rachel sunk back into the bench. What Mary Aaron was saying was true. The Amish faith was one of complete forgiveness for those who repented of their sins. The community would embrace Hannah Verkler and wipe away the years that she had been separated from them. If an English girl had suffered what Rachel suspected had happened to Hannah, it would ruin her life. But the religion that many thought was so stern was based on love and the power of a soul to shine through the clouds of human frailty.

"Did she say how it happened? How did these bad men get her? Does she know anything about Beth? Did they take her, too? What about Lorraine?"

"She hasn't said. We're going to have to give her time," her cousin advised. "When she is ready to talk, she may be willing to tell me how she left Stone Mill and how she ended up in New Orleans. But I can tell you right now, she won't speak to the police. Not even to Evan. So don't press her."

"But if she knows anything about Beth's disappearance or what happened to her, then—"

"You, above all, should know how stubborn our people can be," Mary Aaron interrupted. "Try and force her, and you may never learn a thing. She's grateful that you came for her, but she doesn't trust you. She thinks of you as an Englisher."

Rachel thought for a moment. "Last night, I got the impression she was afraid that someone would come after her. Do you think she's really in danger?"

Mary Aaron shrugged. "Hard to say."

"Do these men know where she's from? Know her family?"

"I don't know that, either," Mary Aaron said. "I've been thinking about it, though, and I think it's best if she doesn't go home yet. In case the bad people know where she came from." She looked up at Rachel across the table. "I was thinking that she could stay with you. At Stone Mill House. Just until she can square things with her bishop and elders. And maybe we can find out if she knows anything that could help us find out what happened to Beth."

"She doesn't want her parents to know she's all right?"

"She wants to see her parents and let them know that she's okay, but she doesn't want the community to know yet. I have a feeling that once she's baptized, she'll leave Stone Mill. No one will ever find her again. Not the men she's afraid of, not even the police. But for now, can you let her stay with you?"

"Of course. But if she doesn't trust me, then why would she want to stay with me?"

"There's nowhere else."

"If I tell Evan she's at the house," Rachel said, "he'll insist on speaking to her."

"So don't tell him."

Rachel should have been surprised by her cousin's suggestion, but she wasn't. In the last two weeks, she'd learned a lot about Mary Aaron that she hadn't known. "I can put her upstairs in my apartment. No one goes up there. And I think you're right; no one in the community, Amish or English, should know yet."

"Just us, Hannah's mother and father, and her bishop."

"That's five people." Rachel grimaced. "How do you keep a secret if five people know?"

"Six," Mary Aaron corrected. "You'll have to tell Ada. Nothing goes on in the house that she doesn't find out."

"Will she keep quiet?"

"As the grave."

Rachel considered that thought. Mary Aaron was right. Ada was no one's dummy. It would be impossible to hide Hannah in the house without her finding out, and if she did, she'd be hurt that they hadn't trusted her enough to tell her. *Only among the Amish,* she thought. Give a secret to six Englishers and the whole county would soon know it. She smiled at her relapse into the culture of her upbringing. The Plain people had a tradition of keeping apart from the world and—if need be—from members of their own community. "I agree," she said.

The restroom door opened, and Hannah emerged, looking like a daughter of the church, untouched by the outer world. The conversation between Mary Aaron and Rachel ended abruptly.

Mary Aaron began to make a show of stacking the dirty plates and gathering up the silverware. "*Goot* pancakes," she observed, "but the eggs taste different. Maybe white chickens."

"I'd better make the most of this stop." Rachel got to her feet. "Ask the waitress if we can have iced tea and pie to go. Once we get on the road, I'd like to make time." She smiled reassuringly at Hannah as she walked past her into the ladies' room.

From the bathroom stall, Rachel called Evan again.

"Where are you?" he asked.

She closed the lid on the toilet seat and sat down. "In Mississippi. We stopped to get something to eat. I think we'll drive until I get tired. I'm hoping we can make Virginia today. We'll stay somewhere tonight and drive the rest of the way tomorrow."

"What did Hannah tell you?"

Rachel closed her eyes. What Mary Aaron suggested had happened to Hannah was beyond an Amish mother's worst nightmare. Beyond any mother's nightmare. "Nothing. Mary Aaron says she won't talk to me. She doesn't trust me."

"But she called you."

"Because I have a phone, I imagine. I don't know. Right now, she's not talking to me. Just to Mary Aaron and only a little."

Evan groaned on the other end of the line. "Does she know anything about Beth?"

"I don't know," she repeated, trying not to be annoyed. "Mary Aaron thinks we need to give her some time. She may be able to tell us something in a few days." Rachel considered what she was going to say next. A part of her thought she should bring Hannah home and never say a word about what Mary Aaron had told her, but another part of her . . . What if Lorraine was in the same kind of danger Hannah had been in? What if these men had been the same ones who had taken Beth?

"So you're trying to tell me that Hannah calling you from New Orleans has absolutely nothing to—"

"I think she was kidnapped," Rachel interrupted.

"What?"

"I think she might have been kidnapped and taken to New Orleans."

"Was she kidnapped from Stone Mill?" he asked, incredulously.

She continued on her own train of thought. "I think she was being held there, Evan, and made to—" She couldn't say it.

He was quiet for a moment. Then he said, "She was wearing a schoolgirl's uniform and lipstick?"

"Yes," Rachel said.

"Rachel . . ." He hesitated. "What we might be talking about here is the sex-slave trade."

Rachel took a deep breath. "I know."

"You have to try to find out what you can," he said.

"I know." She stood up. "I need to go. They'll be coming to look for me."

"You said she was in the French Quarter?" he asked.

"Yes."

"Okay. I think I'll give the local police a call. Maybe even check with the FBI. See what I can find out."

"I have to go," Rachel repeated.

Evan was quiet on the other end of the line for a second. "Stay safe."

"I will." She disconnected and stood there for a moment. Then she heard the bathroom door open.

"We're going to step outside to get some air." It was Mary Aaron. "Meet you at the car."

"See you in a minute," Rachel called.

After dropping the rental car off and picking up Rachel's Jeep at the Harrisburg airport, they arrived in Stone Mill after dark on the following day. Once in the valley, they drove Mary Aaron home, leaving her at the end of her lane.

Mary Aaron hugged them and promised to come over as soon as she could. Hannah got into the front passenger's seat.

Rachel and Hannah then headed for the B&B. They were traveling along Buttermilk Road, which connected much of the Amish community to the town, when Hannah surprised Rachel by speaking up. "Could you stop? Here?"

The girl had barely spoken to Mary Aaron since they'd left New Orleans the day before, and to Rachel even less. Hannah had seemed to be hardly aware that anyone else was in the car.

"Sure." Rachel braked immediately, thinking maybe Hannah was carsick. She'd had a touch of it earlier in the day. "Are you feeling bad?"

"*Ne.* I— I just want to get out here. Just for a minute."

Rachel looked over to see Hannah staring out the window into the darkness. The only thing nearby was an Amish school. "You want to stop here?" Rachel asked. "At the schoolhouse?" She eased onto the shoulder.

"*Ya.*"

Rachel wanted to ask why, but something made her keep her questions to herself, for once. The thought that Hannah might have changed her mind about coming home and intended to run passed through her mind. But what could Rachel do? She wasn't holding Hannah prisoner. Rachel suspected that someone else had already done that, and she couldn't do anything to break down the tentative bonds of friendship they'd formed.

Rachel slowed the car to a crawl as she turned into the steep driveway lined with tall evergreens. Summer vacation hadn't ended yet, and weeds clogged the rutted lane. Rachel could barely make out the one-room schoolhouse in the headlights, but directly ahead, a homemade swing hung from a big oak tree. Just beyond stood a seesaw hewn from a single pine log.

Hannah slid out. Rachel was torn between following her and waiting in the car so as to give her privacy. She stayed put and lowered her window. Fortunately, Hannah didn't go far. She walked over to the homemade rope-and-board swing, sat down on it, and pushed off. Minutes passed as Hannah swung in the dark. A mosquito buzzed around Rachel's head, and she swatted at it. Another five minutes. Hannah hadn't done anything but swing.

Rachel was about to get out of the car when Hannah suddenly stood up and walked back. As she opened the door, the overhead light flashed on, and Rachel saw that the girl's cheeks were wet, as though she'd been crying, but she hadn't made a sound.

"You okay, Hannah?"

"*Ya,*" she answered softly, closing the door, drowning them in darkness again.

"Ready?" Rachel asked, her voice way too cheerful for the mood in the car. Hannah didn't answer, so Rachel turned the key and backed out of the drive.

She continued on to Stone Mill House. Once inside, she led Hannah up the steps to the third floor. She pulled the shades and told the girl, "You'll be safe here."

"*Danke,* Rachel Mast," Hannah said with quiet dignity, moving easily from English to the Deitsch dialect. "Mary Aaron told me that you were a good woman." Her gaze fell on the German Bible lying on the nightstand beside the bed. It was a leather-bound volume that George, a dealer in rare books, had given her the first Christmas after she'd returned to Stone Mill. "Is it all right if I read your Bible? I have not had one . . . where . . . where I was. It would comfort me."

"Of course. Feel free to use any of my things that you want." Rachel gestured toward the bathroom. "There are towels and a robe in there. And there's fruit, snacks, and cheese in the fridge. Please make yourself at home here."

"I appreciate your kindness to a stranger."

Rachel gathered up some clothing and a few personal items, dropping them into a canvas bag that had been at the end of her bed. "You're Mary Aaron's friend, and that makes you my friend. I'm so glad you called me, Hannah. And happy to have you back safe. We've been so worried about you."

"*Ya,*" the girl agreed solemnly. "Me as well."

Rachel went to the door. "I'll stay in one of the guest rooms. No one will bother you here. You can lock the door behind me if it makes you feel better. Sleep well."

"I think I will." She glanced around the spacious room with its high ceiling and pale yellow walls. "This is a peaceful place. Plain."

"Yes, exactly. Plain." Rachel smiled at her. "Good night." She heard the lock click into place as she started back down the steps, and she felt a wave of compassion for Hannah and, with it, the realization that the young woman was a survivor. *At least she's alive.* Only Lorraine, of the missing girls, was left unaccounted for. She could only hope that she had found a place for herself, as Lucy had, and that she was safe from whatever evil had ensnared Hannah.

Rachel left her things in one of the guest rooms and headed down the stairs. She was tired. There had been three cars with out-of-state plates in the yard, telling her that she would have guests to care for in the morning. She wanted to go to bed and get some sleep after the stress of the long drive, but Evan had insisted that she let him know as soon as she arrived. She hoped he wouldn't insist on coming over tonight. She was torn between wanting to see him and wanting to avoid him so that he wouldn't ask where Hannah was. He'd be full of questions, and she'd be hard put to answer them without telling him everything she knew. Why was it that the amateur detectives in novels never worried about keeping information secret from their partners?

She'd missed Evan. She really had. Having him with her in New Orleans, especially the night they'd snatched Hannah out of the French Quarter, would have been wonderful. She always felt safe when she was with Evan. She could depend on him, but . . .

There was always a but, and Mary Aaron had been adamant

that Hannah would have no part of Evan's questioning. He was an Englisher and a state trooper, and for whatever reason, Hannah had no intention of revealing anything to the police. Evan might not agree or like it—Rachel herself might not like it—but the truth of the matter was that Hannah had the right not to ever speak of what had happened to her in the time she was gone from Stone Mill.

On the main floor, Rachel went into her office. There was a small marble-topped Victorian table with a single drawer beside her desk where the daily mail was left until she could attend to it. She glanced at the pile and spotted several bills and what was obviously junk mail, but sticking out of the stack was a letter with distinctive handwriting. It was from George. She picked it up, noting the rubber stamp notice warning the recipient that it had been sent from a prisoner.

Curious, she opened the letter. The letter consisted of a few simple lines of script—certainly not George's style at all. His missives usually ran to four or five pages.

Rachel~
Come Saturday. Important. Need to talk.
Love to Sophie~
George

She wondered what George had to say to her that was so important. She'd promised him that she'd return soon, but she hadn't intended to go back to the prison the coming weekend. She wondered why he hadn't just called; he had phone privileges at least once a week. Did he have something to tell her that he couldn't say over the phone? Now her curiosity was really piqued.

Something warm and furry brushed against her bare ankle.

"Bishop."

The cat meowed.

Rachel pushed the note back into the envelope, returned the envelope to the table, and stooped to pick up the big Siamese. "Did you miss me?" she crooned to the cat. He rewarded her with a displeased sound—half hiss and half purr. "Poor baby, left all alone." She carried the cat with her to the kitchen and was searching for a packet of cat treats when her cell in her pocket vibrated. Evan.

"I was just going to call you," she said into the phone. "We just got in."

"I'll be there in ten."

"Could we wait until tomorrow?" she hedged. She opened the refrigerator door and peered in. A plate of Ada's fried chicken beckoned. "I'll be here all day. Tons of work to catch up with."

"I wanted to talk to you before I go to talk to Hannah."

He'd obviously made the assumption that Hannah had gone home to her parents' house. "I know you *want* to, but I don't think we can pressure her. I can only imagine what she's going through, emotionally. She wouldn't answer any of my questions, and she was adamant about not speaking to the police. Unfortunately, that includes you."

He was quiet for a moment. "I'll see you tomorrow, then. But we'll have to think of something. A way to convince her to talk to me. Hannah might give us the lead we need to crack this case."

"Here's the problem." Rachel reached for a drumstick. "Anything you learn from Hannah, you have to take to Sergeant Haley, right?" She let the refrigerator door close. "Which means she ends up being told she has to talk to him. She could wind up being subpoenaed and required to testify."

"You're talking about a long way down the road. We have to find the killer, first."

"Evan, Hannah can't appear at a trial, which means she can't make an official statement." She exhaled. "Which means it would be better for her and you both if she doesn't speak to you. At least not yet."

"I can't accept that, Rachel. I have to go where the case leads me, and right now, Hannah's my best chance at finding out what happened to Beth Glick. I'm sorry if Hannah gets hurt in an effort to find Beth's murderer. But finding him is what's important. Who's to say he won't kill again? Do you want to be responsible for that?"

"I hear what you're saying." Suddenly, her appetite was gone. She opened a cupboard door, took down a saucer, and put the chicken on it. "But I know you know what I'm talking about." She turned to lean against the counter. "If Hannah were forced to testify in a trial, it would not only hurt her, but the publicity would devastate the Amish community. Coming forward and making a statement could do more damage to her life than what she's already lived through."

He was quiet again on the other end of the phone for a minute. She knew he was thinking about what she'd said. She waited.

"I'll come by tomorrow. I won't go out to her parents' place until I've talked to you." There was a hesitation on the other end, and then Evan said, "Can you be sure Hannah sits tight and doesn't take off again? Right now, she's the only lead we have."

"Don't worry," Rachel assured him. "She's not going anywhere."

Chapter 15

Hannah's mother and father were at the B&B by eight thirty the next morning, supposedly to deliver a basket of tomatoes for Ada's kitchen. Rachel whisked them up the back staircase, down a hall, making sure to avoid any guests, and up to the third floor. Wanting to give them privacy, she excused herself quickly, but not before she heard Hannah's cry of anguish and joy and saw her rush into her mother's welcoming arms.

Downstairs, Rachel threw herself into her work, hoping that would take her mind off what was going on upstairs and Evan's impending arrival. Hulda came over at nine, bringing back Sophie and giving a full report on the past three days' reservations, cancellations, and a call from the mason, Joab Rust, about the mill house building. Hulda was curious about Rachel's sudden departure earlier in the week, but Rachel didn't dare share any of her secrets with her. Hulda Schenfeld was as good a friend as Rachel had, but without meaning to break her confidence, Hulda would have cheerfully spread the news about Hannah's return all over Stone Mill before noon.

By ten thirty, Hannah's parents had slipped quietly out of the house, and Rachel had fed her guests, checked two out, and seen the others off for a day of sightseeing. Two of Ada's granddaughters were busy hanging out sheets on the clothesline, a niece was polishing the front entrance floors, and Rachel's brother was mowing the front lawn with a push mower. Rachel finally felt free to turn her attention to the gift shop orders that had been waiting when she'd taken off for New Orleans.

By the time Evan arrived around noon, Rachel had gone over the three new orders, set them aside to be boxed up and mailed, and rearranged the displays. Minnie could be counted on to dust and polish so that the gift shop shone like a new penny, but her idea of organizing the merchandise was to line everything up in orderly rows by height.

"I think you've given me my first gray hairs," Evan said as he walked into the gift shop and hugged her. "I was worried sick about you."

"Shouldn't have been," she said. "People fly to New Orleans all the time."

"Right." He gave her a peck on the cheek. "And they go into questionable parts of the city in the middle of the night to rescue girls caught up in the illegal sex industry."

She looked up at him, realizing that the full reality of that possibility hadn't sunk in yet. It just seemed so . . . impossible. "You think that's what it was?"

He released her. "Maybe this isn't the best place to talk."

"No," she agreed. "Maybe not." She hung the closed sign on the door and led him out of the house. She took a flagstone path past the herb garden to a bench beside the pond at the old gristmill. It was quiet there, isolated from the house by fruit trees and a hedge, the only occupants a mallard hen and her six half-grown ducklings. The sun was warm on Rachel's face, and across the pond stretched a meadow where her goats were grazing. It didn't seem like a spot that could be touched by an evil such as sex trafficking.

She sat on the wooden bench and motioned to Evan to join her. He was dressed in a pair of khaki shorts and a yellow polo shirt. She liked him this way, this casual side of him.

She watched the ducks paddle around on the pond. "How

could this have happened?" she asked. "Hannah's one of our own, an Amish girl from a little town in the Pennsylvania mountains. How could someone like Hannah be caught up in something like that?" She closed her eyes. "Maybe we're jumping to conclusions. Maybe Hannah just met the wrong man and—I don't know."

"I put in a call to the FBI yesterday morning," he said. "They reached out to NOLA sex crimes division. NOLA PD had a good idea where Hannah might have been held. It just so happens that a crime hotline got an anonymous call late last week. The informant gave an address not far off Bourbon Street, said that undocumented girls were being held there against their will for the purpose of prostitution."

"I know this kind of thing goes on," Rachel said, shaking her head slowly, "but I just can't wrap my head around it."

"The FBI agent told me that they believe this bunch is part of a larger organization, one indicted in the kidnapping of two underage girls in Detroit last year. One of the girls ended up dead in the Detroit River; the other vanished before the case could come to trial. This is a bad bunch. They sweep up vulnerable young women, force them into drugs and prostitution, and hold them in virtual slavery."

"The FBI knows about them and they haven't been able to put an end to it?"

"This kind of thing isn't as easy to stop as you might think. People who commit these types of crime are smart. They move around a lot. They choose young women who have no family ties, or whose family is far away."

"Or who've run from their family," Rachel mused.

"The agent said the group might be part of a larger, international crime ring. They suspect Russian interests, a very sophisticated operation. They open strip clubs as legitimate businesses, rake in huge amounts of untaxed dollars for a few weeks or a few months, and then pick up and move the girls to another city, where they open under another name."

"Do you think it's possible that Beth was caught up in the same circumstances—maybe with the same people?"

"There's no way for us to know. A SWAT team raided the club in New Orleans in question last night." He frowned. "Wasn't much of a raid. Someone must have tipped them off because they'd cleared out. The place was empty."

"Thank God Hannah called me when she did," Rachel breathed.

"If that *is* where she was, you can see why I need to question her. Why the FBI may want to as well."

Rachel turned on the bench to face him directly. "You want Hannah to give you information when the last girls who tried to help the police with these criminals ended up dead?"

"The FBI could protect her," Evan said.

"Really? The way they protected the girl they found in the river?" She got up and walked a few steps, down toward the pond. "Do you see a similarity here? Where was Beth? Floating in a quarry."

"That doesn't make any sense. We don't even know if Hannah was connected to this operation. And even if she was, it's a leap to think they came after Beth Glick and ended up in a rock quarry in Nowhere, Pennsylvania."

Rachel didn't respond. She stared at the water in the pond, debating whether or not to kick off her flip-flops and dip her feet. The ducklings quacked and swam in circles.

"The agent I spoke to said these guys pick up girls in this country in various ways: at bus terminals, in diners, on the street. They target young women who are desperate, girls looking for money or jobs."

Rachel turned to him. "And you think an Amish girl from Stone Mill would agree to something so immoral?"

"I don't know. People hungry enough, scared enough, make bad choices. More likely, they don't know what they're getting into until it's too late—" He stopped and started again. "Look, Amish kids who leave home can get into all sorts of trouble. You and I both know that. It's their innocence that makes them so vulnerable. If Beth had been a part of this thing, she wouldn't be the first conservatively raised girl who'd tossed aside her prayer *kapp* for—"

"Stop, Evan, please." She held up her hand. "I don't want to hear it. You're right. We don't know. We could make up all kinds of scenarios. But it would all be conjecture. We have to know for sure before we bring the authorities in." She walked back toward him. "Give me a few days to gain Hannah's confidence, to see if I—or Mary Aaron—can find out anything definite. And then, if Hannah agrees, you can question her yourself."

"What if I don't want to wait?"

She sighed and made a small gesture with her hands. "What happened when you tried to talk to Beth's family? You got *nothing*. Believe me, if you try to force this with Hannah, she'll vanish in a day. Her family will hide her, and you won't find her. Not ever."

A silence stretched between them.

"When did we get to be on opposite sides of this investigation?" he finally asked. He was hurt. She could read it in his eyes, but she couldn't back down.

"We aren't on opposite sides." She returned to the bench and sat down beside him. She placed her hand over his. "We want the same thing. We want Beth's killer brought to justice."

"And what about the people who hurt Hannah? Do you want them held accountable for their crimes?"

"Only if it won't hurt her more. Whatever sins they've committed, someday they'll have to answer to a higher authority. But Hannah is here and alive, and she can still have a life."

"And if she wants to help?"

"That's up to her, Evan. It's her decision to make, and neither you nor I can make that choice for her."

He glanced toward the pond. "Is she at her parents' now?"

Rachel felt her throat and face grow warm. This was what she'd dreaded. She couldn't lie to Evan, but neither would she reveal where Hannah was. "No."

"No, as in she's not there right now, or no, as in she didn't go home when you got back in town?"

"She's not ready for people to know she's back. And . . . I didn't know if it was safe for her to go home. What if someone came looking for her? We haven't told anyone who didn't need to know that she's back."

"That's probably smart," he conceded. "Is she with Mary Aaron? At the Hostetlers'?"

"Please don't ask me any more questions. Hannah and her parents asked me not to say."

"But you know where she is?"

She nodded. "I know, but I can't tell you. I gave Hannah my word."

He frowned and looked out over the pond, then back at her. "I hope you don't live to regret that decision. Because if harm comes to another girl"—he held her gaze—"you'll always wonder if you could have prevented it."

"Rachel! It's so good to see you. You look fantastic." George hugged her, and this time, she felt comfortable enough in the prison visiting area to return his embrace. "I'm so glad you could find the time to come up."

She followed him back to the table where he had cans of orange soda and snack-sized bags of potato chips waiting. It looked like a typical Saturday morning in the prison's visiting room. The place was crowded with friends and families, but George had chosen a spot in the far left corner, away from the refreshment area and the guards. She was surprised at how healthy George looked, and wondered how he'd managed to acquire a tan since the last time she'd been there. Curious, she asked him about it.

"Oh." He smiled broadly. "I spend an hour every afternoon in the garden. We grow all kinds of vegetables. It's considered a privilege to work there. Next year, I hope that we can try some different varieties. I've ordered lots of different catalogs from companies that specialize in heirlooms. Hybrids may produce more, but the heirlooms are tastier. Two of my best students go with me, and we continue the lessons there. It's just amazing what the right sort of education can do for a man."

She leaned back in her chair, crossing her arms over her chest, trying to at least look relaxed. "So you're continuing your teaching?"

"Absolutely." George's head bobbed up and down with enthusiasm. "I told you about the second class. Would you believe it's full already? I don't want to boast, but I believe I'm having a positive influence on many lives here. Maybe this is what the Lord intended for me all along."

Rachel couldn't help smiling back. There was so much good in George. She couldn't forget the crime he'd committed, but she couldn't find it in her heart to judge him either. "Ell said she was up last weekend. I'm so glad you got to spend some time with her. You won't believe the changes she's made at The George. She has a real knack for knowing what her customers want. She has a group of kids from the high school doing her window displays, and she's started a story time for preschoolers one morning a week." What she wanted to know was why George had written such an odd letter and why he'd been so insistent that she come. But common courtesy and her upbringing among the Plain people made her fight down her impatience and wait while George chatted on.

"What's new in Stone Mill?" he asked. "Did they approve the library addition for the high school?"

She answered all his questions, shared local gossip and crop reports, carefully omitting her trip to New Orleans and Hannah Verkler's rescue. She produced half a dozen new photographs of Sophie she'd printed from her computer that morning. And finally, when her patience had run out, she asked him directly why he'd summoned her.

George lowered his voice and leaned close. "I came upon some information that might be useful in your investigation."

"My investigation?"

"Into Beth Glick's murder." This time, George's smile was sly. "I know you too well, Rachel. You're playing detective again."

"I'm not playing at anything, George. A girl died in our community. I found her body. It's hard not to take it personally, especially when Beth's killer is still at large."

"I'm sorry, that didn't come out right." He squeezed her hand.

"I'm sorry, too." She offered him a grim smile. "I didn't mean to snap at you. It's just that Evan has been part of the investigation, and the police have gotten nowhere. Of course, none of the Amish will talk to them. I feel like . . . I need to do what I can."

"So the police have no leads?"

"It's not that they're not trying. There just aren't any leads that have panned out," she said, hoping she didn't sound too cryptic. She wanted to tell him about Hannah, about her suspected kidnapping and Evan's suspicion that she might have been involved in a sex slavery ring, but she didn't dare. Bad enough that Evan was upset with her. As much as she would have liked George's input, she had to remember where he was and why he was there.

"But you don't think Beth's murder was random?" He eyed her shrewdly. "Not just a bad guy passing through Stone Mill?"

"So far, I can't say for sure, but my gut tells me . . . no."

"Sometimes you just have to go with your gut," he agreed.

"So if you know anything that might help, I'd appreciate it, George."

"I'll warn you, this may be nothing more than jailhouse gossip." He pushed aside his can of soda and the chip bag on the table. "Men get bored in here. Sometimes, they make up stories to pass the time or to gain attention. But what I heard, I don't know." He shook his head slowly. "It had a ring of truth. I can't tell you who told me. He's one of my students. Basically, a good soul who got a bad start in life. The usual: abandoned by his father, raised by a druggie mother who was more interested in her worthless boyfriends than her children. He was in trouble by the time he hit his teens, but he's finally made the decision to turn his life around. I couldn't do anything to jeopardize that."

"What did you hear?" she asked. This had to be important. George had to have believed there was truth to this; otherwise, he wouldn't have had her come, would he?

"You can't tell anyone where you heard this." His gaze grew intense. "I'm serious, Rachel. There are too many places in here where a man my age could fall prey to an accident. One moment he's hoeing cabbages in the garden, and the next he's slipped, fallen, and cracked his head open on a rock."

She nodded. "I understand. I won't implicate you. You have my word."

"Good enough for me." He smiled and offered her the bag of potato chips. "Smile at me. Act as though we're talking about the good weather. I wouldn't want any of my *colleagues* to overhear." He lowered his voice. "What I was told is that someone in Stone Mill is neck-deep in the kidnapping and selling of young women."

Rachel's eyes widened in shock.

"And he's Amish."

Chapter 16

All the way home from the prison, Rachel kept going over and over in her head what George had told her. She could hardly believe it. Was it really possible that someone of her parents' faith was involved in such a terrible crime? One of their own neighbors? Was that why Hannah had refused to give them any information?

What Amish person would risk his immortal soul by selling their own into slavery?

Rachel's first impulse, when she had gotten back to her car, had been to call Evan. But she had to confirm or disprove the accusation before she went to Evan. Right now, the information bordered on gossip, or could be seen that way. And even then, she knew she could never reveal to him, to anyone, where she'd gotten the information.

Despite Mary Aaron's warning, Rachel felt as if she had no choice but to try to talk to Hannah again. She needed to at least get her to say if she'd left the valley on her own, if someone had helped her flee, or if someone had taken her against her will. Was Hannah protecting someone nearby because she was afraid? But if she feared someone in Stone Mill, why had she come back? It didn't make sense.

When Rachel had left the B&B that morning to see George, Hannah's mother and father had been with her upstairs. Maybe she could enlist their help in trying to persuade

Hannah to cooperate—if for no other reason than to protect her sisters, cousins, and nieces. Surely the parents would see the wisdom of convincing Hannah to confide in her. And if George's information was a fabrication, then it was best to snuff out the lie then and there.

When Rachel reached Stone Mill House, she saw that the Verkler buggy was no longer in the yard. So much for getting their help.

Ada had already left for the day; on Saturdays she only came in for a few hours in the morning. The staff always left when she did. Today would be a busy one in Amish homes because all the cleaning and cooking for Sunday had to be done ahead of time. Among Plain people, the Sabbath was a day of rest and prayer. As for the B&B employees, no one worked for Rachel on Sunday except for a high school girl who manned the phone and took care of guests checking out. Rachel had considered trying to hire another English girl to come in for light housekeeping duty on Sunday afternoons, but Ada had declared her opposition to any outside Englisher help with the house. Managing on her own on Sundays seemed the most sensible solution to Rachel because if Ada wasn't happy, nothing in the house went well.

When she got up to the attic, Rachel found the door to her rooms closed. From inside, she could hear the familiar words of an old hymn. She knocked and identified herself, and the door opened.

"I'm sorry," Hannah said. Her cheeks were flushed a deep pink. "Did my singing bother your guests?"

"*Ne.*" Rachel slipped into Deitsch. "You're fine. Sing all you like. Here on the third floor, no one can hear you." As she entered the room, she saw an ironing board and several baskets of laundry. "I see Ada has put you to work."

"*Ya.*" Hannah's smile glowed. "I like to keep busy. I cannot just sit and stare at the walls. My mother brought mending and my sewing box. Glad I am to help her."

Rachel offered her a bottle of root beer. "I thought you might be thirsty. Ada's recipe is good, very refreshing."

"*Danke.* You have all been very kind to me." Hannah placed the soda pop on the table and returned to her ironing: pillowcases and sheets. Ada insisted that sheets, pillowcases, and cloth napkins be ironed.

"Did your parents stay long?"

"Two hours. It was good to see them. I have missed my family."

Rachel was encouraged. It was the most information that Hannah had volunteered. "I'm sure Mary Aaron will come as soon as she is free. I think she had work to do for her mother today. A lot of canning this time of year."

Hannah nodded. "My father says the bishop will come soon. *Dat* spoke with him. He's glad that I am here until we can make arrangements."

"Arrangements?" Rachel sat down on the edge of the recliner.

Hannah guided the electric iron back and forth, smoothing the wrinkles out of the pillowcase. "I will make confession of my sins," she said. "And ask forgiveness."

Rachel pushed back the dark images that rose in her imagination. Was it possible that Hannah could appear so calm after the ordeal she'd experienced? "You were gone almost two years," she said.

"Two years in October," Hannah said softly.

"Did . . . Were you with those people all that time? The people who held you against your will?"

She folded the pillowcase carefully, placed it in a wicker basket, and took another from the other basket on the floor. When she glanced up, their gazes locked for just an instant, and Rachel winced at the depth of pain she glimpsed there.

"The reason I ask . . . My friend Evan Parks and I are trying to find out who killed Beth Glick and why. He's a state policeman." She paused. "Did you ever see Beth? She left about a year before you did." Rachel waited and then went on. "Did you hear anything about her? I know you don't want to think about that bad time, but it's important that you tell us anything you know that might help us find the murderer."

"I read about Beth in the newspaper." She began to neatly fold the white pillowcase.

"In the newspaper? You mean in New Orleans?"

Hannah nodded. "I saw your name. Your picture."

"The article Bill Billingsly wrote? The one picked up by the Associated Press?"

"I don't know those things. But when I saw your picture, that's when I got the idea. To call you." She added the pillowcase to a growing stack and reached for one from the laundry basket. "The paper said you helped your uncle when the police thought he killed a man. I knew you were a good person from the things Mary Aaron said about you before I left. I knew you would help me, even if you are an Englisher."

Rachel couldn't believe that something Bill had written exploiting the Amish had actually helped someone. Talk about God working in mysterious ways. She watched Hannah slip the wrinkly pillowcase over the end of the ironing board. "Can you help me, Hannah? Can you tell me exactly what happened to you? How you came to leave Stone Mill? How you ended up in New Orleans?"

Hannah's attention was fixed on the iron. "I believe that God will forgive me my sins if I am truly repentant. My bishop says that the English world is one of evil and temptation. That even now it tries to lure me away: my fear, my guilt. My shame," she whispered. Then louder, she said, "I must put it away from me and have nothing more to do with it."

"I can understand that, Hannah, but if we don't stop them, these bad people will keep on doing these things. Did you ever see Beth after you left?"

"*Ne.*" The word was so low that Rachel could barely make it out.

"No, you didn't see her, or no, you won't tell me?" she pressed.

"I did not see her, but even if I did . . ." Beth stopped and started again. "I told Mary Aaron, I will not talk to Englisher policemen. I left here of my own choice."

Which meant she wasn't kidnapped from Stone Mill, Rachel thought. She waited.

Hannah's face flamed, and she set the iron upright on its end. "My mother says that I must forget what happened, that our faith will bring me peace. I was young and foolish. I thought that I wanted to see what was beyond this valley, but I should have stayed at home. I know that now. If I had been obedient to my parents, to the elders of our church, if I had not been led astray, it would not have happened."

"Please, Hannah. I'm not asking you to talk to the police. I'm asking you to trust me, to help me."

"I told you, I know nothing about Beth. I am sorry that she is lost to us. Sorry that she accepted baptism into our faith and then turned her back on it . . . sorry that she may not find the peace that waits for me."

Rachel was becoming frustrated with Hannah, but she knew she couldn't show it. She took a different tack. "Mary Aaron said that you knew Lorraine. Did you ever see *her*? Hear about her from anyone else while you were with those people?"

She shook her head. "You see, I cannot help you, Rachel." She picked up the iron and then put it back down. "I don't want to talk about this anymore. If you want me to go from your house, I will go."

"Of course I don't want you to leave. There is no question of you leaving here so long as you may be in danger," Rachel said. She took a breath. When she spoke again, she took care with her tone, speaking softly, the way Hannah did. "I don't want to trouble you, but my concern for other young women makes me ask. You have sisters. What if one of them—"

"*Ne*. I can't. It makes me too sad."

"Hannah," Rachel insisted, "you don't have to talk about New Orleans. All I want to know is if someone helped you leave Stone Mill."

Hannah pretended to be interested in her shoe. Her mouth tightened into a pout. "Somebody tried to help me. But what happened, it wasn't his fault. The woman had lied to him. She promised that she would take us to a Mennonite church. She said that they helped ex-Amish girls get jobs and papers. I didn't have a social security card or my birth certificate. There was another girl with her. Amish, but from Lancaster. I didn't know her."

"Another girl? What was her name?" Rachel asked.

"She said Anna, but I think that she made it up. When I said, 'Anna,' she didn't look at me."

"And the man who helped you? What did he do?"

"Gave me money. Told me that the woman would take good care of me. She was English. A jolly woman. Fat and jolly."

"Did she tell you her name?"

"Ne." Hannah shook her head.

"What kind of car did she drive?"

Hannah shrugged. "A blue van. I don't know about kinds. Just a van."

"Did you see the license plate?"

"Ne." Exasperated now, Hannah grabbed the pillowcase and threw it back into the unironed basket. "It was nighttime. I was afraid, and I was excited to go. How do I see a license plate?"

Hannah's last words bordered on curt. Rachel was quiet again for a moment, giving Hannah time before she asked, "The man who helped you. You must have known him."

"I told you. No one meant for this to happen. It wasn't his fault. He took me to meet the woman. On the highway, in the diner parking lot. He said, 'This is Hannah. She's a good worker. Take care of her.' He didn't know that she would take us to the bad men."

"Where did she take you?"

"Harrisburg. We stopped at a gas station. The men were there in another blue van. The woman said that they were Mennonites and would take us to the church." She looked up and tears welled in her eyes. "They didn't do that." She rubbed at the tears with her fists. "The woman lied. The men who said they were Mennonites lied."

"Oh, Hannah, I'm so sorry. Please tell me what I can do for you." Rachel crossed to her and tried to put her arms around her, but the young woman pushed her away.

"You can't help me. Only being saved will help me. Once I'm baptized, it will be all right." She stared at the floor. "Everything will be all right, and I will never think about it again."

Two Saturdays later, in the evening, Hannah's father and mother, her bishop, and several of her church elders came to the B&B and climbed the stairs to the apartment, much to the delight of several of Rachel's guests. The visitors were all agog that *real Amish* were apparently staying at Stone Mill House. Rachel made no explanation. The less said the better, and the misunderstanding could only help her business.

It had been a long week for Rachel. Evan was clearly displeased with her because he knew she knew where Hannah was and wouldn't tell him. Twice she'd attempted to get together with him for lunch or dinner, and he'd had some last-minute excuse. To be fair, several of the troopers were out with a virus, and Evan was working a lot of overtime.

She'd also had no luck with extracting information from Hannah. In true Amish tradition, the young woman held to her word. Neither Mary Aaron's nor Rachel's own pleas swayed Hannah one iota from her stand. And thankfully, Ada and Hannah's family had kept her presence a secret so that Evan hadn't learned where she was staying and added to the problem.

Not three weeks from the time Rachel and Mary Aaron had whisked her away from her captors, the church community had come to a decision on what was to be done with Hannah. Rachel hoped for the best, but was afraid to be too hopeful. Mary Aaron had no such fears. She was positive that a solution would be found to bring Hannah back into the faith with the least amount of pain for anyone.

When the bishop and the others came downstairs an hour later, Rachel saw that Hannah was with them. They all filed through the house without a word and left by the kitchen door to climb into waiting buggies. Four of Rachel's guests rushed to the front windows to watch as horses and carriages clattered down the drive. Rachel only smiled, giving the impression, she hoped, that she knew exactly what had happened.

Tuesday afternoon was a scorcher, and Rachel was glad for the central air, which George had insisted she install for her guests. A couple with two children checked in, and there were the usual emails to answer and craft orders to fill. Rachel had gone out to the kitchen for a glass of lemonade when Ada reminded her that she'd promised to cut mint for iced tea. "We're nearly out, and I want to make fresh for supper," Ada said. "And you might take some ice water out to Joab. Lifting stone in this heat. Hard work. He must be parched."

"Do you think he'd like lemonade?" Rachel got the stoneware pitcher out of the oversized refrigerator.

"The man drinks water, nothing else." Ada plunged her hands into a bowl of bread dough. "A little stingy with his words, but a decent mason. Not afraid of work."

Ada had recommended Joab, and Rachel knew they weren't relatives. From Ada, this was high praise. "Uncle Aaron likes him better than his brother Eli, that's for certain," Rachel said. She poured a glass of lemonade and took a sip. Tart, just the way she liked it. She perched on a stool, finished her drink, and then went to the old pine cupboard for another glass.

"No need for one of my good glasses." Ada turned the

dough out onto her breadboard, floured her hands, and began to knead the mixture. "Only get broken outside. Use one of those quart Mason jars. He likes lots of ice."

Rachel sighed and did as she was instructed. It might be her house, but it was Ada's kitchen. She picked up a wicker basket and a pair of scissors, packed the blue glass jar with ice, and went back to the summer kitchen to fill it with cold spring water. As an afterthought, she scooped up a gingerbread cookie the size of her palm cooling on the stone shelf. "Even a man who drinks only water couldn't pass up Ada's gingerbread," she said to Sophie. The bichon frise looked dubious but trotted after her as they exited by the back door and crossed the yard.

The old gristmill stood at the back of the property beside the pond and the remains of the old millrace, the flow of water that had once turned the water wheel. Willow trees bent gracefully over the water, and a pair of ducks paddled in the water. Rachel could picture a wrought-iron table and chairs, ferns, and wildflowers here in the deep shade—if the project ever got done. The building was going to take a lot of repairs to be restored. Now, it was piles of cut stone, sagging doors, and endless expense.

As she approached the building, the mason came around the corner, an empty bucket in one hand. "I brought you some water," she said. "And a cookie."

"Not much for sweets." He took the Mason jar. "Grateful for the water, though. It's some hot for September, *ya?*" He tipped the container up and swallowed large gulps. "But autumn's coming. Like as not we'll soon be wishing it was warm instead of cold."

"How's the job coming?" She dropped the cookie into her basket, thinking she might have to eat it herself.

"Passable. Be done when it's done, not a day before."

Rachel walked around the gristmill to survey the ongoing work, complimented Joab on his fine craftsmanship, and then picked up her basket and went to the herb garden. The dog followed. She was cutting mint leaves in the herb garden when Mary Aaron appeared.

Sophie barked and leaped up and down as if she had springs in her legs as Mary Aaron pushed through the garden gate.

"Down," Mary Aaron ordered as the little dog launched itself at her.

"Behave yourself," Rachel chided. Sophie ignored them both. Rachel knew she should do something about the dog's behavior, but there never seemed time, and she was adorable.

Wisps of sweaty hair clung to Mary Aaron's forehead, and there were damp stains under the arms of her maroon work dress.

"Come on your scooter?" Rachel asked.

"*Ya,* better than walking in this heat. At least there's a little breeze."

A little, Rachel thought. *Maybe.* The hills between the Hostetler farm and the town were steep, and Rachel knew from experience that using the scooter, better known to her people as a push-bike, was good exercise and required far more physical energy than riding an ordinary bicycle. Conventional bikes were not permitted by the Old Order Amish in Stone Mill because they were considered too fast and worldly.

"Have you seen Hannah since she left here?" Rachel used kitchen shears to cut mint.

"No. I don't know *where* she is, but I know *how* she is. She's fine. Safe, content. Bishop Abner made the announcement at supper last night that he had spoken to Hannah's bishop. She made her confession before her elders yesterday morning and has been received back into the fold."

"She told them what happened to her?"

Mary Aaron spread her hands, palms up. "Not any particulars, I bet. More of a general confession. Sinners don't have to say *exactly* what they did wrong. Especially in a case like this." She glanced away.

Rachel dropped the mint into her basket. "You must be thirsty," she said. "You want something to drink?"

"In a bit." Mary Aaron sank onto the grass, removed one sneaker, and shook out a piece of gravel. "I thought there was something in there."

Rachel folded her arms and waited, one brow arched impatiently. She knew Mary Aaron. Her cousin had something to tell her, something important, and she was stalling just to tease her. "What else?" Rachel asked. "I know there's more."

Mary Aaron noticed the gingerbread cookie in the basket.

"Joab didn't want it. Go ahead."

Between bites, Mary Aaron said, "I am to tell you that Hannah's parents are thankful for what you did for her." She offered Rachel half.

Rachel accepted the treat and took a big bite. "What *we* did," she reminded her cousin, joining her in the grass. "I couldn't have done it alone." For an instant, memories of the muggy streets of the French Quarter flooded back, and a shiver ran down her spine. "You're the one who got out of that car and found her. You're the one who slammed the door in the creep's face."

Mary Aaron pushed the last of the cookie into her mouth and wiped the crumbs off her dress. "*Ya,* but for one of us to help our own, that's one thing." She shrugged. "They consider you English; that's different. They wanted me to thank you for them."

"I don't expect thanks any more than you do."

Mary Aaron put her shoe back on and tied the lace firmly. The sneakers were navy blue, unadorned with logos or piping. She pulled her knees up and pressed them to the ground so that her blue dress would modestly cover most of her legs. "And they wanted me to tell you that you're invited to Hannah's wedding supper on Thursday."

Rachel sat up a little straighter. "She's being *married* Thursday? *This* Thursday?"

"*Ya.*"

"But . . . but how is that possible?" Rachel stared at Mary Aaron. "She's only been home . . . How could they come up with a husband—a wedding—so fast?"

Mary Aaron plucked blades of grass and tossed it at her. "Do you think that Hannah is the first girl who ever had to be married in a rush?" She smiled slyly. "Remember Eva May's wedding to the Troyer boy last spring? There was no long engagement there."

"I do remember."

"The two had been making mischief, and Eva May was in the family way." Mary Aaron watched Sophie push a bit of cut grass with her nose. "Their marriage banns were read and they were bound all in the same week."

"Eva May was pregnant before they were married?" Rachel knew her jaw dropped. "But she's a preacher's daughter."

"The daughter of a preacher maybe, but still human. Which of us is perfect?" Mary Aaron frowned. "Not me. Not even the bishop, I suspect. We all have our own small sins, don't we? I think Eva May was foolish. But she admitted her mistake and was truly repentant. Should I point a finger of reproach at her now? It's much the same with Hannah."

"Hannah's pregnant?" Rachel blurted. The thought hadn't occurred to her. She'd suggested that Hannah see a physician, out of concern for her health, but she'd never considered that she could be pregnant.

"*Ne,* Hannah is not in the family way. She went to her doctor yesterday and had tests to be sure that all is well. I meant, like Eva May, she needed to be settled with a husband quickly." Mary Aaron's face turned serious, and she stood, brushing grass off her dress, then offering her hand to help Rachel to her feet. "You do think too much like them Englishers," she said. "Have you forgotten all you learned at your mother's knee? Hannah is no longer the same girl who had those bad things happen to her. She is made new in spirit.

If there had been a babe, would it be the fault of the *kind*. The baby would have been a gift from God, like every other child."

Rachel looked into her cousin's eyes as she stood. "It's a beautiful way of looking at it."

"It's our way," Mary Aaron reminded her gently. "The Amish way."

"Does she even know him? The husband-to-be? Is he from here?"

"*Ne,* from Wisconsin. He's a little older than she is, a widower with three children. Hannah's father will provide a good dowry. It's a good match for both of them."

Rachel couldn't wrap her head around it. "But if they're strangers . . . How can Hannah agree to marry a man she's never met? What if they hate each other?"

Mary Aaron put her arm around Rachel and gave her a quick hug. "You worry too much. Where is your faith? This is a good solution. Thomas will be pleased to have a young and devout wife, a mother for his children, and she will be happy to have her own home and a new beginning. All will be well. You will see."

"I suppose." She'd heard of arranged marriages among the Old Order people, but she'd never known someone who'd married without some sort of courtship. Rachel didn't know how she felt about the hasty marriage, but she was relieved to know that Hannah would be safe. If anyone from her old life was looking for her, he'd never find her. And neither would the police. The problem was, whatever Hannah knew would go with her. Rachel sighed. Another lead would end with a stone wall.

"Now, you're not to mention the wedding to Evan," Mary Aaron warned. "Hannah's mother asked me to make that clear."

Rachel hadn't thought about that but would have guessed that would be the case. She didn't like keeping information from Evan, but once again, this wasn't her business to share.

"Are you going to the wedding? Will you go with me?" Rachel picked up her basket. She had wanted to cut some basil, too, but she'd promised Mary Aaron something cold to drink. She'd come back for the rest of the herbs in the morning.

They started toward the house, with Sophie trailing behind them.

"Timothy and I have been asked to be part of the bridal party, so we'll be there all day," Mary Aaron said. "The Verklers have invited you to come for the evening wedding supper. It's being held at her uncle's house."

"Are you going to tell me where he lives, or do I have to drive around the county looking for a farm with a lot of buggies parked in the yard?"

Mary Aaron giggled. "Your *mam* said that you can go with them. The whole family is invited to the supper."

"You spoke to my mother?"

"*Ya.* She said they'll pick you up at six, and that you should dress English, but modest. What you wear for Plain is not so . . ." She giggled again. "Not so good."

"So I'm going to Hannah's wedding with my parents in their buggy?"

Mary Aaron grinned at her. "I hope so. I wouldn't want to have to go back to your *mam* and tell her that you refused to be seen with her."

Chapter 17

It was nearly seven in the evening when Rachel, wedged between her mother and her father in the front seat of the family buggy, arrived at the site of Hannah's wedding supper. It was still light, and the ride along the narrow country road—with the sound of buggy wheels, the familiar clip-clop of the horse's hooves on the road, and the whispers and giggling of her younger siblings—filled Rachel with happiness. It was good to sit close beside her *mam*, and even if her mother didn't actually speak directly to her, it was clear she was happy to have her eldest daughter with her. Rachel's *dat* seemed pleased to have her with them as well, and he humored her mother, passing information back and forth between her and her mother without losing his patience.

"Is a good match, Aaron tells me," her *mam* said as her *dat* reined the horse into a farm lane lined with buggies. "This Thomas Miller, he owns nearly five hundred acres and leases more in Wisconsin. Beef cattle he raises. And he has a house of logs and stone. Where it lies Aaron didn't know. Ask your daughter if she has heard."

"*Ne, Mam,*" Rachel said. "I didn't even know where the wedding supper was being held." Not that it was a big secret now—she could see at least a dozen cars and trucks, including Ed and Polly's delivery van and Hulda's black Volvo sedan.

By tradition, the wedding service and dinner began in late morning and continued on until midafternoon. That was usually attended only by the Amish, but the supper was much more informal and Englishers and a larger crowd of neighbors and friends were often invited.

Just behind them, in another buggy, came Rachel's brother Paul; his wife, Miriam; and their two children. Rachel's sister Sally had told her that their sister Annie and her husband, Benjamin, had stopped by earlier, and sister Lettie had chosen to ride with them. Rachel was looking forward to seeing all of her sisters and brothers and her niece and nephew.

"One of these days, maybe we'll be holding a wedding supper for you, *ne?*" her father teased. "Even if you pick an Englisher, we're still your family. You know I have a dowry saved for you."

Her mother stiffened and sniffed, clearly voicing her disapproval.

"Now, Esther," *Dat* soothed. "Didn't you say the same thing to me not a week past?"

"Three more girls to provide for, not to mention the boys. It's not much of a wedding we can provide for Englishers. And you can tell her that for me." Rachel's *dat*'s hands were firm on the reins, his eyes bright and kindly in his bearded face. Tonight, he'd worn his black felt, wide-brimmed hat and his *mutze,* the longer, more formal coat with the split tail, clothing usually reserved for worship services. Rachel thought he looked quite distinguished. For her own outfit, she'd chosen the same suit that she'd worn for Beth's funeral, which she supposed met her mother's standards because she hadn't complained.

"God will provide, Esther," her father reproved gently. "And when Rachel marries, whoever she chooses, we will do no less for her than each of the others."

"Did I say we wouldn't?" Her mother's tone was meek, but she smoothed imaginary wrinkles out of her immaculately ironed navy skirt with a vengeance. "I love my children equally, but the only true marriage is one in our church."

Her father guided the horse into an open spot between two other buggies and turned to give instructions to the younger children. "You may go and seek out your friends, but do not stray from the supper area, and heed your mother should she need anything. And if your actions are any less than they should be, the next time, you'll remain home with enough chores to keep you busy until long past dark."

He got down out of the buggy and opened the back door, holding it wide so that Rachel's brothers and sisters could scramble out. Then he came around to assist her mother. It was an act that never failed to touch Rachel. Helping his wife in and out of a buggy was one of the few times that they ever touched each other in public, but it was obvious to any who witnessed the act that they were devoted to each other.

Will anyone ever love me like that? Rachel wondered. *I hope so.*

"We'll leave at ten sharp," her father said to Rachel. "If you'd like a ride home, be here promptly. If you aren't here, we'll assume you've found other young people to take you."

Her mother turned a soft cheek for Rachel to kiss, nodded, and walked away in search of her own friends. Rachel's father smiled and shrugged. "You two are like a pair of banty hens," he said, "all ruffled feathers."

Rachel chuckled. "I suppose we are," she agreed. "But *Mam* was born a Hostetler, and they're not known for accepting change easy."

"I like to think of it as a trait of . . . consistency," he said, and his eyes lit with mischief. "I was warned about her stubbornness before I took her to wife. Thankfully, I didn't listen to that good advice. If any team was well matched for a long pull in harness, it's the two of us."

"I'll be here on time if I need a ride home," she promised. "I'm so glad I came with you."

Eli Rust came around the row of buggies and called out to

her father. Her *dat* strode off to join his friend. From every direction came the sounds of Deitsch conversation, calls of greetings, and easy laughter. Even an observer who didn't speak the German dialect would have recognized, at once, the difference between this gathering and the somber one that had been Beth Glick's wake.

Rachel walked toward the house. It was a small, circa-1940s bungalow, but the size of the dining area was of no concern this evening because supper was being served outside. As with communal Sabbath dinners, long tables had been erected with benches on either side. The tables were already laden with bowls of fried chicken and duck, roast turkey, chicken and dumplings, spare ribs, sausages, potato, macaroni and gelatin salads, platters of sliced onions and tomatoes, cooked carrots, lima beans, and applesauce. Young boys walked up and down the outside of the tables with fly whisks, chasing insects away from the food, while teenage girls filled glasses with water.

An array of carefree children, dressed as miniature adults, ran and played, tugged at their parents' hands, or rode high on a father or older brother's shoulders. Not a single youngster whined or cried, fought over a toy, or acted out. Although Rachel hated to make comparisons between English babies and Amish-raised, there was no doubt that the more rigid style of parenting seemed to produce happier and less-demanding children.

Tubs full of ice standing under the trees held pitchers of lemonade and bottles of soda pop; all, Rachel suspected, had been donated by Polly and Ed. The Amish were their best customers at the grocery store because they rarely left the valley to shop. The Waglers appreciated their patronage and never failed to show their gratitude by donating food for Amish celebrations.

There had to be more than a hundred people of all ages gathered there to honor the bride and groom. Groups of bearded men stood around, talking crops and livestock and telling jokes. In other areas of the yard, women traded recipes, gave or asked for advice on child rearing, and shared news of illnesses, coming betrothals, and visits from distant relatives.

It was custom for the sexes in Amish gatherings to socialize separately. When it came to sitting down to partake of the meal, the women might wait for a second seating or they might sit at another section of the table. It wasn't that Amish women were considered inferior to the men; interaction wasn't forbidden, but conversations naturally tended to cater to one sex or the other. Most men would have felt awkward amid a covey of females, and women preferred the easy give-and-take of their own kind.

The only exceptions to this unwritten code were courting couples, and young people seeking boyfriends or girlfriends. Weddings and other celebrations were one of the few places where teenagers and unmarried adults could meet possible marriage partners and were much anticipated. Rachel noticed her sister Lettie deep in conversation with a cousin; both girls were pretending not to watch the young men unloading benches from the bench wagon and carrying them to the tables. The two might be too young to think of marriage, but they weren't too young to survey and critique the available candidates.

Across the yard, a couple came down the back steps of the house. Rachel recognized Hannah, even though her white prayer *kapp* and blue dress were identical to many of the young women present; brides didn't wear special wedding dresses. Walking beside her was a short-statured, average-looking man of perhaps forty years of age. The stocky bridegroom, for Rachel assumed that this must be the mysterious Thomas, was shadowed by a chubby little boy, while Hannah held tightly to the hand of a slightly older girl. To Rachel's surprise, Hannah was smiling at her new husband, more animated and engaged than Rachel had seen her since their rendezvous in New Orleans. And Thomas, in turn, seemed equally absorbed with his new bride.

Rachel glanced around in hopes of seeing Mary Aaron, but her cousin was nowhere in sight. If the groom was from Wisconsin, Hannah would be traveling there soon; if any information was to be gained from Hannah, Rachel knew they were running out of time. Thinking that Mary Aaron might be inside helping with the food, Rachel started toward the house. She had gone only a few feet when she was waylaid by the Waglers.

"Rachel! I thought that was you," Polly exclaimed. "Have you met the groom? Such a nice man. Well spoken. Seems devoted to his children. There's a third, I understand. Too young to make the journey. Stayed with grandparents." She waved her hand, expansively taking in the guests and the tables laden with food. "Can you imagine? Putting this wedding together in so short a time!"

"It is impressive," Rachel agreed.

"As many years as I've lived among the Amish, I've never ceased to be amazed at their ways," Polly continued. "Good people, though. Salt of the earth. But hard to figure out. Why do you suppose Hannah is marrying so quickly after her return?"

"I don't know." Rachel offered a quick smile, glancing at Ed, who seemed eager to escape. His gaze kept wandering to a group of Englisher business owners. Polly was a talker. Rachel imagined celebrations like this gave him the opportunity to escape his wife's chatter. "Hard to say."

"Right. Who knows what young people will do today?" Polly exclaimed. "Maybe she met him while she was away, working out there."

Rachel knew that was the rumor being passed around for the benefit of those who didn't know the truth about Hannah's time away. An untruth, perhaps, but one that would shelter the community from scandal.

Polly beamed. "But Hannah does make a lovely bride, doesn't she? Ed was just saying so, weren't you, Ed?"

The Waglers had dressed for the occasion. Ed was wearing a Hawaiian shirt with a green, white, and orange leaf pattern, buttoned up and worn with a navy tie, while Polly might have been a candidate for admission to a convent in her midcalf-length, long-sleeve, black knit dress, white Peter Pan collar, and Mary Jane shoes. Her purse, Rachel noted, was a black leather designer clutch. Expensive. Rachel knew Ed liked to play cards for money and traveled to Atlantic City once a month. Or so Hulda had told her.

"She does, doesn't she?" Ed agreed, nodding at Polly, then glancing in the direction of the knot of men again.

The Waglers always agreed. At least, Ed always seemed supportive of his wife's opinions. While Ed was almost always in a cheerful mood, Polly could be plainspoken at times. In truth, it seemed to Rachel that Polly, who some thought was a little ditzy, was the brains behind the successful Wagler grocery enterprise. And Rachel had no doubt that Ed held his wife in high regard.

Polly looked to Ed. "We're boring you with women's talk, aren't we? So on with you then." She made a shooing gesture. "I'll find you later."

"Good to see you, Rachel," Ed said and quickly slipped away.

"I meant to call you today. I did get in a case of that organic wheat flour you were asking for," Polly told Rachel. "I have to warn you that it's pricey. So much so that I doubt I'll find many other customers for it."

"That's fine," Rachel assured her. "Organics are more expensive, but my guests appreciate healthy food. I'll come by and pick up the order tomorrow."

"No such thing." Polly tucked her pricey handbag under her arm. "I'll have Ed deliver it. That's what we bought that van for. A customer as good as you are, no need for you to come in. Anything else you want, just call first thing. I'll send it over with Ed tomorrow.

"Oh, look." Polly pointed. "That wooden butter churn on the steps. I see people putting envelopes in that hole in the top." She looked up at Rachel. "I better get that envelope from Ed before we forget it."

Mary Aaron had warned Rachel that due to the distance the bride and groom would have to travel to get back to their home, guests were bringing money instead of the usual gifts. It seemed a sensible solution to Rachel, especially since Thomas might already have most of what they would need to set up housekeeping. She passed Polly her envelope and took the opportunity to escape because she'd just seen the groom step away to speak with Bishop Abner and Hannah was standing alone.

Knowing that this might be her last opportunity to learn anything from her, Rachel approached her. When Hannah saw her walking toward her, she smiled and hurried forward, hands extended. "Rachel! I was afraid I'd miss you."

Rachel took Hannah's hands in hers and looked into her eyes. Hannah gazed back with such an open expression that Rachel thought, *Maybe she will be all right.* "Are you certain this is what you want?" she asked. "Will Thomas be good to you?"

"He is my husband," Hannah answered. "He needs me, and I need him." Her lower lip trembled slightly. "He knows the truth, and he accepts it as it is—something that happened in the past. We will not let the bad things keep us from making a good life."

"I'm glad. I was so afraid for you," Rachel admitted. "Afraid maybe you'd been coerced into this marriage."

"I am a practical woman," Hannah said. "It is better for me and those I love if I am far from Stone Mill. Our faith will sustain me . . . sustain my new family."

Two young Amish women were making their way to a table where the desserts were being put out. Each carried a huge tray covered with paper plates with slices of pies and cakes. The girl with the glasses flashed a quick, shy smile at Hannah as they passed.

"My sister Lorna," Hannah explained. "And our cousin Vi."

Rachel remembered Vi from the young people's singing she and Mary Aaron had attended. She was cute and plump, with freckles on her turned-up nose and bright blue eyes. The sister, Lorna, Rachel didn't recognize. She was a thin girl in her late teens with acne and glasses. In contrast to Vi's laughing countenance, Lorna seemed timid, even sullen.

Rachel waited to speak again until the girls were busy unloading their trays. "Hannah, I'm sorry to keep harping on this, but it's really, really important that you tell me who gave you a ride out of Stone Mill the night you left."

Hannah put her hands together, threading her fingers. She gazed at the grass at her feet.

"If you tell me who it was, maybe I can figure out how what happened to you happened. How you got there," she said, trying to be cryptic because, as the sister and cousin set out desserts, people were coming to get them.

"Please, Hannah," she whispered desperately. "I ask only because of what happened to Beth."

"I pray for her soul every day," Hannah answered. "I can do no more."

Rachel wanted to grab the young woman by the shoulders and shake her, but the sister glanced over her shoulder at them. Rachel took a step closer. "Is there nothing else you can tell me, Hannah?" she whispered.

"None of that matters now because I have closed that door. Nothing can make me open it again." She lifted her gaze to meet Rachel's. "No one can make me speak of it again." She reached out and squeezed Rachel's hand. "Thank you for being my friend. For helping me when I needed it. I won't forget you." She let go of Rachel then and walked away, calling to someone.

Rachel stared after Hannah, a little shocked that she'd not

been able to get any more information out of her, certain this had been her last chance. She was surprised by the tears that stung her eyes. She turned away from the festivities, seeking some quiet spot to be alone, suddenly afraid that the horror of Beth Glick's death would fade into legend and no one would ever find out who killed her or why.

Chapter 18

"Rachel!"

Rachel turned to see her sister Annie standing with hands on her ample hips and staring at her. "Mary Aaron said she saw you walking this way." Smiling, she came forward to give her a hug. "Didn't you bring that handsome young man with you?"

Annie liked Evan. She never mentioned that he wasn't Amish, and she never ceased trying to find out if their relationship was going to lead to marriage. Happily married herself, Annie was determined to find a husband for her older sister and all of her unmarried girlfriends.

Rachel returned the affectionate embrace. "He's working. I was hoping to see you. Is Ben here? I haven't seen him."

"I've been on kitchen duty." Annie hooked her thumb in the direction of the house. "Ben went to the wedding with me this morning, but we've got a mare in labor. You know my husband and his livestock." Annie rolled her eyes. "Sometimes, I think he loves them horses more than me."

"I doubt that." Rachel was genuinely pleased to see her. No matter how down in spirits anyone might be, Annie could always lift them. She was the most like their *dat* in her easygoing personality. Rachel patted her sister's belly. "You're starting to show."

"*Ya,* I am." Annie grinned. After two years of marriage,

she and Ben were expecting their first child in January. "*Grossmama* says, carried high like this, it's bound to be a little woodcutter."

Rachel couldn't suppress a smile. "*Grossmama* says *every* pregnant woman's having a boy. And she's right half the time. It's what most parents want to hear, isn't it?"

"Not my Ben. He says he'd welcome a girl just as much as a boy. You know he hopes for a big family. His mother had fourteen. She says she never would have managed if her first two hadn't been girls. They're so much help with the younger children."

"That would be your practical Ben." She squeezed Annie's hand. "Better you than me. I can't imagine having fourteen children."

"Whatever God sends us. *Mam* had nine. Can you imagine not having Levi or Sally? He has a plan for us, Rachel, and we only find true happiness if we can accept His plan."

Rachel smiled but didn't respond. This belief in God's plan was the Amish way, a way that they had lived by for hundreds of years. So why hadn't she bought into it the way everyone else had? Did she lack faith? She wondered if Annie ever had doubts, but that was too personal a question to ask, even of a beloved sister. Annie certainly seemed content with her life.

"I miss you," Rachel said instead. "We never seem to find time to visit."

"I know. I'm sorry. It's my fault." Annie wiped her hands on her apron, though they weren't wet. "I was busy *before* Ben's grandfather had the stroke. Now, I'm trying to help Ben's mother and sisters care for him *and* keep up with my housework and quilting. I can't believe you sold another quilt off that website. What you're doing for us, for the whole community, you can't know how much it means to us."

"Your work is so beautiful," Rachel told her, uncomfortable with the praise. "All I have to do is put up the pictures, and the customers find me. How's Ben's grandfather doing?"

Annie shrugged her broad shoulders. "He wanders sometimes, but he's such a sweet person, always laughing. He still weaves willow market baskets on his good days. You'd never know he's ninety."

It was like Annie to make light of caring for the elderly man. Among the Amish, seniors were venerated and never placed in nursing homes, no matter how severe their health problems or dementia. Joe Lapp's escapades were legendary. Evan had told her that a state trooper had once picked him up rolling down the highway in his wheelchair, more than five miles from his daughter's farm.

"I came out for a breath of air, but I should get back inside. We could use your help in the kitchen. It's almost time for the women's sitting. Unless you're hungry . . ."

Rachel tucked her arm into her sister's. "I'll wash if you'll dry."

"Deal."

Arm in arm, they walked together toward the house. "You know, *Mam*'s worried about you," Annie confided.

"Anything in particular this week? Or just general concern for my soul?"

"She's worried that you'll never marry and give her grandchildren." Annie paused. "She knows you and Evan have been seeing each other almost a year."

Rachel hesitated, not sure if she wanted to talk about this. "He wants to court me."

"But you don't want him to?"

Rachel glanced at her sister. "I don't know what I want."

"He's a good man."

"He is, and he's a dear friend. I don't know if I'm ready for more than that, though. If what I feel for Evan is love."

"*Mam* says first comes respect, then marriage. Love will follow." Annie beamed, and when she smiled like that, she was beautiful, in Rachel's eyes. "But with Ben, I knew. Even before he knew. I set my *kapp* for him, and he never had a chance." Annie patted the place over her heart. "In here, I felt it, like I couldn't breathe when he was near me."

"Sounds painful," Rachel teased, and they laughed together. What was wrong with her that she couldn't make up her mind? Was it what she'd told Evan—that her worry about finding Beth's killer didn't leave room for anything else? Or was it something more? She cared more about Evan than any other man she'd ever met . . . but did she want to *marry* him?

Amanda, her fifteen-year-old sister, came out the back door, a basket of rolls in her arms. "*Mam* wanted to know where you were," she warned Annie. "Dirty dishes piling up."

"We're on our way," Rachel said.

They met with their mother as they walked into the kitchen. She handed an apron to Annie. "Tell your sister she will ruin her fancy clothes."

Trying to keep a straight face, Annie repeated what their mother had said.

Rachel took the apron from Annie. *"Danke."*

"Tell her that we are glad of her help." Their *mam*'s voice grew tender. "And we're thankful that she is safe here with her family this night." Picking up a bowl of macaroni salad nearly the size of a wagon wheel, she balanced the weight on one hip and carried it past them and out the kitchen door.

"The dishes." Annie gestured toward the overflowing sink. They exchanged meaningful glances and chuckled, sharing the bittersweet humor of their mother's expression of her love. "I think *Mam*'s softening," Annie teased.

"*Ya,*" Rachel agreed. "Another fifteen years and she'll be referring to me as 'that foolish Rachel' instead of just 'she.' "

The other women laughed. Rachel tied the apron around her waist and began to wash dishes. Soon, caught up in the laughter and friendly talk of a half dozen other young women, she found herself not just content but happy to join in the work. Odd as she might be, she was still one of them.

Later, other women who'd already eaten came into the

kitchen to take their turn at the sink, and Rachel and Annie followed the cleanup crew out to the long table. The food was every bit as good as she'd thought it would be. She stuffed herself, then agonized over the choice of dessert. Hannah's mother's Moravian hickory nut cake or a wedge of *apfelstrudel* with whipped cream? She'd just opted for the cake and sat down again when Mary Aaron's Timothy came up behind her and tapped her on the shoulder. She glanced up at him.

"She wants you to come," he said under his breath. "Around the back of the house. There's a cellar-way door."

"Mary Aaron?"

"*Schnell.*"

Rachel stood, handed Timothy her slice of nut cake, and threaded her way through the milling women and children. It was fully dark, and although the eating area was well lit by lanterns, she had to rely on moonlight to make her way around the house. The dwelling wasn't large, so it was easy to find the open cellar door and the cement steps leading down to the basement. As Rachel put her hand on the railing, a shadowy figure appeared at the bottom of the stairs.

Rachel nearly jumped out of her skin. "Mary Aaron?"

"*Ya.*"

"You scared me."

"Watch the steps," she warned. "They're steep."

As Rachel joined Mary Aaron in the cool cellar, she became instantly aware of the sound of someone crying. "Hannah?" she whispered.

"*Ne,* her sister Lorna." Mary Aaron caught Rachel's hand and led her deeper into the cellar. "She's really upset, but she said I could bring you. Tread carefully. Let me ask the questions."

"What's going on?"

"Shh." Mary Aaron raised her voice. "Lorna. I'm back . . . with Rachel."

Mary Aaron led her across the packed dirt floor. Ahead, Rachel saw a gleam of yellow light through the cracks of a black barrier. They rounded a corner, and Rachel saw Lorna standing in the middle of a pantry, weeping. A kerosene lantern hung from a peg in a ceiling beam. The yellow light illuminated tall wooden shelves stacked with jars of home-canned peaches, green beans, corn, and tomatoes. Along one wall hung slabs of smoked bacon and strings of dried onions. The low-ceilinged room was heavy with the smells of curing sauerkraut and dust.

Mary Aaron went to Lorna and put her arms around the girl. Lorna buried her face in Mary Aaron's shoulder.

"It's all right," Mary Aaron soothed, patting Lorna's back. "It will be all right. Tell Rachel what you told me. It's important, Lorna."

"I'm afraid." Lorna's voice was muffled by Mary Aaron's hug.

"That's okay. It's okay to be afraid."

Lorna sniffed loudly, and turned her teary face in Rachel's direction. Rachel wished that she could see her more clearly, but the darkness in the cellar seemed to suck up the flickering light from the lantern.

"Tell Rachel why you're so upset," Mary Aaron urged, taking a step away from the girl.

Lorna shook her head. "I shouldn't have come to you. It was wrong."

"No," Mary Aaron insisted. "It was the right thing to do. And very brave."

Rachel waited.

"My cousin," Lorna whispered, taking off her glasses to wipe beneath her eyes.

Rachel's gaze went to Mary Aaron, then back to the girl.

"I don't know what . . . what exactly happened to my sister when she was gone," Lorna said in a thin, hesitant voice. "I know it was bad. *Mam* and *Dat,* they kept whispering, and *Mam* cried and cried. She never cries, my mother, but she cried more than I saw her all the time Hannah was lost to us. Three times the bishop came, and once all the elders were with him. Every time, they would shut themselves into the small parlor. They told me to take the children up to bed, even though it was too early for them to sleep." She slid her glasses back on. "Maybe I shouldn't say any more. I don't want anyone to get into any trouble."

"*Ne.*" Mary Aaron shook her head. "You coming to me could keep her safe." She glanced at Rachel. "Lorna overheard you talking to Hannah a little while ago and got scared." She looked at Lorna again. "Tell her about your cousin."

"I think I should go back. My aunt sent me for peaches, but I . . ." Tears began to run down her cheeks again. "I'm so worried about Vi."

"Tell her why you're worried," Mary Aaron prompted.

Lorna clasped her hands and began to wring them. "She's leaving. Vi. She's going away like Hannah did."

Rachel had to bite down on her lip to keep from peppering Lorna with questions. But the girl was already skittish. She didn't want to scare her.

"Whatever it is that happened to Hannah," Lorna went on, "it must have been bad or *Dat* wouldn't have found her a husband so fast. She wouldn't be leaving for Wisconsin. You wouldn't have spoken to her the way you did." She looked at Rachel, then down at her feet. "I'm sorry. I shouldn't have been listening in, but . . . Now I don't know what to do. I don't want anything bad to happen to Vi."

"You're right to be worried," Mary Aaron said gently. "Hannah came back to us. Beth Glick didn't."

"I don't know anything about Beth." The girl opened her arms and let them fall to her sides. "I don't even know what happened to my sister. I just . . ." She exhaled a shaky breath. "Vi has always been my special friend," Lorna explained. "I couldn't bear it if something awful happened to Vi, too. I tried to talk to her before Hannah came back. Now—" There were more tears. "I don't know what to do. Vi's already talked to someone. Vi's already made plans to go."

"Talked to whom?" Rachel asked.

"Rachel," Mary Aaron warned softly.

But Rachel couldn't keep quiet any longer. She stepped directly in front of Lorna. "Do you know who it is? Is it a stranger or someone Vi knows? Is it the same person who helped your sister?"

"I think . . . maybe it is."

Rachel grasped Lorna by the shoulders. "You have to tell me who."

Lorna hung her head. "A man," she murmured. "I don't know who. Vi wouldn't say." She looked up at Rachel, her eyes tearing up again. "But I think . . . I think it is someone from here. Somebody who helps kids get away." Her last words were only a whisper.

Rachel looked at Mary Aaron. "We've got to talk to Vi. Tonight. Now. She could lead us to Beth's killer." She turned eagerly to Lorna. "Could you get Vi to come down here?"

"Ne!" Lorna shrank back. "She wouldn't talk to you. She'd think I betrayed her trust. She'd be so angry with me for telling that she won't listen to me either."

"She's right, Rachel," Mary Aaron said, grabbing Rachel's arm. "If we confront Vi, she might tell the person who's helping the kids get away. And he might be right here at this wedding supper tonight."

"So what do we do?" Rachel whispered.

"I have an idea."

The following morning, Rachel and Mary Aaron met at Wagler's Grocery, where they had arranged to meet Lorna, at ten o'clock. When they didn't see the Verkler buggy, Rachel went inside and bought coffee and doughnuts. Ed and Polly had erected hitching posts for their Amish customers to tie their horses when they came to shop, and nearby, in what had once been a vacant lot between Wagler's and the newspaper office, there was a maple tree, a well-tended flower bed, and three picnic tables. In good weather, families often lunched on sandwiches and drinks that they purchased in the store. Mary Aaron waited at one of the picnic tables.

Friday was the day that many of the Amish did their shopping, so the store was busy, with buggies coming and going. Lorna and Hannah's parents didn't care to do their shopping in town among the Englishers, so the chore often fell to Lorna, making it a good place to meet. "I can meet you there without causing anyone to notice," Lorna had said when they'd parted after the conversation in the cellar the previous night. They'd asked her to bring Vi with her, and she'd promised to do so.

A buggy was just driving out of the parking lot when Rachel, carrying a bag of doughnuts and a cardboard tray of coffee, joined Mary Aaron. "Any sign of her?" she asked, setting down the coffee so she could wave to Naamah Chupp, driving the buggy.

"No, but she'll be here. I just hope she was able to get her cousin to come with her," Mary Aaron said. "If Vi would talk to us directly, it might make all the difference."

The coffee was inexpensive, hot, and strong. The cups were a generous size, and the doughnuts were excellent. Not homemade, but close to it, and delivered daily. The Waglers might be small-time with only one grocery, but they clearly went out of their way to treat their customers well. Ed had been one of the first business owners in town to support Rachel's idea of developing Stone Mill for ecotourism, and she appreciated it so much that she purchased as many of her supplies through Wagler's as she could, even if she could have saved money by shopping with the larger out-of-town chains.

Fifteen minutes passed. Rachel watched the street and tapped her foot nervously against the table support. She was seriously considering eating a second doughnut. "We should have tried to find Vi last night," she said. She eyed the doughnut bag.

"*Ne*. We did the right thing, sending Lorna to talk to her."

Mary Aaron licked her fingertip and touched some cinnamon sugar on her napkin. She licked her finger again. "We didn't have any other choice. We can't force people to talk. You have to know that by now."

"You're right. I know you're right." Rachel tucked a wisp of hair behind her ear. "But suppose Vi—"

"I think that's Lorna coming now," Mary Aaron interrupted. "That's the Verkler buggy. I recognize the bay with the blaze."

Rachel glanced toward the driveway. There were definitely two women in the buggy. Rachel tried to contain her rising excitement.

Lorna drove the horse across the parking lot to the water trough. She climbed down off the seat and loosened a strap on the harness so that the bay gelding could lower his head to drink. Someone got down on the far side of the buggy.

"That girl's too young to be Vi," Mary Aaron said quietly. "I think it's a younger sister."

"You go on inside and start filling the cart," Lorna said to her companion. "I'll be there as soon as I water Jack and tie him up." She handed the girl a small coin purse. "You can get yourself a soda pop and some candy, if you want." As soon as she was gone, Lorna motioned to Rachel and Mary Aaron, who hurried over, leaving the coffee and doughnuts behind.

"Where's Vi?" Rachel asked in Deitsch. "I thought you said you could get her to come with you."

Lorna looked embarrassed. In the daylight, Rachel saw a strong resemblance to Hannah. Lorna was a pretty girl in a wholesome way. And now that she wasn't weeping, she had an honest and pleasing face.

"You're not going to believe this. She's gone," Lorna said, adjusting her glasses.

"Gone?" Mary Aaron demanded. "You mean she still ran away, even after you told her how dangerous it might be?"

An extended-cab pickup truck pulled in to a parking place,

and one of Hulda's nieces got out and removed a baby from an infant car seat in the back. She waved and called, "Hello."

Rachel returned her greeting, and the young mother and her child went into the grocery.

"*Ne*," Lorna said with a shake of her head. "Well, she *did* run away, I guess, but not like Hannah. She went *with* Hannah this morning."

"With Hannah?" Rachel echoed. "I don't understand. How did she go with Hannah?"

"After I left you, I found my mother and told her I wanted to spend the night with Vi. Since we had so many relatives at our place and Vi lives just next door, *Mam* didn't mind."

The horse raised his head, snorted, and shook drops of water over Rachel's capris. Lorna took hold of the bridle and led the animal to the nearest hitching post. Rachel and Mary Aaron walked with her.

"I did just what you said," Lorna said quietly. She tied the horse to a large iron ring. "All night I talked to her, told her what you said, told her that something bad happened to our Hannah when she was gone and it might happen to her. I told her that whoever pretended to be her friend out there might be evil. And I asked how she knew that she could trust the man she was supposed to meet."

Rachel pointed to the picnic table where she and Mary Aaron had been sitting together, and the three of them walked over. Lorna continued to speak. "First, Vi argued with me. She said nothing bad happened to Hannah. That Hannah had just come home because she didn't like the Englishers and that I was making it all up. But then I think she got scared when she started thinking about it. I think she realized Hannah's wedding *was* a little quick. And she'd noticed the bishop and elders coming and going a lot. Her living right next door to us."

Rachel was trying to take in everything Lorna was saying. "So you spent the night with Vi. How did she end up going with Hannah?"

"My mother helped. Vi and I went to her, and I told her that Vi didn't want to stay here." Lorna peered at Rachel, who was sitting across from her, through her glasses. "I didn't come right out and say it, but *Mam* realized that Vi was thinking about leaving. She was the one who came up with the idea that Vi go with Hannah. She told her it would be good for her and good for Hannah. To help her cousin get settled in her new life. And who knows, she might meet a suitable man up there to marry. Then the cousins would be close and Hannah wouldn't be so lonely."

"Vi's parents let her go, just like that?" Mary Aaron leaned close. "So quick a decision?"

"My aunt, she knows how Vi is. I think, for some time, she and my uncle have been afraid Vi would run away. Better she goes with Hannah than be lost to the world."

Rachel looked away. She was, of course, happy that Vi would be safe, but she knew there would be no talking to the young woman now. She was gone. And so was Rachel's possible lead. She was beginning to feel like a complete failure. She looked at Lorna and reached across the table to squeeze her hand. "You did a brave thing, Lorna. You might have saved Vi's life."

Lorna's thin mouth quivered. "Now both Hannah and Vi are gone. Hannah is my sister and I care for her, but Vi was my special friend. I kept her from going to the English, but she went away anyway."

"Did you ask her who she was meeting?" Rachel asked. "Who was going to help her?"

Lorna shook her head sadly. "I did ask her, but she wouldn't tell me. I'm sorry I wasn't more help."

Mary Aaron put her arm around the girl's shoulders. "You kept Vi safe. That's what matters most."

"But what about Beth? We still don't know what happened to her."

"The police will figure it out," Rachel said, trying to sound convincing. She reached for the bag of doughnuts. She was definitely having another.

"I have to go." Lorna got up from the table. "My sister will be looking for me." She started to turn away, then looked back at Rachel and Mary Aaron. "One thing I did find out. I don't know if it will help you or not, but maybe. Vi wouldn't say who was going to help her leave Stone Mill." She pressed her thin lips together. "But she said it was going to be this weekend."

Chapter 19

Mary Aaron sat down in Rachel's recliner. The two had come upstairs to escape the heat of the morning and to be alone to discuss and think through what they'd learned from Lorna. There was no central air on the third floor, but a room air conditioner in one of the windows hummed, blowing icy air into the room. "It might be worth turning English," Mary Aaron teased, "if I could sleep so cool in the summer."

Rachel chuckled. "It's probably the last modern invention I'd be willing to part with, but I don't know that it's worth changing your life for."

Rachel had set up a place to read with good light, a coffee table, and a bookcase. She had a desk to do paperwork and a white dry-erase board mounted on the wall for planning. When finances permitted, she hoped to finish the small kitchen area, making her suite an efficiency apartment. For now, a microwave and a stainless steel electric teakettle on an old table and a dorm-sized mini fridge served her needs. As much as she loved welcoming guests to Stone Mill House, it was always nice to have a private retreat.

"Hot or cold tea?" Rachel asked her cousin, switching to English. They usually spoke English at Stone Mill House. She wasn't sure why. It had just become an unwritten rule. She used Deitsch at Mary Aaron's, and they used English in her own territory. "I think I have a Mason jar of sweet tea I brought up yesterday." She lifted one shoulder and let it fall. "It's not fresh from this morning, but it's probably not bad."

"Hot tea, I think. I know, in weather like this, I'm not supposed to want hot tea, but I feel like I need a cup. Always helps me think."

"Me, too." Rachel carried the kettle to her bathroom, filled it up with water from the faucet in the claw-foot tub, and returned it to the table. She flipped it on and retrieved two clean mugs from atop the microwave. She dug into a little willow basket her sister had made her and held up a couple of tea bags. "I've got Assam, Irish breakfast, and . . . herbal mint."

"Irish breakfast." Mary Aaron picked up a restoration magazine off the table beside the chair and began to flip through the pages. "I can't believe Vi took off like that."

"I can't believe her parents saw the wisdom of letting her go."

"Thank God," Mary Aaron murmured, looking over the top of the magazine. "I know it doesn't help us to track down whoever killed Beth, but at least Vi is safe."

Rachel stood there, a tea bag in each hand. "So Vi's safe. She won't be getting into someone's van this weekend, but what if there was another girl last night at the wedding supper planning the very same thing?"

Mary Aaron nibbled her lower lip and studied a hangnail. "Usually, only one girl a year leaves, sometimes no one. After what happened to Beth, I can't imagine anyone will dare go any time soon. They've got to be scared."

"Not scared enough, apparently. If Lorna hadn't been brave enough to speak up to her cousin, Vi would have gone." The teakettle began to rattle as it heated to boiling. "Do you think Vi told the person who was supposed to pick her up that she wasn't coming?"

Mary Aaron shook her head slowly, returning the magazine to the end table. "I don't see how. Lorna spent last night with Vi. Lorna said she didn't convince Vi not to leave until after they were back at the Verklers'. And then Vi left with Hannah and Thomas before daylight."

"Right." Rachel nodded. Her thoughts were flying all over the place, from here to there, not settling on one single thing. She had to think about this logically. There had to be a way to catch the man who was supposed to give Vi a ride out of town. And that man, she had a feeling, was the same man who had helped Beth leave Stone Mill. She knew she couldn't immediately jump to the conclusion that he was the one who had killed Beth when she tried to come home, but it was certainly a possibility. A possibility that she felt was becoming more likely every day. She knew she didn't have any proof, but she'd always had good intuition, and from the beginning, her intuition had led her down this path. Yet that didn't make sense, not if the contact was Amish. She'd never heard of any Old Order Amish who'd committed murder.

Rachel opened a tea bag packet and dropped the bag into a white mug that said *The George*. On the other side was a picture of a book and below it, *Read Fast, Life Is Short*. "So . . . as far as we know," she said, thinking out loud, "this man who was helping Vi still thinks he's picking her up."

"I suppose. Unless someone who knows that Vi's left told him she was gone."

"There's that possibility," Rachel said slowly. "But I doubt Vi's parents will be broadcasting the fact that they had to send their daughter to Wisconsin to keep her from running away to be English. It'll take a few days for word to get around, especially to the men in the community. Every woman in Stone Mill will know before any man except Vi's father." The kettle whistled, and the automatic switch clicked to turn it off.

"Okay, so let's say this man is expecting to pick up Vi." Mary Aaron kicked off her blue sneakers and tucked her feet up under her. Wrinkles creased her forehead as she considered the puzzle. "You know, none of this fits. You said somebody said that an Amish man was making arrangements for these kids to get away. Hannah talked about a van. No Amish man owns a van."

"Wasn't that the woman who took them to the phony Mennonites who had the van? Or did Hannah mention two vans? I should have written that down. I'm not sure." Rachel dropped her Assam tea bag into a green Wagler's Grocery mug. "Maybe the Amish man borrowed one?"

"Maybe." But Mary Aaron sounded unconvinced.

Rachel poured water into one mug and then the other and then set the teakettle back on the table. She walked over to the wall, erased a to-do list on the white dry-erase board, and picked up a blue marker. "Okay, what do we know?"

"We know a man helped Hannah leave, and a man was going to help Vi."

"Right." Rachel drew a big stick figure of a man.

"And your source—and I still can't believe you won't tell me who it is—said it was an Amish man."

Rachel added a long, pointy beard and a stovepipe-type hat. She had zero artistic ability, but it was good enough for both of them to know what it was. "We know, from Lorna," she said, speaking slowly as she thought her way through the facts, "that Vi was leaving this weekend."

"Which means tonight, tomorrow night, or Sunday night?" Mary Aaron said. "And we know Hannah said he drove a van," she added quickly.

Rachel wrote *Friday? Saturday? Sunday?* across the top of the board. Then she drew a rectangle with wheels next to the stick figure of the man. "We know kids leave at night, after their parents have gone to bed," she said. *She* had left at night. She could still remember, after all these years, lying in bed, fully awake, fully dressed, waiting for the sounds of the household to quiet.

"So . . . after dark," Mary Aaron said. "After the parents have gone to bed. Ten?"

After ten, Rachel wrote. Then she stood back and stared at the whiteboard, the marker in her hand.

Mary Aaron stared. "It's not enough," she declared, lifting her hands and letting them fall to her lap. "We don't know where they were supposed to pick her up. It's a big valley. If we don't know where, we can't find him."

Rachel put down the marker, went to the mugs, and pulled out one tea bag and then the other, tossing them in the trash can under her desk. She added sugar cubes from a cup on top of the microwave, then a splash of milk from a pint Mason jar in the refrigerator.

Mary Aaron rose from her chair to come over and stand barefoot in front of the whiteboard. Her blue scarf had slipped down so that it barely covered the bun at the back of her head. Rachel could tell by the look on her face that she was thinking. Thinking hard.

Neither had actually come out and said that they were going to try and meet the van that was to take Vi from Stone Mill, but both of them knew that was their intention. If they could just figure out where to go . . .

Rachel looked around for a spoon. Unable to find one, she grabbed the dry-erase marker, holding it from the cap end, and stirred her tea. She handed Mary Aaron her tea and the marker.

Mary Aaron slowly stirred her tea. "Where would they meet?" she asked out loud. "Somewhere easy for kids to get to."

"So, somewhere within walking distance," Rachel said, going over to stand beside her cousin.

"Somewhere that if someone saw them, it wouldn't seem out of place, even after dark." She handed the marker back to Rachel.

Rachel wiped it on the pant leg of her jeans. "So, probably not in town."

"But on a road where a van wouldn't look out of place, either."

"So, not in town but *close* to town."

Mary Aaron nodded, cupping her mug in both hands. "On

a paved road, not a dirt one. Englishers stick to paved roads after dark. They don't wander out our way often."

"My source says it's an Amish man."

Mary Aaron cut her eyes at Rachel. "An Amish man with a van." She grimaced. "Still sounds *narrisch* to me."

Crazy. Maybe this whole idea that they could solve a case the police couldn't was crazy. Rachel sighed and sipped her tea. Mary Aaron was right. There was no Amish man in Stone Mill who owned a motor vehicle. She had heard of an Amish community where the members all drove black cars, but such newfangled ideas certainly hadn't come to the older orders. Did that mean that George's source was wrong? That was certainly possible, but it made sense that it would be someone Amish, rather than someone English, helping kids. Young people, girls particularly, didn't have much contact with Englisher males. It just wasn't done.

"Where would he pick her up?" Mary Aaron said, obviously thinking out loud. "Where was Vi going?"

Rachel stared at the Amish stick figure she'd drawn. "So, Vi and Hannah's families live right next door to each other," she said thinking out loud. "How about Beth? How far are the Glicks from the Verklers?"

"I don't know. Kind of far. Two, two and a half miles maybe."

"Show me." Rachel held up the marker.

Mary Aaron drew a long line. "This is Buttermilk," she said, indicating a road that led into town. Then she drew two shorter lines. "Hannah's and Vi's families are here on Acorn." She made an *X* on the west side of Buttermilk. "And Beth's family is farther out of town, here on Oak." She made an *X* on the east side of Buttermilk.

"That's not so far," Rachel said.

"It is when you're a girl walking at night."

Rachel set her tea on the table, still staring at the board. "No one would think it was odd to see a van at night on Buttermilk."

"No. There's that new Englisher development, the one built on the old Tragler farm." She made an *X* farther south on Buttermilk.

"So where would kids go on Buttermilk to wait for a ride out of town?" Rachel closed her eyes, thinking. She took the same road out of town when going to her parents' house or Hannah's.

"I don't know," Mary Aaron said. She took another sip of tea. "This is a waste of time. It could be anywhere."

"It could be," Rachel said slowly, trying, in her mind, to imagine driving that piece of road after dark. The last time she'd gone that way at night, it had been with Hannah on the way home from New Orleans. After they'd dropped Mary Aaron off.

It came to her in a split second. "The schoolhouse."

"What?"

Rachel turned to look at Mary Aaron, remembering that night how Hannah had asked her to stop. "The night we got home from New Orleans," she said quickly, with excitement, "after we dropped you off, Hannah asked me to pull over. I thought she was carsick. But we were near the schoolhouse. She got out and went and sat on the swing. The one in the tree near the driveway."

"She wanted to swing?" Mary Aaron asked. "At night?"

"I thought she wanted to stop because . . . I don't know, she had good memories from her school days or something. She was crying. I thought maybe she was crying for that lost innocence. But now—" Rachel stared at the board, but she looked right through it. She was seeing Hannah's tears. "She was crying because that's where everything went wrong. When she went *there* that night two years ago and left with that man in the van."

Mary Aaron stared at her. "You think?"

The more Rachel thought about it, the more she was sure. "Yes," she said firmly, walking over to the table to set down her mug. "Where's my cell phone? Where did I put it?" she asked, looking around.

"On the bed." Mary Aaron pointed.

Rachel made a beeline for her unmade bed.

"Who are you calling?" Mary Aaron asked.

"Can you get me a dress and a *kapp?* And a man's pants, shirt, and straw hat? We need them tonight."

Mary Aaron set down her mug. "I . . . I guess."

Rachel hit *1* on her speed dial. "Evan," she said when he picked up. She turned around to meet Mary Aaron's gaze. "Can you be here at seven thirty tonight?"

"Why?" he asked.

Rachel met Mary Aaron's gaze. "We're going on a stakeout."

"I feel ridiculous." Evan slouched farther down in the buggy seat and pulled his straw hat lower.

"You look fine," Rachel said, trying to hide her amusement.

Evan looked Plain. They all looked Plain. Since the purpose of staking out the schoolhouse was to discover the identity of the local who was helping kids leave the valley, she and Mary Aaron had agreed that the three of them would have to appear Amish. With Timothy's help, they'd supplied Evan with a man's everyday pants, shirt, and hat, and convinced him to wear them. She'd borrowed a dress and scarf from Mary Aaron.

They'd wanted to be at the location and well hidden before dark so that if the suspect arrived, they could see him before he saw them. So, Rachel and Evan had met Mary Aaron at the old covered bridge and dressed in the Plain clothes in the woods. The three of them were now wedged into the only seat of the Hostetlers' pony-drawn, open courting buggy. It was a tight fit, but a sight that no local would look at twice.

Young people out for an evening's fun were a normal sight. Certainly no one would recognize Trooper Evan Parks in Plain clothes.

Talking Evan into Amish garb had been more difficult than Rachel had believed it would be. And it didn't help her cause that Mary Aaron's friend Timothy was both shorter and chunkier than Evan, so his pants were high-waters, his shirt loose, and his hat large enough to settle over his eyes.

"Stop whining," Rachel advised. "If you ever make detective, you might have to wear stranger clothes than these. I can just see you with fake tattoos, a skullcap, and a leather motorcycle jacket." She wouldn't admit it, but Mary Aaron's dress wasn't easy for her to put on, and not simply because, instead of buttons, the garment was fastened together with straight pins. Rationally, Rachel knew that the Amish clothing and head covering were just for tonight, but still, donning the familiar garment brought a lot of conflicting emotions.

The pony's hooves made a pleasing sound as they clip-clopped along Buttermilk Road. "I would have gotten the closed buggy if I could," Mary Aaron said, in an effort to appease Evan. "But *Dat* would have asked where I was going and how many people I intended to take with me."

"This is fine," Rachel assured her. "It's not as though we're going to try and chase down our suspect in the buggy."

"I can't believe I let you convince me this is a good idea," Evan muttered.

"Maybe it is and maybe it isn't," Rachel told him. "But wouldn't you rather be here with us, just in case?"

She took his silence to mean agreement.

They arrived at the schoolhouse after sunset. Rachel and Mary Aaron had guessed that any Amish girls or boys leaving home would do so after their parents had gone to bed. They wanted to be in place in plenty of time.

"I'll put the pony in the shed," Mary Aaron offered. Her voice echoed and then was swallowed up by the towering trees that surrounded the small clearing. "We don't want anyone to see the cart. Young people intending to sneak away would probably walk here."

Or run, Rachel thought. It was impossible to shut out the

memory of that night more than fifteen years ago when—scared half to death—she'd carried a single, battered suitcase to a bus stop along the highway and climbed aboard the first arriving Greyhound. She'd had to pay for her ticket with one-dollar bills and a handful of change. If it hadn't been a rainy night with few passengers, the impatient driver might have refused to allow her on board.

I could easily have ended up like Hannah, she thought, *or Beth.* Amish youth risked so much when they went out, ignorant and usually broke, into the English world. They weren't prepared. They had none of the street smarts that Englisher kids had. They were easy prey to drugs, alcohol, and immoral people who wanted to take advantage of their innocence. She could understand why the community wanted to keep them in the church. Church doctrine stated that the Amish were God's chosen people and salvation lay in following the teachings of Jakob Ammann.

She respected the church and traditions, but some things had to change. Eight years of education wasn't enough for twenty-first-century America, and it was time for the elders to realize that the real danger to their faith was trying to hold their sons and daughters so close that they were unable to fend for themselves in the modern world.

"Quiet place," Evan mused.

"It is." Rachel moved closer to him, glad of his big, reassuring presence. She wasn't easily spooked, but mist was rising off the low ground, giving the deserted school yard an eerie feel. She'd always thought of one-room schools as happy places, echoing with the laughter of children, but tonight this place seemed lonely and a little frightening.

Thick, old-growth timber pushed in on either side of the school yard, diminishing the size of the schoolhouse and the shed and making Rachel feel small and insignificant. It was too early for the moon to illuminate the clearing, and they had to rely on the beams of their flashlights to see more than a few yards into the darkness.

"Thank you for coming tonight," Rachel said, looping her arm through Evan's. "I know you had to take a personal day to make it happen."

"I'm just glad you called me." He held his flashlight up, looking around. "I wouldn't want you two out here alone at night. Just in case you're right about this."

A twig snapped, and Rachel jumped as a figure materialized only an arm's length away.

"So," Mary Aaron said, "are we just going to hide here in the trees? It might get uncomfortable if we have to wait long."

A mosquito whined in Rachel's ear. Simultaneously, she heard what could only be a *slap* and a grunt from Evan's direction. "I'd rather not," Rachel said. "Do you think the schoolhouse is open?"

"Now we're trespassing?" Evan asked.

Mary Aaron chuckled. "The good thing about the Amish is that they don't call the police for every little thing. And they don't bring lawsuits, either."

"We aren't vandals," Rachel argued. "We're here for a good reason. I doubt anyone will mind."

"Inside might be smarter, anyway. There are big windows all around." Mary Aaron added her support to the plan. "And the school is raised on an old stone foundation. We'll have a good view of the suspect when he approaches from either direction."

"The *suspect*? Maybe you two should apply to the state police academy," Evan suggested. "You seem to be enjoying this way too much."

Rachel became conscious of what felt like a needle drilling into her ankle. "Ouch." She brushed away the offending mosquito. "That's going to leave a welt." She glanced at the dark shape that was the schoolhouse. "We should have thought about repellent before we left the house."

"I did." Mary Aaron pushed a spray can into Rachel's hand. "I put some on in the shed. Sprayed the pony, too. We keep it under the buggy seat in warm weather." She looked to Evan. "What do you think? Should we go inside? It could be hours before Vi's man shows up."

"*If* he shows." Evan took the mosquito repellent from Rachel, tucked his flashlight under his arm, and sprayed her back and legs. Then he passed the can to her. "Get the back of my neck. I think I've got bites on my bites."

Mary Aaron chuckled with amusement as she shut off her small flashlight. "If we're going around front, I think it's better if we shut these off."

Rachel turned off her flashlight. Evan turned off his.

Mary Aaron then led the way to the open porch on the front of the one-room schoolhouse. As Rachel made her way up the three steps, she heard the ghostly call of a screech owl from the trees. The doorknob rattled as her cousin turned it.

"Locked." Mary Aaron sighed. "Gully wash! Guess it's back to the trees and the mosquitoes." She turned back to them. "Unless one of you can pick a lock."

"Not me," Rachel said.

"Okay, so now I'm breaking and entering," Evan grumbled. "Luckily, I'm prepared."

"You have a key?" Rachel asked. It was pitch-black on the porch. There was a faint glow, so she supposed there must be some moonlight, but the fog seemed to blot out and distort images around them.

"Swiss Army knife." Evan pulled the penknife from his pocket. "Comes with a tiny screwdriver blade, among other things."

"Wait," Rachel said. "Maybe—"

"I can get this," Evan insisted, rattling the doorknob. "Can you turn on that penlight, Mary Aaron? Right on the keyhole."

"But," Rachel interrupted, "I think—"

"I said, I can get it." That was Evan's take-charge tone. *Trooper Evan Parks to the rescue.*

She bit back a response as she watched, by the light of

Mary Aaron's flashlight, as Evan inserted the blade and fumbled with the lock.

"I just have to get it lined up right." Evan's breathing took on a decided pattern of impatience.

Rachel stepped around him and stood on her tiptoes. Stretching, she reached the top of the door frame and felt around. She gave a small sound of delight when her fingers brushed the cool metal outline of a key. "Maybe try this?" She held the key in the beam of the flashlight.

He accepted it without comment, slid it into the lock, and opened the door. He stepped in, and she and Mary Aaron followed. For a few seconds there was absolute silence, and then Evan began to laugh softly. "How did you know there was a key there?"

Rachel shrugged. "Smartest place to keep it if different people are letting themselves in."

"Of course. I rest my case," he said. "You should be the detective. Not me."

Abruptly, Rachel's mood became somber. "We need to remember why we're here. Someone died."

"You're right." Evan squeezed her shoulder. "Let's do this right. Mary Aaron, you take one of the front windows. I'll take this one, and you can watch the north, Rachel. If you need to use your flashlight, keep the beam low to the floor. We don't want to scare off our man."

Rachel found a chair and dragged it to a spot by the window. Outside, she saw nothing but darkness. There was the scrape of wood against wood, and then no sound but the three of them breathing in the darkness. After what seemed a long time, she asked, "What time is it?"

Evan's watch glowed blue as he pushed the button. "Nine fifteen." Another quarter hour passed before he broke the silence. "I think we can talk. As long as we're not shouting, I don't think anyone could hear us outside."

Rachel shifted restlessly. She'd been staring out through the window with such intensity that she was developing a headache. Every time a pair of headlights came down Buttermilk Road, she tensed, waiting for the vehicle to turn in. Once, they heard hoofbeats and an approaching buggy. The hair had risen on the back of her neck as she listened. Hannah had said a van had picked her up, but what if it was a buggy coming for Vi?

The notion revolted her, but she was afraid George's information might be true. It was logical that the man helping kids leave would be Amish. Who would Amish girls trust most? Certainly not an English stranger. They'd been taught to be suspicious of Englishers from babyhood on . . . even to fear them. It was a foolish belief in this day and time, but it still held true.

The buggy rolled by.

"We should play a word game," Mary Aaron suggested. "To pass the time. How about Twenty Questions?"

"Sure," Evan agreed. "Stakeouts are notorious for being long and boring. You up for it, Rachel?"

"Why not?" She leaned against the windowsill. The mist had thickened, and the last pair of car lights had only been pinpoints moving past in the blackness. "You go first, Mary Aaron."

"Got it," her cousin said.

"Animal, vegetable, or mineral?" Evan asked.

Mary Aaron giggled. "Mineral. I think, *ya,* mineral."

The window glass was cool against Rachel's cheek. It eased the itching from a big mosquito bite.

"Rae-Rae, your turn to ask a question," Mary Aaron prompted.

Rachel opened her eyes to see the flashing lights of another buggy coming down the road. Her pulse quickened.

They all watched in silence as the buggy kept moving on past the school, blink-blink-blinking, until the lights faded in the mist.

"Is it a buggy?" Rachel blurted out.

Mary Aaron scoffed. "You're not supposed to guess yet.

You get twenty questions. You're supposed to ask how big it is."

"Yeah, Rachel, follow the rules," Evan teased.

"All right. Is it in this schoolhouse?"

"Warm," her cousin answered. "But not exactly."

"*Warm*? That's cheating," Evan teased. "You're only supposed to answer yes or no."

Mary Aaron laughed. "Yes or no."

"Is it the woodstove?" Rachel asked, switching to Deitsch. Evan understood the Pennsylvania Dutch dialect, but not as well as they did, and he was hazy about the slang. He protested loudly, but the game went on amid mock accusations that the two of them were in league with each other against him.

Another hour passed and then two. Passing vehicles became fewer. Sometime after eleven, they gave up on Twenty Questions and began to go over the case from the beginning, examining each detail, rehashing the testimony of all the Amish young people whom they'd questioned, searching their minds for any clues they might have missed.

All the while, they kept watching the road. At quarter after two, Evan called a halt to the stakeout. "I doubt if they'd show later than this," he said. "Mary Aaron should get home."

"I was so sure he would show up." Rachel sighed, pressing her fingers to her temples.

"It was a long shot, anyway," Evan said kindly.

"We're not giving up this easily. We're coming back here tomorrow night," Rachel told him. She looked to Mary Aaron for support. "I'm not willing to give up. 'This weekend' could mean *Saturday* night."

"You expect me to dress up like this again tomorrow night?"

"I think Rachel is right," Mary Aaron said. "Tomorrow night he will come, this bad man. For sure. Tomorrow night."

Chapter 20

The following night, Evan walked over to Rachel and sat down on top of a child's wooden desk. She sat lower to the floor, in a pint-sized chair. "It's time we think about wrapping this up," he said.

Rachel shook her head slowly. "I was so sure he would come for her," she said as much to herself as to him. "I was so sure it would be tonight. Didn't you think he would come for Vi, Mary Aaron?" she called softly across the dark schoolroom.

"*Ya,* I thought he would come," Mary Aaron agreed. She sounded as disheartened as Rachel felt.

"And it *was* sound reasoning, Rachel." Evan removed the straw hat and wiped his forehead with his hand.

The air was still and humid inside the schoolroom, and smelled of chalk and an apple left behind in one of the desks. Suddenly, the scents seemed cloying, particularly the distinct smell of the chalk.

Earlier, bored from sitting for so long and playing another long round of Twenty Questions, Rachel had wandered over to the chalkboard on the back wall. A class had been working on state capitals. They had to have been playing some sort of game because someone with mature handwriting—the teacher, she guessed—had written abbreviations for the states, and then in children's scrawls were the capitals. Someone had written that the capital of Arkansas was Austin. It had made Rachel smile.

She glanced up at Evan. The moon had risen and now cast light through the windows so that she could see his face. "I'm sorry I dragged you here two nights in a row. Last night you had to take a personal day. Tonight was your night off." She exhaled, fighting frustration. "This was a complete waste of your time. Everyone's time."

He covered her hand on the desk with his. "From what I hear the detectives say, most of their jobs involve sitting around waiting for something that never happens." He shrugged. "Nature of the beast, I guess. It was worth a try." He chuckled. "As much as I care for you, Rachel, I wouldn't have come with you if I had thought it wasn't."

She gave him a quick smile. He was being so sweet about this whole mess. He was such a good guy. She really did need to put some thought into where their relationship was going. She already knew what he wanted. She needed to seriously consider her feelings for him. She couldn't just keep putting him off with excuses because she didn't want to deal with her own emotions.

She glanced out the front windows; the panes were clean, and the moonlight glistened off them. School had started the previous week. She suspected a cleaning crew of Amish women and girls in the school district had washed the windows. She remembered her own days of washing schoolhouse windows. It had been more like an afternoon party than a work detail, with all the women and girls she knew gathered together, laughing and talking as they worked.

"I thought I could figure this out," Rachel said quietly. "I *really* thought I could help you find out who killed Beth."

Mary Aaron rose from the chair where she'd been sitting and walked toward them. "Maybe you have to be content right now to know that you were able to bring Hannah home safely and that you were able to protect Vi from harm."

"And who knows?" Evan put in. "Something on the Glick

case could turn up over the next few weeks . . . or months. Criminals talk. They can never keep their mouths shut. I can't tell you how often arrests are directly related to the guilty party bragging to someone on a bar stool next to him."

They were right. Everything they were saying was right. She just hated . . . she hated to admit it to them, or herself. "I guess we should go home." Rachel rose, feeling utterly dejected. She had been *so* sure they would catch the man tonight. Especially after he hadn't shown up the night before.

Headlights suddenly appeared in the distance, headed south, out of town. All three of them stared at the lights as they grew bigger.

"What time is it?" Mary Aaron asked quietly.

Evan reached into the pair of Timothy's work pants that he had worn again. The light on his phone glowed. "Eleven fifteen," he said. He locked it, turning off the light.

"The car's slowing down," Rachel whispered. "I think it's slowing down," she repeated, scared and excited at the same time.

"It's a van," Evan observed.

"Should we get down?" Mary Aaron asked, crouching and watching.

Rachel ducked down. "It's turning in!"

Evan leaned over, taking Rachel's sleeve and then Mary Aaron's. He kept his gaze on the approaching headlights as he began to back up, taking them with him. "Let's move to the back door. He might get suspicious if we walk out of the schoolhouse."

As the van pulled into the driveway, the headlights flashed briefly into the front windows. The three of them froze. Thankfully, the headlights went out.

Rachel heard Mary Aaron pick up the suitcase she had brought with her again.

Evan, Rachel, and Mary Aaron stepped into the shadows, away from the moonlight coming in through the windows, and slowly walked backward toward the door just to the left of the chalkboard on the back wall. The windows didn't run the full length of the sides of the building, all the way to the back, so once they were fully in shadow, Evan stood upright again.

Rachel pressed her hand to her chest. Her heart was pounding, and she felt like she couldn't take a deep breath. Somehow, planning this stakeout, thinking the man would come for Vi, didn't feel at all like the reality of it. Being right didn't seem to matter at the moment; mostly, she was just scared.

Evan unlocked and opened the back door, which led directly onto a stoop. "Careful, there's a step down," he warned in a whisper, taking Mary Aaron's hand.

She stepped out into the night, and Rachel moved behind her. As she passed Evan, she placed her hand on the small of his back to keep her balance in the dark . . . and felt something hard and cool tucked into the waistband of Timothy's pants. She looked up at him, surprised, though why, she didn't know. He was a state policeman. He carried a weapon in a holster every day. But somehow, in this setting, in an Amish schoolhouse, it seemed shocking. "You brought a *gun?*" she whispered.

"You think I would come without it?" She could feel his gaze on her. "Rachel, my first responsibility is to protect you and Mary Aaron."

Rachel stepped out onto the stoop without his assistance. Mary Aaron was already down the steps. "What do we do?" she whispered. She sounded scared . . . but determined. She knew what could be at stake here.

"We follow our plan," Evan said firmly in a whisper. "Rachel, you walk to the van as if you're here to meet him. We'll hang back a little."

Her feet on the grass, she turned back to him. "Do you think that's smart? If he sees you two, it might spook him. He might take off."

They walked toward the back corner of the building. They heard the sound of a door opening, then the sound of shoes crunching on the gravel driveway.

"There's no way I'm letting you out of my sight," Evan whispered. "If he does spot us . . . he'll probably just assume we're here to see you off. A brother and sister, or friends." They stopped at the corner of the building. Once they walked around it, the driver of the van might be able to see them.

"Stay close to the building as you walk toward him." Evan grabbed Rachel's arm. "I just want you to confirm that he's here to pick up an Amish girl. Do not, *under any circumstances*, get into the van."

"Take this." Mary Aaron pushed the suitcase into her hand. "And be careful." She pressed a quick kiss to her cheek.

Rachel nodded and peeked around the corner. She gripped the suitcase handle with her now sweaty hand. With only the moonlight, she could see much more than the outline of the van. It was white, with writing on the side . . . maybe on the door. And she could see the man's form. He was neither tall nor short, neither thin nor fat. Just a man. But an Englisher, not an Amish man. That was obvious from his clothing: pants, white shoes that might be sneakers, and a short-sleeved shirt with big flowers on it.

"We're right behind you," Evan whispered.

Rachel took a breath and stepped around the corner. She kept her head down so he couldn't see her face. She didn't know if the driver was specifically expecting Vi or just an Amish girl. And then there was the chance he might recognize her. Her hand went to her white prayer *kapp*. Oddly, she found the texture of the fabric comforting.

She heard the footsteps of Evan and Mary Aaron behind her.

"Someone there?" the man called from near the van.

Rachel thought she might recognize his voice, but then wondered if it was her imagination. "*Hallo?*" she answered tentatively in Deitsch. "*Ya,* I'm here." She got as close as the front of the schoolhouse but remained in its shadow.

"Is someone else there? Did Joe bring you?" the man called. He took a step toward Rachel, then stopped.

"*Ya,*" she called, trying to make her accent heavy. "*Meine bruder und schweschder.*"

"I'm sorry? English, dear. I don't speak the Dutch. Not much, anyway."

Rachel was almost sure she recognized his voice, but her heart was pounding so hard in her ears that she couldn't be sure. "My brother and sister," she called meekly. "Come to . . . say good-bye."

He didn't say anything for a second, and she sensed he was getting nervous. "Well . . . we need to make this quick. They won't wait for us on the other end. So . . ." He lifted a hand and let it fall. She still couldn't see his face.

Rachel heard Evan and Mary Aaron behind her. She took another step and then another. She couldn't make out the man's features because of the way he was standing, with shadows across his face, but she was almost close enough to read the side of the van.

Two more steps and the words on the side of the van came into focus. Her breath caught in her throat, and she took another quick step toward the man. "Ed?" she cried.

His head snapped around, and he looked right at her. He took a step toward the van and snatched open the driver's door.

"Ed, how could you?" Rachel demanded.

In the light, he saw her face. "Rachel?" He looked her up and down once. "What are you doing here . . . in Amish clothing? Is Viola here?" He looked around. Then he must have realized he'd just incriminated himself; his eyes filled with tears.

"Vi's not here," Rachel said sadly. She dropped the suitcase and continued to walk toward him. "But if she had been here, where would you have taken her? The same place you took Hannah?"

He exhaled heavily. "Rachel—"

"Do you know what happened to her?" Rachel's voice trembled with anger. "You sold her into the sex trade, Ed. How could you have done such a thing. How—"

"Rachel, don't." Evan came up quickly behind her. "Mr. Wagler, it's Trooper Parks. Step away from your vehicle."

"You sold Hannah!" Rachel repeated, still walking toward him.

"Rachel!" Mary Aaron tried to grab her arm.

Rachel shook her off. "Is that what you did to Beth, too? And *then what?* She came back, so you killed her to keep her from telling people what you did?"

"No." Ed shook his head violently. "That's not what happened. I didn't know. I didn't know." He took a stumbling step back. "I had nothing to do with Beth's death. I just arranged . . . I got her a job."

"You got her a job as a prostitute," Rachel flung at him.

He backed against the side of his van, his head hitting it with a bang. "I didn't kill Beth! I didn't even know she'd come home. I swear to God, I didn't."

"Rachel." Evan grabbed her arm and held her back. With his free hand, he punched numbers into his cell.

"9-1-1, what's your emergency?" a female voice said on the other end of the line.

"How could you, Ed?" Rachel demanded. She broke free from Evan's grip and walked away. "How could you?" she whispered.

How could he? Rachel was still asking herself the same question the next day when she went out to the barn to let out her goats. How could Ed Wagler have been involved in selling Amish girls to a sex-trade operation? Ed was such a nice guy. It didn't make sense.

Rachel had neither seen nor spoken to Evan since they parted the previous night, her in the courting buggy with Mary Aaron and him in a police cruiser with Ed. Evan had looked a sight climbing into the police car in high-water Amish pants, but he hadn't been concerned. What mattered to him was getting Ed into questioning and making sure proper procedures were followed. One look into Evan's eyes had told Rachel they'd pretty much gotten a confession out of him, but she'd read enough detective novels to know that nothing Ed had said in the school yard would be admissible. What would count was what he said when he was questioned by the police, with his lawyer present, after hearing his Miranda rights.

Rachel had a slight headache and had had one since she got up. She had decided not to go to church, but instead spent the morning reconciling her checkbook, paying bills, and playing catch-up on boring paperwork. She was carrying the bushel baskets she'd borrowed from her father outside, thinking she'd return them finally, when her cell phone rang in the back pocket of her jeans. She pulled out her phone and checked the screen. It was almost two in the afternoon. She'd begun to worry about why she hadn't heard from him. "Evan . . ."

"You home?" he asked. He sounded tired.

She had a million questions, the biggest one being, had Ed Wagler confessed to killing Beth? Instead she said, "Yes. Want me to come get you?"

"No. I'm on my way to get my car. I'm almost there."

"You want me to make you some lunch?" She lifted the latch, swung open the gate, and the goats sauntered out into the field.

"No food. Not sure I could hold anything down." He sighed. "I'll be there in five minutes."

"See you then," she told him.

Rachel was waiting for Evan on the front lawn when a police cruiser pulled up and he got out. "Thanks," he said as he closed the door.

Rachel walked over to the driveway as Evan walked up it.

He was no longer wearing Timothy's clothing, but the khaki pants and blue oxford shirt didn't look familiar either. He was still wearing his work boots. He must have known what she was thinking because, as he walked toward her, he indicated the clothes. "Something someone had in his locker. I still haven't been home yet. Headed there for a shower next."

She nodded. "You want to go sit?" She pointed in the direction of the swing under the arbor.

He stood there for a minute, hands on his hips. "How about we take a walk? I've been sitting too long. The detectives let me listen in on the questioning. I need to stretch my legs."

"Walk it is." They crossed the driveway and started across the back lawn toward the gristmill house. There was a nice path that went around it and into the woods behind the property, an old deer path she'd cleared for her guests for their strolling pleasure.

"So," Evan said. He didn't seem all that happy.

"Did Ed confess?"

"I really shouldn't be talking about this."

"I already know more about the case than the police," she argued. "And you know I won't say anything to anyone. Who would I tell?"

He hesitated. "Ed did confess." He glanced at her. "But . . . it's not the confession we were—" He stopped and started again. " 'Hoping for' is not quite the right phrase. But you know what I mean."

"Okay." She drew out the word, not quite following but trying to give him the opportunity to speak.

They circled the building site and walked to the edge of the millpond. "Ed's definitely going to jail," Evan said. "He confessed to taking money in exchange for delivery of Hannah and Beth."

Evan scratched his chin; he needed a shave. "Here's the thing, Rachel. Ed did sell the girls, but he didn't kill Beth."

All she could think of was that Ed Wagler was clearly not the man he appeared to be. How could the police believe anything he said? "How do you know that?"

"He has an alibi, Rachel. I made a few phone calls this morning."

"On a Sunday morning?"

"I started with the hotel in Dayton, Ohio, where he was at a Hometown Grocers' convention. When the police call, people tend to be willing to talk, even if it is Sunday morning. Ed Wagler was definitely there. According to a woman I talked to in Pittsburgh, he gave a presentation. I still have a few phone calls to make, but . . . Ed Wagler didn't kill Beth Glick."

She thought on that for a minute. "He said he took money in exchange for the girls. Did he say why?"

"Did you know Ed was a gambler?"

"I know he used to go to Atlantic City once in a while with Willy O'Day."

"He goes once a month to Atlantic City, every month. Stays all night. Blackjack. Big gambler. Big loser," he added.

They walked past a willow tree that shaded the path and a section of the millpond. She heard ducks squawking but couldn't see them. The mother and ducklings she had seen the other day, she guessed.

"Apparently he has serious debt. Didn't want his wife to know. Didn't want to lose his business. It's a pretty standard story. He says someone came up to him at a casino and said she was looking for undocumented workers. Females for maid service and child care and such."

She shook her head, meaning she wasn't following.

"The woman was looking for people in the country illegally. Women without social security cards. He said it occurred to him that the Amish women he was giving rides out of town to obviously needed work. He says he thought he was doing them a favor."

"He didn't think it was odd that this woman was offering

him money?" she asked in disbelief. "Ed never struck me as stupid."

"But apparently he was foolish. Maybe naïve."

The path they were following entered the woods, and it was immediately cooler. Rachel had checked the weather report while on her laptop that morning. Cooler temperatures were expected early in the week, for which she was thankful. "So, he picked up girls at the schoolhouse and then took them where?"

"To someone else. He didn't know who. There was a meeting place—sometimes at a rest stop, other times a diner. A respectable-looking woman would pick the girls up. Honestly, Ed was crying a lot. Sometimes he didn't make a lot of sense. We had to stop twice because he thought he was going to be sick. It could take weeks to sift through his statements."

"Hannah pretty much said the same thing," she mused. "About meeting someone in a van. I guess Ed left her with someone who then drove her to someone else. At some point, she thought Mennonites were picking her up. That they were going to find her a job." She glanced at Evan. "I still can't believe Ed would be part of something like this. How did he not know something bad was going on here?"

"He said the thought crossed his mind, but . . ." He pressed his hand to his forehead and let it fall. "I don't know. We believe what we want to believe, I guess."

"What did he say about Hannah?"

"He basically gave the same story as he gave for Beth. He just drove her to meet this woman."

"Did he say how many girls he delivered to this mysterious woman?" She ducked under a low-hanging branch, making a mental note that it needed to be pruned. "What about the boys? You know very well that he helped Enosh."

"Apparently, sometimes he really did just give kids a ride out of town."

"Like Lucy Zug? She seems to be doing well."

"Exactly."

She glanced up at him. "You ask him about Lorraine?"

"Yeah. She was one of the girls he helped *find a job*."

She closed her eyes for a second, then opened them. "We may never know what happened to her." They'd stopped on the path.

Evan was just standing there, hands in his pockets. "No."

Rachel gazed up at a patch of blue sky peeking through the treetops. "So if Ed didn't kill Beth, who did?"

"Could be what we guessed from the very beginning. A random act of violence. Beth was at the wrong place at the wrong time."

"A random act," she repeated. It made perfectly logical sense. She knew that. But it didn't . . . feel right. "Did Ed say anything about who else was involved? Here in Stone Mill? These girls didn't just approach him in his store, did they?"

"I don't know. We went over a lot of stuff, Rachel. After a while, I don't know if it was an act or what, but he seemed confused."

"Ed, confused? That doesn't sound like the Ed I know."

"Neither does the man who agreed to accept money to transport young women to strangers in the middle of the night."

"Good point," she conceded, and started to walk again. "Have there been any other murders similar to Beth's in the area? I know no other Amish have been murdered—I'd have heard about that—but . . . runaways? Strangulations leading to drownings in old rock quarries?"

"Nothing that fits the circumstances of Beth Glick's murder, but it's something Sergeant Haley is looking into." His cell phone in his pocket rang, and he stopped and pulled it out. "It's what you do after a month passes and you have no leads. The detective—Sorry, Rachel, I'm going to have to get this. Evan Parks," he said into the phone.

He turned away from Rachel, presenting his back to her. "You've got to be kidding me." He paused. "Yes, sir. Where?" He paused. "I understand, sir. I'll see you there."

When Evan turned back to Rachel, his face seemed paler than it had a moment before. "Ed Wagler had a heart attack during transport to lockup."

She covered her mouth with her hand, in shock. "Is he—"

"I have to go." He turned and started back the way they'd come. "He's still alive, but they don't know if he's going to pull through."

Chapter 21

At six on Monday evening, Rachel parked her Jeep next to her father's barn. As she got out, she checked her cell. No calls, but she took note that the battery was low. Luckily, she wasn't planning on making or receiving any calls while she was at her parents'. She really *did* need to get a new phone or a new battery, though. She'd hardly talked on it all day, and the battery was still drained. Making sure the phone was on silent, she stuck it into the pocket of her skirt and walked around to open the back gate of the Jeep. She'd finally remembered her father's bushel baskets; she'd had to take the backseat out of the Jeep to fit them all in. She removed the three stacks of baskets, set them by the open barn door, and then headed for the house.

She found something so comforting about walking through the barnyard on a warm September evening, with the peaceful lowing of the cows and the cheerful shouts of her brothers and sisters drifting over the farmyard. The younger kids were playing softball in the meadow. She waved, and several waved back.

Normally, she would have joined them, but tonight she kept walking because she felt like she needed to talk to her parents. With eight siblings and a never-ending assortment of visiting friends and relatives in residence in the big farmhouse, she had only rare and precious moments alone with them. Somehow, talking with her parents even after she'd left Stone Mill and then returned, made her feel more capable. More confident.

Rachel needed a boost of confidence right now. She was so frustrated by her inability to track down Beth's killer. So disappointed, not just in the state of the investigation but in herself. She'd been *so* sure when they caught Ed Wagler and he'd admitted to being the one who sold the girls into shame, that the case would be solved. But it wasn't, and if Evan was right, if it had been a random killing, then they might never know what had happened.

One of the dogs gave an excited yip and scampered, tail wagging, to greet her. She found her parents sitting on the back porch with a bushel of freshly picked lima beans between them. Her *dat* and *mam* each had a big yellow Tupperware bowl in their laps, and they were shelling limas for canning and freezing.

Her *dat* looked up, and a slow grin spread across his face. "Rachel, it's good to see you."

Her mother glanced at her, and for an instant their gazes locked. Rachel felt a warm flush of pleasure as she read the affection and genuine welcome in her *mam*'s eyes. A heartbeat later, her mother fixed her attention on the bowl of shelled beans in her lap.

"Come, join us," her father urged. "We've got a lot of lima beans to finish up before dark."

"Better you'd call some of the kids to help, Samuel," her *mam* said. "They've still got plenty of energy. They should be using it to good ends."

"*Ach*, Esther, leave the young ones to have their sport. Tell the truth. You enjoy the quiet as much as I do." He chuckled and patted the empty rocker beside him. "How often do we get to visit with our Rachel, now that she's gone out amongst the Englishers?"

He had pulled off his shoes and socks, and left them by the back door. That meant that his chores were done for the day, and he could relax in the comfort of his home until time for evening prayers in the parlor. Her *dat*'s prayer ritual never took long and he never got preachy. He would remind the children of the positive actions they'd taken that day and of the way the Lord had blessed them with His grace. He would instruct them to think of how they could best use their time on the morrow, remember any in the neighborhood who were ill or grieving, and tell them how thankful he was for home and harvest and family.

His prayers had once been the highlight of Rachel's day, and they had never failed to bring her comfort and a sense that God, like her father, was watching over them. Those memories had cradled and strengthened her in her journey to find her purpose in life, and continued to do so.

Taking an extra bowl from the stack on the porch, Rachel gathered several handfuls of unshelled lima beans and settled into the creaky wooden rocker. For a while, none of them spoke; they just rocked and shelled beans. Then, casually, her mother began to tell her father about the carrots and potatoes she and the children had brought up from the garden that afternoon and how many pints of grape jelly she and the girls had made.

Rachel's *dat* shared his plans for acquiring a new Dorset ram and traveling with their son Paul to a fence-building workday for a needy family on the coming Saturday. Rachel listened, letting the familiar farm news flow over her, seep into her pores, and ease her discontent with her own failures.

And after a while, as she'd known it would, the talk turned to Ed Wagler and the terrible thing that he'd done. Even though it hadn't been forty-eight hours since his arrest, it had made the morning papers, as well as national news. Of course, no one knew the part she and Mary Aaron had played in the stakeout; all parties involved had agreed that information had nothing to do with the case and need not be publicized. The fact that Ed had had a heart attack while being transported by the police had been widely publicized, as well as speculation as to whether or not the police were somehow responsible for his life-threatening condition.

"The bishop has asked us to pray for Ed," her *dat* said, "but it's a hard thing after what he's done."

"I never trusted that Ed," her *mam* said. "Never liked the way he weighed out cheese. He knew I always wanted three pounds of Swiss, but it always went over. 'A little heavy,' he'd say. 'Is that all right?' Pushy, even for an Englisher, he was." She emphasized her words by snapping the bean hulls violently.

Her father reached over to pat her mother's hand. "Peace, Esther. It's not for us to judge. Ed must answer for his sins."

"He knows he did wrong," Rachel offered. She wasn't sure that she could forget or forgive, but was glad that Ed had been able to provide a solid alibi for his whereabouts the week Beth had been murdered. It was easier to believe that some stranger was capable of murder rather than someone she'd known and liked. "He claimed he was as shocked about Beth's death as everyone else and that he hadn't seen her since he gave her a ride out of the valley. He said he knew nothing that would help the police find whoever did kill her." She thought for a minute. "I was there when Evan took him in for questioning. I really think he was sorry for the part he played in Beth's leaving."

"Sorry he was caught, more likely," her mother said tartly, and then added, "Samuel," in case Rachel might assume that she was speaking to her.

Rachel's *dat* continued looking at his wife, and her mother's cheeks took on a hint of rose color.

"But I will pray for his soul," her *mam* allowed. "For I truly hope he won't die before he's had his opportunity to repent."

"Whatever else Ed Wagler has to answer for, he isn't a murderer," Rachel said. "Which means that the murderer is still out there. I have tried so hard to come up with something to help the police, but I'm about out of ideas." She swallowed against the tightness in her throat and reached for more limas.

Her mother gathered up the buckets of shells and carried them to an empty bushel basket at the edge of the steps. Rachel knew that the lima bean shells would be shared between the pigpen and the chicken yard. Nothing went to waste on an Amish farm. Even vegetable peelings, used coffee grounds, and worn-out clothing could be repurposed. She watched as her mother strode gracefully back to her chair. Esther Mast was still an attractive woman, and the lavender dress and spotless white *kapp* accentuated the strong planes of her face. No hint of gray tinted her arched brows, and the laugh lines and wrinkles only added to her character. *I hope I look as good as she does when I'm her age,* Rachel thought.

Rachel's mother refilled her yellow bowl, returned to her rocking chair, and began to shell beans with a renewed urgency.

"Maybe what Ed did had nothing to do with Beth coming home," her father suggested thoughtfully. "Could be that she was coming home and wickedness crossed her path."

"That's what Evan says the police think," Rachel said. "A random act of violence. It happens, even in places like Stone Mill."

"Lots of violence here in the olden days, back when the Indians warred with the Englishers," her mother said. "My *grossfader* had it from his *grossfader*. Mostly our people were friends to the savages and they left us alone, but sometimes, when tempers ran high and the militias raided the Indian towns, our blood ran, too."

"Maybe the police are right, but I just keep thinking there's a missing puzzle piece," Rachel said, looking at her father. "Something someone isn't telling. I've talked to kids who left and turned English, and I tried to talk to Hannah Verkler before she went away, but no one wants to tell what they know."

"It's the Amish way," her mother said, looking directly at

her father. "Keeping secrets. The practice's been handed down generation to generation from the martyr times in the Old Country." She sighed. "You'd think that some of these young people would use their heads. If they'd told about Ed a long time ago, Beth might be alive."

"I thought about Eli Rust's son, you know, the boy that left and joined the Marines," Rachel said. "He might not be afraid to talk to the police." She found a shriveled bean and tossed it into the bucket with the empty hulls. "But Mary Aaron said he's overseas with the military and won't be home for six months."

"I remember when he ran away," her father answered softly. "It was a shock to his father."

"I was not surprised. That Rust family has always had a name for being wayward," her *mam* said. "Always in one kind of trouble or another with the bishop. You remember when Eli bought that John Deere tractor and thought he could use it for getting lumber off that timber section? Didn't think he'd get caught."

"A farmer buying a tractor is a long way from encouraging youngsters to run from their church and families," Rachel's *dat* pointed out.

"I'll not carry gossip against one of our own, but he did let his son spend too much time with that brother Joab of his." She gave her husband a meaningful look. "Maybe that's where the son got the idea to leave in the first place."

"No need to bring up such old news, Esther. What a man does when he's twenty shouldn't come back to bite him when he's fifty."

Rachel's curiosity made her want to ask what exactly Joab Rust had done when he was twenty, but she knew better. Her mother would say, given time, but she had to be patient. She concentrated on her bowl of limas.

"You might tell her to go have a chat with that Joab, Samuel," Rachel's mother said after several minutes of silence stretched between them. "Could be he knows a thing or two about running off to the English."

"Joab? We're talking about Joab Rust?" Rachel looked from her mother to her father.

"Maybe she doesn't know," Rachel's *mam* went on. "It could be important. It's not gossip. It's all true. Could be people need to know."

"What should I know?" Rachel asked.

"I don't say a man should be judged on his past. Only that the past still exists. Just because a man—"

"All right, all right." Patience exhausted, her father threw up his hands. "You'll not rest until I tell her, although it's not worth mentioning, in my opinion." He tugged at his neatly trimmed beard, and he turned to Rachel. "What your mother is trying to say, which she can't since she doesn't speak to you, is that Joab ran off before he was baptized into the church. He went to Canada to harvest corn."

"Wheat," her *mam* corrected softly. "It was wheat. But if she wants to talk to somebody about how you run away from Stone Mill, Joab Rust would be her man."

After Rachel left her parents' house, she drove to Joab Rust's place. She didn't see how Joab leaving more than twenty years ago could have anything to do with the kids leaving today, but it wouldn't do any harm to talk to him. Maybe her mother knew more than she was saying. It was often the Amish way and her mother's way.

As she pulled into the farmyard, a border collie ran out to bark at the Jeep, but otherwise, it was quiet. A child's push-scooter leaned against the back porch, and a cow poked her head out of the barn window. Chickens scratched in the yard, but none of the Rust family appeared. Rachel slipped into her canvas sneakers, walked across the tidy yard to the back door, and knocked. When no one answered after a minute or two, she returned to the Jeep. Apparently, no one was home.

She was just getting back into the Jeep when she heard the distinctive *thwack* of an axe splitting wood. She stopped and listened for a moment. The sound was coming from out back; the sound of an axe cutting could carry some distance. She got out of the Jeep, walked around the barn, and gazed out across the field, in the direction of the woods. The sound of the axe was definitely coming from that direction. A dirt lane ran along several outbuildings, across the field and into the woods. She thought about walking out there, but it was getting dark and she felt . . . uneasy. It was probably Joab in the woods, but what if it wasn't?

"What would Evan say?" she said out loud. *Use common sense.* That's what he would say. She got back into the red Jeep and followed the rutted road past the outbuildings, through an overgrown pasture to where the road ended at a gate at the woods line.

Rachel got out and scanned the thick woods. Here, the wood splitting was much louder, but the sound seemed to bounce off the trees, making the woodcutter more difficult to locate.

When there was silence, Rachel called into the woods, "Hello? I'm looking for Joab."

"You found him."

She hesitated, glancing back at her Jeep, then into the woods. "It's Rachel . . . Rachel Mast."

His response was another *thwack* of wood.

"There was no one up at the house," she called into the woods

"Wife and children gone to her sister's next door." *Thwack.*

Rachel lifted the loop of rope that held the gate closed, went through the gate, and dropped the rope over the post again. "I was wondering . . . if I could talk to you for a minute?" She took a step toward the sound. Once inside the woods line, it was immediately darker. Much darker.

Thwack.

"Do you . . . have a minute?" She took three more steps into the woods and finally spotted the outline of a bearded man in a white shirt, dark pants, and a straw hat. He swung an axe over his head and dropped it.

Thwack.

She took another step toward him. She could see him better now. "To talk?" she said, thinking that if her words sounded silly to her, what must Joab think?

"About what?"

He kicked a piece of wood with his boot. It hit another, and she flinched. She could smell the scents of freshly cut wood and forest vegetation. She heard a squirrel scurrying in a tree high overhead. "Your nephew Rupert."

He upended a section of log that was two feet high and almost a foot in diameter. He took a steel wedge from the ground, set it into a crack in the log and then swung the axe over his shoulder. He brought the flat end down hard on the wedge, and it made a great clang as the log split. "Rupert's gone. Been gone."

"I know. Actually, I . . ." She didn't know why she was nervous. She'd talked to Joab a dozen times in the last month because of the work he'd been doing for her. She'd never felt uncomfortable with him before. Maybe because she'd mostly spoken to him on her own property. Here, on his property, she was in his world. Was her uneasiness just a throwback from her days as a kid when Amish girls didn't often speak to adult men?

She started again. "I ran into Rupert at a diner a few months ago." Only a little fib. What had actually happened was that her Aunt Hannah had taken her to meet Rupert to talk to him. Joab's brother Eli, Rupert's father, had been there. But the details weren't important. "I know he joined the Marines. Scary," she added.

Joab split another log. *Thwack.* The sound was beginning to get on her nerves. She took a step closer. Close enough so that it wouldn't have been safe for him to swing the axe again. "Joab, do you know who helped Rupert leave Stone Mill?"

He stared at her. A long silence stretched between them, long enough to make Rachel feel uncomfortable.

"You didn't come to ask me about Rupert," Joab finally said. He raised the axe, but only to rest the handle on his shoulder.

She felt a sudden sense of panic. What did she say now? Did she make something up? If so, what? Or did she just come out and tell him why she was really here?

She glanced away and then back at him. He was just standing there, looking at her, no decipherable expression on his face.

"I guess you heard about Ed Wagler being arrested?" He didn't respond, so she went on. "That he was giving young Amish folks a ride out of Stone Mill, but . . . involving them in terrible things." Still, he said nothing. "It was in all the papers this morning," she added.

He took his time before saying, "Heard something like that."

She glanced at the pile of split wood at her feet. He certainly wasn't making this easy. "Joab . . . I'm just going to come out and say this. I know that you were close to Rupert, so I was wondering if you know who helped him leave Stone Mill?"

She waited. "Do you know who was the go-between between the girls who went missing from here and Ed Wagler?" This time, she didn't wait for him to respond; she just barreled forward. "Because . . . no matter what the police say, I think someone else was involved." She shook her head. "It just doesn't make sense that girls, particularly, were walking up to Ed Wagler at his grocery store and asking him if they could meet him late at night at the schoolhouse and catch a ride out of town. I think someone else was helping them . . . one of—" She almost said *our own*. But of course she wasn't one of them any longer. "Someone in the Amish community," she finished.

It seemed like it was getting darker in the woods by the second.

Joab took a step toward her, the axe still on his shoulder.

She took half a step back. She had a sudden urge to run, and she had no idea why.

He leaned over and picked up a chunk of wood he'd just split. "He tell you that?"

"Rupert?" she asked, confused.

"Ed."

Rachel stared at him, thinking back. Saturday night, when she had approached Ed, he'd asked her if *Joe* had brought her. *Joe*. Had he meant—

She saw Joab move toward her, but his movement was so quick, so unexpected . . . She saw him raise the chunk of wood, and then her head exploded with pain, followed by darkness.

Chapter 22

Rachel groaned and tried to open her eyes. Her head pounded, and something wet and sticky dripped down over her ear. She felt like she was going to throw up.

With great effort, she managed to get one eye open. Was the other swollen shut? Her head . . . Just opening the one eye made her dizzy. She had to close it for a moment before opening it again.

She stifled another groan, trying to think. Something seemed to be in her mouth. No. Around it. A cloth. A gag . . .

Was she awake, or was she dreaming? Rachel croaked out a sound.

"No need for that," a man ordered. His voice was muffled, but she could make out the words. Deitsch. He was speaking Deitsch. Where was he? Where was *she?*

It was dark, and she couldn't see anything. Was her face pressed into the ground? No, not the ground. A floor.

She listened, trying to gain her bearings.

She heard the sound of a car engine start, and she sensed that she was moving. *They* were moving.

How did she get in a car? She tried to remember what she'd been doing last, but her thoughts were as random as leaves bobbing in the millrace during a downpour. Disjointed images flashed across her mind . . . a yellow Tupperware bowl of half-shelled lima beans . . . a barking black-and-white dog . . . an axe blade striking a section of log.

Thwack. Thwack. Thwack.

A chill flashed through Rachel, and her breath caught and rasped in her throat.

Joab. Joab Rust.

She tried to holler, but the gag in her mouth muffled the sound.

"I said no need for that," Joab said. "No one can hear you."

The engine whined as he shifted awkwardly into the next gear. Rachel *knew* that sound.

It was her Jeep.

She was in the back of her Jeep, with something thrown on top of her. It smelled of sweet molasses and grain. A blanket . . . the old blanket she used to protect the floor of her vehicle when she carried grain for her goats. No wonder it was hard to breathe. Fumes from the underside of the Jeep mingled with dust and the scent of blood . . . *her* blood.

The realization that Joab had struck her with something sunk in. He'd had an axe in his hand . . . but he couldn't have hit her with that. She'd be dead, wouldn't she?

Bile rose in her throat, and she forced it down. If she was sick, she might choke to death.

Think, Rachel.

She wiggled onto her side and inched the blanket up so that she could breathe a little easier. What was wrong with her hands? Why couldn't she move? Slowly, it began to make sense. Her hands were tied in front of her and her ankles were tied. Joab Rust had hit her in the head with something, trussed her up like a goose bound for market, gagged her, and thrown her in the back of her own vehicle.

Why? Where was he taking her? What was he going to do to her?

Everything that had happened in the last few weeks tumbled around in her head: Beth's murder, the trip to New Orleans, Hannah's wedding, Ed coming to the school in his van.

If Ed hadn't killed Beth, if Ed hadn't been the man George's fellow inmate had been referring to, then it had to be Joab. An Amish man. Joab.

In some roundabout way, it made sense. Sort of. Joab had left the Amish as a young man. He'd probably helped his nephew leave. He'd helped all those girls, too. And when Beth came back, he'd killed her. So she wouldn't tell what he and Ed had done to her, to other girls. He'd *murdered* Beth. The word reverberated in her head.

And now, he meant to do the same thing to her.

She strained against the ropes. They bit into her wrists and ankles. Her nausea rose again, and she tried to take deep breaths through the cloth across her mouth.

The Jeep made a turn onto a smooth road. The road had felt . . . soft before. Now it was harder and smoother.

Rachel recognized that she must have been unconscious . . . but for how long? Had it been minutes? An hour? Two? What was she going to do? Panic made her tremble. What *could* she do, tied up like this?

But she couldn't just lie there like a broken doll and wait for Joab to finish her off.

Something was gouging into her hip. She twisted to ease the pressure; then slowly it dawned on her what it was. Her cell! She had her cell in her pocket. It never occurred to Joab to check to see if she had her cell phone in her clothing.

But how could she call for help? Joab would hear her.

Seconds ticked by . . . maybe minutes. Her brain was still processing slowly.

Joab could *hear* her, but in the dark, with the old blanket thrown over her in the back, he couldn't *see* her.

Cautiously, she inched her phone out of the folds of her skirt. The movement was awkward and slow, with her hands tied together . . . but not impossible.

The logical thing to do was to call 9-1-1. But that involved speaking into the phone and having someone speak to her. That would never work.

The smart thing to do, then, was to *text*. She'd remembered reading about 9-1-1 text capability, but was it available in their area yet?

She didn't know. What she *did* know was that she could text Evan.

She clutched the phone so tightly that she was afraid she'd break it.

First things first. She checked the volume to be sure the sound was off. Then she hit the button on the bottom and the screen lit up; it was eight twenty-seven. She did the math slowly . . . She'd arrived at the Rust farm just after eight. She'd walked up to the house, then driven out to the woods. Not that much time had passed. He had to have *just* thrown her into the back of the Jeep.

She slid her finger across the bottom of the phone to unlock the screen. Her hands shook. She tried to keep it close to her body, afraid Joab might, somehow, see the dim light. Her gaze fixed on the little picture of the battery at the top. Red.

"No, no, no," she breathed. It was going to die any minute.

She touched the text bubble on the bottom of the screen.

Help me joan did it gone to kill me, she texted, noting autocorrect had messed up the message. Evan would get it. She hit *send*.

Waited.

Joan? Who's Joan? Where are you? he texted back less than a minute later.

Thank God he has his phone with him was all she could think.

Don't no where back of jeep driving tied up hr can hear me help bat. dying

Coming! he texted. **Hold on. I'm coming. I love you.**

Rachel stared at the message for a long moment before turning off the screen. She debated whether or not to power down the phone to save on the battery. But she was afraid to shut it off, to cut off all possible contact. And she wasn't sure how much battery power was involved in turning it off and then on again.

Evan was going to find her. She knew he was going to find her. In time . . .

In time for what?

She closed her eyes. Her head was still pounding. *In time to save my life? In time to find my body?* There was no way Joab could let her live. He'd killed once to hide his secret. He'd do it again.

But Evan had said he was coming. He had said he loved her. He would find her.

How was he going to find her? *She* didn't know where she was.

Time seemed to stretch. It went on and on. Joab just kept driving.

Rachel wanted to check the time on her cell, but she was afraid she'd use up the battery by illuminating the screen. How was Evan going to find her if her phone died? How was he going to find her, anyway? Maybe the police had a way of tracking her number with a GPS system?

Instead of worrying about her phone, Rachel tried to focus on where she thought Joab might be taking her. It was hard, though, because her head felt as if it was going to explode. She just wanted to close her eyes . . . her *eye* . . . and sleep. But sleep was a bad idea—for obvious reasons. Instead, she tried to pay attention to what was going on around her. First the road was flat, but eventually it changed.

Where were they going?

Out of the valley, she guessed from the way the Jeep began to turn one way and then the other. She could feel the vehicle climbing.

She wanted to text Evan again. She could tell him they were on a winding road. That would help him, wouldn't it? But she was afraid to use up her battery. She needed to bide her time.

It seemed as if Joab kept driving and driving, but she couldn't tell how far they had gone or how much time had passed—her head hurt so badly. She did know that he was driving slowly. She imagined he knew how to drive the stick shift because it was something like driving a tractor, but he was driving slowly.

Eventually, they turned off the smooth road onto what could only be a gravel road, and Rachel began to get scared. What if he was taking her up into the mountain to some remote place to kill her?

She needed to text Evan again.

She turned on the screen on the phone. Her fingers felt stiff. The battery light was blinking red.

"No," she whispered. "No . . ." She went to messages. Because Evan was the last one she'd texted, all she had to do was to type into the text bar. She tried to type quickly . . . as if that would somehow save on battery.

She wanted to tell him they'd turned off the main road, but the first word came off as **Tiebreaker**.

"No. No. No." She held down the *X* on the keyboard, erasing the word. "Turned off the paved road," she whispered. "I'm trying to tell you that we turned off a—"

A white, spinning circle appeared in the center of the phone, and a tear slipped from the corner of her eye. It was powering down! Her phone was powering down! She touched the power button. Maybe she had another few seconds left? The screen showed the dim outline of a battery gone red and then black.

"Evan," she whispered. She squeezed her eyes shut against stinging tears.

How was he going to find her now? GPS only worked

with the phone on! Now what? Rachel knew she had to think . . . think. If Evan couldn't come for her, she had to save herself.

The surface of the road changed again. Now they were on a dirt road. He was driving very slowly now. In first gear.

Rachel couldn't tell if five minutes passed or fifty. She was so nauseated, so scared. She tried to come up with different scenarios with Joab. What was he going to do when they stopped? How would she respond? How *could* she respond, tied and gagged?

She thought about the axe Joab had been swinging just before he knocked her out. Had he taken her off his farm, up onto a mountain to kill her and leave her body where no one would find it? If that was his plan, what was he going to do with her red Jeep? How was he going to hide *that?*

It occurred to Rachel that instead of spending what might be her last minutes on earth thinking about Joab and his intentions, maybe she should be thinking about herself. About God and the reckoning that came after death. But no matter how hard she tried, she couldn't think about any of that, maybe because she didn't know, despite her upbringing, what she truly believed happened after death. She knew what she wanted to believe, but here . . . now . . .

The Jeep came to a sudden stop, and against her will, Rachel cried out in fear.

She heard Joab get out, and she began to shake.

He didn't close his door, but she heard the back gate swing open. She clutched the phone, though why, she didn't know. It wasn't going to save her now. Nothing was.

When he reached for her . . . touched her . . . she cried out and tried to kick at him. Despite the fact that he wasn't a big man, he was strong.

"Why didn't you mind your own business?" he asked her, lifting her easily in his arms.

Her cell phone fell from her hand, onto the ground.

"Why did you have to put your nose in mine?"

"What are you doing?" she asked against the gag. "Why are you doing this?" They were in the woods. She could see the outlines of trees and smell the green of the underbrush. "Joab." Her voice cracked with fear. "Please."

"You cannot stop me," he said. He dumped her in the grass. In a small clearing. It felt like they were in a small clearing.

"I don't—"

He made a motion toward her, and she tried to pull away, thinking he was going to strike her, but instead, he just pushed down the cloth that had been around her mouth so that it hung around her neck. It looked like it was maybe a men's big blue handkerchief. It was hard to tell in the dark.

She sucked in a breath of the fresh night air and then another.

"You know, I've always wanted to ask you . . ."

She looked up at him.

". . . why you came back, Rachel Mast." He sounded bitter. Angry . . . at her. "You made it in the English world. So few of us can."

He's angry because I came back to Stone Mill? "I wasn't happy among the English," she answered. She tried to look up at him, forcing her swollen eye open, to get a better look. The moon was just rising, but it seemed to be reflecting off something. It was dark, but not so dark that she couldn't see him. "Successful maybe, but not happy."

He shook his head, slowly. "I couldn't make it. I tried. But I didn't have a birth certificate to get a social security card. I had a trade, I could have worked at masonry, but . . . no one would hire me for what I was worth."

She stared up at him, her eyes adjusting to the darkness. "That's why you helped the kids leave? Your nephew . . . the others? You were helping them because no one helped you when you tried to leave?"

"I never meant for this to happen," he told her. "I meant to help them."

"Help them. Right." Lying on the ground, still tied up, she looked up at him. "Did you get money, too? For selling the girls?" She made no attempt to keep the anger and bitterness from *her* voice. If she was going to die, if he was going to kill her, she thought she at least had the right to know what had happened.

"What kind of a man do you think I am?" he shouted at her. "I didn't know! I only thought I was helping them get out of Stone Mill." He looked away and then back at her. "I trusted Ed. I didn't know until Beth Glick came back and she told me what he had done. What those people had made her do."

As she spoke, she tried to look around. Tried to figure out where they were. "I still don't understand. But I want to. Tell me what happened. Why did you kill Beth?"

"She came to me," he said in a far-off voice. "She told me what happened to her. She was going to tell her bishop. Everyone. I couldn't let her tell them. I didn't mean for any of this to happen, but I couldn't— No one would have understood. She didn't suffer," he added in a small voice.

"She didn't suffer when you strangled her?" Rachel demanded.

"I'm sorry," he whispered, barely sounding like himself now.

She exhaled, took a moment to steady her breathing and then looked up at him. "Could you untie me, Joab? At least my hands? My wrists hurt."

"I can't do that, Rachel." He grabbed something from his pocket.

A knife! He had a big knife!

"I know you. You will try to stop me. To stop what must be done." He started to lean over her as if to grab her, and she jerked back, as much as she could, lying on her side with her ankles and wrists tied.

"Wait! Wait! You said you didn't know Ed was selling the girls. That makes you innocent. You don't have to do this. You can't. My parents and I talked about you tonight. They'll know to send the police to you if I go missing."

He didn't seem to hear her. "Innocent of selling the girls," he said without emotion. "But not innocent of Beth Glick's death. I panicked when she told me she was going to her bishop. I killed her. I strangled her, and then I threw her into the quarry so no one would know the terrible thing I had been a part of." He was quiet for a moment. "But *I* knew." He pointed heavenward, his voice trembling now. "God knows!"

Then he leaned over and, with one quick movement, grabbed her foot and cut the rope at her feet. "Walk down the mountain," he said.

She looked up at him. "What?" She separated her feet and started to try to stand. She was weak and shaky. "I don't understand."

"It's better this way." He walked back around the side of the Jeep to the driver's side. "Follow the dirt road, Rachel Mast. You know the way."

Rachel somehow managed to get to her feet. Behind her, she was almost sure she heard the sound of another vehicle approaching from the road. "Joab!"

He got into the driver's seat and put on the seat belt.

Rachel just stood there, staring at him. He started the engine. He did not turn on the headlights.

What was he doing? Was he going to just leave her here, unharmed? With her knowing what she knew? Was he going to run? How far did he think he would get, an Amish man driving a red Jeep?

Rachel glanced around, knowing she was in a familiar place. Sensing it. She looked up at the sky and around her again. Something was so eerily familiar . . . the reflection of the moonlight . . . And then she knew. They were at the rock quarry. She was standing in the clearing where she and the other girls had had a picnic only a month before. Ahead of the Jeep, only fifteen or twenty feet into the darkness, was the water-filled quarry.

Joab hit the gas, and for an instant, the tires spun.

Rachel screamed as it came to her what he was doing. "Joab!"

The tires caught in the grass, and the Jeep leaped forward. She took a step toward it. The tires flattened weeds and little saplings as the Jeep shot away.

She screamed again, though why, she didn't know. There was no one there to hear her. She was vaguely aware of headlights coming up behind her. A car. The light illuminated the back of her Jeep, and suddenly the clearing was filled with flashing red and blue emergency lights. It was Evan.

But he was too late.

The Jeep dropped into the water with a huge splash.

Evan threw the police cruiser into park, skidding sideways.

Rachel just stood there as the Jeep, partially illuminated by Evan's headlights, disappeared from sight as the water bubbled up and over it. Evan got out of the car and ran toward her. She noticed that he was wearing a T-shirt, shorts, and flip-flops.

"Are you all right?" He grabbed her by her shoulders, pulling her closer to him so he could see her face. "You're bleeding."

She looked up at him. She was shaking all over. "My hands are tied, but I'm all right."

He let go of her and ran toward the edge of the quarry. She ran after him.

"Evan!"

There were still sounds of air bubbling up, but not like when the Jeep first hit the water.

She saw him lift his arms over his head as if to dive in.

"Evan, don't! It's sinking too fast!" she hollered, coming to a stop close to the edge of the quarry. "The Jeep's too heavy. The water's too deep. He's gone."

He slowly lowered his arms. He knew she was right. He hesitated and then turned to her. "You're all right?"

Somehow she managed to smile, even though tears were running down her cheeks. "You came for me."

He threw his arms around her, his voice ragged. "Of course I came for you, Rachel." He pulled her against him. "You know I always will."

Epilogue

The following evening, Rachel sank into a chaise lounge under the spreading beech tree behind Stone Mill House. She had become the town's main attraction now that rescue divers had recovered poor Joab's drowned remains from the bottom of the quarry. For the last three hours, neighbors, friends, and relatives had been stopping by to express their concern for Rachel and offer thanks for her part in finding Beth Glick's killer. Several families were there now, standing around in the yard and on the lawn, sharing in the mountains of ham, fried chicken, salads, pies, and cakes that everyone was bringing. Among her people, Amish and Englisher, food was love.

Rachel was grateful for the outpouring of support, but a part of her just wanted to hide alone in her room. She hadn't had a chance to really process what had happened. She'd been at the hospital until morning, getting stitches and an MRI, due to her concussion. Then she'd gone to the police troop to make her statement. Her brain felt as though she'd been put in a sack and dropped off the barn roof. Fortunately, her headache had retreated to a dull buzz and the pain where she had been stitched up over her left eye was only a minor annoyance.

"More visitors," her mother said to Mary Aaron, leaning in front of Rachel to do so. "*Ach,* is that Bishop Abner's buggy? It is. There's Naamah, and who is that with her?" She lowered her voice to a whisper. "It's Joab's wife, Lottie, and his oldest son getting out of the back. Lord bless them. Wouldn't you think they'd have a heavy enough burden of sorrow to bear? That's true grace to come see our Rachel today."

According to Mary Aaron, who'd spent the day at Stone Mill House fending off curious phone calls from the press and friends and caring for the B&B guests, Rachel's *mam* had arrived at noon, before Rachel had returned from the police station. Her *mam* had immediately taken charge of the kitchen, putting even formidable Ada in her place in preparation for her daughter's homecoming.

Rachel was beginning to feel a little overwhelmed and wished that Evan were there. He had remained at her side all night at the hospital, then at the troop, his solid presence steady and reassuring. But when he'd brought her home to Stone Mill House, he'd had to leave her. He had needed a shower and a change of clothes and then had to get back to work. He'd promised he would be back as soon as he could.

Rachel had been so certain that once Beth's killer was brought to justice, all her questions would be answered and the sadness that had haunted her since her discovery of the dead girl would be lessened. But somehow, that emotion had been absorbed and magnified by discovering that one of their own had been the culprit. There was no comfort for Rachel in Joab's death. And while other Amish families in Stone Mill could sleep easier at night, Lottie Rust and her children had to live with the shame and loss of a beloved husband and father.

As shocked as Rachel had been when she'd thought that Joab had meant for her to die in the quarry, seeing him take his own life had stunned her. Suicide wasn't unknown among the Amish. The church community concluded that Joab had lost all hope of salvation and that was why he had done what he did. Sadly, they believed that Joab was truly lost, and because he didn't live long enough to publicly repent and ask forgiveness, there could be no hope of redemption. Rachel didn't know how she felt about any of that, but the one thing she did know was that Joab wasn't an evil man in his heart, just one whose wrong decisions had brought tragedy to an innocent girl and his own destruction.

"Mary Aaron?" Rachel's mother's voice sounded anxious. "Is she all right?"

"Rae-Rae?" Mary Aaron's hand brushed Rachel's arm. "Did you hear me?"

"Sorry." Rachel shook off the mental cobwebs. "I was just . . . thinking." She looked up to see the latest arrivals crossing the lawn toward her. She made an effort to rise, but her mother restrained her with a gentle gesture.

"Tell my daughter that there's no need for her to get up," her *mam* said.

Mary Aaron barely suppressed a smile as their glances connected. "Your mother says—"

"I heard her." Rachel caught her mother's hand and held it fast, taking comfort from the familiar warmth and strength. "I hear her," she added. And for just an instant, her mother looked full into her face and Rachel read the love and worry in her eyes.

I love you, Rachel mouthed.

Her mother's lips moved soundlessly, forming in Deitsch, *And I you, child.* Then, she got to her feet to greet the bishop and the others. "So good of you to come." She embraced first Naamah and then Joab's wife, graciously accepting the casserole and pound cake that the women had brought.

Rachel's sisters materialized just in time to receive the additions to the bounty of food.

"I'm so sorry," Joab's wife murmured, approaching Rachel. Her eyes were red and swollen, her face pasty white with loss. "All night and all day, after . . . after we learned of what . . . what had happened, we kept you in our prayers."

"And your family in mine," Rachel replied, getting up to return the embraces.

Joab's son didn't speak, but he didn't need to. His presence was enough to assure Rachel that the Rusts didn't hate her. They were struggling to accept the unacceptable, and in true Amish way, their sorrow was the sorrow of the whole community.

"We are holding a special prayer service on Sunday at your Uncle Aaron's home," Bishop Abner said. "We hope that you'll be well enough to come. And your English friend Evan is welcome."

"I'll be there," Rachel promised. She didn't intend to let a few stitches and a bump on her head turn her into an invalid. "And please let me know when the funeral is being held for Joab."

Joab's wife nodded, and Naamah slipped an arm around her shoulders. The women murmured a few words of farewell, the son nodded, and Bishop Abner folded his arms and smiled down at Rachel. "The Lord works in mysterious ways," he said. "His wonders to perform."

Rachel thanked him for coming and for bringing the Rusts. The community would close around them, holding them up, helping and supporting, and life would go on in the valley. Their faith was strong, and her people were resilient, possessing a strength born of centuries of unity and caring.

As Bishop Abner and the others drifted away, Rachel's cell vibrated in her pocket. She had found it on the ground at the quarry and kept it with her all night long. Evan had been passing by her house when she'd texted him from the back of the Jeep. He'd gone inside and grabbed her laptop to use to pinpoint her last location with the *Find My Phone* app he'd installed months earlier. By the time her battery died, he'd already figured out where Joab was taking her. It was Mary Aaron who had thought to charge it when Rachel returned home. As she pulled it out of her jeans' pocket, her mother waved her back to her chair.

"Tell her to rest," her *mam* ordered Mary Aaron. "I'll get her some lemonade from the kitchen."

"I'll come with you." Mary Aaron glanced back at Rachel and flashed a conspiratorial smile. "So Rae-Rae can take her message in private."

How's the head? It was from Evan.

Rachel sank down and leaned back against the cushion. **Better,** she texted. She kicked off her shoes and curled her feet up under her. **Will you be done soon?**

Her phone rang a few moments later. She answered quickly, feeling self-conscious, surrounded by Amish family and friends. It was Evan calling. "Hey," she said softly into the phone.

"I'm probably going to be a while," he said. "Sergeant Haley wants to sit down and put all of the pieces together. I'll be working with him for the next few days."

She smiled, feeling suddenly exhausted but so glad to be alive. "That's good news, right?"

"Yeah. I guess."

They were both quiet for a moment; then she said, "Thanks for staying with me last night. And today. I don't know if I could have gotten through it all without you."

"That's not true, but you're welcome. What are friends for?"

Rachel knew this was where she was supposed to respond that they were more than friends, but she didn't say anything because she didn't know what to say. She still didn't know how she felt.

The silence that followed became painfully awkward.

"I better go," he said, finally. "The sergeant's waiting for me."

"Will you come by later?" she asked.

"You want me to?"

Her response was genuine. "I do."

"I'll be by later, then. In the meantime, keep that cell phone battery charged."

They were both laughing when they hung up.